D0594513

"FIRE AND ICE, YOU BURN ME," HE MURMURED.

When he saw her naked, watching him, he paused for a heartbeat, then gathered up her hands in his and brought them to his lips. He kissed her palms, her fingers, before he embraced her and drew her closer. At last Sabrina looked up into her lover's face. It was hard to believe she had ever seen it frozen over, expressionless. Now the eyes were darker, liquid with tenderness. His mouth was soft and full. . . .

"Come to me," she whispered. "Come to me."

Other books by
Roberta Gellis

THE KENT HEIRESS

Roberta Gellis

A DELL BOOK

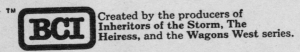

™ **BCI** Created by the producers of Inheritors of the Storm, The Heiress, and the Wagons West series.

Executive Producer: Lyle Kenyon Engel

Published by
Dell Publishing Co., Inc.
1 Dag Hammarskjold Plaza
New York, New York 10017

Produced by Book Creations, Inc.
Lyle Kenyon Engel, Executive Producer

Copyright © 1982 by Roberta Gellis
and Book Creations, Inc.

All rights reserved. No part of this book may be
reproduced or transmitted in any form or by any
means, electronic or mechanical, including photocopying,
recording or by any information storage and retrieval
system, without the written permission of the Publisher,
except where permitted by law.

Dell ® TM 681510, Dell Publishing Co., Inc.

ISBN: 0-440-14537-6

Printed in the United States of America
First printing—November 1982

THE KENT HEIRESS

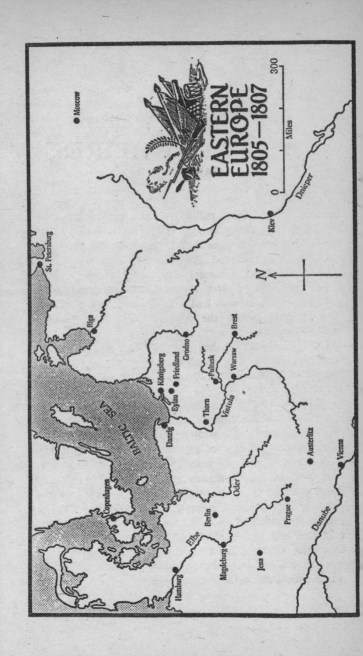

EASTERN EUROPE 1805–1807

Miles
0 300

Moscow

St. Petersburg

Riga

Dnieper

Kiev

Königsberg
Friedland
Grodno
Brest
Eylau
Poltusk
Warsaw
Danzig
Thorn
Vistula

BALTIC SEA

Austerlitz
Vienna

Copenhagen

Oder

Berlin
Prague
Danube

Elbe

Hamburg
Magdeburg
Jena

N

CHAPTER ONE

Sabrina, Lady Elvan, pulled her rich cashmere shawl a little tighter over her bare white shoulders. Near the window it was cold, despite the roaring fire. She looked out on a sparkling fairyland. The new snow had melted just a little when the sun had come out during the day; now that it was gone again, a layer of ice had formed. It glittered as if the entire boulevard had been seeded with diamonds. The buildings across the way glittered, too. White on white—exquisite.

Beautiful, beautiful, her eyes told her. Ugly, ugly, her heart whispered. Everything in Russia was like that—an incredible dichotomy that drowned the senses and sickened the soul.

St. Petersburg looked like a city built by gods—wide streets, beautiful buildings. While other cities huddled in filthy, sloppy misery in winter, St. Petersburg glittered and sparkled in its covering of ice and snow. But Sabrina knew it hadn't been built by gods; it had been built by slaves who died by the thousands from cold and hunger and beatings. Everything else was like that, too: gorgeous outside and ugly inside. The huge rooms inside the sparkling houses also sparkled and glittered, ravishing the sight with gold leaf and jeweled ornaments. All too often, though, they were unclean, the furniture dusty and greasy. That was the result of using slaves who could have no hope for advancement nor pride in their work.

7

No, Sabrina told herself severely. She was being unfair. Many of the serfs were treated well, and there were dirty houses in England, too, where the mistress was too high-and-mighty or too lazy to make sure the housekeeper kept the maids to their work. There were as many wretched people on English lands, also. Bad landlords could ruin the farmers, and neglectful ones permitted stewards and bailiffs to extract bribes so that tenants starved. It was useless to blame Russia because she was unhappy. It was William's fault.

Slowly Sabrina turned away from the window and returned to her dressing table. She stared sightlessly into the glass, automatically hanging a complex necklace of sapphires and diamonds around her throat and pushing the hooks of the matching earrings into her ears.

But it was not her own elegant appearance that Sabrina saw. What appeared in the mirror was another scene entirely. She was looking again into the small drawing room, with its cozy grouping of sofa and chairs—right into the mirror behind. A few moments before that Sabrina had returned home from her scheduled round of morning visits, barely half an hour after leaving the house because she had forgotten her visiting cards. Having been told that Countess Maria Fedorovna Latuski was not at home, she had reached into her muff and found the card case missing. Then she remembered she had left it on the table in the small drawing room.

Sabrina shuddered. She had found the countess, instead of the cards, in the drawing room—found her in William's arms. So shocked had Sabrina been that she stood mute and paralyzed. The high back of the sofa cut off her view of the couple from below the chest. Unable to believe, in that first half second, what the expression on her husband's face and the movement of his body implied, Sabrina's eyes had passed to the mirror behind them, which revealed a head-to-foot view.

8

Perhaps a low whimper of shame or rage had forced itself from Sabrina. The sound was not enough to disturb the countess, who had her head buried between William's shoulder and neck and was gasping and trembling in the penultimate stage of her climax, but William's eyes shot open. Sabrina wanted to shrink away. In the instant before her mind comprehended what she was seeing, she had been racked with all the shame, guilt, and embarrassment William must feel. And then she *saw* his expression. If her first shock had numbed her, this second turned her to stone.

William looked . . . irritated. He was annoyed—but apparently no more annoyed than if she had walked in on a delicate diplomatic negotiation or interrupted him when he was writing a difficult letter. There was no sign of guilt, or shame, or even embarrassment. No tinge of extra color rose in his cheeks. Without interrupting the thrusts of his hips, he freed one hand and gestured at Sabrina to go away.

She staggered out of the doorway as if the flick of his hand had thrust her backward physically. Blindly, without knowing what she did, she found her way upstairs to her own dressing room, shed her heavy furs, and sank into a chair. Slowly the total deadness that had made her respond automatically to William's gesture of command faded into indignation. How dare he! In her own drawing room! She had never suspected William of such crudity! Such bad taste!

And then Sabrina was shocked all over again, this time by her own sentiments. She should have been torn by pain and humiliation, burning with jealousy, frantic with grief. What she felt was the same kind of irritation—perhaps stronger, but essentially the same—as William had displayed. Again the first shock was followed by a stronger one. She did not love William any longer—if she ever had!

What was she to do? Now tears filled Sabrina's eyes.

She realized she did not want William, had not wanted him for a long time—not even in bed. At first his caresses had been almost unendurably thrilling, the culmination of hours of delicate pursuit—a whispered word or two, sultry glances, fleeting touches, all built expectation so that she was halfway to climax before she got into bed. William was an expert at that technique, but it had failed after Sabrina had seen him use it on other women. That was when she still believed he was faithful and that the languorous looks he cast on other women were only harmless flirtations. Still, after noticing, she had found it difficult to obtain satisfaction in lovemaking. William never bothered to arouse her fully, and frequently was done before she came to climax.

Sabrina had at first blamed herself. Now she understood. William's preliminaries to lovemaking were all public. Women like Maria Fedorovna could not spare more than fifteen minutes or so to make love. William expected his women to be ready and to be in a hurry. He wanted to get right down to "business."

The ugly image of that "business," of the countess's dress crumpled on her abdomen, of William's breeches drooping around his knees, made Sabrina nauseous with revulsion. Love? Was that love? Sabrina shook with distaste. William was incapable of love. Sabrina covered her face with her hands and wept. She knew she could cut this affair dead where it was, that she could keep her husband relatively faithful by finding various methods to make herself the object of his pursuit—because William did not really care who the object was. Sabrina choked. That was horrible, horrible. The thought of William courting her again, glancing at her sidelong, touching her insinuatingly with the tips of his fingers . . . it was unbearable.

The door opened. Without lifting her head, Sabrina said, "Go away!"

"Now, Sabrina," William reproved sharply, "I know you

are angry, but I cannot have you acting up in a silly way right now. Why the devil did you come home?"

Sabrina's hands dropped. Her head snapped up, eyes and mouth open in astonishment. She had thought it was a servant who came in. It had not occurred to her that William would dare confront her.

"You are upset to no purpose," William went on. "It was an accident. It meant nothing."

"In my home! In my drawing room!" Sabrina gasped.

For the first time, William had the grace to look self-conscious. "I told you it was an accident," he snapped. "I met her on the doorstep. It was impossible not to invite her in. I didn't know, after all, that you weren't home."

"Liar!"

"Don't be a fool," William snarled. "I have no time for your 'finer feelings.' I've told you a hundred times already, this has nothing to do with you. I wouldn't have bothered to talk to you about it, except that the political situation is particularly precarious. I cannot afford to have you pouting and sullen."

"But you can afford to indulge your—your—"

"That has its political purpose, too," William interrupted angrily. Then, seeing Sabrina redden with rage, he added, "I didn't mean things to go so far—I swear it. I tell you again, it was an accident."

"One accident too many," Sabrina spat. "I'm finished! I'm through with you!"

"This is no time for childish tantrums," William shouted. "Will you allow your petty personal foibles—"

"Petty foibles!" Sabrina shrieked.

"Yes!" he screamed. "Petty! Petty! Infantile! There isn't another woman in the world who wouldn't have had the common sense and good manners to pretend she hadn't stupidly walked in on what wasn't her business. Instead of that, you're prepared to add a completely irrelevant factor

11

that may cause the collapse of the whole British mission here."

"That's a lie!" Sabrina cried. "You only say it to force me to condone your lecheries."

But her voice trembled uncertainly. Sabrina knew that there might be truth in what William said. Czartoryski, the foreign minister of Russia, who had always urged alliance with England, had fallen out of favor. Tsar Alexander had not yet dismissed him from office—in fact, Czartoryski was hosting the ball that she and William were invited to that very evening. If they did not attend—even if she alone did not go—there might be political repercussions.

It was ridiculous that a personal quarrel between a man and wife should cause echoes in international politics, and in most cases it would not. Now, however, the tsar was behaving so peculiarly and the diplomatic situation was so strained that even the smallest incident might precipitate serious consequences. Quite false rumors might be attached to the "migraine" Sabrina would plead to excuse her absence from the ball; and even if the truth were known, it could be used as an excuse for action taken for quite another reason. Sabrina bit her lip.

"It is not a lie," William said emphatically, but in a normal tone of voice. "I have told you that what happened was an accident. I had no intention at this time. . . . It was impossible to avoid. It would have given great offense if I had refused—and I would have needed actually to refuse—and I couldn't chance that yet, not until I'm sure it's not Czartoryski alone but the whole Polish party that is out of favor."

"Another excuse?" Sabrina asked sardonically, but her voice, too, was merely conversational.

"It is not an excuse," William replied. "You *know* Alexander is sleeping with Maria Naryshkin, and, whatever else she is, she is Polish to the core. At present he is completely besotted with her. I'm informed that Novosiltsov and Stroganov will be dismissed also—the whole liberal group, in fact—but there's no special reason Czartoryski's fall should affect the other Poles. No one could call most of *them* liberal. In any case, Countess Latuski is too friendly with Naryshkin for me to offend her with impunity."

It was true. Of course, if William hadn't started the flirtation, he wouldn't have been placed in a situation where offense was possible. However, that thought was just a cynical flicker through Sabrina's mind. Expecting William not to flirt was the same as expecting pigs to fly. Sabrina had come, at long last, to a willingness to admit to herself that she didn't care with whom William went to bed so long as it wasn't with her. She knew she had been furious only because he had not had enough respect for her to be ashamed of being caught. And probably it was true that what happened had been an accident. Usually William was very discreet . . . although he had been growing more and more careless.

"So you *must* attend this ball, and you *must* behave toward me just as usual. Do you understand me, Sabrina?"

Obviously she had missed something while her mind had been busy. It didn't matter. Sabrina acknowledged that this was no time to stir up a hornet's nest in the diplomatic community. She would, indeed, have to attend the ball and behave normally toward William. Her lips twisted as she realized it would not be at all difficult. It had been a very long time since she had displayed any overt sign of wifely affection.

Suddenly Sabrina was aware of herself, still staring into the mirror. No, it would be no trouble to behave as usual to William. Once her rage at the insult done her was past, she found she did not *feel* differently about him. Her eyes grew troubled. Was this William's fault or her own? She focused on her own face, and the lips made a sardonic grimace. The fault was not there. Sabrina knew she was beautiful. Diamonds and sapphires sparkled in her hair, so pale a blond that William had called it "moonlight hair." Her eyes were pale, too, and in spite of perfect features her face would have been without character, except for the fortunate accident that her brows and lashes were darker than her hair—an ash brown—and there was an odd ring of darker color around the circumference of her irises.

Sabrina leaned forward. Silly eyes. They tended to open very wide because the lids were thin, and that gave her an expression of slightly surprised innocence—or, the less kind would say, stupidity. The sardonic grimace deepened. It would have been much better if she were stupid. Life would have been sweeter, easier, happier. If she only were as stupid or innocent as she looked, she would either never have discovered what William really was or would have accepted it.

Did William still think she was stupid or innocent? He had when they first married, she now realized; Sabrina acknowledged that she had been innocent then—but she had been only sixteen years old. Besides, how could she be anything but innocent after living with Leonie and Roger since she was nine years old?

In spite of her general unhappiness, Sabrina chuckled suddenly. Unlike most parents or guardians, Leonie and Roger made no effort to keep her mind pure. Well, no, Roger would have, perhaps, but he was no match for Leonie, who believed that ignorance on any subject led to misery rather than bliss. But knowing all the sins in the world by their names hadn't convinced Sabrina that her husband could commit any—not *after* he married her. Roger hadn't; even Leonie, who was jealous as a cat, admitted her accusations were far more preventative than realistic.

A frown wrinkled Sabrina's alabaster brow. Had she just determined that Leonie's theory was wrong? Would ignorance have kept her happy? Sabrina shuddered and

14

drew her shawl up over her shoulders again. No, Leonie was not wrong. If William's repeated infidelities had remained unknown to her longer, the blow of discovery would have been much, much worse, and what had happened this morning would have killed her. In the beginning she had refused to believe the hints and winks of her "friends"—and what thanks had she had? William had simply behaved more and more blatantly until it was impossible to ignore the truth. He had not even bothered to lie! Sabrina gritted pearly teeth whose whiteness belied their strength. She remembered her first heartbroken accusation and the way William had responded.

"Now, now, my love," he had soothed, taking her into his arms and patting her back comfortingly, "you shouldn't bother your pretty head about such things. You are my wife. No one can take your place. Never you mind what people say. They'll respect you all the more for taking no notice."

Sabrina had thrust him away so fiercely that he staggered back. Her pale coloring made her look fragile, but she was really quite strong. She was tall for a woman and, although slender, was well muscled from much walking and riding. Had they been in England at the time, Sabrina might have left William in her first fury and returned to Roger and Leonie. However, she and William were in Vienna, and there was no easy way home.

That difficulty alone might not have discouraged Sabrina, but as her immediate rage cooled she recalled that she and William were not private citizens. They were members of the British diplomatic staff in Austria, and as such her actions might reflect on her nation as well as on her husband. Her obligations to William might be ended, but those to England were not. But she could not, would not, be wife to a man who betrayed her. He would have to learn that. Three years ago, in Vienna, she had been

15

young enough to believe that William's addiction to chasing other women could be cured.

At first her course of treatment had seemed to work well. Sabrina had turned herself into the ice maiden she outwardly resembled. In fact, an igloo would have been warm and comfortable compared to William's home. In public she was formally polite; in private she did not see or hear her husband at all. He no longer existed. She did not inquire whether he would be home for meals or inform him when she would be out. There was never a place laid for him; the servants were soon totally demoralized from receiving no instructions, and Sabrina's door remained locked.

William's first reaction was contempt; he had handled sulky beauties before. He had not been married to them, however. When it finally occurred to him that the situation would not pass in a few days but was permanent, his idea of a cure was to slap Sabrina into submission. She defended herself so ferociously, however, with teeth and nails and kicks and bric-a-brac that he ended as bruised as she—and in more delicate spots. In fact, William had been totally unprepared for her reaction; apparently he had believed that a single slap would reduce her to whimpering tameness. Her violence intrigued him. It was after the fight that he cut short his illicit affair with an Austrian beauty and began to try to win Sabrina back.

He had been contrite, wryly apologetic, explaining that he had not thought she would care. Everyone did it, after all; however, if she felt so strongly, of course he would not, ever again. It had seemed reasonable enough to Sabrina at the time. She had known before she married William that he was "quite a lady's man." Roger had warned her; her foster brother, Philip, had warned her; Leonie had warned her. Actually, Roger had wished to forbid the courtship altogether. Leonie, too, had not been happy about it, but William had insisted so passionately that his affections were fixed at last and had behaved so impeccably that they had yielded. Besides, there was little else they could do. The damage was already done. Sabrina was head over heels in love with her practiced charmer.

She had still loved him in Vienna, so it was not surprising that his peace overtures were accepted. And for a precious half year it had worked—or she had not caught him. Part of that time they had been back in England. Sabrina felt a thousand years older, but she was only seventeen. Perhaps he had been faithful; perhaps it was only easier to be discreet in England. He was as loving and attentive as when they first were married, but she had seen the anxiety in Roger's and Leonie's eyes—and she had seen Philip, once as much a lady's man as William, become as steady a husband as Roger ever was.

Sabrina smiled again when that thought crossed her mind. Megaera had a temper as hot as her flaming hair and could shoot a pistol as well as a man. It would be dangerous to cross her. The smile died. Philip was not faithful because he was afraid of his wife. He was faithful because he adored her. They were friends, too, just as Roger and Leonie were friends.

Tears welled into Sabrina's eyes, and she looked hastily down at her dressing table. Mechanically she began to choose rings and slide them up on her long white fingers. The skin on her hands was so delicate that a tracery of blue veins was visible below the surface. The tears did not fall. It was too late for tears. Still, that was the most painful part—she had not wanted her husband to be her friend. She had scorned the down-to-earth realism with which her cousin Leonie regarded her husband. She had some romantic, half-baked dream of a marriage in which her husband would always be her lover.

Horribly, she had achieved it! She had unerringly picked a man who was only capable of being a lover. When pursuit and wooing were no longer necessary,

17

William lost interest—especially in a woman bound to him by law.

It was quite clear what had attracted William to diplomatic life. He was perfectly suited to it. He never tired of dressing and dancing and making elegant conversation. He could pursue indifferent or hostile men for friendship as eagerly—and successfully—as he pursued women for love. Sabrina laughed shortly and stood up. She loved the diplomatic life, too. She adored the fun of disseminating information William wanted spread—oh, so innocently, as if she were telling secrets overheard—and gathering hints and rumors to pass back to the British Foreign Office. She knew she was the perfect diplomatic wife. If only William . . .

Still, it wasn't worth the effort to hold him. It would go on forever and become more and more degrading. Sabrina took a last look at herself in the mirror and grimaced again. Perfect, exquisite—white on white—an ice-white moiré, embroidered with snow crystals in silver, dropped low off shoulders as white as the dress. The cashmere shawl, bleached to the whiteness of snow, and as soft, draped gracefully over her arms. The only touches of color were her blue eyes, the glittering points of blue fire where her sapphires burned amid the white glitter of diamonds, the delicate rose of her lips, and the pale, pale gold of high-piled hair.

No, Sabrina thought, her problem was not in behaving normally to William tonight. Her problem was with the future. Sabrina wanted and needed to be loved. She had grown up in a household filled with love. She had seen a new love ripen between Philip and Megaera just as rich and fulfilling as that between Roger and Leonie, although different in detail. Too late she knew that she wanted that for herself, and it was impossible to attain with William.

All afternoon Sabrina had struggled with that realization. Now it was easy enough to understand why she had

18

never considered taking a lover to pay William back for the shame and pain he had inflicted on her. A lover was not the answer to her need. Sabrina shivered. How peculiar that word was—lover. Usually the last thing a woman obtained from a lover was love.

After the political crisis was over, she could leave William, go back to Stour Castle, and live with Roger and Leonie—but that would not be a normal life, no matter how much they loved her. Anyhow, that was not the kind of love she needed. There was another difficulty there. If she confessed her misery to her guardians, they would blame themselves. It *was* their fault in a way. They should have known better than to allow her to marry William, no matter how infatuated she was. How could they have been so stupid, so careless? Sabrina blocked that train of thought hard. There was no use putting the blame on others, particularly on those who loved her only too well. Or who took the first opportunity to be rid of her? No! That was insane.

It was her problem, and she even knew the solution. Roger was a very influential man. He could pull strings as strong as ropes in the government and, likely, even reach into the Church. Her marriage could be annulled or she could obtain a divorce. Unfortunately the cure was at least as bad as the disease and might be worse. A divorce would not permit her to remarry, and even if an annulment could be obtained, she would have made herself into a pariah. There would be very few men who would be interested in marrying a woman who had put away her husband for infidelity. Everyone would know the true cause, no matter what formal reason was given for breaking the marriage. In addition, an annulment initiated by his wife might ruin William's career, and Sabrina did not really want to hurt William. He could not help being what he was.

That sounded very noble, Sabrina thought cynically, but

the truth was that she did not wish to lose the excitement of the diplomatic life, either. And she would be ruined far more completely than William. He might well be taken back into the service as soon as the scandal died down. Her situation, even though she was the injured party, would be far worse. Not only would she be deprived of the foreign travel and excitement that she loved, but she might even be excluded from English society—déclassé because her husband was a lecher and she had dared to complain.

A scratch at the door broke the bitter thought and made Sabrina start. She had not realized how long she had been lost in unpleasant daydreams. *"Entrez,"* she called, thinking that it was very useful that she had been raised in a bilingual household. Her French was pure, accented only slightly by the patois of the Côte d'Or, and as fluent as her English. She was, thus, a great favorite with both the embassy wives, who needed an interpreter, and the Russian ladies, who made heavy weather of the halting French of many English wives and daughters.

The door opened to reveal a small, round woman, neatly gowned in gray merino topped with a black spencer. Her face was good-natured with a short, pert nose, twinkling blue eyes, and a pretty mouth. If it had not been for the few streaks of gray in her simply dressed brown hair, and her mature body, she would have looked little more than a girl. Cocking her head to examine Sabrina critically, she nodded curtly.

"Verra nice. Himself is below all ready and wonderin' what's keepin' ye."

Involuntarily Sabrina smiled. "I thought I told you to go to dinner, Katy."

"I'll go when I'm ready. Ye needn't fash yersel' that I'll starve." Her eyes were troubled as she opened the door wider and stepped back. "Go down now, luv. Ye can't hide from life."

"I wasn't hiding," Sabrina said, rather indignantly. "I was thinking."

"This isna the time for it, Brina. Himself is all atwitter. There'll be someone important at this party, I'm thinking."

"Really?" Sabrina felt brighter at once. She dropped a kiss on Katy's cheek and moved quickly past her and down the corridor toward the stairs.

Katy watched her go, then closed the door and stood with her back to it. The good humor had faded from her face. If she had not been a faithful daughter of the Church, William, Lord Elvan, would have been dead by her hand. But murder was a deadly sin, and she had been taught a sin never solved anything, only brought more trouble. Nor would it do any good to show her rage against the man to her beloved nursling. Brina had not quite made up her mind, and to speak against him would only make the stubborn girl defend him. That might push Brina in the opposite direction from the path Katy wanted her to take.

"Wanted" was too strong a word. Katy was as undecided as Sabrina herself, as aware as Sabrina of the dreadful results of "her child's" leaving her husband. What Katy wanted was that Brina should be happy, and it was quite clear that she would also be forced to leave the life she loved if she left William. That certainly would not make her happy. And Brina deserved happiness. She had had tragedy enough in her short life.

Katy shook herself and moved into the room, beginning to tidy the slight disorder Sabrina had left on her dressing table. As she closed the jewel box, hung up a dressing gown, and collected discarded garments for laundering, Katy's mind slipped back into the past.

Like her cousin and guardian, Lady Leonie, Sabrina was a granddaughter of the earl of Stour. In fact, if Brina's father had lived six months longer, Brina rather

21

than Lady Leonie would have inherited the vast estates of Stour. Katy clucked her tongue. Good luck to Lady Leonie and no harm to Brina. Leonie would have turned every penny over to her cousin if she thought Brina wanted it or if it could do her any good. Cut out her own heart for Brina, Lady Leonie would.

It was not the estates that mattered but how Lord Stour had died. He had been bringing his family back from Ireland to England when a sudden squall struck the vessel in which they were traveling and the boat sank. Lord Stour, his wife, and his son had drowned. The nursemaid with Stour's two little daughters, Alice and Sabrina, had found temporary safety in a lifeboat. This tiny craft had been blown far north of the vessel's route and had finally capsized in the surf near the island on which Katy lived.

The nursemaid was devoted to her charges. She clung to them even in the face of death, protecting them as well as she could from the battering waves. No one knew exactly what happened, but it was likely that the elder child, nine-year-old Alice, had become hysterical, had been torn loose from the nursemaid's grasp, and had drowned. The little one, Sabrina, not yet four, had clung trustfully to what was safety to her and had survived. But the beach onto which the nursemaid finally crawled was deserted at night, and the woman was nearly dead from exposure and exhaustion. She had collapsed there. By the time they were discovered, the nursemaid had taken a fatal chill.

She lived three days, raving with fever. There was little Katy's parents could do for her. Over and over the nursemaid cried for the child she had lost. Once or twice she said the names "de Conyers" and "Stour," but she gave no more information. At first they had hoped she would recover. By the time they realized she was dying, she could not respond to questions. Thus, she never said enough for Katy or her parents to make head or tail of the child's identity.

The little girl had been very sick too, but Katy tended her with a passionate devotion engendered by the loss of two infants of her own, and again Sabrina survived. The Larsons knew from her rich clothes that she came from a fine family, but she could tell them nothing of value in tracing her people. Her name was "Brina," and she chattered volubly of Mama and Papa and William and Alice and Nurse, but not of where she lived—her answer to that was "with Mama and Papa in the house" because some of her "friends" lived "outside the house," presumably in cottages on the estate.

The Larsons did what they could, asked every person with whom they came in contact whether the names "Stour" or "de Conyers" meant anything, but they lived in an isolated area on a small island, and they could not afford to leave their work to inquire too far afield. Meanwhile they kept the child, unsure of how much to tell her or whether it would be a kindness or cruelty to remind her that she was not theirs, that she might be nobly born.

As the months passed, hope of finding her people dimmed, and they even began to wish—for their own sakes—that Brina's family would forget her. She was a delight to them all. Sugar baby, Katy called her, for her whiteness and sweetness of disposition. It was natural that she should be most precious of all to Katy Petersen, who had lost her husband a few months before and had no living child of her own. The months added up to years. Katy almost forgot that Brina was not her daughter. She taught the child to spin and sew and knit, and Brina did all the chores that any six- or seven-year-old was expected to do in an isolated fishing and farming community.

By 1795, although Katy and her parents still asked about "Stour" and "de Conyers," they did so by habit, certain there would be no result. In the spring, however, a stranger not only rode into their village but dismounted and asked for Katy's house. In that instant Katy knew that

Brina was lost to them, lost forever. It wasn't like her sister marrying a man on another island or her brother going to sea. They came back to visit, even if infrequently, and she could imagine what their lives were like. When Brina left, it would be as if she had died. She could never come back, and even if she could, she would be a different person.

But it had not happened that way. The stranger had not taken Brina away, and when at last Lady Leonie and Mr. St. Eyre had come, they had asked Katy to stay with Brina and with them. They had taken Katy and the child to the inn with them that night, and their patience and tenderness were a marvel. They had not tried to change Brina's ways all at once. Mr. St. Eyre had to leave the next day; he had business affairs and government duties that could not be put off, but Lady Leonie stayed at the inn for over a month.

Little by little, Lady Leonie had introduced new clothes, new ways of speaking, sitting, eating. It was all a game that Brina soon came to love, all done with laughter, and not a word implied contempt for the old ways or shame for lapsing back into them. Although she never said it in words, what Leonie was telling Brina over and over was that to each person in each place there was a "right" way. When a person changed place, new "right" ways must be learned. That did not mean the old ways were wrong. In fact, the new ways would be wrong in the old place. Brina must remember both ways—and all new ways—and use each in the right place.

Toward the end of the month, Leonie had asked Katy to join her in her parlor after Brina was asleep. *This is the end,* Katy thought. *Now I'll be sent away.* But it was just the opposite. Lady Leonie begged her to come with them to England so that Brina's life would not be completely broken again.

"I would like it best if you would live with us, Katy,"

she said. "Roger and I thought we would settle on you a sum that would bring an income of about three hundred pounds a year——" She misunderstood the shock mirrored on Katy's face and hurried on, "Oh, please, do not be offended. I know money cannot pay for what you have done for Brina, but it is all we have to offer. We cannot let you keep her."

"I know that!" Katy exclaimed, horrified now at the thought of what she had wished to deprive her darling. "Ye dinna need give me aught. I'll come—but what will I be?"

Not being stupid, Katy had already seen the difficulty. She could learn the new ways, too—perhaps she could—but to ape the actions and manners of the great was unnatural and made her miserably uncomfortable.

"What do you mean?" Leonie asked.

Katy was frightened, just as frightened at the notion of living among the nobility as at losing Brina. Even the pain of losing her sugar baby could not have forced Katy into such a situation—but Brina's pain was far more compelling to her than her own. Generally Sabrina was a very happy little girl, but she had one deep-seated trouble. She seemed to think she had done something that had lost her her parents. Why, she would cry, had they left her? As if that were not bad enough, recently the child had been asking whether Katy was tired of her, too, because Katy had hinted that Brina would be going away with Lady Leonie. And then, with too bright eyes, she had asked whether, after a while, Leonie would grow tired of her and leave her also. A solution had to be found.

"I canna be a lady," Katy said slowly. "I wouldna like it and—and yer servants would know. Ye can make them behave, but I'd be lonely. I'd have nothin' to do. I'll come—but as Brina's maid. Then I'll have friends among the servants, ye see, and I'd still be with Brina as much as she wants me."

Lady Leonie considered that, then nodded. "Why do we not combine the plans, Katy? There will come a time when your parents will need help. Perhaps you will wish to return to them, but perhaps you will not. It will be best then if you have enough of your own money to do what you think best."

Truer words were never spoken. It took some years before Katy really believed the money was hers and got over feeling guilty whenever she spent any on anyone but Brina, but she was used to it now. Her parents were willing to take a little from her, too; they believed she was paid for her duties as a companion—and that was proper. And they hadn't even lost Brina, who spent at least one month every summer with them—still feeding chickens and lugging water—until she married.

Katy shook herself. She was as bad as Brina, standing like an image with the soiled undergarments in her hands. Everything had been perfect until Brina married that . . . Katy groped hopelessly in her mind, unable to think of a word foul enough to describe Lord Elvan accurately. He had fooled them all. Then she sighed. He hadn't only fooled all of them, he had deceived himself as well.

A lot of women wouldn't have cared that he played around; they would just have looked for a man for themselves. But Brina wasn't that kind. Something had changed, however. Katy knew that. The first time, in Vienna, Brina had been bitterly hurt; the second time she was more angry than hurt—and she wasn't as relieved and happy when he came back to her. This time Brina was acting really queer. She didn't seem hurt at all, only . . . tired? Bored? She was more uncertain than anything else.

CHAPTER TWO

As she hurried down the stairs, somewhat impeded by the huge footman who held her carefully by the arm, Sabrina wondered how William would act. He had gone out immediately after she agreed to attend the ball and "behave herself," leaving a message that he would not be in to dinner. She wondered also whether William's impatience was owing to an important Russian official who would be at the ball or because the present object of his affections would be there. Her double doubt was resolved as soon as she entered the drawing room.

"Of all days for you to be late, Sabrina," William exclaimed. "I told you the tsar himself is expected to look in, and if he does—"

It was obvious that William intended to act as if that morning's incident had not taken place at all. Sabrina felt a flicker of pique, but that faded into relief. It really was easier that way. Not to be beaten by his sangfroid, Sabrina said, "I don't believe it," as soon as the servant went off to bring her furs. She watched William pull on his marten-lined greatcoat. He seemed totally unaware of a possible double meaning. "Alexander hasn't the nerve," she went on, acknowledging she would get no rise from her husband. "He tried to sneak into St. Petersburg at night two weeks ago, and he hasn't showed his face at a single function. Besides, Alexander is said to be disenchanted

27

with our host, Prince Czartoryski. Then certainly he would not come to the foreign minister's ball."

William growled but made no direct reply because a footman had returned and was tenderly inserting Sabrina into her ermine wrap. It was a bulky garment, completely lined with ermine fur and faced with marten, but it would keep Sabrina as warm as a heated room in the subzero temperature of a St. Petersburg January. Although she did not resist, Sabrina still resented being dressed like an infant, even having her arms lifted and pulled through the sleeves. The house servants, except for Katy and William's valet, Charlot, were Russian and had been trained to act as if their masters and, even more particularly, their mistresses were feebleminded, paralytic infants.

It was annoying, but to send the servants away caused them such fear and even grief that Sabrina had yielded. It was, after all, her purpose to be as "Russian" as possible, to convince her hosts that she loved them and their ways. It was part of her success as a diplomatic wife that she was so sensitive to the balance between seeming to toady and seeming to appreciate the good aspects of a foreign culture. There was a limit, however. As it was, every time she went up or down the stairs, she was supported on one or both sides by footmen. For the first six months she had spent in Russia, Sabrina had thought she would go mad.

The behavior of the servants, especially their terror when Sabrina initially refused their attentions, had given her the worst impression of Russian noblewomen. She had struggled against the feeling because contempt has a way of revealing itself, no matter how determined the facade. That would have been a disaster. A quite remarkable amount of diplomacy was actually conducted in lacy boudoirs and at feminine tea parties. News flew between sips of tea and intimate whispers. Much of it was false or only half true, but sifted together with the half-truths and falsehoods the men told each other, both officially and unofficially, trends of favor could be guessed.

Fortunately Sabrina had discovered that physical idleness had no effect on the brains of Russian ladies. In fact, they wielded far more power and influence than most European females. They were not minors under the law; they administered their own money and property if they desired and, very frequently, dominated their men. Moreover they were not in the least mealymouthed—a disease growing more and more prevalent in England, where far too many things could not be said or were discussed only in whispers.

The liking and respect Sabrina soon developed for the various princesses and countesses permitted her to accept other customs as harmless eccentricity. There was a deliberate hypocritical blindness in this, Sabrina knew, but it was her duty to her own country to be liked and trusted—which would have been impossible if she went about preaching. So she bit her tongue when the Russian servants acted as if she were a senseless doll.

Conversation between herself and William had been suspended while the footman buttoned up Sabrina's coat, wrapped her fur scarf carefully around her head so that it would not crush or damage her hair, and inserted her hands into a huge ermine and marten muff—carefully holding the muff so that Sabrina would not have to support its weight. Another footman had come in and set a hat on William's head, then eased his gloves onto his hands. William gritted his teeth. A third footman arrived to announce that the sleigh was waiting for the "little father" and "little mother."

Regardless of the bitter weather, all three footmen accompanied William and Sabrina out of the house to help them down the stairs until the grooms, hurrying up, could take over the support of their master and mistress. William's breath hissed in with frustration, but he made no protest. He was an excellent diplomat, willing to endure any discomfort to show respect for his host country.

Once they were safely closed into the luxurious sleigh, he picked up the conversation they had abandoned while surrounded by servants. Although they customarily spoke English to each other and the servants were supposed to know only Russian and French, both Katy and Charlot had reported a suspicion that English was understood. This had not surprised either William or Sabrina.

"It's true enough that Alexander doesn't trust his foreign minister's policy anymore," William confirmed, "but he's too proud to make a clean about-face. That would be admitting openly that he's been wrong from the beginning. Besides, he doesn't trust anyone else, either. Worst of all, he doesn't trust himself. At least, that's what Lord Gower says."

"Then why would the tsar show up at Czartoryski's ball? In fact, after a disaster like that battle at Austerlitz, with thirty or forty thousand Austrian and Russians dead or prisoners and the rest still scattered all over Poland and Germany as well as Russia, I don't understand any government official giving a ball."

"To save face. There's a lot of the Oriental in Russians."

"Tsar Alexander might want to and need to, but Czartoryski? Isn't he finished as foreign minister, William?"

"Yes . . . No . . . How can one be sure? This isn't a rational government. It's—it's a figment of a man's imagination—or, rather, of a woman's who's been dead for years."

"You mean Tsarina Catherine?" Sabrina asked.

"Yes, indeed. First she has her grandson Alexander educated by a damned republican—that La Harpe. Then she changes her mind, after everything blew up in France, and starts clamping on the screws so her own people won't get any revolutionary notions. Then she dies and her lunatic son Paul takes over. Can you imagine trying to run a country this size like an army camp—uniforms for everyone, hours to do this and that, making dress styles illegal—"

"But William," Sabrina protested, "he really *was* a lunatic. Why should you have expected him to act rationally?"

As she said the words she winced internally. Of all people, it seemed to Sabrina, William should be the most understanding of irrational urges. Was it rational never to be able to care for a person who cared for you?

And was her own behavior any more rational? Eighty or ninety percent of married women of her class would call *her* a lunatic, to consider leaving a kind, polite, generous husband, who was willing, even eager, to include her in the fascinating work he did, only because of an affair now and again. Lady Melbourne had confessed herself humbly grateful to her husband's mistresses, who diverted his attention and left her free to pursue her own love affairs. The duchess of Devonshire had invited her husband's mistress to live permanently in their household and cherished Lady Elizabeth Foster as her dearest friend.

Now, sitting in the carriage, listening with half her mind to William's penetrating analysis of the situation, Sabrina wondered with the other half of her mind whether she *was* insane. Why couldn't she compromise? So she no longer loved William—so what? Most of the women she knew did not love their husbands. Some devoted themselves to their children, some chose to have affairs of the heart— and sometimes of the body, too—of their own. Even those who did love their husbands often accepted the existence of a mistress. "Men will be men," they would say with a shrug. "It doesn't mean anything." Why couldn't *she* accept that?

She watched William's animated expression as he described how the Tsarina Elizabeth had taken Catherine's son Paul away from her and given him an ineradicable hatred for his mother. This had become mutual over the years, violently intensified after Catherine had encouraged a military rebellion against her husband, Peter III, and rewarded the men who murdered him with her body as well as her trust. Of course, Peter III had been madder than his son Paul—although possibly Paul was not Peter's son. Owing to the unsavory situation, Catherine had repeated Elizabeth's actions—removing Alexander and his brother Constantine from their parents' care and influence.

It was hard to guess, William continued judiciously, whether this had done the present tsar more harm or good. Certainly it had been good for Russia. The four years of Paul's reign had been a hell that even the Russians—who were accustomed to insane rulers—had found unacceptable. If Alexander and all his brothers had been raised by his father and had been in accord with Paul's ideas, either the palace coup that had unseated (and murdered) Paul would not have taken place or the country might have suffered anarchy.

"What do you mean, you don't know whether being raised by his grandmother was good or bad? Surely it couldn't have been worse than being raised by an insane martinet," Sabrina protested.

She could respond with interest to anything William discussed, she was thinking as she spoke. She could admire the flash of his dark eyes, the straight, fine nose, the well-curved lips. She could respect his intelligence and enjoy his perceptions—but she could not feel a quiver of sexual response or, far worse, a spark of affection. There was no warmth in William. There was no excuse for fondness or tenderness. He was only capable of the hot lust of pursuit or cold usage. He was not talking to her because he was interested in her. He was giving her information so that she would not make a faux pas and therefore could be useful to him.

"Perhaps not," William responded, "but being filled with

a mess of republican idealism and then told 'right-about-face, march to absolutism' by his grandmother and finally being dumped into four years of militaristic lunacy—all drill and parade with no rhyme or reason to it—didn't do him much good, either. Particularly when the only way out was to have his father murdered."

"William! I can hardly believe he agreed to that."

"No . . . In fact, he asked for assurances that Paul would only be forced to abdicate. But Alexander isn't stupid, Sabrina. He knew it wasn't possible to have two tsars with diametrically opposed ideas. As long as Paul was alive there would be a strong focus for the opposition. Every tsar who had been deposed before had died—if not immediately, then within a few weeks or months."

"I suppose he lied to himself," Sabrina said with sympathy. "So many people do."

"Yes," William agreed without a shadow of self-consciousness. "Anyway, it's a very touchy subject. If it comes up, just look blank, as if you never heard a word about it. After all, that was in 1801. You were only a child. No reason you should have known. I was only trying to explain that Alexander doesn't always let his left hand know what his right hand is doing. That is why he might attend Czartoryski's ball."

Sabrina chuckled. "That should make him a first-class politician."

"It should," William remarked dryly, "only very often his head doesn't seem to know what *either* hand is doing. He was taught too much idealistic nonsense totally unsuitable at this time in this country. He hasn't the maturity or patience to work toward those ideals slowly. So when he's had a disappointment, he wants to throw the baby out with the bathwater—only he doesn't want anyone to see him doing it. He'll keep Czartoryski for window-dressing for a while."

"Poor man. Does he know?"

"I should imagine so. Czartoryski's clever enough. It's too bad. He had some good ideas, and he was reasonably pro-British. He'd even discovered a way to make Alexander acceptable to the Polish nobles, and they would have fought with the Prussian-Russian army—only Alexander hemmed and hawed, so Bonaparte got to the Poles first."

"Would it have made any difference?" Sabrina asked doubtfully.

"Probably not. I'm no military man, but from what I can gather, the defeat was virtually assured by Alexander—who's no military man, either, though he may have thought he was with all his father's drilling on the parade ground—taking control. He did about everything wrong that could be done. Oh, here we are. Sabrina, drop the women—Novosiltsov's and Stroganov's mothers and sisters, too. Both are out of favor. I don't mean cut them dead—"

"I wouldn't even if you did mean it," Sabrina snapped. She knew the needs of political friendships, but the coldness of William's order was ugly. "That would scarcely recommend me to my other friends, would it? I'll manage."

"It may not be as easy as you think," William warned. "Drowning people cling rather desperately to any support in sight. Just remember there isn't anything you can do for them anyway, and we don't want to be tarred with the same brush. There are some signs that Alexander is looking around for someone else to blame for his troubles. I don't want it to be the British."

As he spoke the sleigh was threading its way through the large number of other similar vehicles waiting in the street. Sabrina kept her eyes on her muff. She could not bear to look at the coachmen and grooms huddled together or curled up asleep under the sleighs. The temperature was probably below zero already, and a sharp wind was blowing. No provision ever seemed to be made for those poor creatures. They waited outdoors for many hours without the slightest protection.

Sabrina was glad William never permitted it, although she wondered if it was not his concern for the horses more than for the men. In any case, both were protected. Invariably William found an errand for the men to do or a necessity for them to return to the house for some hours. She heard him giving instructions but did not really listen. Her mind was busy with the problem of avoiding women she had heretofore cultivated. Foreign Minister Czartoryski had no women in his household—at least none presented at formal balls, but the others . . .

The sleigh door opened again, letting in a blast of air so frigid that it stung her eyes and nose. Hands reached out to help her down from the sleigh. Their own grooms handed William and Sabrina over to Czartoryski's servants on the stairs, and in another moment they were in a reception chamber, being tenderly divested of their outer garments. Opposite were doors, either gorgeously or ostentatiously decorated, depending on one's taste. Sabrina would have preferred less gold leaf and fewer convolutions in the carving, but ostentatious or not, they were beautiful. They were flung wide to show an impressive staircase. In winter the reception rooms on the upper floors were used because they were warmer, and it was necessary to use every possible device to conserve warmth. Although two fires blazed in the reception room, Sabrina had been very glad of the cashmere shawl that protected her bare shoulders and arms.

Once they entered the rooms above, Sabrina allowed the shawl to drop and rest in the crook of her elbows. She was, as always, dazzled for a moment by the brilliant lighting of the thousands of candles glittering back from crystal ornaments, from jewels that made her own look paltry, from rich fabrics embroidered in silver and gold, from the bright-colored, overdecorated walls and ceilings.

She had noticed in the past that her pale eyes were more sensitive to light, particularly sudden changes from dark to bright, than were other people's.

While she was still half-blind, she heard her husband utter a soft exclamation. He extricated his arm skillfully from her hand, which had been resting on it, and plunged into the crowd. Before he was completely swallowed up, Sabrina's vision had cleared enough to catch sight of him making his way toward a short, dark-skinned man with small, bright eyes and a very high, aquiline nose. She could hear music coming from the ballroom beyond, but William was obviously not going directly there. Her first feeling was one of relief. At least her husband was not obviously pursuing the inamorata of the moment. Her next sensation was one of intense surprise. What was Prince General Bagration doing here?

His presence was quite startling. He was a firm believer in and supporter of Prince Marshal Kutuzov, whose plans had been ignored and superseded by the tsar, causing the defeat at Austerlitz. Furthermore, Prince Bagration was of volatile disposition, like many Georgians, and had been heard—or so rumor had hissed in Sabrina's ear—to have said certain things about the tsar's advisors that implied he would not, to say the least, court their company. In fact, Sabrina noticed, Prince Bagration did not look happy. Her eyes swept beyond him for a glimpse at the rest of the group, hoping to find an explanation of his presence in his companions. Instead, a most unladylike screech of joy and amazement was forced out of her.

"Perce!"

Sabrina surged forward, elbowing people out of the way quite rudely. For a split second after she had shouted Philip's friend's name, she thought she must have been mistaken. What in the world would Percivale Moreton be doing standing attentively at General Bagration's elbow? But Perce's head had turned instantly at her call, and although he had missed seeing her in the crowd, she was certain it was he. She knew Perce almost as well as she knew her foster brother, Philip. Perce and Philip were inseparable childhood friends, and since Perce's family lived in Cornwall, he had spent most of his short school holidays with Roger and Leonie at Stour Castle or Dymchurch House.

As soon as Sabrina began to move, Perce saw her. Pausing only to excuse himself to his companions, he worked his way toward her with as much determination as she was showing and hugged her as enthusiastically. Then he pushed her back a little to look at her.

"Brina, you're breathtaking. How the devil did you work up that hard glitter?"

"It suited the weather," she said.

She was smiling, but there must have been something in her voice that betrayed her. Perce knew her as well as she knew him, after all. She had been the "pesty little sister," trailing along behind him and Philip, begging to be included in their games and excursions. Considering that she was seven years younger—and a girl—they had been generous. They had yielded to her entreaties often, too often for the safety of her clothing, the cleanliness of her person, or the proper development of the delicate sensibility expected of a young female of high breeding.

The smile died out of Perce's eyes. As it did, Sabrina suddenly realized that he did not look quite right, either. There were dark shadows under his eyes, hollows in his cheeks, and lines around his mouth that she did not remember.

"What's wrong?"

The anxious question came from both simultaneously, so that each had to laugh. Sabrina sighed and shrugged.

"A long story," she said. "And you?"

Perce shrugged also. "Austerlitz," he replied even more succinctly.

"Austerlitz?" Sabrina echoed. "What were you doing there, in God's name? What are you doing in Russia in the first place?"

"A long story," Perce said, and they both laughed again.

Sabrina looked around and saw Countess Latuski bearing down on her. Either the woman had no idea Sabrina had seen her with William or she was eager to force a confrontation. Sabrina took a firm grip on Perce's hand. "Can you get away for a little while?"

He glanced quickly at Prince Bagration and saw him listening to William, who was talking eagerly. "Yes, but I can't leave and I have to be where I can see when the prince moves."

"We can go over to the window." Sabrina nodded toward one of the huge double windows that formed six embrasures down the length of the room. Although they were partially covered by heavy, swagged draperies, they leaked frigid air and people generally avoided the area.

"You'll freeze," Perce protested.

"I have my shawl," Sabrina assured him, drawing it partially up over her shoulders as she spoke, but her eyes flashed toward the woman plainly trying to approach them. It was clear that Sabrina hoped to discourage her by moving away obviously.

Perce nodded and turned—but they had not been quick enough. The woman Sabrina was trying to avoid reached them and began to gush, delivering en route several invitations. "You are in beauty tonight, great beauty," Countess Latuski twittered, "and I see you have already captured one of our special guests. You must grace my little breakfast, and the ball, and bring—" She stopped suggestively, not having had Perce presented to her.

"You overestimate my allure," Sabrina said flatly. She still had no idea whether the countess was ignorant or was pushing for Sabrina's tacit concurrence in her relationship with William. "This is Percivale George Evelyn Moreton,

my brother Philip's closest friend. Countess Maria Fedorovna Latuski, may I present to you, Lord Kevern."

Of course, Philip was not Sabrina's brother; he was not
related to her in any way, but it was too difficult to explain each time that Leonie was her cousin, not her
mother, and that Philip was her cousin's husband's son.
Sabrina noticed that sometimes when she had explained
the relationship and then had occasion to mention some of
the innocent things she and Philip had done together, she
received suggestive leers. That was sickening! In her heart
Philip was her brother, and she knew the feeling to be mutual. It was easier to call him brother and be done with it.

Perce bowed to their unwelcome companion with great
grace, but his face had all the animation of a dead fish.
"Honored, I'm sure," he said in English.

The countess looked at him in surprise.

"He said he was honored, he was sure," Sabrina translated literally, knowing that the meaningless English idiom
came out as a cynical, veiled insult in French.

Perce continued to look utterly blank, as if his French
were not good enough to make him aware of just what Sabrina had said. The countess's interest in him diminished
visibly. She had obviously been about to invite him more
specifically than her unfinished "bring—" but was now
reconsidering.

"Owing to the presence of Lord Kevern in St. Petersburg, I am afraid I don't know how much time I will
have free over the next few weeks," Sabrina said.

No quiver of voice or expression betrayed that she knew
Perce's French was as fluent as her own, although he
spoke it with an abominable English accent. In fact, Perce
learned languages more quickly than anyone Sabrina
knew, and spoke each with the same strong accent. He
claimed, and she believed him, that he was only marginally aware of the difference in his speech and that of
others. It was interesting to Sabrina that he was also tone-

deaf, or nearly so. He could recognize the rhythm of music well enough to dance, but he admitted that the tunes all sounded pretty much alike to him.

She turned to him and asked in English, "Will you be free to visit us for the next week or so?"

"I think so, but don't count on it. I don't know how long we're supposed to stay in St. Petersburg—and if someone steps on Prince Bagration's toes . . ."

All the while he spoke, Perce looked about as intelligent as a village idiot, his face empty, his eyes blank and glazed. Sabrina smiled with spurious regret at Countess Latuski.

"I will be much occupied showing Lord Kevern the city," she said. "I fear this may cut into my engagements. Perhaps if he finds other amusements . . . I will write and let you know."

The countess now had the option of clearly asking Sabrina to bring Perce to the functions to which she had invited her or of leaving them rapidly. Apparently she decided the latter was the better of the two options. Again Sabrina was not sure whether this decision was a retreat in fear of a more open rebuff or whether Perce's seeming dullness and bad French had put her off. Maria Fedorovna made some quick excuse about seeing someone waving to her and left them. Sabrina and Perce exchanged a single glance of understanding and continued their interrupted attempt to find a modicum of privacy.

As they reached the window and took refuge partly behind and partly alongside the heavy swag of drapery, Sabrina chuckled. "I love it when you go blank like that, Perce," she confessed. "You look like a cross between a dead fish and the village idiot. It's enough to discourage the most violent lord-sucker and toady alive."

"Was that what she was?" Perce asked doubtfully.

The brief haunted expression of indecision and dislike that he had seen when Sabrina noticed Countess Latuski coming toward them had given him the impression that she was more than just a social nuisance. He had put his back to the window so that Sabrina was sheltered from the worst of the draft. He did it out of habit, quite unaware of the protective gesture born of years of blocking drafts from his much-loved mother and sisters, who, to his mind, were most inadequately clad in their thin muslins or silks.

The shock of seeing so dearly familiar a person had brought back to Sabrina all the happiness of the years when Perce was another "brother." Then the countess's intrusion into those memories had brought into horrible clarity the ugly happening of that day and the equally ugly choice she was now to make, with the knowledge that whichever path she chose would lead inevitably to unhappiness. Now the little act of consideration, Perce's obvious desire to spare her any discomfort, even the small one of being chilly, demolished any barrier of pride Sabrina might have erected around her misery.

"No," she said, "that isn't all she is. She's the woman to whom William was making love in *my* drawing room this morning. The trouble is, I don't know whether she is unaware that I saw them or whether her sudden passion for me is to force my tacit acceptance of the affair—and I'm not sure I care. Then there's this other stupid tie-in with the tsar's mistress, Maria Naryshkin—they're friends—so that I don't dare openly spit in her face. On top of that, I've just discovered that I—I don't care with whom William goes to bed, so long as it isn't me! I don't love him anymore, Perce. I don't want to be his wife. I don't want to bear his children."

Perce had opened his mouth in shock at Sabrina's first disclosure, but hadn't interrupted her. "My God, how long has this been going on?" he asked in an odd voice.

Sabrina looked up at him, but his face had gone blank again. Even she could not read anything in that fishlike stare. She shuddered. "For two years. I can stop him. I have in the past. But—but it isn't worth it to me. Oh, Perce, I made a dreadful mistake. I'm not jealous—really I'm not. It's—this is what's so awful—that William isn't worth the effort to keep him."

Perce's lips moved, but he didn't seem to be able to find his voice or the words he wanted to say. Tears sprang into Sabrina's eyes. If Perce reacted this way merely to the confession that she didn't love her husband or want to keep him, how would the rest of the world react to an annulment or divorce? Resentment followed despair.

"You haven't heard the worst yet," she snapped. "I'm considering an annulment or divorce. Do you think that's a good idea?"

"Don't!" Perce sounded as if someone had him by the throat. "Don't ask *me*! I'm the last . . . For God's sake, Brina, I'm in love with you! You can't talk to me about this!"

Sabrina recoiled as if she had been struck in the face. It was almost as bad as if Philip had made sexual advances to her when she had brought him a broken toy to fix. She had expected sympathy, concern, grave counsel. What she really hoped for, of course, was a big brother to dry her tears and pat her back and show her her doll all mended. That her adult mind knew quite well broken marriages could not be mended like broken toys was irrelevant. Her heart had a childlike corner that had infinite faith in her big brothers' abilities to mend anything.

"I'm sorry—" Perce began, but Sabrina had already turned and fled.

He stood watching her disappear into the crowd, calling himself ten times a fool. He hadn't meant to say it. He knew Sabrina had classed him with Philip. He was neuter gender to her, a safe friend. Now he had destroyed that, destroyed her faith in him, and probably blackened himself with William's soot. She would think of him as just another predatory male, eager to prey on any attractive, unhappy wife.

But he hadn't known! His confession of love had been a result of shock, of a sudden brief vision of heaven within his grasp. He had never guessed there was any trouble between Sabrina and her husband. Philip hadn't said a word. Well, why should he? And it was possible Philip didn't know, either. Sabrina might have been afraid to say anything to Philip, who was rather prone to impetuous behavior. She could have feared that Philip would try to mend Elvan's ways with a horsewhip or a pistol.

I never know anything at the right time, Perce thought bitterly. He hadn't realized that he loved Sabrina until she was lost to him, already completely devoted to Elvan. It was his sudden dislike for Elvan—a man he had always found pleasant enough until Sabrina began to love him— that had revealed Perce's true feelings to himself. It was too late then. Sabrina was already waging a determined war to be permitted to marry the man she had chosen. To present himself as a suitor at that point, a suitor her family would have favored strongly and would have pushed at her every way they could, would have earned Perce only her hatred. Quite aside from the fact that she had never thought of him as other than a brother, it would have seemed to her a deliberate betrayal, a cheap device to distract her from a man her guardians felt was too unsettled for her.

Like Leonie and Roger, it had not occurred to Perce that Elvan would not be a faithful husband, or, rather, that he would be so indiscreet Sabrina would discover his lapses. That Elvan was known to have had many affairs was irrelevant. He had never before pursued an unmarried girl. He had given every evidence of being completely smitten. Men in their thirties frequently tired of ephemeral affairs and wished to settle down and start a nursery. What was more, it was inconceivable to Perce that any man who

43

had won Sabrina, a woman as intelligent and high-spirited as she was beautiful, would ever want to look elsewhere.

While Roger and Leonie delayed, hoping Sabrina's infatuation would fade, Perce had continued a frequent visitor to the family. Had he seen the faintest sign that either Lord Elvan or Sabrina was losing interest, he would have leapt into the breach to widen it and win the prize for himself. Unfortunately, no uncertainty on either side ever showed. All Perce had accomplished was to fall more and more deeply in love himself. Thus, when Roger and Leonie had finally given permission for the marriage, Perce had found the situation too painful. In general, after that, Perce had avoided Sabrina and her husband. There had been nothing obvious, of course, and Elvan's employment in the diplomatic service had soon removed them from England altogether.

Perce winced, thinking what a shock his announcement must have been to Sabrina. Ugly, disgusting, to profess love to a woman who was already hurt by her husband's betrayal—as if the confession of her injury had somehow cheapened her, had incited him to instant lust. It must seem like that, he thought sickly. What else could she believe, when she must have been even more unaware of his past desire for her than he was of her dissatisfaction with her husband.

CHAPTER THREE

The next morning Sabrina opened her eyes and looked at her bed-curtains with faint puzzlement. She felt light and happy and could not imagine why. Then she realized she had had a very pleasant dream. The actual events were vague, but an overall feeling of joyous pleasure remained. She smiled and sat up, hearing the rings of the curtains rattling on the rods as Katy pushed them away from the windows. In a moment Katy would draw the bed-curtains and bring her hot chocolate.

The curtains were drawn, but Katy held no tray and she jumped a little as if surprised to see Sabrina sitting up. "Are ye all right, then, luv?" she asked.

"Of course I'm all right," Sabrina replied in surprise. "Whatever do you mean?"

"Whatever do I mean?" Katy echoed. "Ye came home last night like a walkin' corpse. I was all ready to call a physician to ye—only I didna know who, and ye didna have a fever. . . . What happened at the ball?"

"The ball?" Sabrina was the echoer that time.

What happened at the ball? Sabrina did not really remember anything clearly except Perce's voice when he said, "I'm in love with you." The words caught her mind again, but she pushed them away. She had been so surprised, so shocked. Had she done or said anything really stupid? Had anyone noticed she was not herself? She tried to recall startled expressions or remarks, but she could hardly remember talking to anyone. Then she gave a small sigh of relief. William had commented on the way home that she had disappeared into the ballroom and had danced every single dance. He had thought it a clever device to avoid talk that, at this uncertain moment, might be dangerous. Nothing else came back to her. She hoped, then, she had not misbehaved in any obvious way.

"Brina!" Katy's voice was anxious again.

"Perce was there," Sabrina said.

That wasn't what she had intended to say. She didn't want to talk about Perce, not even to Katy—especially not to Katy, who had always been fond of him.

"Lord Kevern? What's he doin' in Russia?"

"I don't know," Sabrina confessed. "We—we didn't have time to talk about it."

Suddenly she remembered that he had looked ill and tired. Austerlitz! He had said he was at Austerlitz! In the battle? Perce? He must have been! He was with General Bagration, who had fought a desperate rearguard action when much of the rest of the army had panicked. Prince General Bagration was the hero of a lost cause. His action had permitted old Field Marshal Kutuzov, commanding the Russian forces, to rally a few remnants of the army so that the tsar and others could retreat safely. Sabrina had never thought of Perce in a battle. It wasn't a pleasant idea. If anything happened to him . . . Perce hurt? Dead? A big hollow opened inside Sabrina.

"Well, that still doesna explain why ye came home lookin' like a poleaxed ox."

The sharp comment was a relief. It broke the anguish wakened by the thought of losing Perce. Stupid thing to worry about, Sabrina told herself severely, now that he was safe. But she didn't want to answer Katy's remark. She wouldn't lie to Katy, but she couldn't confess what had happened, either. All she could do was shake her head.

Katy's eyes narrowed, but she asked no more questions. That stupid, vicious clot of a husband must have shamed Brina publicly. Katy seethed, but she kept her expression bland. No use adding to Brina's troubles. Besides, Brina was looking better now, more thoughtful than sad. Whatever Himself had done, it seemed to be pushing Brina to some kind of a decision.

It wasn't often that Katy misjudged her nursling, but she was far out this time. Her question had, of course, brought Sabrina's mind right back to Perce's saying he was in love with her. But the words came from a new face, not from the boyish lips that had told her stories and kissed her bruised knees and laughed at her. The lips that had said those words were thin with pain, and there were lines of bitterness around the mouth. The dark-shadowed eyes had seen a great deal since Perce used to make blank fisheyes to conceal her little sins or since they glinted with mischief when he teased her. Between then and now, they had looked on the shambles of Austerlitz—and what else? Bonaparte had trapped the Russian and Austrian armies at Austerlitz, and over 26,000 men had lost their lives in the battle against the French invaders. What *was* Perce doing in company with Russian generals?

Sabrina uttered an exclamation of frustration when she realized she had no idea where he was staying or how to reach him.

"What's it now?" Katy inquired as she set the tray of chocolate and dry bread and jam over Sabrina's thighs. She sounded relieved, and she was. Brina's remark had been in a natural tone of irritation.

"I didn't get Perce's address," Sabrina replied.

"Why would ye be needin' it?" Katy countered. "Sure he'll be here soon as he thinks it decent. And dinna be worritin' that he hasna yer direction, either. He only looks like an idiot—sometimes. He's got rare brains, Lord Kev-

47

ern. He'll know he can find ye by askin' at the ambassador's."

"He might not be able to come," Sabrina replied, skirting the truth. "I think he's here on some secret government business—and don't say a word to anyone, especially to Charlot. I know he's been with William for years and years and is loyal to him—but he's French, and—and Perce isn't William."

"A greater truth you never spoke," Katy said sharply.

"My goodness, Katy," Sabrina exclaimed, setting down the chocolate she had been about to sip. "Do you think Charlot would help Bonaparte? Send information or—"

"Dinna be silly, Brina. Charlot's no more interested in Bonaparte than I am, and for all his French accent he was born in England. I meant what ye said about Lord Kevern and Himself. There couldna be two men more different."

Couldn't there be? Sabrina sipped her chocolate as Katy went out into the dressing room and came back carrying underclothing and went out again. As soon as she said she was unhappy with William, the chase had started, Sabrina thought bitterly. Only Perce wasn't as skilled as William. He had started with his mouth instead of his eyes. That was stupid. Any woman . . . Sabrina's mind backed up and considered the last completed thought. Whatever Perce was, he wasn't stupid. He wasn't clumsy, either. It was very rare, indeed, for Perce Moreton to set a foot wrong in any undertaking.

Oh, Perce got into trouble, lots of it, all the time—but that was youthful, deliberate deviltry. He wasn't like Philip, barging blithely ahead where angels feared to tread. That pair was like a ship, with Philip the bowsprit and Perce the rudder. He wasn't a very cautious rudder; he'd go along with Philip head on into the rocks to see if they'd jump aside and for the hellish joy of dodging a near thing—but he did dodge. He had it all planned out.

No, Perce wasn't stupid and wasn't clumsy, but blurting

out "I'm in love with you" was both. It was the wrong time, too, and Perce never missed on his timing. He always knew just when to say the word that would make Roger start to laugh and save them all a whipping. He knew just when to approach Leonie to get permission to do something that wasn't "quite proper." So Perce had done something both stupid and clumsy and at the wrong time. Why?

Because he hadn't intended to say it. Because it had been forced out of him by shock—or by an overwhelming emotion. Because he was shaken up so much that he had stated the naked truth.

That was all very logical, Sabrina thought, but the conclusion was insane. When could Perce have fallen in love with her? She hadn't even really seen him for years—not since she'd married William. She stopped there, jam-filled spoon suspended over her bread. Not since she'd married William! That could have been a coincidence. They had only been in England for three months after the wedding and another five months in 1804. She spread the jam over the bread slowly, thoughtfully. No, it wasn't a coincidence. It so happened that Perce was an old friend of Meg's as well as of Philip's. It was too odd that he wouldn't visit even once in five months.

Well, hurrah for logic. A fat lot of good it did when it provided conclusions crazier than plain guessing. A man doesn't fall in love with a girl who isn't there. Or does he? Was it because he missed her? But that was ridiculous, too. Perce used to visit often, but he didn't live with them. There were often months between visits. He had had plenty of chance to miss her before she ever set eyes on William.

Absently, Sabrina ate her bread and jam and sipped her chocolate. She was never going to find the answer this way. Her logic was full of holes. Perce could have said he loved her because he thought she needed it said, because he thought she was hurt by William's playing around and needed to feel loved.

Whatever his reason, Sabrina knew she couldn't let the matter rest where it was. That would mean losing him. Also, there were too many questions unanswered, one of them damned dangerous. She had said to Katy that Perce must be involved in government business, but she wasn't really sure of that at all. It was a possibility and a good excuse for his inability to visit. But it was just as possible that this was another case of Perce looking for trouble to make life interesting. If so, she was going to have to do something about that. Bonaparte wasn't going to stop. There would be more battles. Even Perce's perfect timing wouldn't help him dodge bullets.

Sabrina put aside the remains of her breakfast and got out of bed. She threw off her nightdress and slipped on her undergarments, pale yellow silk pantalettes, edged and flounced with natural lace and buttoned at the waist. Sabrina ran a hand automatically along the hip. Wrinkling meant she was gaining weight, the well-fitted garment pulling a bit at the seams. No wrinkling. In fact, the fabric slipped about more than usual; she was getting thinner. Sabrina sighed. She was unfashionably slender already.

A narrow breastband followed. Many women no longer wore them, having cast them aside with their corsets in the name of freedom, but Sabrina had rather full breasts and found herself uncomfortable without some support. Besides, with necklines as low as they were these days, there was the danger that a full-breasted woman would bob right out of her dress if she moved energetically. On the other hand, Sabrina did not use or need the bodyband that controlled the abdomen. Hers was flat and hard still, although she really did not get enough exercise these days.

A simple chemise and petticoat, also pale yellow silk with lace trim, followed. Sabrina sat down and drew on her stockings. These were rather heavy wool, not at all fashionable but more practical than thin silk with the temperature below zero and the floors cold. Her long skirt would hide her concession to practicality. She tied her garters above her knees just as Katy, who had heard her moving around, came in carrying her dress. This, too, was pale yellow silk, its bodice so short that it came barely one third of the way up, exposing about two thirds of her breasts. Katy clucked and mumbled as she twitched the dress into place, fastening the tiny buttons at the back.

"Well, I agree with you," Sabrina said in response to Katy's grumbling. "I think it's idiotic to wear low-necked thin silk dresses in the middle of a Russian winter, too, but William's position must be supported. He can't have a dowdy wife. Frankly, I'd like to try traditional Russian dress, but there's so much bad feeling about it because of the last tsar's stupid laws that I don't dare."

Katy came around in front, having done up Sabrina's buttons and looked at her. "I didna say a word about the dress," she remarked as she pulled a rich gold overdress up Sabrina's arms. "What's wrong with ye, Brina?"

"What *did* you say?" Sabrina asked guiltily. Her mind had been miles away and she had answered Katy's usual complaint without really listening to her.

"It wasna important, but ye're actin' queer, luv."

"I'm just worried, Katy. Whatever I do is going to make trouble. . . ."

Her voice drifted away. She was talking of her marriage, of course, so why did she think of Perce? She was going to have to see him. It didn't seem possible to concentrate on anything else. But Sabrina was very much afraid Perce would not come or even write to her. He must have seen that he had offended rather than reassured her. In that case, he would do his best to avoid her. She would have to send him a note, but she didn't know where to send it. Well, William could find out for her. Sabrina grabbed for her shawl and hurried down to catch William at breakfast.

Perce was having a very similar argument with himself, although he had not enjoyed pleasant dreams. In fact, he had hardly slept at all, and his memory of the ball, unlike Sabrina's, was all too vivid. Nonetheless he, too, felt he could not allow matters to rest where they were and was racking his brains for a way to approach her—no, not so much that. Elvan, damn and blast him, would arrange the approach. Perce was trying to think of some explanation for what he had blurted out that would permit Sabrina to look at him without feeling sick.

Damn Elvan! Curse, rot, and damn Elvan! It was all his fault. If he hadn't made Brina miserable to start out with, the whole situation wouldn't have occurred. If he had just kept his damned mouth shut about personal matters when he was talking to General Bagration, that kind, thoughtful Russian would not have withdrawn his invitation to Perce to stay at his estate near Moscow. Elvan had told the prince of Perce's long friendship with Sabrina's family. Bagration had smiled on Perce kindly and said he could come to his estate another time, that Perce should stay and taste the joys of St. Petersburg in the company of his friends right now.

For a while after realizing that protest was useless, Perce had given some thought to murdering Elvan. He knew quite well why that sly son of a bitch had been so passionate in urging him to stay. Elvan thought he had found a nice safe escort for his wife, a cavalier servente who would take her anywhere and keep her occupied so that Elvan himself could concentrate on his romantic escapades.

Perce sat on the edge of his bed and held his head in his hands and groaned. If he had known! If he had only known! He had been so furious that only Bagration's rather abrupt departure soon after the supper had been served had prevented Perce from telling Elvan the truth. Perce sighed. That was one time it was lucky he had never been able to get Elvan alone. If he had confessed, it might have made serious trouble for Brina. Unfaithful husbands always seemed to be suspicious. Logic never influenced such suspicions. It made no difference that he and Sabrina had not exchanged more than a few words at a public ball since her engagement, had not even been in the same country most of the time. If Elvan wanted to dream up an affair . . .

There was no use crying over spilt milk. He would have to . . . Suddenly Perce jerked upright and snatched his watch off the table. What a fool he was! Instead of confessing he loved Sabrina, he should have told Elvan the other truth to his face—that he didn't intend to play cavalier servente so that Elvan could whore around with another woman. Grinning viciously, Perce began to strip off his nightshirt. He would catch that sly, sneaking bastard at breakfast and put a flea in his ear before Sabrina came down. As for Brina . . . Perce shrugged. He would leave his card. If she wanted to see him, she would write.

He shouted for the Russian serf who served him. Sergei was a bear of a man, thick and dark and broad. He was solidly built with rock-hard muscles and massive short legs. His face was flat and open. Dark, bright eyes twinkled under bushy brows, and a broad forehead was hidden under curly black hair touched with graying streaks.

Sergei had been someone's serf—Perce had never been able to figure out to whom he had belonged—but he had been singled out for the army when he was little more than a boy, and by virtue of long separation from his home he was as much a free man as any soldier could be. Perce had come upon Sergei very soon after he arrived at the Russian army camp. Having had no previous connection with any army, British or foreign, Perce was not accustomed to the brutality with which the troops were treated, and Sergei was about to be whipped for some infraction of the rules. Although Perce knew he should mind his own business, he had asked what the man had done, mostly through pantomime. From expression and gesture, he guessed it was a minor matter, usually settled by paying a fine—only Sergei had no money. Casually, Perce had flipped the sergeant a gold coin.

"Take it out of that," he said in French, hoping someone would understand him. Then he looked around at the ragged troop and tossed over several more guineas. "And get your men something decent to eat and some shoes."

How much any of them understood of what he said, he didn't know. Perce could comprehend some Russian but could speak only a few words—all unsuitable for this occasion. Obviously the sergeant realized that Perce had paid Sergei's fine, because the man was released and allowed to put on his shirt. That was all Perce really cared about. If the money disappeared into the sergeant's pocket, it would still benefit the men by improving the sergeant's temper.

Thus he was somewhat surprised five minutes later to find Sergei trotting behind his horse. First he thought the man wanted to thank him. However, he was stunned, after an interpreter had been found, to discover he had bought Sergei. Realizing he was in out of his depth, he had sought out his friends on General Bagration's staff and discussed the matter with them. It was made clear to him that it would be a great cruelty to dismiss or even to attempt to free Sergei. The man had long lost touch with his relatives and did not even seem sure from what part of Russia he came. Perce was somewhat worried about what he would do with Sergei when it was time to leave Russia, but he set about using him to learn Russian while he taught the serf French and trained him to be useful in other ways.

Over the nine months that Perce had been with the Russian army and a guest of various officers of that army, Sergei had proved invaluable. Perce made no pretense of being able to understand him. In a sense Sergei had a real slave mentality. He *had* to belong to someone, but had no particular loyalty. Perce had bought him and was now his personal "little father." He would, and nearly did more than once, die for Perce. If, however, Perce sold him, he would be equally loyal to his new master. Once Perce had even tried to discuss the matter but could get no more out of Sergei than that the "soul" was sold.

Not that Sergei was unfeeling. One of the reasons Perce never got to the bottom of the selling of souls was that Sergei became so frantic with terror at the thought of being sold to someone else. He, who faced bullets and cannon without flinching, fell on his knees and wept and begged Perce to inflict any punishment on him for his wrongdoing but not to sell him. It took Perce nearly an hour to explain to his servant he had done nothing wrong, that the question had been asked only out of curiosity. Whether he had convinced Sergei, Perce didn't know. For weeks the man had looked hunted and haunted, trembling every time someone visited Perce or whenever he had to accompany his master anywhere. He had not quite recovered from his fright, even several months later.

On the other hand, Sergei was never cringing or even dependent in a slavish way. He assumed that Perce held the ultimate responsibility, but he was quite clever in general and could be fiendishly inventive when it came to practical matters like obtaining food and shelter on the march and in dangerous situations. Perce was not sure he would have survived the retreat from Austerlitz if it had not been for Sergei—and certainly not with his baggage intact. Another oddity was the complete lack of formality with which Sergei treated his master and dealt with him. He might fling himself on the floor and kiss Perce's feet while begging pardon for a mistake, but in an ordinary situation he laughed and joked and gossiped in a way no English servant would dare imitate.

Now, in answer to Perce's shout, Sergei stuck his head in the door and asked, "What do you want?"

"My clothes and my horse—and quickly," Perce said in Russian.

"Quickly, quickly," Sergei grumbled. "Always everything quickly. Take the sleigh. It's too cold to ride. And what about food? You can't go without eating."

"Mind your own business," Perce responded. He had long since gotten over being shocked by Sergei's unsolicited advice and merely answered the man in his own terms. "It will take too long to get the sleigh ready. I want to catch someone at breakfast—an Englishman, not a Russian," he added as he saw Sergei's mouth open to say that it was too early for any sane man to be eating breakfast.

Sergei snorted, stopped arguing, and withdrew his head. In his estimation all English were crazy. They were like babies in some ways, always speaking the truth and always rushing around doing tasks that could be done just as well the next day or even the next month. In other ways they were even stranger. They never cried or even laughed with open, hearty roars. Of course, Perce was the only Englishman Sergei really knew, but he assumed they were all alike. He felt a fierce devotion to his gently imbecilic master, a need to protect him because of his innocence and childlike gullibility. If not for him, Sergei told himself, his master would have been robbed of everything and befooled by every little man in Russia.

He sent Perce's current French valet to him and went to saddle the horse himself. There were many French body servants in the cities of Russia. They had long been favored by the nobility and were hired and dismissed erratically because of the volatility of many Russian personalities. Sergei did not in the least resent the valet, whom he looked down upon for not "belonging" to Perce.

The Frenchman might starch a neckcloth to perfection, but he did not dare speak to the master in the way Sergei spoke, and he would be dismissed when Perce rejoined the army. Sergei could not be dismissed. He "belonged."

Perce rode as quickly as he could to the house Lord Elvan had rented. Fortunately the ice layer that covered the snow on the main streets had already been broken by sleighs of farmers or purveyors of firewood and coal or peat. Still, a sober trot was the fastest pace that was safe. And it was cold! Perce had adopted the Russian fashion in outerwear, a necessity if one wished to stay alive, but his nose and cheekbones stung with cold and his fingers and toes felt stiff inside his furred boots and gloves.

A muzhik ran from some scanty shelter to hold his horse at the steps of Lord Elvan's house. He was as round as a barrel, with layer upon layer of rags topped by a filthy sheepskin, his feet shapeless blobs under similar wrappings. Even so, Perce wondered why the man did not freeze to death. He was barely keeping himself from shivering under his furs, and he had been riding; the muzhik had most likely been sitting still. Perce told the man to keep the horse moving but not to go far. If he found Elvan and their conversation lasted more than a few minutes, the animal would have to be stabled.

As he came up the stairs the door was flung wide. This was quite common, Perce had discovered. Most large households had one or more serfs who did nothing but watch for visitors. The reason was readily comprehensible. It was not practical or hospitable to keep a visitor standing outside in the winter weather of St. Petersburg while a footman came from somewhere to answer the bell. It was in the entry hall that one gave one's name and stated one's business. If the host was at home and wished to see his visitor, he was led to a reception room to remove his outer garments and then to a drawing room or saloon or office as appropriate.

Perce, however, was not kept waiting at all. As soon as he gave his name he was led inside, the footman chattering volubly, as was customary with Russian servants, explaining that word had been left by Lord Elvan that Lord Kevern was to be admitted at once any time he came. Perce smiled grimly. That order was not likely to stand very long. He did not listen to the remainder of the servant's chatter, being too intent on honing his speech to make it sufficiently explicit and insulting. And if Elvan chose to take offense, so much the better! There was no law against dueling in Russia.

Perce took a deep breath, wondering if it would be possible to goad Elvan into a duel deliberately. No! It would be murder. Sabrina would not tolerate that, and it would make endless trouble for his father. Besides, Elvan was no fool. He might get angry, but he would be most unlikely to challenge Perce no matter what he said, particularly as he might know Perce was very handy with both sword and pistols.

The door to the breakfast room opened. Perce stepped forward on the heels of the servant who was announcing him. His mouth opened to begin his elegantly nasty speech, and just hung. Sabrina was getting up from her chair with an expression of anxiety on her face.

"Perce! At this hour? Is something wrong?"

The servant had left, closing the door behind him. Perce cast a single, haunted glance at it before he could subdue the cowardly impulse to take to his heels and avoid the confrontation.

"I didn't expect to see you," he said when he hooked up his jaw. "I came to speak to Elvan."

Sabrina laughed. "I could guess from your face you didn't expect to see me." Then she paused and frowned. "William left very early this morning. I have no idea why. I didn't catch him myself." She was about to say he hadn't told her he had to get to the embassy early, but he might have done so and she had not remembered. She had not been "all there" the previous night. "Is it business?" she went on. "If it's important and you don't want to go to the embassy, I can send a servant for him."

"I don't want to go to the embassy," Perce said, repressing a shudder at the thought of having the discussion he planned in an office where anyone could walk in. "The matter isn't urgent. It can wait until some other day."

Sabrina stared at him, a flush rising under her delicate skin. "It isn't urgent, but you arrived here before William should have finished breakfast? Yet you don't want to go to the embassy. The matter couldn't be personal, could it? Oh, no! And I'm sure it has nothing to do with me—has it?"

"I assure you I had no intention of discussing anything you told me. I'll catch Elvan somewhere around the city. I'm sorry to have troubled you, Sabrina."

Despite his fair skin, Perce almost never blushed. Sometimes his face flushed with repressed anger, but ordinarily his emotions were well under control. He had a very cool head and had not been embarrassed by any circumstance for years. Just now, however, he could feel his ears burning and was aware that his face was as red as a beet. He turned away quickly, reaching for the door.

"Don't you dare run away, you coward," Sabrina shrieked. "You come back here and sit down and explain yourself."

"My horse," Perce said desperately.

"Sit!" Sabrina ordered, pointing to a chair. Then she called, "Sasha!" The door opened promptly, and Sabrina gave orders to stable Perce's horse. When the door closed again, she turned to Perce, who was still standing, and said, "Well?"

"Damn it, Brina, you can't order me around like a slavey," Perce exclaimed.

"I'm so sorry," Sabrina said, sweetly poisonous. She dropped a curtsy. "Please, sir, pretty please, will you be so good as to sit and *explain to me what the hell you think you're doing?*"

Laughing, Perce dropped into a chair. "You can give me some breakfast. A condemned man always gets a last meal."

"By all means."

Sabrina took a plate and went to the sideboard, heaping smoked fish, grilled sausage, slices of ham, and eggs in various forms on it. She delivered this and poured a cup of tea, automatically adding cream and withholding sugar. She had poured a great many cups of tea for Perce over the years and did not need to ask how he liked it. When she had put the cup by his plate, she returned to her own seat. Perce said nothing, staring a little blankly at the food. Sabrina felt ashamed of herself. Naturally Perce would try to help her, and naturally the first thing he would think of was to warn William to behave himself.

"You look dreadful, Perce," she said quietly, "all blue around the eyes. I shouldn't have run away from you last night. I was just surprised."

"Why don't you say 'disgusted.' That's what you mean. I know what it sounded like, Brina, as if I thought, oh, here's another ripe one. But I swear it wasn't that way at all. Damn it, Brina, you know I'm not in the petticoat line and never was. I just—" He closed his eyes. "I just didn't expect to see you—just stupidity because I wasn't thinking about your connection with the British embassy—and you looked so damned beautiful. And then you sprang that thing about wanting to be free of Elvan." He opened his eyes again and looked directly at her. "The words just came out before I thought."

"I know. I should have known immediately. That's why I said I shouldn't have run away. But I figured it out after a while." She smiled. "You're far too clever to come out with a stupid remark like that if you had intended—intended to seduce me. But, Perce, what are we going to do?"

"What do you mean—what are we going to do?" he asked, forcing the words through stiff lips. Could Sabrina mean she was going to take his confession of love seriously?

Tears came into Sabrina's eyes, and she lowered them. "I don't want to lose you, Perce, but—"

"You couldn't ever lose me, even if we never spoke another word to each other. Anything you want, any way you want it, it's yours. Can you forget what I said? I'll never say it again, or try. . . . We can just be friends."

There was a little silence. Neither of them seemed able to finish a sentence. Everything they *wanted* to say to each other was better left unsaid. Finally, Sabrina looked up. "Can we?" she asked, doubt and hope mingling. "Won't that . . . hurt you?"

"If it doesn't hurt you, Brina, it won't hurt me."

That was a thumping lie. It would hurt like hell to be near and not be able to touch, but it would be bearable because he knew she didn't love anyone else and the situation wasn't hopeless. Besides, now that she knew how he felt, perhaps Brina might see him with different eyes. It wasn't a very safe way to think, but if she really didn't care for Elvan anymore and was thinking of separating, Perce wanted to be right there with open arms.

Sabrina continued to look at Perce somewhat doubtfully. She was not suspicious of what he had said. She believed that Perce would not express his love either verbally or physically. It was the statement that it would not hurt him that bothered her. Either it was a lie—and Perce had never lied to her before—or her second guess had been the correct one. He had said he was in love with her because he thought she needed to hear it to restore her self-respect after the blow William's infidelity struck her.

There was a twinge of disappointment, which Sabrina repressed quickly. It was better that way. She would be a monster to desire that Perce really be in love with her. It would be torture for him if she couldn't honestly return the love. Couldn't she? He was eating now, rather eagerly, as if their conversation had restored his appetite. She was aware of the neat movements of his long-fingered hands and of the barely visible sparkles on his cheeks and chin where the light caught golden stubble as he chewed. He had come out so quickly he hadn't bothered to shave.

Certainly no one would call Perce handsome. His face was what was considered "typically British," long and thin with a broad forehead, a high-bridged nose, which made him look haughty, and a lantern jaw. His hair was his best feature, full and guinea-gold and softly curling. His eyes were nice too, when he didn't make them glazed and blank: a lively gray that glinted when he laughed. He was tall, taller than William, and much slenderer. Sabrina had always thought of Perce as willowy, but now that she looked carefully, she realized that that, too, was a deliberate impression. His shoulders were broad enough so that his coats needed no padding to widen them.

It was ridiculous, but Perce did look different. Somehow there didn't seem to be anything left of the boy she had played with so freely. If he loved her, would it really be impossible to love him back? Perce lifted his head to tilt his teacup and drain it. Sabrina felt oddly shy, as if she suddenly found herself with a stranger.

"I'll get you some more tea," she said hastily.

"That's my girl," Perce replied as he handed over his cup.

The words and gesture were blessedly familiar. Sabrina did not blush, as she had feared she would when he spoke. Nonetheless, it was a man, an interesting man, to whom Sabrina handed the refilled cup. *Don't be silly,* she warned herself. *There's no question of could or couldn't love him.*

62

*He only said what he did to help you. He wouldn't say
"That's my girl" to someone with whom he was in love.
But wouldn't he? He had just promised. . . . Stop it,* Sa-
brina ordered herself.

"Perce, what are you doing in Russia?" she asked to
break the round of unanswered and unanswerable questions.

CHAPTER FOUR

"I'm not quite sure," Perce said.

Sabrina drew a sharp breath and spoke in a lowered voice. "I'm sorry. I didn't know there was anything secret about it. Let's talk about something else."

"Whoa, now, I didn't say there was anything secret about it, and it wouldn't be secret from you in any case. You know how to hold your tongue, Brina. I was telling you the exact truth. I'm not sure whether I'm here because it's necessary to watch which way the army will try to push Alexander or because my father thought it would be a good, interesting way of keeping me safe."

"Safe? Austerlitz?"

A shadow passed over Perce's face, followed by a mischievous smile. "I don't think Fa planned on Austerlitz." Then the smile faded. "I don't think anyone, except maybe Bonaparte, planned on Austerlitz."

"Perce, begin at the beginning, please."

"You can't mean that," Perce replied, smiling again. "The beginning is pretty far back. Let's skip the details and say that owing to both my younger brothers' stubbornness about fighting Boney, they nagged Fa into letting them join the services."

"Yes, so Robert's in the army, and Fred's in the navy. But what does that have to do with you being in Russia?"

He looked past her, his face going expressionless. "Fa's in good shape. There wasn't much for me to do on the es-

64

tates. After Boney started the war again, I couldn't bear it, Brina. To me it seemed as if I were the only one sitting on my hands and doing nothing."

"But Perce—"

"I know why, damn it! I know I'm the eldest and the Moreton estates come to me, but I . . . Well, you know Fa; he's a reasonable sort of person. Fond of me, too, even though he sometimes thought I was an idiot. Well, the less parents know, the better, usually. Anyway, he saw I was pining away."

Sabrina snickered, and Perce grinned back at her. Nonetheless there was real sympathy in her eyes and acceptance of it in his. Sabrina understood very well the need to be in the action. That need was all that was holding her to William. If it had not been for her delight in being a diplomatic wife, she would have packed up and left William as soon as he began this latest affair.

"As I said," Perce went on, "Fa's reasonable and he knows I have this knack for languages. We were thinking of my going into the Foreign Office on the diplomatic end, and then this alliance between England and Russia came up. There was a question in the Lords because Alexander blew so hot and cold—"

"He always does."

"Yes, but his closest friends and advisors didn't seem to be in tune with the really powerful families. Well, you know what happened to Paul when he got too far out of step. He was murdered."

"Yes, William was talking about that last night. But surely Alexander is in no danger. He's a darling, even—" Her voice stopped.

"Even if he is a fool," Perce finished. "Yes, perhaps. I don't know him. No, I don't think he *is* in any danger, at least not of being assassinated by the army. The truth is, Brina, that it's the army that changes tsars in this country, and the diplomatic staff has virtually no contact with the army."

"Lord Gower tries to—"

"Don't be defensive," Perce interrupted with a smile. "I know he tries, but no one on the general staff is going to say anything different from the official line to a foreign diplomat. They might drop a tidbit here and there, but not a brick like a prospective mutiny."

"I suppose not, but I'm sure no one wants to be rid of Alexander."

"No, it's Czartoryski and his crowd they want to be rid of."

"Yes, that's true. Lord Gower is worried because he doesn't want the British involved in Czartoryski's disgrace —if he is disgraced. On the other hand, it's Czartoryski who always wanted an alliance with England. Most of the others are pro-Prussian, and there are even quite a few who are pro-French."

"Not in the army," Perce said bitterly. "But to get back to my part in this. Fa talked to Roger, and Roger suggested that I come out as an idle young man with more money than brains—I can do that part hands down—and try to attach myself to the young men surrounding the generals. I was supposed to hang around the key regiments and see what information I could pick up and relay to the British Foreign Office."

"But the Semeonovsky Regiment was stationed in St. Petersburg until . . . oh, Perce. . . ." She realized he had been avoiding her. Surely that meant he did love her, that he wasn't only trying to make her feel better.

"I didn't stay in St. Petersburg long, and I didn't want to be connected with the embassy crowd," Perce said quietly. "Besides, the officers of the Semeonovsky Regiment are too sophisticated, and they're quite devoted to the tsar. He's one of their officers—or was. I wouldn't get worthwhile information from such a loyal group. Fortunately, I was able to get an introduction to one of Bagration's aides-de-camp. We became pretty good friends, and I just went along when the army moved out." He stopped and pushed away his plate, which was not quite empty.

There was a short pause. Sabrina's mind skipped between the overt subject and Perce's casual remark about the embassy and the Semeonovsky Regiment. Perhaps he just hadn't thought about her being in St. Petersburg. With that notion came a renewed awareness of how much had changed between them. Previously she would have cried, *You beast! You never even thought I might want to see a familiar face.* And he would have laughed and answered, *Business before pleasure, my girl,* or possibly even *Pleasure before business.* That kind of ease was gone. Sabrina missed it, but not as much as she would have expected, because the old comfort was replaced with a more enticing sensation. There was a tingling excitement in Perce's company now that she had never experienced before.

"What happened, Perce?" she asked, keeping to the safety of an impersonal subject. "At the battle, I mean. Was it really that Austrian general's fault, that Weyrother?"

He looked without seeing at his half-empty cup of tea. "I'm no general. I never even trained with the militia. I have no way to judge on my own, and my informants are prejudiced as hell. The blame was certainly dropped on him, and from what I can make out, what he did was incredibly stupid. Maybe the plans he devised could have worked if everyone had understood them, but about half the army didn't even know what they were."

"But why was an Austrian making plans for the Russian army? I thought Marshal Kutuzov was supposed to be in command."

"Again, remember my sources are prejudiced." Perce shrugged. "But I tend to agree with them. Look, all the talk is to obscure one point and one point only. From beginning to end, all the deaths, everything, the whole fiasco, was Alexander's fault. No one will say it. They talk about Weyrother and the lack of training of the Russian troops and of the 'unconquerable' Napoleon Bonaparte. Maybe a little of all of it is true, except the last. Bonaparte isn't unconquerable. Kutuzov could have beaten him."

"At Austerlitz?"

"No. Kutuzov had no intention of fighting him, at least not then and there."

"But Bonaparte would have attacked," Sabrina protested. "At least, that's what I've been told."

Perce laughed. "One lesson I have learned about military tactics: You can't attack an enemy that won't fight unless you corner him—and old Kutuzov's too smart for that. The old man looks half asleep all the time and talks like a rheumatic old maid, but he knows war. He's clever and sly and brave as a lion when he needs to be. You should have seen him, streaming blood—he was wounded several times—and cool as if he were talking tactics in a drawing room. Alexander would have been captured, and the whole war would have been lost instead of one battle, if it hadn't been for Kutuzov."

"You must be right," Sabrina agreed. "That's why Alexander tried to sneak into St. Petersburg in the middle of the night. And that's why he hasn't shown his face. He isn't stupid. *He* knows it was all his fault, even if no one will say so. But why, Perce? Why did the tsar disregard Kutuzov's advice? Before the battle when we all thought the Russians and Austrians would . . . William was really hopeful that Boney would get his comeuppance this time."

"I can tell you what General Bagration says. For one thing, Kutuzov is not in the least heroic. He always looks sleepy. Maybe he is sleepy, or his eyes bother him. He lost the sight of one eye in a battle some time ago. He's not a young man, and he's had a hell of a hard life. And all he talks about is physical comfort: Will there be good beds, good food, and good wine in the town to be picked for headquarters."

"Well, that does seem—"

"Damn it, I don't care how it seems. He's right! I tell you it makes a big difference if you've had a decent meal and a decent night's sleep before you go into action."

There was real passion in Perce's voice. Sabrina thought, *He's been through it.* She reached across to touch his hand. He looked up at her. It was as if a fiery spark passed between them. Sabrina snatched her hand away, and Perce dropped his eyes to his teacup. There was a brief, breath-held silence.

"The other consideration is that Kutuzov wouldn't tell Alexander exactly what would happen if the allies attacked," he went on quickly.

There was a slightly rough quality to Perce's voice. Otherwise nothing in his manner betrayed any special awareness. Sabrina knew she was blushing. She could only hope that Perce would not look up at her again. He didn't, continuing to speak about Kutuzov and the battle as he idly arranged and rearranged the unused silverware on the table. He explained how Alexander had forced Kutuzov to order the attack even before all the units were in position and described the heroism of General Miloradovitch's division and how the tsar's brother Constantine had ruined the one chance to counterattack by bringing in the reserves too early.

"Still," he sighed, "maybe it wouldn't have mattered. The fighting was so bad that Kutuzov's aides just couldn't get through to us."

"Us!" Sabrina exclaimed. "You *were* in the fighting. Perce!"

He looked up now and smiled deprecatingly. "It was an accident. When Bonaparte's Marshal Murat rode into Vienna on November thirteenth instead of pursuing the Russian army, Kutuzov nearly wiped out some advance columns of French. Boney must have burned off Murat's ears. He came racing up into Moravia, and he fought Bagration at Hollabrunn. We stopped them but couldn't hold them. Mikhail Ivanovitch, my friend, and several other aides had been wounded in the previous action, and I was just helping out in the emergency. Before I knew it, I, well, I was sort of on the staff."

"Perce! You'd better get yourself off the staff. Your father will have a fit."

"No, he won't, at least not when he understands the situation. I can't quit, Sabrina."

"You mean you don't want to."

"I don't know," he said soberly. "After it's over I'm always scared witless and sick as a dog. It's horrible, and yet during the battle it's exciting as hell. That's not my reason for sticking to it, though, not really. There's some pretty bad feeling about the English, a lot of talk about how we're cowards—rich cowards, but cowards nonetheless, who pay others to risk their lives. If I quit now, after Austerlitz, I'll only confirm that view."

"Do they call Trafalgar cowardice? The British navy nearly wiped out the French and Spanish navies in one battle!" Sabrina asked indignantly.

"Most of these men don't understand sea battles. Also, Trafalgar was far away and just words. I'm here and real."

"If they want to believe we're cowards, they'll just say you're a crazy exception," Sabrina insisted.

"Some might. Those who have fixed anti-British feelings will, I suppose. But those who are willing to accept whatever evidence comes to hand may add me in."

"Don't, Perce! I don't want you to be a dead noble example."

He laughed but didn't look at her. "I don't intend to be."

"But bullets aren't very smart," Sabrina protested. "They might not know what you intend."

Perce's eyes rose quickly and fixed on her. "You're sure there will be more bullets? I mean, are you sure Alexander will continue the war? Austria agreed to a truce immediately after the defeat at Austerlitz. Maybe the Russians will follow suit."

"I didn't think there was any doubt about Alexander continuing the war," Sabrina answered, her eyes widening. "Does General Bagration think Alexander wants to make peace?"

"He doesn't know, but he sure as hell thought there was a big smell of bad fish when Kutuzov was ordered to go to Czartoryski's ball. The old man was worried. He said he was too ill with his wounds. Maybe that's even true. He isn't young. Anyway, Bagration decided to go in Kutuzov's place. He knows he's clean—a hero in spite of the disaster, but if the tsar wants to cover his mistake with Austria's General Weyrother, he could try throwing the blame on Kutuzov."

Sabrina frowned. "That sounds as if it might be true. He might even convince himself that it *was* Kutuzov's fault. William said last night that Alexander doesn't let his head know what his right or left hand is doing—and they're usually doing opposite things."

"Yes, but what does that mean for the war? Do the people at the embassy think he'll pursue the war or just look the other way while Boney eats up the rest of Europe? I know that's what I'm supposed to find out, but I swear Bagration doesn't know and is just as worried as I am."

"No one's *seen* Alexander. He's sent out some notes, but no one's spoken to him that I know of," Sabrina replied anxiously. "But William says he's immature—"

Sabrina saw one of Perce's fair brows lift. His lips quirked as if he were about to make a caustic remark, too.

Sabrina was sure Perce was thinking of William's own immaturity. She felt warmed, although she was grateful he had not spoken, because she could not think of how to respond to such a remark.

"Children don't like being trounced by infeiiors," she hurried on, "and I'm pretty sure Alexander has this feeling that a genuine Russian tsar is very superior to an upstart Corsican corporal. Don't you think he'd want to hit back hard and be revenged for Austerlitz?"

"You may be right. I hope so. But why try to associate Kutuzov—oh, damn! I'll bet he's just trying to get rid of Kutuzov himself."

"What if he does, Perce? Is that going to affect the war?" Sabrina asked.

He shrugged dyspeptically. "I don't know. It depends on whom Alexander appoints to take Kutuzov's place and whether the tsar has learned his lesson about interfering in military matters. You know, Sabrina, I think I'd better go to the embassy and have a word or two with them. Who's reliable and has a brain?"

There was an awkward pause. Perce made an indeterminate sound of irritation, and Sabrina said, "William," in a small voice. "But he *is* a good diplomat," she added. "He has brains and uses them."

There was another brief pause while Perce very obviously did not say what he was thinking.

"Try Mr. Stuart, then, the secretary of the legation. He's busy, though. Perce, you can't avoid William, not if you intend to stay in St. Petersburg. We go to almost every large social function. To see him at the embassy about a matter of business would be a good way to—to bury what you know in—in formal politeness."

"And learn to accept it? Is that what you intend to do?" His voice was hard.

"I don't know," Sabrina replied. "You said I shouldn't talk to you about it."

"I won't give you any advice."

Perce knew he was being stupid again, but he couldn't resist. He wanted to hear her say she didn't care for Elvan. He wanted to know how far her "not caring" went.

"I don't know what good talking about it will do if you won't say what you think."

"You know what I think."

But she didn't know. Nonetheless, Sabrina realized there was a good reason to tell Perce the situation clearly and unemotionally. If he were sure she wasn't in agony, it would be easier for him to be civil to William, and that was necessary in the tight society in which they moved.

"You have to understand that I could stop his playing around," Sabrina said calmly. "I told you I had done it before. William—he's just a born hunter, or chaser. Once he has a woman . . . there are a few happy weeks or even months. I guess he likes the intrigue, the sneaking around, and the danger of getting caught. And then he gets bored, I suppose. It's the hunt that matters. I just don't want to play, that's all. He—what he has to offer me isn't worth the effort."

"Then . . ."

Sabrina waited, but Perce had set his teeth over whatever else he had to say, so she went on. "Naturally, the first thing I thought of when I knew I'd made a mistake was to pack up and go home. But it isn't as easy as that, even though I probably could find an excuse that wouldn't damage William's career."

"Wouldn't damage his career? I'd like to damage his hide with a horsewhip," Perce choked.

Sabrina smiled and started to reach out to touch him, but she remembered the sensation their last contact had given her. She wasn't ready for that—not until she was surer Perce's ferocity was caused by more than just a desire to protect her. After all, Philip would have reacted the same way, perhaps even more ferociously. She changed her movement to picking up and putting down a spoon on the table.

"My motives aren't really very noble, Perce," she said wryly. "I don't want William, but I do want this type of life. You must understand, I have something real to do. I'm as much in the diplomatic service as William. I have my work, and he has his. He goes to the office, and I go visiting. But sometimes I know more than he does. Women are very powerful in Russia."

"I never thought about that," Perce admitted. "Yes. I see. Elvan wouldn't be nearly as effective without you."

"Now you're trying to make a patriot and martyr out of me, when all I am is greedy for excitement." Sabrina smiled at him. "It's very kind of you. I can lay 'that flattering unction' to my soul. Maybe it will obscure the fact that my personal prospects won't be very bright if I divorce William."

Perce opened his mouth to assure her he would be ready and waiting to receive her, then closed it. He wouldn't be able to marry her if she were divorced, and there was a strong possibility—in fact, a near certainty— that she wouldn't be received by society. She wouldn't be invited to balls or given vouchers to Almack's, and she would be ostracized in public places. His gray eyes blazed almost white with rage.

"Stupid!" he snarled.

Sabrina had caught her breath at the intense flare of emotion that passed over Perce's face. The furious word that followed was a dreadful shock. "Perhaps so," she said icily.

"Not you," Perce snapped. "The whole situation is stupid, but I'm afraid you're right. I'm glad I said I wouldn't advise you. Frankly, I don't know what to say."

"I don't think anyone can say anything useful," Sabrina sighed. "It's just a decision I'll have to make. Either way, it will be . . . unpleasant. I'll have time to think it over.

With the political situation so unsettled here, I wouldn't want to add even a straw to the embassy's problems. Probably no one would notice, but it is barely possible that some silly significance would be attached to my leaving Russia right now."

"But maybe there's a way around it. No! Whatever decision you make, I'll back you any way I can, Brina. And I'll do anything else I can to help, but—but you'll have to tell me what it is you want me to do."

"The first step is to promise to treat William civilly." Sabrina chuckled at Perce's outraged expression. "You must, Perce. I can't have you standing around glowering at him. And as long as you're free to do it, I'd like you to—to visit me, if—if you don't mind. It's a comfort to see you."

With some effort, Perce unfastened his set jaw. He had said he would not declare his love or make physical advances. Perhaps he would not abide by that statement absolutely, but today was too soon. He knew he wasn't thinking clearly. He needed time to consider what Sabrina had said when he wasn't dazzled by her presence. There were hints that she might be getting interested, but maybe he was reading too much meaning into glances and hesitations and a single touch.

"All right," he said gratingly. "I'll be sweet as sugar pie."

"Not in that voice or with that expression on your face, I hope," Sabrina protested, laughing. Then she sighed. "Why did you come here this morning? You didn't really intend to horsewhip William or—or challenge him?"

"Well, I did think of challenging him," Perce admitted, "but I knew he wouldn't accept. He would be right, too. It would have been murder. I couldn't have done it, anyway. I had thought of a horsewhip, but I'm afraid I allowed political consequences to prevail over personal feelings. It wouldn't have been very edifying—or too edifying, perhaps—to have such a scandal in the British community."

Sabrina smiled at his reasoning, but she hadn't been distracted. "Then why did you come?" she insisted.

"My reason isn't very flattering to Lord Elvan." Perce found it impossible to say "your husband." It was a warning. If Sabrina didn't want to hear ill of the man, she could stop him, but she said nothing. Perce went on with a certain satisfaction, "After you went into the ballroom, I wandered around a bit to cool off. Later, when I was with General Bagration, Elvan came up to us again particularly to tell the prince that I was an old friend of yours. He said it in such a way that Bagration released me from my acceptance of his invitation to accompany him to his estate near Moscow."

"But William was probably only trying—"

"He was trying to do exactly what he did! I saw the satisfaction in his face when Bagration withdrew that invitation, and he was positively fulsome about his assurances that I would not be lonely or neglected, that I was practically part of your family."

"Well, it's true, Perce. And you probably put on your dead-fish face so William didn't know you were furious with him."

"I'm sure he didn't know," Perce agreed, furious again. "He was trying to use me to keep you safely occupied so that he would be free to—to pursue his present object."

"Yes," Sabrina said after a short, thoughtful silence. "You're right, of course. As you were a childhood friend, it wouldn't cause gossip if you escorted me, and—and we are easy with each other, Perce." Suddenly Sabrina blushed hotly. "At least . . . Well, but even if that was what William wanted, I don't see what that has to do with your coming to see William this morning."

"I intended to tell him I wouldn't play—and why," Perce growled.

Sabrina sat looking at the table. Her blush had diminished; now it intensified again. "But why shouldn't we . . . play?" she asked. "I'd rather be with you than with William. And I'd like to give him a dose of his own medicine. No matter what story he tells people, a lot of them are going to be sympathetic to him if you and I are seen together very often. I've never allowed anyone to be my escort more than twice and even then at long intervals. In fact, the more William talks about you as my childhood friend, the less anyone will believe him, if—"

"If I look smitten. That won't be hard."

"No, not you," Sabrina pointed out. "If *I* look smitten."

Perce sat perfectly still, staring at his clasped hands on the table. "I said I'd do anything you wanted, Brina," he said slowly.

"Good!" she exclaimed, her ice-blue eyes brighter than usual. "Then you'll have a very good reason to be civil to William. He is always *excessively* cordial to the husbands."

"Oh, is he?" Perce pushed back his chair and stood up. "I've been here long enough. I want to get to the embassy before noon." He took out his card case and a small gold pencil, scribbled his address on the card, and left it on the table. "I suppose you have a raft of invitations. Let me know what time to pick you up or where to meet you."

Sabrina was startled by his sudden action, at a loss for how to respond. Then it was too late. He was out of the room, asking the servant to send for his horse. After that she heard nothing and knew he had been taken back to the reception room where he would dress for the outdoors again. Sabrina could catch him before he left, but what was there to say? Had he been offended by what she had asked of him? He hadn't looked or sounded angry, just hurried.

A silvery chime sounded behind Sabrina, and she realized Perce had been facing the clock. That was certainly a reason for what he had done, but she remained uneasy.

Had he run away because he felt her pretense of infatu-ation would be painful? Would it be *all* pretense? Sabrina again felt that tingling excitement she had experienced when she touched him.

It was ridiculous! She had known Perce for more than ten years. Was it just because he had said he loved her? Would she respond in the same way to any man just be-cause William was off on the hunt again? That was ridicu-lous, too. She had had offers enough in Vienna and hadn't responded. It wasn't really the same, though. In Vienna she had still been thinking in terms of keeping William faithful. Sabrina sighed with exasperation. Life was always so complicated. It was bad enough to have to decide whether she could bear to continue living with William now that she knew she no longer loved him—if, indeed, she had ever loved him. To add the problem of Perce and what to do about him on top of the other was the outside of enough.

Nonetheless she felt surprisingly cheerful, not weighted any longer with a burden of depression. She moved to her own sitting room and began to examine the invitations for that day with absorbed interest. Often William chose where they would go. Sabrina had always acquiesced in the past because she had never cared which function they attended or whose box they shared for the opera or ballet. She had assumed that William's choices, when he did not ask her to choose, were based on political considerations. Now it was more likely that William's choice would be dictated by which function his light of love was going to attend.

Well, then, let him go there. Unless it was, coinciden-tally, the affair Sabrina had chosen, he could go alone. She chuckled wickedly. So William wanted to find her a cavalier servente, did he? Doubtless he intended Perce to accompany both of them to the places he had selected; that would make Perce a friend of his as well as of Sabrina's. William was about to get a rude surprise. Having found an escort for her and having probably told—or being about to tell—the world that it was his choice, he would discover that he had freed her to do as she liked.

When he fled Sabrina's breakfast parlor, Perce felt dizzy with confusion. There was one consolation in which he could take intense satisfaction: He had not lost Sabrina completely by the preceding night's stupidity. She had apparently reasoned the incident through and come to the conclusion that he had not meant to insult her. It was just like Brina to say he wouldn't have said such a stupid thing if he intended to seduce her. But *did* he intend to seduce her?

Shaking himself free of the too assiduous footmen, Perce made his way carefully down the stairs to where his horse was waiting for him. After his demonstrations of impatience with Russian ways, it would do his dignity no good if he slipped on an icy patch and fell down. This kept his mind occupied for the few minutes until he was mounted, but then his own embarrassing question resurfaced.

He was in no doubt that he wanted Sabrina for himself, but on what terms was he willing to take her? The answer to that was easy: any terms at all. But that didn't answer the initial question. Was he going to try to seduce her? The answer "any terms at all" implied Sabrina's concurrence; seduction implied resistance or, at least, uncertainty on Sabrina's part that he would have to overcome.

Perce did not like the implications in seduction. He wanted Sabrina very badly, but not if she were unwilling or if loving him would make her more unhappy. However, he wouldn't mind overcoming a few religious scruples, if Sabrina had any, and he would overcome any concern for Elvan's pride or feelings with enthusiasm. In fact, Sabrina seemed far too concerned with her husband's welfare for Perce's taste.

This brought a very unpleasant idea forward. He knew Sabrina would not use him deliberately, but could she be doing so without realizing or admitting to herself her real purpose? Could she be so hurt by Elvan's promiscuity that she had convinced herself she no longer cared for him when she really did care? Could all her talk about wishing to retain the interest and excitement of being a diplomatic wife be only an excuse to continue the marriage when her pride told her to be rid of her husband? Could this notion of giving Elvan a taste of his own medicine be a device to win him back by making him jealous?

But Sabrina had said she could have stopped the affair, that she had stopped him in the past. In that case, she really was sick of Elvan, so perhaps she would not be unwilling. Perce found that his breathing had quickened. It seemed to him that Sabrina had been looking at him with an unusual intentness, as if his features had somehow changed. He remembered vividly how, after looking at her with affectionate indifference for years, he had suddenly, too late, realized how beautiful she was. Well, she certainly wouldn't find *him* beautiful, soon or late. Damn Elvan, he was extremely handsome. But Sabrina's intentness might mean something.

Surely, it might mean she was worried about him. She had said he looked dreadful. That was rather flattening to the spirit if one believed that beauty was in the eye of the beholder, but Perce cheered up again when he remembered how she had touched his hand and reacted as if she were burnt. He had felt burnt himself. He had looked at his hand, surprised that it was not marked by the flash of heat he had felt. And the way Sabrina had blushed. Perce could not remember Sabrina ever blushing when she talked to him before. Quite uplifted, he went into the British embassy and asked for Lord Elvan.

CHAPTER FIVE

Politically, life in Russia apparently came to a standstill in the last weeks of January and the first of February. The tsar seemed to have been paralyzed by the horror and defeat of Austerlitz. He did not wish to make scapegoats of his friends; indeed, that would only reflect badly on him in the end, for he should have known better than to listen "only to a few giddy-headed young men," which was what his confidants Novosiltsov and Stroganov reported was being said. Those around him, his own mother included, urged him to cut himself loose from his ties to those who shared his disgrace.

Unable to go forward or back, Alexander did nothing. Although he came out of absolute seclusion, he seemed afraid to act in any way. It was apparent that Sabrina's analysis had been wrong. Alexander might be immature, but he had been taught to revere power. Far from resenting an inferior Corsican corporal who had beaten him, Alexander feared Bonaparte. The tsar now desired only security, a place from which to watch and wait. He had no more interest in his old allies. Pressed to act, he would only say, "Let us remain totally passive and not make any move until the time when we are attacked on our own soil." It was a dictum that reduced several of his more knowledgeable generals to tears.

Perce and Sabrina were grateful for the political limbo, though each felt an occasional twinge of conscience because prospects for the war against France were not bright. As diplomatic and intelligence personnel, they should have been distressed at the rapidly dimming possibility of defeating Bonaparte. As patriotic English citizens, they should have been worried because England was again virtually alone against the greatest military power the world had ever seen. Both reminded themselves of this periodically, but personal concerns were far more significant to each. Thus it was a relief to know that political events did not require their attention.

The evening and the few days after Perce and Sabrina had breakfast together were very peculiar. Each was so confused, so undecided about what the other really felt that they met almost as strangers, but not complete strangers. It was as if two people had corresponded for years, until each knew the other's tastes and character with sureness, but had never met. Now, face to face, new aspects of each personality were exposed.

One laughable result of this relearning process was that, quite without meaning to, they gave the impression that William was lying or mistaken when he insisted they had been family acquaintances for years. Since William was not stupid, he was well aware of the winks and nods behind his back and the sympathetic sighs of certain ladies who would not be loath to comfort him. This infuriated him since he *knew* what he had said was true. During their courtship Sabrina had not always been the perfect young lady every time he called. He had seen her himself any number of times romping with Philip and Perce like a kitten with two puppies. He *knew* she regarded Lord Kevern as a brother. If she had not, she would never have permitted him to accompany her everywhere. Sabrina was always very careful that there be no hint of scandal about her. William knew he could have stopped her with a word, but he did not wish to. Just now, when he was about to

82

seize his prize, it was very convenient that Kevern keep his wife occupied.

Totally unaware that she was accomplishing a purpose she had forgotten, Sabrina ignored the evidence that William was having a dose of his own medicine. Perce was peripherally aware, but he was more concerned with his interactions with Sabrina. Far from acting "easy" with each other, there was a shade of formality in their gestures and conversation for those first few days. By the end of January most of the awkwardness of their new relationship had been absorbed or smoothed away. Insensibly, they were drifting into a delicate courtship, erasing the last shreds of the brother-sister comradeship of the past.

Neither could remember ever being happier. The days flew by, glittering as much with joy as with ice. The political impasse did not, of course, affect the social scene. Theater parties followed sledge races, masquerades alternated with balls, and morning entertainments of promenade or a visit to the booths and exhibits that provided a daily fair on the frozen Neva filled any time not dedicated to dressing for more formal activities.

Thus far, Perce had not said a word of love, nor had Sabrina invited one. They seldom touched, except when dancing, seldom even looked at each other, yet each was becoming so sensitive to the other that presence alone was as exciting as a physical caress. The effects were most visible on Sabrina. The ice maiden was warming into a delicate fairy beauty, subtly inviting. A pale pink flushed her cheeks, deepening the blue of her eyes and making her moonlight hair more ethereal. Her mouth was softer, less guarded. Men who had admired her from a distance, accounting her exquisite but coldly unapproachable, drew near and began to court.

Sabrina turned playful, which might have had a disastrous effect on Perce, except for two considerations: It was he her eyes sought, touched, and dropped away from when she laughed and talked to others. And it was always he who had the last dance so that, if William had not come to the affair, she could ask him to order her furs and see her home. This did not discourage the others. Some took him for her lover and hoped to win her away; others had their own mistaken notions of English propriety. Lord Elvan had virtually said he had selected Lord Kevern to escort his wife while he spent his time as he preferred with Countess Latuski. Sabrina's new approachability was associated not with Perce but with her knowledge of her husband's activities. Kevern, many assumed, was Elvan's watchdog, and they were careful in his presence.

Perce was also protected from jealousy by the delight Sabrina took in detailing the various overtures made to her and the dreadful accusations that were made about his strict surveillance of her behavior. They laughed heartily over that notion. Perce had his own bits to offer. Friends of those who desired Sabrina had become most attentive to him, proffering all kinds of invitations in the hope of distracting him from his watchdog activities. He accepted some of the invitations, warning Sabrina in advance so that she would accompany William on those afternoons or evenings, or else remain at home.

On the sixth of February, Perce told her he would not be able to escort her on the ninth. Sabrina was rather annoyed with him because she did not want to attend the dinner to which they were all invited that night. Perce would not change his plans, however. Partly that was for the reason he gave Sabrina: The dinner was being given by William's inamorata, and Perce felt Sabrina should go without him to show *she* had nothing of which to be ashamed.

The other reason was more personal. Perce was finding it harder and harder to control his physical desire. He was, in fact, almost constantly in a state in which he feared that he would embarrass himself. Relief was imperative, but he did not wish to visit any of the whorehouses to which he had been introduced by his military friends. For the night of the Latuski dinner, he had been invited to a private party—of a certain type—and he was determined to go.

It was most fortunate that Sabrina had no idea of the truth, or she would have been furious. Not that she was unaware that gentlemen without other outlets relieved their needs with paid companions or that she even disapproved of it in general. Philip had been more than usually prone to such activity before his marriage to Megaera and had made no particular effort to conceal his pleasures from her. Sabrina would have been furious because she was having problems of her own along the same lines, and she had no such convenient way of satisfying her needs.

Using William was out of the question. Sabrina had locked her door against him as soon as he looked elsewhere. A man could be forgiven for paying whores when he had no woman of his own, but Sabrina had been available and willing. She would never accept another woman's leavings, either emotional or sexual, no matter how great her need. Sabrina had discovered that, although women might be slower to arouse, they were just as sensual as men. William had awakened her sexually and given her a strong taste for the pleasures of the bed. Unfortunately, Sabrina also found she needed to enjoy her partner to enjoy the act. Thus, even before he started to wander this last time, she had been less and less satisfied with William's lovemaking.

Sabrina was well aware that she wanted a man and that the specific man who was arousing her was Perce. She was equally aware that he wanted her. On the few occasions when she caught him really looking at her rather than briefly meeting her glance and looking away, his eyes had a particular shiny glaze that she recognized. There were other signs she recognized too, a fulling of the lips, a certain tension that culminated sometimes in a rapid physical retreat. But Sabrina, once burned by thinking she was in love and finding herself with the wrong man, had grown cautious.

Was it love they both felt, or was it an attraction generated by William's behavior and the suggestive propinquity into which they had been thrust? It was entirely possible that Perce had initially only wished to comfort her but had been stimulated into desire by the situation. Men, as Sabrina knew, caught fire easily. She also knew Perce would never cause her to suffer the rage and shame to which William had subjected her. Having committed himself to her, he would be utterly faithful—but at what cost?

He was the heir of Moreton and needed a son to succeed him. Of course he had two brothers—if Robert and Fred survived the war. Even so, was it fair to ask Perce to give up the future prospect of a wife and family? Only if she could obtain an annulment could she give him that, but perhaps even then she couldn't. She had conceived only once, and then had miscarried. And what if Roger couldn't obtain an annulment? Then there could be no marriage. It would be a high price to pay for love, and if it were not love but only a wish to protect her magnified into desire, that would be a real tragedy. Sabrina knew she and Perce should be apart, should have time to reconsider the emotion presently running away with them. However, he would not go unless she sent him away, and she could not bear to do it.

On the morning of February ninth Sabrina was reconsidering this problem, rather grateful that she would not see Perce at all that day. When she thought his name, a faint thrill ran through her, and she clucked her tongue aloud at herself. Sensations like that made her distrust herself. They were fine for a sixteen-year-old being courted by a Casanova like William. They were wrong for a woman of nineteen who had been rudely awakened from a dream of love by sad experience. Another rude awakening—either because her infatuation had passed or because she discovered that her lover, however loving and faithful, was *not* in love with her—would not leave much of Sabrina de Conyers intact.

She smiled and shrugged when she realized she had reassumed her maiden name in her own mind. That was significant of how she felt about William, but she had not tried out Sabrina Moreton. Was that also significant? It was a triviality, but worrying. She thought about it and about Perce's lands in Cornwall. She was sure she would love Cornwall. Philip's and Meg's descriptions made it sound fascinating, and they would come often to Bolleit if she were at Moreton Place. But it was ridiculous to dream of that. Roger might not be able to arrange an annulment. Divorce was possible, but then she would not be able to marry Perce. She might just as well stay married to William and take Perce as a lover. She shivered.

Even if Perce was truly in love now, how long could that last under the strains of an illicit relationship? And Sabrina knew she would hate it herself. Not to mention the horrible complication as soon as William noticed. He would begin to pursue her again. Sabrina closed her eyes and swallowed hard. The thought of such a dreadful situation had generated a physical nausea in her.

"Madame."

Sabrina jumped, but it was only Sasha bending forward with a note on a salver. Sabrina took it eagerly. She had intended to stay at home today to bring some order to her emotions, but the paths along which her thoughts wandered were definitely unpleasant. If this were a last-minute invitation, she would be glad to accept its diversion. The speculation was cut off when she saw the handwriting. William! Why would William send her a note? She could only think that some business had interfered with his attending the Latuskis' dinner that evening, and he had written to warn her of it. Fine! She would not mind missing that party at all. She opened the note without urgency, and the words leapt out at her.

"Pitt died on the twenty-third of January. I am ordered home by the ship that brought the news. If you can be ready by tomorrow, I believe it would be best for you to travel home with me. In haste, William."

The prime minister of England was dead! The multitudinous implications flooded into Sabrina's mind, leaving her shaken. Pitt had been the driving force behind the war against Bonaparte and for the alliance with Russia. Now that he was gone, the policies of Britain might alter drastically. Naturally someone from the embassy staff must go at once, yet in the present delicate situation it was impossible for Lord Gower to leave. In any case, he could not be given new instructions. If the ministry changed, it was likely that Lord Gower would be recalled, since he had always been a powerful adherent of Pitt's and would be suspected of pushing Pitt's policies even if the new ministry had different ideas. Yes, William was the logical person to go.

Sabrina stood up. William was right. It would be best for her to go. There was no telling how long he would be delayed in England, and she could not remain in Russia alone. She could, of course, take the next available transportation, but then if William were sent back to Russia in a hurry, her ship might cross his. The result would be that she would reach England and immediately have to turn around and come back. That would be ridiculous.

The thought was so definite that Sabrina stood perfectly still examining it. Why should she return to Russia at all? She certainly did not feel a need to be with William. Was it because she felt it to be her duty? Yes, a little, perhaps, but . . . Perce! Well! That answered rather definitely the question of how she felt about him. She hadn't been thinking about him at all, but deep inside her he was enough of a lodestone to have made her decide instantly and definitely to return.

"Oh, goodness! Perce!" she said aloud.

He would not know. She glanced at the clock. If she sent a note at once, it might catch him before he left his rooms. She burst out of the breakfast room, sending Sasha to fetch Katy to her sitting room at once. Then she ran up the stairs, thrusting aside the footmen who would have accompanied her and slowed her down. Pushing aside the heap of invitations on her writing table—she would somehow have to find time to send excuses to all those whose invitations she had accepted—she reached for paper and a quill. Even as she was thinking through the wording of her excuses, she scribbled her note to Perce. It didn't matter what she said to him.

Katy rushed into the room, breathless with hurry, as Sabrina folded and sealed her note, calling for a footman to carry it. "What—" Katy cried, but Sabrina waved her into silence while she instructed the footman, emphasizing the need for great haste and pressing into his hand coins to pay for a hired conveyance.

"We must leave for England tomorrow," she said to Katy. "Can you and Charlot get us packed and ready?"

"Tomorrow!" Katy echoed. "What's wrong, luv?"

"For us, personally, nothing," Sabrina assured her, "but Mr. Pitt died on the twenty-third of January, and the government must be in a turmoil. William has been ordered home for new instructions. We must go on the naval vessel that brought the news, I suppose." Then Sabrina put a hand to her forehead. "Dear God, I don't know whether there will be room or suitable quarters for you, Katy."

"Dinna worrit about me. Just tell me whether ye expect to be comin' back here."

"Yes, I expect so, but I'm not sure. Oh, dear!"

"Dinna worrit now," Katy soothed. "We'll manage fine.

I'll set the laundry maid to packin' yer little things. She knows how to fold them fine, and Himself's smallclothes, too. While she's at that, Charlot and me, we'll just step round and mark the things that are ours. Then, if we dinna come back, someone from the embassy can come and see to the packin' and shippin' them home."

"Yes. Yes, do that," Sabrina said distractedly, but she hadn't been thinking of the possessions that would have to be left behind, ornaments and paintings that she and William had purchased to add a warmer, more personal note to the ready-furnished house they had rented. She had been thinking that it might be a very long time before she saw Perce again. She had almost jumped up to call the footman back, but knew it was too late. Surely Perce would come before they left. But what had she written in that note?

Never mind, Sabrina told herself angrily, and drew her appointment calendar toward her abruptly. She began to write notes of apology, refusing to allow herself to formulate the thought that Perce might not come to say goodbye, might view her sudden departure as a release from an entanglement that had become more intense than he originally projected. She completed the notes and was piling them together to be given to the footman for delivery when an incredible uproar broke out on the floor below. She heard a footman cry out in frightened protest and then Perce's voice shouting her name.

Sabrina flew out of her sitting room and almost collided with Perce, who was leaping up the stairs with his greatcoat still on and a pistol in his hand. The footmen were pounding up the stairs behind him, recovered from their initial shock and determined to protect their "little mother," even at the cost of their lives.

"Stop!" Sabrina shrieked at them.

They obeyed, but largely because they saw the pistol

drop to point at the ground the instant Perce saw their mistress.

"Go. Go," she ordered them. "You know well that this is my dear friend and he would not harm me." And then, turning to Perce, who was clutching the banister and gasping for breath, "What's happened? Perce, what's wrong?"

"You're asking *me* what's wrong?" he choked.

"What are you doing with that gun?" she cried.

He stared at her for a minute until he caught his breath. "What the devil did you expect when you sent me a note saying, 'Something dreadful has happened. Come at once.' Then your butler told me you weren't receiving anyone. I thought . . . I hate to tell you what I thought."

"Oh, heavens! Is that what I wrote? I—" She grasped his arm and pulled him into her sitting room. "I'm so sorry. I had no idea. . . . How stupid!"

While Sabrina sought for words, Perce shoved the pistol into a pocket, unbuttoned his greatcoat, and pulled it off. "Sabrina, what *has* happened?"

"Pitt's dead. He died on the twenty-third of last month. William has been ordered home. We must leave tomorrow."

He threw the greatcoat on a chair and turned back toward her. Sabrina was blushing furiously.

"I only meant to tell you that we were leaving," she went on in a small voice. "I can't imagine why I should have written anything so silly. I suppose I wanted to be sure to see you before we—"

But there was no need for Sabrina to try to explain what she had done. Perce had taken two steps, caught her in his arms, and prevented her from speaking at all by kissing her. She returned his embrace with passionate urgency, clinging fiercely to him when she felt his lips releasing hers. But he was not withdrawing, only lifting his mouth to whisper "Darling, darling" before he kissed her feverishly again, pressing his lips to her ears and throat.

Neither heard the door open and then close softly almost at once. Katy stood with her back against it, a stunned expression on her face. She had noticed, of course, that Sabrina had been in excellent spirits recently and had wondered whether the husband had cut short his affair. Then, when she saw that the door between his dressing room and Sabrina's bedchamber remained locked, she had begun to associate Sabrina's happiness with Lord Kevern's presence in St. Petersburg, but not for this reason! Silently Katy wrung her hands. Himself was no good, no good at all, but this could only bring more grief.

She could not have convinced either Sabrina or Perce at that moment. They were still locked together, feeding on each other's passion. Sabrina slipped her arms under his coat the better to feel his body. He had worked one of her short sleeves off her shoulder and was kissing that and the tops of her breasts, while she ran her lips up and down the back of his neck. One of his arms clutched her close, the other stroked her and picked at the tiny buttons on the back of her dress.

Outside the door, Katy saw Charlot emerge from the drawing room across the stairwell with a sheaf of papers in his hand. Probably he would go to his master's dressing room, but it was possible he would be bringing those lists to Brina. Swallowing a cry of terror, Katy fled down the corridor to the entrance to Sabrina's bedchamber. She ran through the room, then through the short passageway that served as a wardrobe, being lined on both sides by cupboards and closets. At the end of the passageway was the door to Brina's sitting room.

"Brina," Katy called loudly, "are you all right? What was all that noise?"

Her voice sounded strange to her, but she hoped the muffling of the door would conceal it. She hoped Brina had heard her, hoped that it would stop her, but she couldn't take the chance. She sped back through the passageway and bedchamber without waiting for a reply and popped out of the door. The footman near the stairway looked at her curiously, but everyone had been running around like mad, so Katy's hurry did not seem too odd.

Charlot was nowhere in sight. Katy took a deep breath. Should she go back and enter the sitting room on some excuse? But she was afraid she would give herself away and make Brina more miserable. Well, at least she could give them a little time. She asked the footman where Charlot had gone and followed the valet. There were plenty of arrangements they needed to talk about, and she could tell him not to bother Brina.

Sabrina would not have noticed if Katy had croaked like a frog. Perce had just succeeded in loosening enough buttons to slide her dress and chemise off one of her full breasts. The call through the door was like a knife in the back. Sabrina muffled a cry of frustration and fear against Perce's hair and clutched him to her convulsively. He froze in the act of reaching for her nipple with his lips.

"Yes," Sabrina tried to say, but the word came out as a low, creaking gasp. She drew a shaking breath and tried again. "I'm all right, Katy. It was only a misunderstanding with the footmen. Perce is here." Her voice trembled dangerously, and she stopped to steady it. "We have something to discuss. I don't want to be disturbed."

But it was too late. What might have happened in a spontaneous and overwhelming flood of recognition and desire they could have forgiven themselves and each other. To pause and lock the doors and begin again would somehow cheapen what they felt. Gently Perce drew Sabrina's chemise and dress up over her shoulder. She uttered a sob, and he drew her close and kissed her lips. Then he turned her around and rebuttoned her dress.

"God knows I want you, Brina," he whispered, leaning his head against hers, "but this isn't the way."

"No," she agreed, "and I was just thinking before

93

William's note came that it would be better if we were apart for a little while. I can't think when I know you're within reach, Perce."

"I don't need to think," he said, smiling slightly. Then he sighed. "But you do. I know what I want, and it's easy for me. But you'll be the one to suffer. You aren't one to sit home and sew a fine seam, Brina. You want to be out and doing." He paused, sighed again. "I suppose I should be grateful for your sake that Katy called in to you." Then he stiffened and, his hands tightened on her shoulders, turned her around to face him. "Did you say Mr. Pitt was dead?"

Sabrina stared at him, nodded, and suddenly giggled, although tears had risen into her eyes. It was quite clear that Perce had been so caught up in how she summoned him, and its results, that he had given no thought as to why.

"Good God!" he exclaimed, stepping away from her. "What is to happen now? Are we to have Mr. Addington back as prime minister? That would be a disaster. The man doesn't know his own mind, much less what's best for the country."

"William's note didn't say any more than— Yes? Come in."

Charlot opened the door, following his scratch. One did not in general scratch at a sitting room door. Charlot, the most correct of servants, knew that quite well, but Mrs. Petersen had warned him that Lady Elvan was busy, so he felt a warning was necessary.

"I am sorry to bother you, madame," he apologized. "Mrs. Petersen said you did not wish to be disturbed, but I felt I must ask about the gold candlesticks and the clock with diamonds. Should they be left with all the other things?"

"No, indeed. Thank you, Charlot. Anything small and particularly valuable should be taken, of course, but not the paintings or the rugs."

He bowed and stepped back out of the door, closing it carefully behind him. Both Sabrina and Perce looked at it speculatively for a moment, then Perce's brows rose questioningly. Sabrina shook her head.

"I doubt Elvan knows any more than was in his note," Perce said, but his eyes were asking a question that had nothing to do with politics. "The news of Mr. Pitt's death must have been sent out immediately. Even the ministers can't have known exactly what would happen."

"Yes," Sabrina agreed. "But I've forgotten my manners in all the excitement. Will you take a glass of wine, Perce?"

"At this hour, ale, if you have it, thank you."

She went to the door, grateful for the first time that Russian houses did not use bells as English ones did. The huge number of serf-slaves that the rich used in Russia eliminated the need for mechanical contrivances. In most houses a man was stationed at every door so that master or mistress need only call out for service. In many houses the servants actually waited inside the rooms. Russians, Sabrina thought, did not have the same need for privacy that the English did. In any case, Sabrina followed custom for the public rooms, like the drawing room or dining room or breakfast parlor, but she had forbidden the invasion of the private sections of the house, the bedchambers and dressing rooms and her own private sitting room.

In this instance the rule was fortunate, as it permitted her to go out into the corridor to see whether Charlot was listening at the door. She had no intention of catching him at it, of course. That was the reason for the stupid verbal exchange about refreshment: to give the valet time to get away. Charlot was not in the hallway. This meant nothing. He might have slipped into any room along the way, or he might have been completely innocent. The latter was most likely. Charlot knew Perce was a frequent visitor, accepted by his master. Scratching at the door before entering was, for Charlot, completely natural. Sabrina shivered. She would never have thought about Charlot listening in the hallway before she fell into Perce's arms. It was a horrible prognostication for a future full of misery and suspicion.

Sabrina beckoned to the footman near the head of the stairs and gave her order. Then she went back inside, shut the door, and walked straight into Perce's arms again. "What are we going to do?" she whispered.

He held her close without passion, comfortingly. "I'll do whatever you want, Brina. You're the one who'll be hurt, so you have to decide. Are you sure he wasn't spying? I don't care, but if Elvan is suspicious, I don't want you traveling with him alone."

"No, it's not William; he's too—too conceited to believe I'd find anyone else attractive."

"Don't you believe it, Brina. Men who chase are often the most suspicious." He stood away from her, holding gently to her upper arms and looking at her intently.

She shook her head. "Not William, not in the way you mean, anyhow. I had to be pretty blatant with flirting when we were in Vienna. And he didn't get angry. He just dropped the woman he was after and started on me. If he noticed anything special about us, I'm sure his first reaction would have been to pay me a great deal of attention." She shivered again and said in a low voice, "We never would have thought anything was wrong if we hadn't . . ."

Perce pulled her back into his arms for a brief, hard hug, then let go of her completely. He went to the chair near her writing table where her shawl lay. She had dropped it when she ran out in response to his voice. Perce picked it up and put it around her tenderly. He had found the answer to the question he had asked himself when he first hoped Sabrina could love him. He was not going to seduce her. She would be utterly and completely miserable, and he wouldn't be much happier.

"I know you aren't really cold, darling," he said. "And I don't know what we're going to do, but cheating on your husband isn't the solution. You aren't made that way. Well, neither am I."

CHAPTER SIX

The trip home was a cold, cramped misery. The naval
sloop had never been meant to carry passengers, of course.
It had one advantage, however, in that there was no place
to put Katy unless she and Sabrina shared quarters. This
eliminated any possibility of an attempt by William to enjoy his marital rights. Nor did their arrival at Dover give
him any opportunity. Sabrina informed him that she
would go directly to Stour Castle. He looked a little oddly
at her then.

"But Lady Leonie and St. Eyre will probably be in London. I imagine St. Eyre will be interested in the organiza-
tion of the new government."

"Possibly," Sabrina replied coldly, "although it is a
month since Mr. Pitt died and very possibly my cousin, at
least, is at home. In any case, I can see no reason to be
shaken up in a post chaise for seven or eight hours when I
can be at Stour in two."

"Very well, my dear," William said pacifically.

There was a gleam in his eyes, however, that made
Sabrina stifle a sigh. Countess Latuski was out of reach,
momentarily at least, and William had become aware of his
wife's coldness. Soon, if he did not find a more interesting
prey, he would be hot on her trail. Sabrina could not help
laughing as she found herself sincerely wishing he would
find a tempting woman at once. Then her eyes filled with

tears. It was really dreadful to feel like that about one's husband.

The post chaise came, and Sabrina stepped into it. Katy fussed around her, putting hot bricks at her feet and a rug over her knees. Sabrina thanked her and even discussed where the basket of delicacies and wine—a thoughtful touch on William's part, which made Sabrina more uncomfortable—should best be placed. She hardly heard her own voice; she felt like one of those strange automata that made sounds without life. If only she could make up her mind what to do! She had been so sure when she parted with Perce. Being with him always seemed the only important goal. But she had had time to think on the voyage; there had been little else to do. Now her path did not seem so clear at all. Nothing really answered whether Perce was truly in love or just caught up in an infatuation caused by the circumstances.

Sabrina did not doubt the genuineness of his sexual excitement when he seized her and kissed her. The desire had been real enough and hot enough, but that was common in men. And it had cooled very quickly. He had said he wanted her, but followed the statement with rather frequent reminders of the unpleasant consequences of a break with her husband. And he had been very quick to renounce the possibility of pursuing a love affair. That didn't seem natural in a man.

Not natural for a man like William, perhaps, but was it unnatural for Perce? Everything she remembered could easily be the result of real love, the kind that considered one's partner's needs before one's own. But Sabrina had no personal experience with that kind of love. She had seen it; Roger and Leonie had it, and so did Meg and Philip. She suppressed a shudder. Whose fault was it? Was it because of what William was that she could not believe in that kind of love for herself, or was it because of what she was herself?

Only Sabrina knew Perce responded to her emotions even when she tried to hide them. He had seen how she hated the fright Katy's voice had given her. Katy! How could she be afraid of Katy? She knew Katy would lie for her, probably would die for her. It was because she was ashamed. She didn't want even Katy to know that she considered being unfaithful to her husband. Considered being? She *was* unfaithful: her mind was, and her body would be gladly if it had a chance.

Perce said it wasn't the way. Because he didn't really want to be committed? How could she know? Oh, nonsense! That first night at the ball, the words had just burst out of him. *Accept that*, Sabrina told herself. *It's stupid to pick Perce apart. It's stupid to think he could be so idiotic, so cruel, as deliberately to continue a farce of love. Accept that he is as truly in love with you as you are with him. Does it make anything easier?*

In a sense it did. The problem reduced itself immediately to a single question. Which did Sabrina want more, the life to which she was accustomed, or Perce? And the answer to that was easy: Perce. Somehow he would make life interesting for her, even if they had to emigrate to find excitement.

But the simplicity was deceptive. To get Perce, an annulment of her marriage would have to be obtained. To obtain an annulment one needed grounds, even false grounds. Roger would have to cook up the grounds since none of the common ones could be used. She was not barren; she had conceived and miscarried. Thus her husband had done his marital duty and could not be accused of denying her her natural rights. William would have to cooperate, too. Sabrina shuddered.

That was a mistake. Katy began to fuss at once. Sabrina felt like screaming at her, but she bit back her irritability and agreed that the cold in England was different from that in Russia, less cold but more penetrating. Sabrina even knew why Katy was fussing, which was not normal for her. Obviously she sensed Sabrina's misery. *Why can't I be like everyone else and accept my husband for what he is*, Sabrina thought. She was going to make every single person who loved her utterly miserable.

Even William! Sabrina restrained another shudder. The first whisper of an annulment would turn his full attention to her. He would woo and plead and show the world a totally devoted husband, bewildered and hurt. He would never agree. In his way, she supposed, William did love her. She was his safe harbor, the place to which he returned from his adventuring. He expected her to bear his children—and she had to admit he had been most understanding, not railing at her or blaming her when she lost the child—to act as his hostess, and to support his diplomatic activities. He did not ask love of her. Society would consider him a near ideal husband and her a fool for objecting to a little affair now and again.

There really was no hope of an annulment, Sabrina feared, unless Roger could bring some violent pressure to bear on William. And how Roger would hate that! Although he would have preferred a more settled sort for Sabrina's husband, essentially, Roger liked William as a man. What was worse, he would be devastated by knowing that Sabrina's marriage was so unhappy that she would risk social ostracism to escape it. Leonie, too! Both would blame themselves for Sabrina's unhappiness. And their distress would be all the bitterer because to a certain degree it was their fault.

No, Sabrina thought, *I cannot, simply cannot do this to them. They love me too much. Do they deserve to be punished for that? I can bear remaining married to William. It will grow easier with time. I will have many, many pleasures*. Her mind checked there, having received a sharp nudge from her body. She would not have Perce, and he would not have her . . . if he wanted her. Oh, no!

101

Not again! She would not begin at the beginning all over again.

Determinedly, Sabrina pushed all problems out of her mind and began to talk to Katy of the possibility that Leonie would be at Stour. They reminisced of other winters spent at the castle, of the various amusements available, whether they had missed Lady Arthur St. Eyre's annual ball. Katy perked up visibly as Sabrina talked and smiled. Home would heal her, Katy hoped, pushing away the knowledge that home could not change her husband's character or reduce Sabrina's passion for another man.

Although both suppositions were true, Sabrina did feel better as soon as the porter in the gatehouse had opened the park gates. He exclaimed in surprise, but gave Sabrina the welcome news that Leonie was in residence, and the horses started up the long, curving drive to Stour Castle. Sabrina could see that the "wilderness" Leonie had planted in the southeast was doing well. The entrance was a good half mile from it, but one could see the trees quite clearly. They had been too small to be seen from the entrance the last time Sabrina had been home. A renewed quiver of unhappiness passed through her. It was wrong to think of Stour as "home." Elvan Manor should be "home," but Sabrina had never developed any affection for that most elegant and commodious house.

Warmth enveloped her as she thought of Stour's wild mixture of architectural styles, its myriad confusing passageways, towers, nooks, and crannies. It was so large that she had become really lost in the top-story warren of rooms while playing hide-and-seek with the boys. Of course, that was not long after she had come to Stour from the island. Warm comfort changed to a flash of passionate heat as she remembered how Perce had found her and held her close to him, kissing her to comfort her. She knew there was no more in those kisses than what he bestowed upon his sisters, but she wondered how *she* had been such a fool. No, she had simply been too young. There was no sense thinking about it.

And there at the end of the long drive was the beautiful Inigo Jones front, graceful and plain with Corinthian pilasters. To either side were the older portions, Elizabethan wings with projecting mullioned windows, carved cornices, and ornamental doorways. Each wing terminated in a strong octagonal tower, the walls immensely thick and the windows only thin slits. The rooms in the towers were used only when Stour was overfull; they had been places of refuge in case of attack, not meant for residence. However, there was plenty of room without them.

When they pulled up at the portico Sabrina was too impatient to wait. She got out at once and was running up the steps as Cobworth, the butler, opened the door.

"Lady Sabrina!" he exclaimed. "Oh, pardon me, Lady Elvan. How glad we all are to see you home."

"And I to be here, Cobworth. Where is Lady Leonie?"

"In the small drawing room, madam, unless she is back in the nursery again. Mr. Philip left little Master Roger with us while—"

"Sabrina!" Leonie shrieked, rushing out of a doorway down the corridor. *"Petite, petite, bienvenue, bienvenue."*

Fortunately Sabrina had divested herself of her outerwear while Cobworth gave her the most essential family news. She was thus free to embrace and be embraced without having her arm half in and half out of her pelisse or having her bonnet knocked to the floor. There was no tame pecking of cheeks or squeezing of fingers in Leonie's welcomes.

"Ah," Leonie sighed after hugging and being hugged, kissing and being kissed, *"Que je suis heureuse!* How happy I am! I knew William was sent for, but I did not know whether you, too, would come. And Katy?"

"She's seeing to the luggage. You know she insists on

103

doing things like that. I'm so sorry to hear that Meg and Philip aren't here."

"No, Meg's poor papa, he leaves us at last. The good doctor, he wrote to ask Meg to come. Her papa has been asking for her, the doctor said. It cannot be much of a grief to her, but of course she would wish that he should be as easy as possible."

"So you have Roggie all to yourself," Sabrina teased. "How is he?"

"Wicked! Oh, how could it be otherwise with that naughty Philip for papa and that Meg with her red hair for mama? Come up and see for yourself. No, better come and have a cup of tea. Dinner is early—six o'clock—but you must be cold."

"I am a little chilled," Sabrina admitted, "but can't we have tea in the nursery? Do you have a tartar for a nurse?"

"Not at all, but Roggie should be taking his afternoon nap, and Weeper—is not that a dreadful name for a nurse—good as she is, would be furious if we wake him. Nor would I blame her. He is cross as two sticks if he does not sleep."

She led Sabrina to the room in which she had been sitting, rang for tea, urged Sabrina to a chair by the fire, then stood back just to look at her. In a moment the expression of excited pleasure faded. "*Ah, qu'as-tu?*" Leonie cried. "*Ma petite,* what is wrong?" Her hand flew to her mouth. "*Stupide! Bête!* Like a fool I talk of the child, and—"

"No!" Sabrina protested. "Leonie, for heaven's sake, do you think I don't love Roggie? I swear I'm not grieving over that miscarriage. It wasn't ever real to me. I mean, I hadn't thought of it as a child yet."

It was true. Oddly enough, she hadn't known she was pregnant until about a week before she miscarried. Just about the time she missed her first flux, there had been a political crisis. When it was over, she had forgotten she had not menstruated. Then at the time she missed her second flux, she had realized that William was growing restless again. He had not quite fixed on a woman, but he was, quite obviously, looking. The miscarriage had checked him. Sabrina had to admit there was nothing mean about William. He had given her his full attention for several months, as if to prove he did not blame her.

"Then what is wrong?" Leonie asked.

Sabrina's heart failed. She couldn't, she simply couldn't tell Leonie the truth and see the guilt and pain in her beautiful golden eyes. "How can you ask?" she protested. "It was the most horrible passage, freezing cold and wet and not enough room for a mouse to turn. It was rough, too, and the ship was so small. It pitched and rolled—"

"Brina," Leonie interrupted, "you have sailed with Philip and Perce in a—a cockleshell and loved every minute of it."

"Not in the middle of the winter or for weeks at a time," Sabrina said reasonably, smiling.

"*Petite*," Leonie sighed, "it is not *mal de mer* in your eyes." She shook her head. "There is only one thing, I think, you should not wish to tell me, because it is my fault you suffer. It is William." She covered her eyes for a moment.

"It's my fault, not yours," Sabrina said quickly. "It's not a fault to want someone you love to be happy."

"It is the duty of the elder to guide the younger. Do I give Roggie a sharp knife because he cries for the shiny thing? Oh, Brina, Brina . . . But it was not only giving in because I could not bear to see you cry. It was Roger who fooled me."

"Roger?" Sabrina knew Roger liked William in a general way, but he had never favored the marriage. He had opposed it more vigorously than Leonie at first, and had yielded less willingly.

"Because Roger was a great one for women before we

105

were married. Do you see? He was not happy with Solange, his first wife, and he sought out others, many others. And I believed William would be the same, that he
had had enough of *affaires*. Oh, *petite*, we inquired and
inquired, and never before had William looked seriously at
a young girl. And in many ways, Brina, you were not like
other young girls. We waited, thinking he would weary, or
you would. But he was so steadfast and spoke so reasonably to Roger. . . ."

"I know. Don't blame yourself, Leonie. You *told* me he
had had many affairs. Roger told me. Even Philip told me.
I talked to him about it myself. He swore to me that those
days were over for him, that his love for me was true. Leonie, I don't think he was lying. I think *he* believed I
would be his last, true love." Sabrina laughed bitterly.
"Maybe he believes it each time."

Leonie blinked back tears. It would do no good to
weep. "*Eh, bien, petite,* then what do you wish to do? We
will help you any way, *vraiment.*"

"I don't know. Leonie, don't cry. You mustn't think I'm
suffering; at least, I'm not suffering the pangs of 'despised'
love. I can stop William any time I want. I just . . . don't
care . . . not about him. I just suddenly realized . . . he
isn't worth the effort. That's dreadful, isn't it? That's
what's really dreadful."

"Not about him!" Leonie picked out the significant part
of the statement unerringly.

Sabrina blushed painfully and shook her head. Before
she could speak, the door opened and Cobworth brought
in a tea tray. He made a business of setting it on a table,
which he carried to Leonie's side, and of laying out cups,
cakes, biscuits, and thin sandwiches. By the time he left,
Sabrina's complexion had returned to normal, and she had
decided what to say. She would not mention Perce. That
would be unfair to him. If things did not work out between them, she did not want any awkwardness or

coldness to rise toward him from her family. Sabrina got up and took a sandwich and the cup of tea Leonie had automatically poured for her.

"I'm not having an affair myself, I promise you," she said quietly. "And I want you to be sure that William and I are not quarreling. There is no bitterness. I can't be bitter about someone who isn't worth the effort of holding. Or, if I am bitter, it's at myself for being such a fool. William is what he is—and he is never unkind. None of the affairs means anything once it is over."

There was a brief silence. Then Leonie asked bluntly, "Are you sleeping with him?"

"Of course not," Sabrina snapped. "Do you think I would take the leavings of another woman?"

"But you said none of the affairs means anything—" Leonie began.

"And neither do I anymore," Sabrina interrupted stonily.

"*Petite*, you cannot live in this way for long," Leonie said.

"Perhaps not," Sabrina admitted, and hesitated.

Should she mention the idea of an annulment? But it might take a long time, and once the action was started it would be out of the question for her to accompany William back to Russia. But Perce was in Russia!

"I said I didn't know what I wanted to do, and I don't think this is the time to do anything anyway," Sabrina went on. "That's why I assured you that I am not unhappy. I can wait. It isn't as if William were a monster who mistreats me. And I like the life. William and I work very well together on the diplomatic end. Considering the political situation in Russia, it would be best if I returned. I have friends, a certain circle of influence. Women wield a surprising amount of power in Russia."

Leonie looked and felt puzzled. She did not wish to push Sabrina into any action, but she was rather surprised at her cousin's willingness to let so emotional a matter hang in limbo. For all her ice-maiden appearance, Sabrina was both impetuous and warmhearted. Leonie's own heart contracted painfully at the thought that bitter hurt and several years' practice in misery could teach caution and patience.

She had been studying Sabrina's face all through the conversation, however, and her distress diminished. Leonie was a keen observer of expressions and involuntary movements owing to her own precarious background. Now, while Sabrina hungrily consumed her sandwiches and tea, Leonie recovered from her shock and was able to sort out her impressions more carefully. First, she realized that she was not really shocked at all. Sabrina's confession had merely confirmed her growing fear that all was not well with the girl's marriage. Second, she recognized that whatever she had seen in Sabrina's expression, it was not patient, grief-stricken resignation. Third, the eagerness with which Sabrina was eating struck Leonie. One does not eat with the speed and appetite of a coal-heaver when one is discussing something painful enough to close the throat and knot the stomach.

Relaxing, Leonie nibbled on a cake and sipped her own tea. Sabrina grinned and helped herself to another sandwich; although she bit and chewed in a most ladylike manner, the rate of her consumption was remarkable. Between swallows she explained that the food aboard the naval sloop, even officers' stores, had been close to inedible—and that was when the cookfires had not been swamped by high seas in the middle of preparation. At all other times it was completely inedible.

"In any case, nothing like this was served," Sabrina concluded, reaching for a tea cake this time.

"Please proceed," Leonie laughed. "If you are thoroughly filled by the time I must present you at dinner to our guests, they will not receive the impression that I have

108

raised a vulture. Eat now so that Lord Ellenborough and Sir Samuel Romilly will be deceived and think you properly delicate."

Sabrina raised her brows. "Ellenborough and Romilly?"

"Lord Ellenborough is the new chief justice, and Romilly has been appointed the solicitor general."

Having absorbed this, Sabrina continued to feel puzzled. Although Roger was a barrister and had close ties in the legal community, most of his government connections in the past had been with the Foreign Office. He had been most closely aligned with Pitt, but his impartiality, experience, and knowledge had made him acceptable even to Addington, Pitt's enemy.

"The chief justice and solicitor general? Is Roger working with them on some legal bill?" Sabrina asked.

Leonie put down her tea. "Oh, my dear, you cannot know what has been happening since Mr. Pitt died. None of his friends felt able to form a government, and the king was obliged to call on Lord Grenville to be the new prime minister. That meant Mr. Fox would also hold office, since he and Grenville are friends and political allies. Of course, Fox insisted on having the Foreign Office. It will mean quite a change in England's policy. Fox has always been against the war. He has always believed that worse was said about the republicans than was true."

"Including that bloody lunatic Robespierre?" Sabrina commented caustically. "Well, he's dead and can't do any more harm, but if Fox feels the same about Bonaparte, we may be in serious trouble."

"*Bien sûr*, and that is why Roger is no longer connected with the Foreign Office. Harrowby suggested that Fox speak to Roger. He did, but what Roger said did not agree with Fox's notions."

"Good heavens, can no one make Fox understand?" Sabrina cried. "Bonaparte will swallow all of Europe. The tsar is sitting in a corner sucking his thumb. He cannot believe in the people who could accomplish something, so he will not support their plans, and the others are so incompetent he cannot trust them, either. If England does not animate him, Alexander will do nothing."

Leonie shrugged. "Fox insists that Bonaparte attacks because he is threatened, that if we offer peace seriously, he will accept."

"Boney very well might," Sabrina replied, "but only because it would give him more time to consolidate his gains and build up his army."

"But is it true, *petite?*" Leonie asked anxiously. "Or do you and I and Roger and Philip believe this because what happened to me during the French Revolution has poisoned us all?"

"Well, it certainly hasn't poisoned General Bagration or Marshal Kutuzov, both respected commanders of the Russian army. They believe it," Sabrina pointed out. "And so does Perce."

Sabrina had said the name without thinking, but the moment it was out of her mouth, color flew into her face. She got up hastily and turned toward the mantelpiece, where an elegant marble clock sat ticking. Leonie had looked away when she mentioned her fear that she had infected her family with a hatred of French republicanism. Sabrina's sudden movement drew her eyes. Although the girl's face was not visible, Leonie could see her throat and part of a cheek, and they were rosy. She was startled, but the color could have been caused by a number of things.

"Gracious, how the time has flown," Sabrina remarked before Leonie could think of a way to ask tactfully for the cause of the blush. "Roggie must be awake by now. Let's go up, because there isn't much time. If we aren't going to be *en famille*, we must dress for dinner."

Leonie blinked. She had been warned off. It was rather painful, but she knew she must accept it. Sabrina was fully a woman now, and although she would never complain

110

nor offer a single word of recrimination, Leonie knew she had made a botch in the matter of her cousin's marriage. Sabrina had good reason not to trust her judgment.

"But what shall I say to Roger?" Leonie cried.

"Nothing, I think," Sabrina replied. "He has enough to worry him, and I am quite sure that, whatever Fox thinks about making peace with Bonaparte, William will want to discuss matters with Roger. It would be hard for him to act naturally—you know how protective Roger is."

"Will William be able to act naturally?" Leonie asked, relieved that Sabrina was not cutting her off completely. To her surprise, Sabrina laughed.

"William is not aware that there is anything to be unnatural about," Sabrina said. "Oh, he knows I am displeased with him, but if he has given the matter any thought at all, he expects that I will yield to his wooing, as I have done several times already. It depends on what happens at the Foreign Office."

"At the Foreign Office?" Leonie asked, completely at sea.

"Yes. If Fox relieves William of duty and we must remain here, I will have to make a decision. Or if William is kept in England for very long . . . I don't know. But if he is sent back to Russia quite soon, I want to go with him, so I would rather nothing was said."

Leonie nodded. She agreed that Roger should be spared further worry if possible, and it was quite clear that Sabrina was in control of herself and believed she could control the situation. It was also clear that she was deeply troubled, but there seemed to be as much eager excitement as pain in that trouble. Leonie concealed a sigh. There was nothing more she could do for Sabrina now, except love her and assure her that whatever decision she made, she would be supported. But why did Sabrina want to return to Russia? Duty? Perhaps. Sabrina had a fine patriotic fervor and took great pride in her responsibilities as a diplomatic wife. But that would not account for her tense excitement when she spoke of going back.

"Yes, let us go up and play with Roggie," Leonie said.

It was not her business to interfere, Leonie told herself firmly. When she should have interfered, she had taken utterly the wrong course. If Sabrina asked, she would speak the feeling of her heart this time. She had stood up and started toward the door when Sabrina threw her arms around her and kissed her. Leonie returned the embrace with joy and relief. She had a good part of her thanks already. The only thing that could make her happier was to see her beloved Sabrina happy herself.

It was almost impossible to worry about anything in Roggie's presence. He was an extremely happy baby, so accustomed to love that he greeted Sabrina with crows of delight, even though he could not possibly remember her. Nor did Weeper make them feel unwelcome, as many nannies did. She was not at all like her name, being plump and jolly and obviously quite accustomed to invasions of "her" nursery. In fact she seemed glad to leave the baby to his "grandmother" and "aunt"—neither of whom was really related to him at all—and get on with some other chores.

They had a lovely time, crawling about on the floor to the everlasting detriment of their gowns, feeding Roggie a pretea or postlunch, showing him pictures, and laughing over his antics. Weeper came back to find both ladies sitting cross-legged on the floor, inducing Roggie to toddle a few steps from one to the other.

"That's right kind of you, madam," the nanny said. "He's proper wore out and he'll be glad to play quiet a while. I'm not bidding you go, but it's near dinnertime."

"Oh, *ma foi*," Leonie cried, snatching Roggie into her arms to kiss and catching a glimpse of the sky as Weeper drew the curtains, "it is growing quite black outside."

Even as she spoke they heard the sound of a carriage

112

coming up the long drive to the house. Leonie thrust Roggie into Sabrina's arms and fled. Sabrina kissed the little boy and spoke soothingly as his face crumpled in indecision whether or not to wail at "gamma's" sudden departure. However, he was easy to distract. Sabrina played with him a few minutes more, a quiet game of pushing colored blocks into a line and then a circle. She wondered amusedly whether Leonie would stop to put herself to rights or would greet her guests with her hair all anyhow and the marks of Roggie's sticky fingers on her dress. Leonie was not at all conventional about such things.

When she had made the blocks sufficiently interesting, Sabrina bent over the child and kissed him, saying, "*Au revoir*, Roggie. I'll come back soon. You be a good boy and play with Weeper now."

There was another momentary indecision, but Weeper was there with a bottle and a cuddly blanket. Roggie went willingly into the familiar arms, and Sabrina stepped out of the nursery. She hurried toward her room, partly soothed, partly envious. She wanted children. However, when she inevitably thought of her miscarriage, it was relief she felt. If she had borne that child, she would have no choice. She could never have left her baby, and no woman who left her husband, no matter how valid the reason, would be allowed to take his child.

As Sabrina dressed she considered her desire for a child in and around Katy's conversation. It was rather frustrating, for her thoughts were broken, but by the time Katy carried away the soiled clothing, Sabrina had decided without the smallest doubt that she didn't want William's children. He would be a dreadful father, not cruel but totally uninterested. She paused a moment, her hands upraised to pin a long curl so that it would fall gracefully over her shoulder. No wonder he was so pleasant about that miscarriage. He didn't care. Sabrina set her pin and shook her head. She was being unfair. William was kind.

On the other hand, Sabrina thought, smiling into the mirror, she would love to have Perce's children. She knew just what kind of father he would make. Hadn't he endured her, read to her, played with her, tied his handkerchief around her knee and kissed her when she skinned it? But that could never happen while she was married to William. And what if Perce didn't want her to be the mother of his children? *Nonsense,* she told herself, focusing on the beautiful countenance that looked back at her from the mirror. Why shouldn't Perce want her?

Deep inside, not in specific words but in feeling, something said, *No one wants you. Mama and Papa and brother William and sister Alice went to heaven and left you behind. Roger and Leonie let you marry the wrong man just to be rid of you. And now William doesn't want you.* Sabrina stood up abruptly. It wasn't the same thing at all! Her family had drowned. They had not deliberately abandoned her. Roger and Leonie had yielded to *her* arguments and pleas. And William was just different from most men. He never wanted any woman for long. Surely that was true. Surely it wasn't anything she had done that had driven him back to his old ways. She had asked! That first time she had begged him to tell her if it was her fault, if she had displeased him in some way. All he would say was that she was imagining things, and when she would not accept that answer, he glibly announced that it had nothing to do with her at all and if she looked the other way everything would be fine. But what if it was her fault?

However, all that happened after the dinner gong sounded was calculated to make Sabrina laugh at her own self-doubts. Roger's joy in seeing her was too deep and warm to misunderstand, and after all, Roger had lived with her far longer than had William. If there was some fault of manner or speech she displayed that had rubbed William raw over time, it must be something William alone noticed. It was apparent she was a total joy to Roger.

His guests showed no distaste for her company either—far to the contrary—and she had accomplished that over an initial reluctance, too.

Their reluctance was not personal, of course. However, Ellenborough and Romilly had come to discuss business and were rather put out when they found their host's nineteen-year-old foster daughter a surprise guest. Neither gentleman really wanted to make conversation suitable to a frivolous young woman. But Sabrina had not been a diplomat's wife for three years in vain. When Romilly politely asked her about her stay in Russia, expecting a spate of nonsense about balls and gowns, he heard a brief, womanly, but totally political remark on the effect of the defeat at Austerlitz on the Russian government.

Surprise faded into interest and interest into pleasure. Sabrina was neither strident nor opinionated. She let the men lead the conversation and answered their questions, but not with her own interpretations. After all, to give most men a woman's opinion could only convince them the concept was silly. Nonetheless, her opinions were carefully selected to create the impression Sabrina wanted to produce.

The subject did not follow them from the drawing room into the dining room since it was not of deep importance to Ellenborough or Romilly. By the time the first course was removed, they were deep in a discussion about a proposed act to abolish the slave trade, quite at ease with the knowledge that serious talk would not bore Sabrina.

From the attitude of these distinguished guests, it was difficult for Sabrina to think of herself as repulsive in any way. Her company and conversation were sought with eagerness rather than mere politeness. Altogether, when the evening was over, she went to bed in a far happier frame of mind than she had enjoyed since she left Russia.

The next few days did nothing to change her mood, although on the fourth day she received a sheaf of hothouse flowers and a most loving note from William.

Leonie raised her brows at this, but she made no remarks. Sabrina was somewhat amused at how easy it was for her to interpret William's gestures. The note, despite its loving terms, said nothing about Sabrina coming to London or William coming to Stour. The loving terms and flowers indicated that William had not yet found a woman he wished to pursue, but neither had he decided to set about rewooing his wife.

Sabrina was relieved as well as amused. For a while longer she would be able to avoid a confrontation with her husband. Moreover, the London social season was beginning. Company would be flooding into town. With any luck at all someone new would cross William's path, or an old love, now indifferent, would recall his attention. Sabrina resolved to delay her arrival in London as long as possible to give him every opportunity to find fresh prey.

CHAPTER SEVEN

Sabrina was still at Stour Castle when Perce's letter arrived in the middle of March. It was beside her place when she came down for breakfast, and she barely repressed a cry of joy. Leonie looked up at her as she started to open the letter before she sat down, but Sabrina was too busy to notice the attention she had attracted. She found that she was almost as excited as if Perce himself had appeared. He had never written to her before.

The weeks at Stour had been so calm, peaceful, and happy that Sabrina had begun to wonder whether her sudden passion for Perce had been real or nurtured by the hothouse atmosphere in which she had been living. No question arose about her indifference to William. On that subject she grew more certain with every note and gift she received from him. Significantly, none of the notes urged her to join him.

Sabrina had recast her initial analysis of this dichotomy. She no longer believed William was undecided as to where to bestow his attentions. Now she was convinced that the loving letters and trinkets that came every few days were designed to convince her—and, more important, her family—of his devotion. William, she was certain, was either on the hunt again or was simply having so good a time in the fleshpots of London that he wished to ensure her noninterference without making her family suspicious.

In the latter, he had failed. Roger was livid, although he

said nothing to Sabrina. Leonie had conveyed this information as well as the fact that Roger chose not to confront William. Any breath of scandal would have been sufficient excuse to discredit the entire Russian diplomatic mission. No matter how ridiculous it was that one man's differences with his wife should reflect dishonor on a whole diplomatic staff, it was a common enough occurrence. Roger was far too aware of the serious problems in relations with Russia to add even a single straw to the fire.

What was most significant to Sabrina was that William's behavior left her feeling totally indifferent. She had agreed with Roger's decision that no issue should be made of William's infidelity, but she had not felt any special anxiety about it. The peace of Stour Castle seemed to insulate her against any strong emotion, and she had unconsciously avoided anything that could disturb that peace. She had never visited the schoolroom, where in inclement weather Philip and Perce had joined her to read and talk, play games, and roast apples and nuts. Equally, she had avoided the room in which Perce had customarily stayed. She had had thoughts of remaining in the passive, contented state in which she was enwrapped.

Perce's letter destroyed the placid, imaginary cocoon even before she broke the seal. The moment she saw his handwriting, every emotion she had felt at their last meeting—the hunger, the joy, and the despair—gripped her again. It did not matter that she knew there could be nothing revealing in the letter. Perce would never take the chance that it might be delivered when she was not at home. Husbands had a perfect right to open their wives' mail, and many husbands did so. Her hands trembled as she pulled the letter from the cover, and her breath sighed out in pleasure when she saw that there were three thin, closely written sheets rather than a single thick piece of paper containing a polite scrawl.

He began, skirting safety, with "My very dearest Sa-

118

brina," and went on to give his excuse for writing to her—that they had parted in such haste he had no chance to thank her for her kind attentions in St. Petersburg. "I find the atmosphere here much changed," he continued, "so much so that I have decided not to stay longer in the city." Sabrina's heart fluttered. He could come no closer to saying that he missed her too much to remain where every ball and theater party reminded him of her.

"I have obtained an introduction to and an invitation from Princess Dashkova, who, I understand, is very pro-English," the letter went on. "I will stay as her guest for a month and then pay my promised visit to General Bagration. If Philip wishes to reach me, a letter under cover to the prince will come into my hands safely. I hope he will write, since I believe the prince will be interested to hear any news from the English point of view." Sabrina flushed slightly. It was not Philip from whom Perce wanted to hear.

From there, the letter concerned events and rumors in Russia. Sabrina read it with devoted interest, although she had already heard most of the information through diplomatic channels. Roger might be ignored by the new minister, Fox, and his immediate appointees, but the long-term civil servants at the Foreign Office were eager to keep him informed since, to a man, they thought Fox grossly deceived by his own long-held opinions.

The tsar, Perce wrote, continued to be almost completely a recluse, except for a most unwise liaison with Madame Maria Naryshkin. Rumors abounded, principally that Alexander was growing more and more unstable, like his father, bursting into unpredictable angers and then succumbing to deep depressions. He told her, too, about the reasonably successful campaign Admiral Dmitri Senyavin was waging against French outposts in southern Dalmatia.

Sabrina smiled tenderly as she read. Perce must have known that all this information would have come through the diplomatic post. He simply could not stop writing, because it was a form of contact with her. She understood. She felt the same. Having finished reading, she turned the sheets over and began again. The words did not matter, only that Perce had written them. Then a sense of anxiety took hold of her. Once more she read Perce's letter, trying to perceive meanings he did not wish to state openly. At once something came; there was no hint of any intended return. In fact, the overall impression was that he expected to be in Russia for some time.

Yes, there it was. "Spring comes very late in this country and, I am told, with great suddenness. I will be interested to see this, although I do not look forward to enduring the heat of another Russian summer."

But Sabrina knew there were negotiations under way for peace. Had Perce simply not received orders yet? Had he decided to stay in Russia in spite of orders to return to England? Or did the secretary of war have opinions different from those of the Foreign Office? If so, he could have sent secret instructions for those agents who were not readily identifiable to continue their work. Impatience swept through Sabrina. She had to get back to Russia. She stood up.

"I think I will go to London," she announced.

Leonie raised her brows. "Before breakfast?"

Color flooded into Sabrina's face, and she sat down again, reaching for her cup.

"Let me pour another cup for you," Leonie said. "That must be stone cold. Your Russian acquaintance writes an absorbing letter."

The servants put the mail out, and Leonie was too polite to pry by peering at Sabrina's letters. Thus she had not seen Perce's handwriting. Sabrina's mind jumped one way and then the other. She would not lie to Leonie, not for any reason.

120

"It's not a Russian. It's Perce," Sabrina said, and flushed again.

"Perce?" Leonie sounded stunned. Her mouth opened again, but she shut it on whatever almost popped out—a miracle of self-control for Leonie. "I hope he is well," she remarked blandly after a short silence.

"He doesn't say," Sabrina replied in a small voice.

Leonie's mouth opened again, and again shut soundlessly over a caustic remark that his health seemed to be the only topic he could possibly have omitted in a letter of that length. But Sabrina did not notice. She stood again, looking worried. Leonie's casual question, asked only to cover an awkward silence, had raised a specter for Sabrina. Was Perce ill? Was that why he had not mentioned his health, why he said he did not look forward to the hot summer? One part of her mind laughed at her. There was no reason for Perce to mention his health; a normal young man would never think of doing so. The other, silly, part of her mind was frightened to death.

She felt an immediate need to write to him. Fortunately she had an excellent reason to do so. Perhaps in the change of administrations, whoever was responsible for giving Perce his orders had been dismissed or transferred. When Philip had gone to France in 1804, he had been responsible only to the foreign secretary himself, and there had been no written orders, only Philip's report after he had returned. Could it be that Mr. Pitt's outgoing war secretary had forgotten to mention Perce to Mr. Windham, the current war secretary? The situation had not been normal, after all. There had been great confusion in the aftermath of Mr. Pitt's sudden death. It was possible that Perce had left St. Petersburg before Fox's moves toward making peace were known.

Sabrina's letter was fully as long as Perce's. She told him how Foreign Minister Fox had been informed of a plot to assassinate Bonaparte, and Fox had passed the information to Bonaparte's foreign minister, Tallyrand, on February twentieth. From this opening, negotiations had been initiated using as an intermediary Lord Yarborough, who had been interned in France in 1803. Lord Lauderdale had just been sent to Paris, so it seemed that there was a real chance for peace between England and France.

As she wrote this, conscience stabbed Sabrina. Roger had nearly had a fit when Lauderdale was sent. He found it incredible that so clever a man as Fox could fall victim to the same tactics that Bonaparte had used so often. The Corsican had made a regular practice of using the period in which he was negotiating peace to build up his army to make war more effectively. But if she said that, Sabrina knew that Perce would never consider coming home.

Clearly stated, Sabrina's guilt was too plain for her to ignore. Duty was duty. Biting her lip, she described Roger's conclusions and then added, "I do not know when, if ever, we will return to Russia. I understand that William is advising the ministry on Austrian-Russian relations. There is a conviction here that the tsar will make peace. In that case, the British legation in Russia will be much reduced." She could not say, *Come home to me.* That would be very wrong, but she knew Perce would understand, as she had understood his *I miss you.*

Eventually she ran dry and signed and sealed her letter. Writing it, however, had crystallized her need for action. The peace of Stour Castle, which she had found so soothing, now smothered her. In her need for action, a confrontation with William faded into insignificance. Many, many wives looked the other way while their husbands played. Sabrina would merely become one in this numerous group. She did not care. She needed to be closer to what was happening. This was easy enough to accomplish. Sabrina had only to tell Leonie, ask Katy to have her clothing packed, and move to her husband's house in London.

122

Sabrina was grimly amused that William was shocked, and none too pleased, to see her. However, his attitude changed when he discovered that she had not come on the warpath. There was another sharp shift back to dissatisfaction when he discovered that Sabrina had no intentions of resuming conjugal relations.

They had just returned from a grand gala given by Earl Fitzwilliam, and Sabrina was still glowing with the pleasure of returning to the social whirl. She looked exquisite. William signaled the footman away and removed her cloak himself, bending his head to kiss her bare shoulder. She whirled away from him, unconsciously rubbing her shoulder as if to wipe away the feel of his lips.

"Don't touch me," she breathed.

William blinked. "Don't touch you," he repeated. "What in the world do you mean? You're my wife. Don't sound like a silly shopgirl."

"Oh, have you taken to chasing them, too?" Sabrina snapped. "I thought your taste was degenerating when you took off after Countess Latuski, but I didn't know how far downhill you had gone."

"Sabrina! Don't be indecent!"

She opened her eyes to their widest extent. "Indecent? I? I haven't been chasing shopgirls—you have."

"Hold your tongue, Sabrina," William growled.

"Certainly," she said, and flounced down the hall toward the staircase.

William threw her cloak at a chair and followed it with his outer garments. He caught her halfway up the stairs, but she wrenched her arm out of his hand, repeating her *Don't touch me* in a vicious hiss.

"Stop being ridiculous," he snarled, reaching for her again.

"If you put your hand on me again," Sabrina said

coldly, "I'll scream the house down. If Katy doesn't kill you, Roger will when I tell him."

William dropped his hand. "What the devil is wrong with you, Sabrina? I just want to talk to you, and you have insulted me and threatened me—"

"Since when do conversations begin with an intimate kiss?" she interrupted.

"I cannot think that very exceptional between a husband and wife who have been apart for some time," William said softly, smiling.

"I'm amazed that you noticed," Sabrina remarked with weary disgust.

"Oh, I noticed," William purred, completely misinterpreting his wife's tone. "You're a silly girl to be so jealous."

Sabrina paused and looked at him. She was irritated by his assumption and decided that this was as good a time as any to clarify the terms upon which she was willing to act as his wife. William was really not a political creature but a member of the diplomatic service. Nonetheless he had received his initial appointment and various promotions during Pitt's administration. Because Fox was not a fool and his party had not been in power for many years, he was calling upon any experienced men who were willing to serve under him. However, Fox had no reason to back William up under adverse circumstances. If William were involved in any scandal, Fox would dismiss him.

Because she was somewhat tired, angry, and apprehensive, Sabrina made a mistake. Instead of turning and going downstairs again, she went on up and into her dressing room. It was a natural place for her to go. In the drawing rooms and parlors of the main floor, the lights had been extinguished and the fires allowed to die. Her dressing room and William's, on opposite sides of the double bedchamber, were still lit and warmed.

It would never have occurred to Sabrina to go to

William's room. That was fitted out as an extra bedchamber, and William had often slept there, even before any differences had arisen between them or at least any that Sabrina had known about. She had never liked it. Roger and Leonie never slept apart unless they were in different parts of the country. William had insisted it was because he could not bear to wake her when he came in late from all-male meetings and conferences. Later Sabrina realized that he had probably been unfaithful all along and that many late nights had actually been spent with other women. Most likely he did not want to come to her bed because he was afraid she would want to make love, or because he thought she might notice the scent or see evidence of cosmetics on him.

However, Sabrina was not thinking of that, and it would not have troubled her if she had thought of it. Her mind was busy arranging what she would say, and she opened the door of her room and walked in, not realizing she had just confirmed William's impression that she was jealous. Worse, he believed that her invitation into the dressing room was an invitation to far more.

Although there was no bed in the room, nothing more suggestive then a chaise longue for Sabrina to rest on, William knew that the room would be empty. Sabrina never allowed Katy to wait up for her when she would be late. Before Sabrina was married, she and Katy had had many tussles on the subject of waiting up. Afterward, Katy had agreed readily. It was much more interesting to have one's husband help with undressing than one's "nurse." Over the year in which Sabrina thought she was happily married, this had grown to be a custom. Katy still did not wait up after ten or eleven o'clock when William and Sabrina were together.

Knowing this, William leapt to the conclusion that Sabrina was subtly suggesting that he overpower her and prove that her jealousy had no foundation. After all, why else would she invite him into a place where she would be totally unprotected, especially after saying she would scream if he touched her. Screaming in the corridor would have made sense. The servants would have heard her. Someone would surely have come running to find out what caused the disturbance.

In Sabrina's dressing room the chances of screams being heard were much smaller. All the bedchambers on the floor, except their own, were empty. The doors and walls were well built. Neither the menservants in their quarters below nor the maidservants on the topmost floor would hear a muted cry. Even Charlot, waiting in William's dressing room to put him to bed, would hear very little, if anything, with the large bedchamber and two closed doors between them.

Obviously, Sabrina had returned because she found him irresistible. On the other hand she could not, without damaging her pride, take him back to her bed. If he overpowered her, she could weep and call him a brute and have what she wanted all along. He was smiling when Sabrina turned, stopped, and said, "William, we—" But he did not stop. He took two steps more and seized her in his arms. Before she could cry out, he had dammed her lips. She struggled, twisting and bending, making furious muffled noises, but her arms had been caught down by her sides. Although she managed to bend her elbows and grasp at his coat, she could not get enough leverage to push or pull him effectively.

Surprise also made Sabrina's struggle ineffectual. Aside from the single attempt he had made to discipline her with a blow nearly two years previously, William had never used violence of any kind, and certainly not in lovemaking. As far as Sabrina knew, her husband was a seducer, not a rapist. Thus, although she tried to get away, she made no attempt to hurt him, merely wrenching her head free to gasp, "Let me go, you idiot."

Encouraged by her ineffective struggles, William murmured, "You are far too beautiful, far too desirable for me ever to let you go."

As he spoke William shifted his arms, raising his right hand to grasp Sabrina's neck and hair so that she could not move her head and he could plaster his mouth on hers again. The grip was strong and painful. Shocked and frightened, Sabrina cried out under the gag of his lips. They had been quarreling the last time he tried to use force to tame her, and she had been so angry she had hardly felt the pain when he hit her. This time her temper had no time to flare, and the bruising grip paralyzed her so that even when he relaxed his left arm to grasp her breast with his hand, Sabrina did not immediately realize she had been granted some freedom. Instead of twisting around to the right and wrenching herself loose, she continued to try to free her mouth.

Further convinced by this seeming lack of initiative, William pulled sharply downward on the minuscule bodice of his wife's evening dress. It was in the height of fashion and barely covered the large pink aureolas around Sabrina's nipples. The yank thus drew the fabric below Sabrina's full breasts to where the material could stretch no more. This pushed the breast upward so that the nipple was tilted provocatively. William could not see this, but it was scarcely the first time he had used the technique. He opened his fingers, felt for a purchase, and pinched and rubbed Sabrina's nipple gently.

In the next moment all hell broke loose. The intimate caress roused Sabrina from fear to fury. Pain could no longer terrify her. She was nauseous with disgust, revolted by the physical sensation his fingers had generated. In a hysteria of rage she stamped violently on William's foot, grasped his hair with her free hand, and tore his mouth from hers. William squawked with agony, letting go of her

127

head and involuntarily jerking his foot out from under hers.

This movement, plus Sabrina's violent pull on his hair, propelled them apart. William's hand, coming away from Sabrina's breast, caught in her dress and ripped it. The sound and sensation, seeming to continue the assault on her, further stimulated Sabrina's resistance. Finding both arms free, she pushed William so fiercely that, off balance as he was, he staggered back. Sabrina did not delay an instant but ran to her desk and seized the heavy inkwell, which she threw as hard as she could.

Since they were no more than ten feet apart and the target was large, Sabrina did not need much aim. The inkwell caught William in the chest painfully, completely overbalancing him and spattering him with ink. His arms windmilled in a vain attempt to find support, but there was none, and he sat down hard on the floor. Sabrina now had the sander in hand, and her arm cocked to throw a second missile.

"Are you crazy?" William roared.

"Filth!" Sabrina shrieked. "How dare you!"

"How dare I? What did you come back for, if that wasn't what you wanted?"

"Wanted?" Sabrina gasped, horrified. "Fool! You've read too many books written by men for men. If you ever try to force me again, I won't wait for Roger to kill you. I'll geld you myself before I cut your throat."

Nonetheless her arm dropped, and she allowed the sander to come to rest on the writing table. Her husband made no move to attack her again, and the affronted indignation on his face, crying aloud that his questions were quite sincere, cooled her rage. She knew his huge conceit. She should have foreseen the conclusion to which he had leapt. She should have written to him first. It was really not his fault. Her unannounced and unexplained arrival must have seemed the result of an irresistible urge.

128

Well, so it was! How was William to have known the urge was not toward him? Even if she had told him she was in love with another man, William probably would not have believed her, Sabrina thought. He would have assumed her confession was another jealous attempt to reawaken his interest in her. Then, how in the world was she going to convince him to leave her alone? He was so sure he was the Casanova of the British diplomatic service. Sabrina watched as he climbed painfully to his feet. He had jarred his tailbone when he sat down so hard. Poor Casanova!

"Resistance is one thing," William said indignantly, "but you have gone too far. I will just leave you to reconsider your silliness. I was willing to play your ridiculous game, but not to have you think you have the upper hand. When you are ready to say you are sorry and beg me to forgive you *and* promise to behave like a proper wife and cease your interference in my affairs, then . . . we will see. I *might* pardon you." He turned to go.

"Wait, William," Sabrina cried as she pulled her dress together and hid her exposed bosom.

He turned back so eagerly and looked so comical in his ink-spattered clothes with his neckcloth all rucked up on the side that Sabrina felt sorry for him. William was not stupid. That speech was a cover for his shock and embarrassment. He knew she had made him look foolish. Perhaps even his monstrous conceit was a form of protection. If so, Sabrina felt no need to puncture it for revenge; she didn't even care enough for him to want revenge. And she didn't want to be on bad terms with him. Let him think her jealous.

"I *am* sorry," she said, "but you misunderstood me. I will not accept from you the leavings of other women."

"That's nonsense," he snarled.

"Not to me."

"A man must be a man. It has nothing to do with you."

Sabrina shook her head. "I should have written to you, but I thought it would be easier to explain in person. Roger is worried sick about this attempt to make peace. I know you agree with him—"

"What the devil has the peace to do with your crazy behavior?" William interrupted furiously.

"If you would allow me to explain, I'll tell you. I just thought it would look peculiar if I didn't come to London once the Season was in full swing. I'm sure Mr. Fox is only looking for an excuse to get rid of anyone who doesn't agree with him wholeheartedly. I thought he might use a rumor that we were estranged to dismiss you. That would be dreadful."

"Why should you care?" he asked bitterly.

"But I do care. You are valuable to this country, William. You will be a very important man some day, and not far in the future, either: an ambassador, and perhaps foreign secretary, if you wish to take a seat in the Commons. Whatever our differences, I don't want to spoil that. And, especially, I don't want you to be dismissed when Fox will need you."

William had been watching her with fascinated loathing, as one might stare at a poisonous reptile, but his expression began to relax under Sabrina's compliments. Encouraged, she continued.

"This peace, if it is ever made, will go sour. You know that. You will be desperately needed to patch up new alliances against Bonaparte, but Fox might be ashamed to recall you if he had dismissed you. It's important to keep your appointment, if possible."

William's eyes narrowed, and his body firmed. He was clever enough to know that Sabrina was petting his pride on purpose, trying to repair the damage she had done. At first he could not understand why she should bother if she didn't want him sexually. She was not dependent on him financially as most wives were dependent on their husbands. St. Eyre had tied up her money so that he couldn't lay a finger on it, and Sabrina had full use of the entire income. William had made no more than a token protest when the marriage settlements were discussed and this fact had been revealed. He had no need of her money and had been completely sure then that he would not need a financial whip to control his wife. The bitter curve of William's lips eased. It was true; he would not need a financial whip. He had found Sabrina's weakness. She was ambitious to be the wife of a political pundit.

"You will suffer more than I if there is a scandal," he warned nastily.

"I know," Sabrina replied with honesty. "I don't want that. William, I swear I will make no more scenes. I will be blind and deaf to your pleasures. I will run your houses to perfection. I will be your hostess, your help in all things to the best of my ability. But I will not lie with you."

He laughed at her. "You are ridiculous! It's you who have read too many books, too many romantic novels with heroes who are mewling pattern pieces——"

"Roger and Philip are not mewling pattern pieces," Sabrina interrupted icily. Then she shrugged. "Perhaps I am not as satisfactory a wife as Leonie or Meg. I don't know. I have tried my best. If I have failed, I'm sorry, but this is how I am made. If I cannot have all of you, then I don't want any."

The admission that it was her fault was soothing. Besides, William did not feel that the loss of Sabrina's sexual company for a few months more would be any deprivation. She was beautiful, even with her hair and dress pulled to pieces, but she was dull, and cold, too, in bed. At first he had thought the young girl would be a delightful adventure, but he had been wrong. Her early, eager response had been minimally amusing but, really, not worth the effort. He preferred women who knew their way around in a situation where the spice of deceit and the fear of exposure generated excitement. Failing that, he liked those who could devise new techniques, and he didn't mind paying for it. Oh, yes, he could do very well without Sabrina abed.

On the other hand, she *was* the perfect political wife. She had grown up with politics, St. Eyre being deeply involved, and young as she was, she knew just what to say, to whom to say it, and when. Her dinners were always perfect, her balls successes, and her behavior was irreproachable. As he recalled that, a tiny quiver of doubt passed through William. There had been several hints in St. Petersburg that Sabrina's relationship with Lord Kevern was not quite as cool as her friendships with other men. Nonsense! She had known Kevern since she was a child. Of course her manner with him would be different. Yes, and probably she had blabbed her whole sad story to him, too, which would explain Kevern's cold reserve toward him.

That was beside the point, which was whether he should accept Sabrina's offer or send her packing. Well, the latter was out of the question. Roger St. Eyre would not only make such a stink that William himself would be ruined, but that hothead Philip would most likely call him out while brandishing a horsewhip. Stupid of him to have married a woman with blindly devoted male supporters. And Sabrina was right about Fox. Fox *would* dismiss him at the hint of a scandal. William shrugged his shoulders and laughed. Talk of hypocrisy! Fox had married his longtime mistress, an actress, no less. Now *there* was a scandal!

"I'm glad you're willing, William."

Sabrina's voice jarred him, and he realized she had taken the shrug and laugh as an acceptance of her proposal. Well, why not? The silly chit probably thought that her beauty would drive him mad because she was close but unobtainable. Yes, that was it! She had withdrawn herself for a month and that hadn't worked—or maybe she thought it had worked because of the notes and flowers he had sent. Now she was going to try flaunting herself around. Eventually, she would realize she could have him only on his own terms, and she would come crawling and pleading.

He shrugged again. "I have too much to do to bother with the tantrums of a silly girl. There are plenty of women just as beautiful and much more interesting than you, my dear. I assure you I wouldn't *dream* of offending your propriety by forcing myself on you." He laughed. "When you are ready, you can ask me, on your knees, and I'll consider whether to favor you with my services."

Sabrina gasped with hurt and shock, but William was out of the room before she could gather her wits for a reply. At first she was furious. She had deliberately refrained from hurting him, not mentioning he was so unsatisfactory a lover that there wasn't much to miss when deprived of his attentions. She had taken the blame for his failure onto herself. She had not told him the full truth—that she would not have him in her bed again on any terms at all because the thought of his caress turned her sick.

Instead of accepting her courtesy graciously—Sabrina was experienced enough to know William would not be generous and share the blame, but she had expected a civil response—he had insulted her brutally. She was halfway to the door before she mastered the impulse to tell him the real truth as she saw it. But that could accomplish nothing. William would only think she was retaliating in kind in a fit of temper. Ask him for his favors? She shuddered at the thought, her skin crawling.

Perhaps she should go back to Stour. But that would surely precipitate just the kind of rumors she wished to avoid, and she would be buried in the country again with nothing to do. Besides, a break with William would destroy any chance of returning to Russia, or even Prussia or Austria. Once on the Continent, Perce could get to her, she was sure. Somehow they would manage to meet. Her eyes closed, and tears welled up behind the lids. She could feel his arms around her and his lips on her breasts. The hand that had held her dress tightly together in William's presence dropped and bared the perfect snowy bosom. But Perce was in Russia.

Sabrina uttered a single sob of frustration and loneliness, then opened her eyes, dashed the tears out of them, and began to undress. It was worth it to swallow William's insults. Anything was worth it if it would get her back to Perce.

The next few months, however, provided no recompense for Sabrina's sacrifice. There seemed less and less chance of any European mission for William. Fox was avidly pursuing the attempt to obtain a peace treaty and was virtually ignoring any diplomat who had served under previous administrations. William had not been dismissed from the diplomatic service, but he was on the periphery, deliberately cold-shouldered so that it was plain that his resignation would be accepted without reluctance the moment he proffered it. He was often very tempted to resign, but his own sense of patriotism and Roger's reasoning made him swallow snubs and even veiled insults.

In this political emergency Sabrina and her family supported William with skill and energy. The bitterness of their quarrel was swallowed up in less personal problems. It was not forgotten, but William was discreet about his sexual adventures and Sabrina behaved impeccably. She was also sustained by the hope that William's lack of assignment might not matter. Perce might be coming back to England soon.

Relations with Russia were growing colder as Fox concentrated on negotiations for peace with France. Secretary of War Windham, in the name of economy, dispersed the forty thousand men and the transports to ship ten thousand at a time to any necessary war zone. Not that Russia desired war or England's assistance. Word came that the tsar had sent the Count d'Ouvril to Paris to negotiate peace.

Sabrina heard that news in June as she was preparing to move back to Stour for a month until the whole family should take a house at a popular watering place for the summer. She spent the next three weeks in trembling expectation of seeing Perce any day. Instead she received a letter. It was not at her place at breakfast time but handed to her privately by Leonie, who had no intention of permitting Sabrina to betray herself publicly if the letter contained news that either overjoyed or distressed her. It was good, Leonie thought, that she had decided on this little ruse, because Sabrina broke the seal in trembling haste.

After reading the first page, she said, "He isn't coming home."

"Why not?" Leonie asked. She had to say something.

Sabrina's lips were pulled into a tight line. "He says the treaty between Russia and France won't be signed. The tsar wants it, he thinks, but there's a very strong prowar party in Russia. Alexander just isn't decisive enough to do anything that big without strong support from somewhere. Also, Perce is pretty sure Bonaparte will be so cocky because of Austerlitz that he'll do something to offend the tsar. Alexander takes offense, at least political offense, very easily."

"Brina," Leonie said gently, "I see that you are disappointed because Perce feels it his duty to remain where he is, but have you decided what you will do when he does come home?"

"*If* he comes home," Sabrina said bitterly.

"If? What do you mean?"

"Nearly getting himself killed at Austerlitz wasn't enough for him. Somehow he's got himself onto General Bennigsen's staff because Marshal Kutuzov and General

Bagration are strongly out of favor. Perce is furious, and I can't blame him. I don't know much about Kutuzov, but Bagration's a fine general, a nice person, and a real hero. Anyhow, Alexander seems to have decided to put the blame for Austerlitz on them, or at least on Kutuzov—"

"Brina," Leonie interrupted. "I cannot understand a word you say. What is Perce doing on a Russian general's staff?"

"It's something to do with the information the War Office wanted him to get, although I'm sure they never intended him to go so far as actually joining the Russian Army. But he has this compulsion about proving that the English aren't cowards. A lot of Russians say we are because our government sends them subsidies but never soldiers. I told Perce he was crazy, that he wasn't going to change any minds by being one heroic lunatic—and probably a dead one—but he won't pay any attention to logic."

"*Petite,* there is no war now. Perhaps we will have peace. Anyhow, I do not see why it is important that he is on Bennigsen's staff rather than Bagration's."

"It's important because that lunatic is certain Bagration won't be given orders for the next battle with Bonaparte, and he thinks Bennigsen will." Sabrina shook her head. "He's determined to be in the fighting, and he doesn't think much of Bennigsen. Can you imagine insisting on being an aide-de-camp to a man you're sure will lose?"

"You are exaggerating, Brina," Leonie said reprovingly.

"No, I'm not." She paused and read further, then drew in her breath suddenly. "I think Roger had better read this letter," she said, getting up. Her face no longer had so bitter an expression. "I have an idea now that Perce meant it for *him.* There's something odd here about his 'favorite correspondent' not answering."

"Perhaps it is meant for Roger. You do answer, I suppose?" Leonie asked.

"Oh, yes. He doesn't mean me. He's had my last letter."

She read the remainder standing and found a single sheet at the end that was really for her. The first few lines caused her color to rise, and she hurriedly folded the sheet and put it away to read more carefully in private. While she was thus occupied, Leonie had summoned a footman and sent him to bring Roger and Philip back to the house. The breathless footman caught them in the stables, and without comment Sabrina handed her foster father the main body of Perce's letter as soon as he came in. He looked mildly surprised, read the first page, turned it, read further, and began to curse. Straining to read over his shoulder, Philip gave up and asked what was wrong.

"Do you know what Perce is doing in Russia?" Roger asked.

"Yes, of course," Philip replied. "He's picking up army opinion on what happens. The army can exert pressure in Russia."

"Yes. Well, he has it from high-level officers that the tsar is negotiating seriously with Prussia to fight again rather than to make peace. They believe that if Britain will offer about twenty-five thousand men, this would tip the scales definitely toward war. The force would be nothing more than an appearance of good faith. He doesn't think his information is getting through to Windham at the War Office."

Philip laughed bitterly. "It would not matter. The man is mad. Can you imagine anything more ill-advised than that disastrous expedition to Egypt? And even if Beresford's attack in South America is successful, which I cannot imagine it will be, can you tell me the purpose of such a maneuver? Can we hold the country in the face of the colonists' resistance? Or, at the price it would cost, would we want to?"

"Then you don't think it worthwhile for me to pass this information along?" Roger asked.

"Worthwhile, no. Necessary, yes. In any case, Viscount

Castlereagh should be told. Even though he's not presently in office, he is very influential," Philip replied.

"Hmmm, yes. You certainly have a point there," Roger agreed.

"Perhaps if it became general knowledge it would be useful," Sabrina suggested.

"Now that's a good idea." Philip brightened, then frowned. "But if it comes from you, that might make trouble for William."

Ways to implement Sabrina's suggestion were thoroughly discussed. William was even summoned from Elvan Manor for consultation. A plan was devised, but it was never used. By the time Sabrina was in a position to spread Perce's information in the proper political and social circles, everything had changed. All negotiations with Napoleon had collapsed by the beginning of August, and Perce's analysis of the Russian situation was found to be quite accurate.

Count d'Ouvril had actually negotiated, and signed, a peace treaty with France in the tsar's name on July twentieth, but when Alexander saw the terms—in which the French had actually conceded many of the points he had demanded—he still flew into a rage and refused to ratify it. He would have refused to sign under any circumstances. The tsar maintained publicly that the treaty sacrificed the interests of Russia in the Adriatic and acknowledged Bonaparte's right to determine the political structure of the German lands without reference to anyone else whose interests might be affected.

This was true, but it was impossible that Alexander should not have known, even before negotiations began, that he would have to accept those points in any treaty made. Obviously the tsar had changed his mind about peace with France. Everyone in the diplomatic community was relatively sure that this could be credited largely to the king of Prussia's influence. But the immediate reason for King Frederick William's animosity toward Bonaparte, the fate of Hanover, was the crowning joke among British diplomats.

Lord Yarmouth had been traveling in France during the peace of Amiens and had been trapped there and interned as an enemy alien when the war was renewed in 1803. Fox had used him as an unofficial ambassador in his early attempts to make peace. Yarmouth had done his duty, but with strong reservations; he was not overly fond of Bonaparte or his government. Soon Lord Lauderdale had arrived to take over the negotiations, but Yarmouth was not excluded entirely.

He had never believed that Bonaparte truly meant peace, and when he learned that there was a secret clause in the agreement with England to wrest Hanover from the Prussians (to whom Bonaparte had originally ceded it) and restore it to Britain, Yarmouth had betrayed that information to the Prussian ambassador. He had claimed that it was a slip of the tongue, owing to incautious drinking in the Prussian's presence. But there was considerable doubt of the likelihood of such an event.

The result of this "accidental" disclosure of the secret clause was that Prussia had already begun to mobilize for a renewal of the war. Alexander's mother, a devout supporter of anything Prussian, immediately began to press her son to support King Frederick William. All the Russian nobility who held lands in Poland added their influence, since their property would be endangered by French action in that area. The officers of the Russian army were burning to redeem themselves after the defeat of Austerlitz. Under these combined influences Alexander had repudiated the treaty d'Ouvril had signed in his name.

Britain's part in all this remained nebulous. Fox had accepted the necessity of pursuing the war, but he was still reluctant. And Windham, having learned nothing from the disastrous expedition to Egypt and the so far inconclusive venture into South America, put no rein on his fatal tendency for numerous small, scrappy actions in peripheral areas. Roger was again advising at the Foreign Office, but his conviction that a strong effort should be made to assist Russia was making little headway. Then Mr. Fox died on September thirteenth and with him all resistance to the active resumption of the war.

One problem was the disputed fate of Hanover. Assistance to Russia meant acting in concert with Prussia. It went sorely against the grain to join hands with the nation that had robbed England of Hanover, their king's ancestral territory.

This stumbling block at last provided Sabrina with what she had so long desired. Special secret arrangements were made for William to go to Berlin to negotiate with King Frederick William. Perhaps British support for Frederick William's claims to absorb a number of other German statelets plus a pledge of financial support in the war against France could be traded for the return of Hanover to British jurisdiction. By the last week in September, Sabrina had her wish. She was back on the Continent, but whether it would do any good now was questionable. She wrote to Perce the day she arrived to say she was in Berlin and sent him a second note a few days later, but without much hope. An aide-de-camp to General Bennigsen would be unlikely to be able to obtain a leave of absence in the middle of a major mobilization for war. Also, Perce might be moving from place to place so quickly that her letters would not catch up with him.

CHAPTER EIGHT

Sabrina's suppositions about Perce's ability to contact her were not exactly correct. Nonetheless, although Perce did receive both her letter and her note more quickly than she had expected, he did not dare ask for leave of absence. His problem was less with mobilization than with the character of the man he now served. General Bennigsen possessed a personality far different from General Bagration's. German-born, Bennigsen had neither the volatility nor the openheartedness of the Georgian prince. He was rather suspicious of his aides, always thinking that they had some personal motive for their actions. So far those suspicions centered mostly on his Russian aides, whom he suspected of seeking promotion at his expense, and Perce did not want to draw suspicion on himself by asking for leave. Bennigsen was also envious of his equals; he was a very ambitious man.

Since Perce did not intend to make a career in the Russian army, he was worried by only one aspect of Bennigsen's ambition: He felt that it warped the general's judgment. Over the past year and a half Perce had learned a remarkable amount about military techniques and maneuvers. Bennigsen, he thought, was far too much inclined to accept reports of doubtful validity—when they fitted with conditions that were likely to make a hero of him. However, he was courageous, and he certainly had the best interests of Russia at heart.

141

The major problem, as far as the war went, was not with Bennigsen in any case. Despite strong urging from many quarters, it was impossible to convince Alexander to give Kutuzov the command of the army that was forming. Nor would he trust Prince Bagration, who was considered both too much under Kutuzov's influence and too young. This left the tsar with a choice between Marshal Kamansky and Marshal Prozorovsky. Since the latter was too blind to recognize his own officers at a distance of three feet, the command naturally devolved on Kamansky, with Bennigsen as second in command.

Although Perce had long expected this, he had not realized just how decrepit Kamansky was. Bennigsen had said caustically that his senior officer suffered from so many ailments that he was never sure which were troubling him at any one time. Perce had discounted this as a characteristic denigration by an envious man, but it was in fact the horrible truth. Kamansky had taken command because the tsar ordered it, but he did not want it and was in no hurry to get into action. No one seemed to be in any hurry in St. Petersburg.

The advantage of the situation from Perce's point of view was that the dilatory behavior of the senior officers and the envy and suspicions of Bennigsen drove the younger men together. Bennigsen had no close ties with his aides. Mostly he left the selection of his staff to others, counting on discipline to provide obedience. Moreover, he was not the most pleasant of masters to serve. He was exacting in small matters, careless in large ones, and when anything went wrong he shifted the blame to someone else—usually his staff. When aides tried to obtain more specific orders, they were accused of stupidity and lack of imagination. When they themselves tried to give form to formless orders, they were accused of trying to steal command from their superior officer.

Under the circumstances the group drew even closer together. Rivalries were suppressed in the need for self-protection. Any information one gathered—and none was above listening at keyholes—was immediately passed to the others, and since one or more aides-de-camp accompanied the general everywhere, Perce's fund of information was better on the suspicious Bennigsen's staff than it had been on the more free-talking Bagration's. With rumor and real information flying thick and fast and inextricably entangled, there was no way Perce would have dared leave his post to meet Sabrina, even if he had not feared Bennigsen would see some dark purpose in any request for leave.

It was not an easy decision for him. Whereas Sabrina was occasionally torn with doubt, Perce was torn by jealousy. First, there was the ever-present jealousy of her husband. Perce did not underrate Elvan's charm. Sabrina had said she was cured of her infatuation, but that had been while her husband's attention was fixed elsewhere. When Elvan's new object was removed and he became aware of her displeasure, he would undoubtedly try to win her back, if only to avoid a scandal. When he thought of this, Perce would examine his face in the shaving glass with near despair. He was not handsome; he was not charming; and he certainly had no particular skill in wooing women.

Even if Sabrina were inoculated against Elvan, as Dr. Jenner's technique inoculated people against the plague of smallpox, there were others who would try to win her. She was very beautiful and very rich, and a discontented wife was like a honeypot for drawing all kinds of vermin. Unhappy as Sabrina was, would she be able to resist the attentions of the practiced charmers who preyed on such women?

Her letters only increased Perce's agony of mind. It never occurred to him in his wildest flight of imagination that Sabrina could doubt the quality or intensity of his feelings. He loved her so much that it used to make him physically sick to contemplate the need to marry elsewhere to ensure heirs for the title and estates of Moreton. He did not dream that his desire to protect her, which made him point out the dangers in their future relationship and prevented him from writing as often as he wished, could be misinterpreted as reluctance or lack of passion. Never did it enter his mind that Sabrina's letters were reserved to provide *him* with the freedom to withdraw from the relationship.

It was a real struggle not to ask for leave and ride off to Berlin. It was more difficult to endure because Sabrina did not ask him to come. However, there were lines in her letter that riveted him to his duty. Thinking it might tempt him to come to Prussia, Sabrina had described the fury of preparation for war. This worried Perce. "Fury of preparation" were scarcely the words that applied to the Russian effort.

If he had still been with Prince Bagration, Perce would simply have taken the information to him. Bagration had reason to trust him and would have assumed Perce was doing his best for his commanding officer and for Russia. Bennigsen seemed to trust no one in the army. If he simply told the general what he knew, Bennigsen would suspect him of planting information to forward the plans of the British, or, still worse, to get Bennigsen into trouble. Of course Perce did want to help the British cause, but in this case he felt British interest was identical with Russian. The main purpose was to defeat Bonaparte.

The best Perce could do was spread the news subtly and write immediately to Sabrina that William should get word to King Frederick William that Russia was not now and would not in the next month or even two be ready to support any action. He found it hard to believe that Prussia and Russia, whose ambassadors had been in earnest consultation since July, should be so mistaken about each other's readiness to move. However, thinking back on some British miracles of disorganization, stupidity, and bad timing in the past gave him reason to fear the worst.

In these fears he was quite correct. Sabrina never received his warning letter. Even at the time he was writing it, it was far too late for anyone to help. The die had been cast at about the time Sabrina and William had arrived in Berlin. During the last week in September the Prussian ambassador in Paris had delivered an ultimatum to the French government demanding that all French troops withdraw immediately from German territories east of the Rhine. War was declared on October seventh, and by the fourteenth of the month the Prussian army had been catastrophically defeated in the twin battles of Jena and Auerstedt—almost completely owing to the ignorance, stupidity, and cowardice of its commanding officers.

The disaster was so complete that out of an army of one hundred and fifty thousand, barely fifteen thousand remained as a cohesive force. Within ten days of the battle Bonaparte arrived at Potsdam, and there was nothing, not a squad of men nor a single gun, to block his path to Berlin. There was no need for him to hurry, since the principal prizes were already gone. King Frederick William, his queen, his high officials, and the diplomatic personnel of any nation at war with France had fled eastward toward Russia and had taken refuge in the fortress city of Königsberg.

The fortress-palace itself was large, but so was the king's party. Some high-level diplomatic personnel were accommodated, but after seeing their situation, Sabrina could only be grateful they weren't housed in the palace. Either she and William were not important enough or the delicate nature of William's mission made the king wish to keep them "unofficial." They were not forgotten, however. Even in his distress King Frederick William remembered to have those of his subjects who lived reasonably close to the palace expelled from their homes to make room for those of his court or those diplomats who could not be housed in the castle itself.

Rather shocked by such high-handed ruthlessness, William sweetened the order for the evicted tradesman with golden guineas so that he found lodgings elsewhere for his family. Sabrina sweetened the situation still further by begging William to allow the cobbler to continue his business on the ground floor of the house. There was no way they could make use of a shop premises, she pointed out, so there was no reason to deprive the man of his livelihood. His tools and lasts were all in the shop and would be difficult to move, and his customers would not know where to find him. Moreover, he would be very little nuisance since a cobbler's work was neither nasty nor very noisy.

Later, upstairs, she enlarged on other reasons for her generosity. "There is bound to be resentment, even more against us as foreigners. If Herr Braunscheid is cobbling shoes below just as usual, few passersby will know we occupy the rest of the building."

"Very clever," William approved. "I hadn't thought of that. The noise won't bother us during the day—you, really, for I'll be out most of the time—and he won't work at night."

William eyed his wife speculatively. The house had two rooms, parlor and dining room on the first floor, with two bedrooms above. On the ground floor was the shop, with a storage room and a cubbyhole for a servant behind it. The kitchen shed was built out behind the house. Neither Sabrina nor William had looked at the cellar, and neither intended to do so. It was almost certainly dirt floored, without windows, and not a fit area in which to live.

Sabrina caught her husband's glance. "Katy and I will share the children's bedroom," she said with determination. "You can have the big bed, and Charlot can sleep in the servant's room."

"You are being ridiculous, Sabrina," William said angrily.

"There are whores in this town as well as in any other," she replied icily.

"Don't be a fool," he snapped. "This isn't London. I will be noticed in such company, and besides, I do not choose to buy the wares such a town as this is likely to display."

"Then try celibacy," Sabrina recommended, rather amused. "You cannot use me like a drab, whenever the urge comes to you. I assure you celibacy is very pleasant and peaceful, once one becomes accustomed."

The last remark was a lie. Sabrina found celibacy preferable to William's attentions, but she had been dreaming of Perce recently and waking up achingly ready, reaching out for him in the empty bed. That did not show in her face, however. In fact, Sabrina did look more peaceful than she had since they arrived in Prussia. Despite the mauve rings around her eyes, lines of weariness that made her look seemingly years older, and being rumpled and filthy from the dreadful conditions under which they had traveled, Sabrina's expression was almost eager and happy. William could not know this was simply because they were farther east, nearer—at least in Sabrina's mind—to Perce.

William regarded his wife warily. It had come to him this past week, while they had struggled northeast from Berlin to Königsberg, that he did not know Sabrina. Not only that, she was the antithesis of everything he thought a woman should be—except beautiful, of course. She was self-willed, indifferent to his opinions or directions, and far cleverer than he liked.

The news of the defeat at Jena and Auerstedt had hit Berlin like a thunderclap, and within the following two days it became clear that the entire Prussian army had either disintegrated or had been taken prisoner. Berlin could not be defended and would have to be abandoned. When the decision was made, William decided that Sabrina had better return to England, since Bonaparte hated the English and was known to look the other way when people of that nationality were insulted or even mistreated by his troops. Sabrina simply refused.

Moreover, William discovered that she had prepared for the coming disaster far more efficiently than he had. Weaned on the tale of Roger and Leonie's adventures in the chaotic France of the Terror, Sabrina had been drawing large sums of money in gold and silver for several weeks. Belts and secret pockets had been sewn so that the coins could be carried on her body and Katy's. She had also purchased two two-shot muff guns and a fine pair of pistols. Ignoring Katy's pleas and protests, Sabrina had taught her how to load each of the guns. William wondered how Sabrina had overcome Katy's objections to staying in Prussia altogether. It was simple enough; Sabrina had only said, *Perce is coming with the army from Russia,* but William was told that it was only the guns Katy feared. She had no objection to the general idea of protecting herself and her beloved nursling. On her hip, beneath her drab and respectable gown, Katy had armed herself with a long, thin, ugly knife, designed for gutting fish. She was not in the least afraid to use that.

At first William had laughed at these preparations, believing the guns to be some romantic expression of bravado. That was while he still believed he could convince or force Sabrina to go home, but everything had happened too fast. The magnitude of the military disaster had exploded rather than growing slowly in the normal way. Terrible stories had come from the port cities about overcrowded and unseaworthy vessels, and Sabrina declared that she was not yet ready to join the rest of her family who had drowned in a shipwreck. William, never having been involved in a panic-retreat, agreed then that Sabrina would be safer traveling north with the court unless a British naval vessel could come to pick up fleeing citizens.

There was no question of William leaving. The military catastrophe at Jena and Auerstedt made it more likely that an agreement to yield Hanover in exchange for British assistance might be extracted from Prussia's King Frederick William. When the court left for Königsberg, William and Sabrina, with Katy and Charlot, followed. It was on the journey that William's eyes were finally opened. Guns were no romantic bravado to Sabrina. She could and would use them, and her silly little muff guns, aimed and fired by her delicate white hands, killed one man and wounded another, thus saving them from being robbed and, perhaps, murdered on the road.

In spite of the disaster that had overtaken the Prussian Army, William was not at all ready to concede total victory to Bonaparte, nor did it matter to him that the Prussians had been defeated. If he could obtain an agreement on Hanover, Britain would insist Prussia stand by it *whenever* Bonaparte was put in his place. Moreover, Sabrina's intrepid behavior and cheerfulness under the miserable circumstances of the retreat had endeared her to Queen Louise, a woman known for her pluck and beauty. So, although he was infuriated by her continued resistance to him, William was not ready to quarrel openly with Sabrina.

Political reasons aside, William was not really convinced that Sabrina was indifferent to him. She showed absolutely no interest in any other man, and no matter how he twisted and turned the facts, he could perceive no reason for her to insist on remaining in Prussia if not to be with him. William was beginning to think Sabrina was simply frigid. Perhaps she had pretended to enjoy the sexual side of marriage in the beginning, found that her pretense could not keep her husband chained to her, and as a result had abandoned the pretense. William didn't mind that, but he felt that when no other woman was available, he had a right to his wife's body. He was thoroughly annoyed by her remark about celibacy, but he turned away with no more than an angry lift of lip and eyebrow. This was not the time or place to try to enforce his will.

Although the Russian high command was not ready to move, General Bennigsen had obtained permission to march sixty thousand men forward into Poland. They set out before word of the Prussian disaster reached St. Petersburg. When and how the news came to Bennigsen remained a mystery even to his aides-de-camp. The general tended to keep as much information to himself as he could. In this case it was justifiable. There was no point in damaging the morale of the officers and men by informing them that their only militarily active ally, Prussia, no longer had an effective army.

However, neither Bennigsen nor anyone else could be certain about the true extent of the disaster. Sometimes events looked worse in the beginning than they actually were, and as yet only early dispatches, from the third week in October, had reached Bennigsen's headquarters. When an army is defeated and scattered in a hopeless rout, it might take weeks for the dispersed units to be reassembled. Furthermore, not all of the army had been involved in the battles of Jena and Auerstedt. Kleist von Nollendorf had been at Halle, Blücher at Lubeck, York von Wartenburg at Radkan. Any or all of the divisions these men commanded might be capable of continuing the fight.

Never afraid to put himself forward to increase his own power, Bennigsen conceived the idea of making personal contact with the Prussian command—whatever was left of it—rather than waiting for information to travel first east to St. Petersburg and then west all the way back to him. No one could blame a general for desiring firsthand information as quickly as possible. There were advantages to sending two of his own aides to look around: Perhaps he could sift the truth from the falsehood in their reports, and that might help him to sift the truth from the falsehood in the reports sent by Kamansky; then he might be able more accurately to interpret the situation in Königsberg.

Bennigsen had guessed what would happen as soon as he heard about Prussia's declaration of war. Those over-cautious fools on the Prussian general staff, particularly the aged duke of Brunswick, would fail to take advantage of the declaration of war. Instead of attacking immediately, overrunning the French strongholds and supply depots, and then regrouping, they had hesitated until Bonaparte brought up his full army and ran over them. Bennigsen was not likely to make that mistake—if he ever had a chance to act.

His own condemnation of too much caution spurred Bennigsen to immediate action, and he began to consider which of his aides he could best spare. Two leapt to mind: Pëtr Pavlovitch and Lord Kevern. Both were recommended by their rank and manners, for it would be useless to send rural boors into a court, more especially a shattered one that might misconstrue any tiny infraction and blow it up into an insult. One more moment's thought to review his other aides decided the general that his original choice was best. Pëtr Pavlovitch was clever, a natural leader; it would be just as well to be rid of him for a few weeks.

The Englishman, on the other hand, Bennigsen trusted —or, rather, mistrusted less than he mistrusted others. He was quick, efficient, and accurate in carrying orders and never seemed to do anything he was told to do. That was a front, of course. Lord Kevern looked stupid and never said much—and when he did speak his French hurt one's ears—but he was *not* stupid. He was a British agent, and at the present moment there was no harm in that. Bennigsen realized that British interests and

151

Russian interests were aligned just now in their common goal to stop the French.

Another matter that concerned Bennigsen was that in trying to lay the blame elsewhere than on themselves, the Prussian generals might have chosen as scapegoat the allied Russians, who had not come in time to assist them. In this, however, he was mistaken. The Russians were potential saviors, if a trifle late; it was the English against whom most animosity was directed. In Prussian opinion, the English were acting like corpse robbers after the defeat of Jena-Auerstedt.

William had been as delicate about it as possible, but the facts of his mission could only be disguised to a limited degree. Actually he was asking King Frederick William to cede all future rights to Hanover in return for rather nebulous support—nebulous because at the time William had been sent out, the newly formed British government was not at all sure what they had to offer. Naturally the bald facts had been disguised as well as possible, and later Lord Hutchinson and his military attaché, Sir Robert Wilson, had been sent out from London with more concrete proposals but the warmth of their welcome by the king and queen was spurious.

Had Bennigsen known of this, he would never have sent Perce and associated himself, even indirectly, with the English. However, he did not know and, suspicious as he was, he was not so foolish as to believe his aides could gather information without knowing the facts. Thus, just before Pëtr Pavlovitch and Perce were to leave, Bennigsen relayed to them the outlines of the Prussian debacle and the retreat of the court to Königsberg, which was basically all he had learned himself from the dispatches he had received.

It was fortunate that Perce had blanked all expression from his face as soon as he entered the general's quarters and that Bennigsen required his aides to stand at attention while he spoke to them. Thus, Perce was already braced to hide any emotion he might feel. Nonetheless, if Bennigsen had not been so self-centered, he could not have failed to see that every vestige of color left Perce's face when he heard of the defeat and the taking of Berlin.

Pëtr Pavlovitch, closer to Perce by the width of a handsome desk—Bennigsen had naturally commandeered the best house in the town for his quarters—heard his companion's breath hiss in as if he had been physically hurt. Pavlovitch's head moved fractionally in a quickly aborted gesture of inquiry. This drew Bennigsen's attention and a brief reprimand. Perce, too frozen with horror even to breathe, escaped notice. For ten minutes more, Bennigsen issued detailed instructions concerning what they were to discover and how they were to obtain this information.

Pëtr Pavlovitch's acknowledgment of his orders woke Perce from his agony of fear for Sabrina. Had she been left behind in Berlin and taken prisoner? Surely not, he told himself over and over. Elvan was no fool, whatever else he was. Surely he would have sent his wife to safety as soon as the first news of the defeat had come. But Perce was not convinced by his own reasoning. There were too many incalculable factors.

Sabrina had never mentioned the situation between her husband and herself in her letters. What if Elvan did not care what happened to her? What if the ship on which he had sent her away had been captured, or overloaded because of the panic? And Sabrina herself was of a daring disposition. She would attempt the craziest antics trying to keep up with Philip and himself. Perce barely stifled a groan when he remembered that they had encouraged her fearlessness with praise and laughter. What if Sabrina had refused to go?

That question hung in his mind even while he replied affirmatively to Bennigsen's sharp questions as to whether he understood his orders. He must have looked more than usually idiotic, for the general then told Pëtr Pavlovitch to explain it again until he was sure Lord Kevern understood what was necessary. Then, mercifully, they were dismissed. Perce began to shout for Sergei to bring his horse before they were quite out the front door.

"Kevern, what's wrong with you?" Pëtr Pavlovitch asked, seizing his friend's arm. "The defeat is bad, yes, but not the end of the war. And perhaps it is not even so bad as it seemed at first."

"The French have taken Berlin!" Perce groaned.

"But the king and queen were not there. Prussia has not yielded, even if the capital is taken."

"Prussia!" Perce snarled. "Who gives a damn about Prussia? Lady Elvan was in Berlin."

Pëtr Pavlovitch blinked. He did not know who Lady Elvan was; he had never heard her name before, but a great many questions he had been too polite to ask his English friend had been answered—at least to Pëtr Pavlovitch's satisfaction. It was clear to him now. This Lady Elvan must be Kevern's mistress. That was why Kevern was so resistant to lures cast out to him by women in St. Petersburg. Pëtr Pavlovitch asked no questions and merely tightened his grip on Perce's arm.

"You cannot go to Berlin," he said. "If it were possible, I would go alone to Königsberg, but it is not possible. Kevern, you are too English, and I am too Russian to go to Berlin for you. But it is in Königsberg that you will find the answer to what has happened to this lady. How does an English lady come to be in Berlin anyway?"

For a moment Perce stood rigidly still, but Pëtr Pavlovitch's painful grip on his arm had checked his first hysterical impulse to ride off to Berlin that minute. His companion's logical remarks sank into the maelstrom of fears roaring around in his mind and steadied them so he could get a hold on them. The last question was even more helpful than the preceding reasoning. Perce shuddered and uttered a deep sigh.

"Her husband is a diplomat. He came to find out whether a pact with England could be arranged after Prussia broke with France."

Having said it, Perce regained self-control. Elvan would have followed the court if he possibly could. Pëtr Pavlovitch was right. The place to find out what had happened to Sabrina was Königsberg. He was still racked with fear, but it was no longer uncontrollable. He urged speed and more speed both in leaving camp and traveling, but he was not unreasonable. He was able to understand that they would be more delayed in the long run by exhausting their horses than by giving the beasts the rest they needed along the way.

It was unfortunate for Perce's nerves that traveling was so slow. The nights were bitterly cold, and twice it snowed. This made the roads as slippery as glass in the early morning and then a sticky morass when warmer temperatures and travelers melted the ice and snow into mud. It was rare that the horses could go faster than a walk, and too often they could do no more than plod along, pulling each hoof from the gluey surface with effort and a disgusting squelch.

Perce was not a very amusing companion during the six days of travel, but Pëtr Pavlovitch was patient. He, too, had been in love. He had also suffered. Nonetheless he felt that Kevern was allowing himself to be carried away. He could only assume it was his peculiar English disposition that caused this. It was logical that a man of high spirit, which Pëtr Pavlovitch knew Kevern to be, must express that spirit somewhere.

Since Kevern did not allow himself to fly into screaming rages or into suicidal fits of despair over the meaninglessness of life or any other profound questions, and since he did not respond with ecstasies to music and expressed his appreciation of art in the mildest and most moderate terms, it was reasonable that he should run mad for love. Even in this Pëtr Pavlovitch felt a faint disappointment. He did not doubt the depth of Kevern's feeling, but his expression of it was faulty. His friend did not rave or tear his hair or weep. He only grew silent and pale and spent all his time during rest periods making sure the horses were attended as though they were sick children. When not engaged in such tasks, he questioned every local person he could about the quickest, shortest route.

This practicality, no matter how disappointing to the emotional Pëtr Pavlovitch, saved them considerable time. Just before the light failed and a heavy fall of snow immobilized them on November twenty-third, they rode into Königsberg to present their papers to the officials in military headquarters. Long before the papers had been passed up the line to a properly august personage, Perce's fears were set at rest.

He had asked whether Lord Elvan was in Königsberg when they first entered the city and registered as foreign visitors. He had been told that both Lord and Lady Elvan were in residence and had even obtained their direction. The question and answer were overheard by the aide who had come to take them to military headquarters. The aide had wanted to know whether Perce was also English and, when Perce admitted he was, had asked a multitude of questions. These Perce answered absently until, when another aide came to escort them the rest of the way, the young man lifted an eyebrow and warned Perce with a grin that Lady Elvan was a woman of whom to beware.

Such a remark naturally drove Perce to ask the next aide whether Lord and Lady Elvan were well known. William was dismissed with a nod—another cursed diplomat—but it seemed Lady Elvan had made a greater impression. Perce was assured she was safe and well, in the highest beauty, just like an angel, that she danced like a

156

fairy—although not recently, of course; there had been no balls—and that she was a great favorite with the queen. But such a woman! A look of disapproval or awe or perhaps regret followed. And then they were at their destination, and the story was interrupted. During the next interlude Perce tried again. Oh, yes, Lady Elvan—again the odd expression, the laugh, the warning to beware.

Relieved of all his fears, Perce began to react with indignation. What *had* Sabrina done to get herself known and talked about this way?

At long last they reached General Estoque, who accepted Bennigsen's letters. By then, Perce could not make up his mind whether he would kiss Sabrina or spank her when he saw her. Released after a mercifully short interview, Perce told Sergei to take the horses and go with Pëtr Pavlovitch to find out where they would lodge. When he had the information, Sergei should come to the cobbler Braunscheid's house where Lady Elvan now lived.

Perce then rushed off, barely noticing the broad, sympathetic smile on Pëtr Pavlovitch's face, but the meaning of it finally penetrated his mind when he was not far from his goal. He stopped and turned. He should have explained that Lady Elvan was his best friend's sister, that he had known her nearly all her life. A brief review of his behavior the past week flashed through his mind. Cursing himself for a fool, he started for the cobbler's house again. It was no use going back now. Pëtr Pavlovitch would never believe the "Philip's sister" story.

Damn that Sabrina, Perce thought. *If she hadn't made herself the talk of the town, I wouldn't have rushed off like an idiot.* If he had explained the "little sister" involvement to Pëtr Pavlovitch first, it might have worked. Now it was too late, and all because Sabrina was acting like a hoyden. How any girl could look so ethereal and get into so much trouble was a mystery to Perce. His sisters didn't look like angels, but compared with Sabrina they acted like them.

He came to the door just as the cobbler, who had stopped work when the light failed, was stepping out. To Perce's request for Lord Elvan, Herr Braunscheid gestured toward the back of the shop and said, "Abovestairs." Perce climbed one flight, but it was apparent there were no candles lit behind the ill-fitting doors. Without thinking that it was not possible that Lady Elvan should be expected to live in two small rooms at the top of the house, Perce climbed the next flight two steps at a time.

One room was dark, the other lit. Perce scratched on the door. Sabrina did not turn from the small dressing table with its awkwardly placed mirror where she was preparing to attend a small musicale later in the evening. Each time she used the mirror, she vowed she would tell Charlot to get a man to move it or to go out and buy a decent dressing table; however, the moment she was not using the irritating piece of furniture it slipped her mind. There were more important worries than needing to bend and twist to see her own face.

Preoccupied with her thoughts and her mild irritation, Sabrina called "*Entrez.*" She had heard the footsteps hurrying up the stairs and had assumed it was Charlot coming to tell her of an urgent message or a visitor. William was out, dining in all-male company at Lord Hutchinson's house, another commandeered, makeshift diplomatic residence, although somewhat grander than Sabrina's own pied-à-terre. Katy was there, too, and had been nearly all day. In their haste and terror most of the courtiers who had fled with King Frederick William had left their servants behind in Berlin. When they arrived in Königsberg, they had snatched at any servants available. Thus the late-arriving Lord Hutchinson had to do with a totally untrained staff, and Katy was trying to prevent a disaster by assisting with the dinner Lord Hutchinson was hosting.

Perce entered in response to Sabrina's summons, automatically closing the door behind him to keep in the heat. His heart had already leapt into his throat at the sound of her voice so that he could not speak, but he was completely paralyzed by the vision that greeted his eyes. First he saw the two beds. Instinctively he looked away from the evidence of his blunder only to have his eyes fall on Sabrina's image in the mirror. She was leaning well forward and down in order to see the curl she was trying to fix in place, and her peignoir had fallen open to reveal her bosom.

It was a brief vision, two or three seconds at most before Sabrina realized that Charlot was not coming toward her. She jerked upright, aware suddenly that her gown was displaying far more of her than was modest. Furiously, she turned to castigate Charlot. Of course, in normal circumstances Charlot would never enter her bedchamber. No male servant would, unless specifically summoned. Nonetheless, servants *didn't* see such things. They were paid to be blind if such an accident should occur.

The angry words were never uttered. For a long breath-held moment Sabrina was as paralyzed as Perce. Then she opened her mouth to call his name, only no sound would come, and she stumbled to her feet to run to him, only she tripped on her gown and would have fallen if he had not jumped forward and caught her in his outstretched arms.

Neither had made a sound, and they did not now as they embraced fiercely and their mouths met. The kiss was like the first sip of soup to the starving. It did not allay but stimulated the need. More and richer sustenance was desired. Sabrina's hands knocked Perce's fur cap to the floor, scrabbled at his high, furred collar. The wide sleeves of her gown fell back, baring her arms, and they came in contact with the melting snow on Perce's shoulders. It was cold! The shock made Sabrina aware that her peignoir was soaked where she had been pressed against Perce and across her back where his arms had gripped her. She would have put up with the cold without complaint to go on kissing him, but the kiss was not enough. She began to fumble for the buttons of his greatcoat.

Perce pulled away wordlessly, his eyes fixed on her as he shed the garment. But even as he was pulling it off his arms and allowing it to drop to the floor, Sabrina was reaching for the buttons on his waistcoat. She was not really thinking of what such a gesture would imply, only of the need to be nearer, really to touch him. Perce was not thinking at all. Every intellectual process was blocked, swallowed up in the tidal wave of desire that flowed over him. For months he had been racked by doubt and longing, and those emotions had been topped by intense fear and spiced with anger. Thought was beyond him. He did not stop with his tunic, which followed his greatcoat to the floor, but tore off waistcoat, shirt, boots, breeches, and smallclothes with frantic haste.

For Sabrina there was the briefest flash of surprise when Perce threw his tunic atop his greatcoat and began to pull off his boots. It was followed by an equally brief flash of recognition that her own action had precipitated his. Both ideas were driven out of consciousness by her flaring desire. She had long been deprived of sexual satisfaction, and the intensity of Perce's passion was vividly communicated by his violent stripping. By the time he had his boots and shirt off and was shoving breeches and smallclothes down his hips, Sabrina was bare, waiting, watching him hungrily.

There was nothing about Perce's lean, pale body to remind Sabrina of her husband's very different appearance. Perce's muscles were long and hard, marked out by thick blue veins. Like many very blond men, he was nearly hairless, except for the golden pubic bush from which his engorged manhood stood up, flushed dark crimson, startling

160

against the whiteness of his skin. He straightened up, reaching out, his hands bent into hard, gripping talons fit to clutch an uncertain prey, but they never took the bruising hold Sabrina expected.

When he saw her naked, watching him, he paused for a heartbeat. His hands relaxed, fell gently on her shoulders, ran down her arms, gathered up her hands into one of his, and brought them to his lips. He kissed her palms, her fingers, his other arm sliding back up hers to embrace her and draw her closer. As his body was hidden by their nearness, Sabrina at last looked into her lover's face. It was hard to believe she had ever seen it frozen over, expressionless. The eyes were darker, liquid with tenderness, the mouth full and soft.

Then she could see him no longer for his head was bent, his lips on her throat, shoulder, ear. He released her hands to stroke her body, to press her against him so that she could feel the hard shaft teasingly just above where she wished to feel it. But she wished for other sensations, too. Her hands, now free, ran over his hard-muscled back, over the small buttocks, between his thighs. He gasped.

"Fire and ice and you burn me," he murmured. "You burn me."

He had relaxed his grip on her a little so that he could lower his mouth to her breasts. Sabrina leaned backward from the waist, shaking inside with excitement and with the sensations that passed over and through her body as lips and tongue played across her skin.

"Sweet, sweet," he sighed between kisses. "You taste sweet. You smell sweet."

His words suddenly made Sabrina aware of Perce's own odor—that of old sweat, of tired horses, of effort, of strength taxed to the uttermost. It was not an odor she normally associated with him; he was ordinarily scrupulously clean. But she did not find it repellent right now. It was male and very exciting. William never smelled, except

161

of scent. Sabrina pressed her hips harder against her lover's body and moved them. An involuntary spasm rippled over Perce. He uttered a gasping, wordless sound of desire.

"Come to me," she whispered. "Come to me."

The floor was strewn with pelts, sheepskin and bear. They were the only purchases Sabrina had made for the house, and they were strictly practical, necessary to mitigate the drafts across the floors. Sabrina's words and action seemed to unstring Perce's muscles. His knees bent, and he sank down on the rug, carrying Sabrina with him. Fortunately it was a bearskin, quite large enough to protect them. A small surprised sound came from her, but it was muffled by Perce's mouth, and the feel of his weight on her eliminated any sensation but the need to have him joined to her. . . .

CHAPTER NINE

"Brina. Brina."

The urgent whisper made her open her eyes. She was reluctant, unwilling to be drawn up out of the delightful lethargy that had followed the cataclysm of pleasure that had engulfed her. Still, she knew an equal joy waited on vision; she would see Perce's face. Sabrina began to smile even before her lids came far enough apart to see. The smile broadened when she saw the anxiety with which he was regarding her.

"Are you all right? Did I hurt you?"

"No," she replied, laughing at him softly. "I'm half-dead, and I'm sure I'll fall asleep at that musicale tonight. That will make a scandal."

To her surprise, instead of laughing with her, Perce's reaction was first anxiety, then anger. "Scandal? You don't need any more scandals. What the devil have you been doing, Sabrina?"

She could not imagine what he was talking about. Sabrina knew her behavior had been unexceptionable—except for this past half hour. "Oh, goodness," she whispered, "did Charlot come up and hear us?"

"No. Oh, my God! On the floor, like animals. Brina, I'm sorry. I—I couldn't—couldn't help it."

Laughter bubbled up in her. "But I thought it was a brilliant idea, Perce. It saved me making the bed, and time is important, considering that my hair is all down again."

He leaned over and kissed her silent, drew her against him, and held her tight. "We'd better get dressed again," he said in a low voice. "This is insane. I never meant . . . Where's—where's Elvan?" He still couldn't bring himself to say "your husband."

"Out. He won't be back until late. Nor will Katy. There's only Charlot. Unless someone sends me a note, he won't come up. We'd know if someone came to the house. The bell can be heard up here." She paused and then asked, "How did you find your way up? Charlot would have put you in the sitting room."

"He doesn't know I'm here. A man, the cobbler, let me in. I asked for Elvan, and he said 'abovestairs.' But there was obviously no one in the lower rooms." He hesitated and then went on very uncertainly. "We'd better get dressed."

"Must we?" Sabrina whispered. "If Charlot doesn't know . . ."

Perce buried his face against her throat. She could feel the muscles of his jaw work. Instead of responding to what she said, however, he asked, "What the hell are you doing here in Königsberg? Why didn't you go back to England?"

Her lips trembled. "I couldn't," she said, wanting but not daring to say that she had stayed in the hope of seeing him. Perce's expression did not invite confession, and she went on, "The ships were crowded. William thought it would be more dangerous to go than to stay. Why? Are you sorry?"

His arms tightened so hard that Sabrina whimpered. "I don't know what I am." His voice grated. "I only know I can't resist you."

He began to kiss her again, making a thorough job of it. It was as if he had no senses but those of touch and taste, as if he must know her only through those sensations. He kissed her cheeks, her neck, her shoulders, her sides, her belly, her hips, her thighs, her toes, and between her toes. Eyes closed, he explored her.

Eyes open, Sabrina watched him, fired by both the assault on her senses and the obvious passion he felt. At last her eyes closed, too, as the sensations became too exquisite to permit sight to interfere. She wanted to urge him to mount her, but she had no voice. Feverishly she caressed him, pulled at him, uttering incoherent little cries. Although he was enwrapped, insulated from reality by his violent pleasure, Perce knew that sound was dangerous. He abandoned the nether lips he had been kissing and dammed those from which the sounds came. Again they came together, and again, all too soon, climax broke over Sabrina like a whirlwind, so fierce a pleasure that she could have screamed as if it were pain.

This time it was she who drew away when she had stopped trembling. "I think we had better get dressed," she murmured in a shaken voice. "If you do that to me again, I think I'll die. And it's black as pitch outside, Perce. What time is it?"

He groaned and levered himself to a sitting position. His clothes were within arm's reach, and he fumbled through the pile until he found his waistcoat, from which he extracted his pocket watch. "If I didn't break it, dropping it like that, it's ten after five."

"Oh, heavens," Sabrina whispered, getting to her feet, "if I don't soon ring for Charlot to bring up what Katy left for my dinner, he'll come to see whether I've fallen asleep."

"Shall I go?" Perce's voice was flat, his face a mask.

Sabrina caught at him as he got up. "No, oh, no!"

He put his arms around her at once and kissed her. "All right, then. I'll just go outside to ring the bell like a proper visitor."

She clutched him tightly, then let him go and laughed. "I don't want you to go even as far as that, not even for

165

five minutes. But you're right. It would be best. Oh, I'm so glad I didn't go home!"

Perce had let go of her when she released him and started to dress while she was speaking. His movements checked infinitesimally at her last remark, but he said nothing. The ships were too crowded, were they? He had no time to argue with her now. When he came back in, he would tell her what he thought of her lunacy.

They crept down the stairs silently in the dark, clinging to the wall to avoid the creaks and squeaks of the staircase. Perce opened the door bolts and stepped outside; Sabrina shut the bolts again and fled upstairs, breaking into giggles as she reached the haven of her room and closed the door. Perhaps guilt or remorse would seize her later, but just now her physical relief combined with Perce's stealthy escape to make her effervesce with joy.

Nonetheless, she dressed herself in trembling haste, thanking God that Katy had laid everything out and chosen clothing that fastened within her reach. Finished, she returned to the horrid little dressing table to examine how badly her hair needed redoing, but her eyes were irresistibly drawn to the bearskin where she had made love so short a time ago. There was nothing to mark her joy. The thick, resilient fur showed not a sign of having held two heaving bodies. But on the sheepskin beyond the bear pelt—Perce's fur hat.

Sabrina gasped and snatched it from the floor, jumping about a foot into the air when the bell pealed. She glanced wildly around for a place to hide the hat, darted toward the closet, away, to a drawer, then stopped. It was impossible to hide anything. Katy would find it. Besides, Perce could not go back to wherever he was staying without a hat. Aside from the fact that Sergei would notice, his ears would freeze. She heard Charlot's steps coming up, shoved the hat under her arm, and pulled her shawl over it so it was hidden.

Charlot announced Perce, but Sabrina made no sense at all out of his words. Just as he entered the room she saw scattered between the rugs clods of mud that had fallen from Perce's boots. If Charlot saw . . . Katy would never leave such dirt on the floor, and Sabrina had not been outside since Katy left the house. She nodded and smiled and said, "How delightful. Yes, certainly, I'll come down at once," praying that those were the right words but unable to gather her scattered wits enough to judge whether Charlot was surprised by a possible non sequitur.

But rescue came as a pang went through her, a pang not of love but, most unromantically, of hunger. She waved Charlot out, saying, "Light the dining room at once, Charlot, please. And bring my meal there. Set a place for Lord Kevern, too."

Did the valet look strangely at her? Inside, Sabrina shook with fear. All her joy was lost, spoiled. A life of intrigue was clearly not for her. But without intrigue there could be no Perce. She lingered behind Charlot long enough to kick the largest clods of mud under a rug. Katy would find them and berate the woman who came to do the scrubbing. *I must remember to get some mud in here somehow,* Sabrina thought as she scurried down the steps.

Perce stood up from the chair in which he was sitting with obvious effort as she opened the door. "Please forgive me for coming to you in all my dirt, Sabrina," he said formally.

She swallowed with shock, then saw his eyes on the door and closed it hurriedly. He could not know that Charlot was not right behind her. She came across to him quickly and handed him his fur cap. His breath drew in sharply, but he took it and thrust it into a pocket of his greatcoat, which was lying across another chair.

"Sorry," he muttered, and passed his hand over his face.

"It's all right. Charlot didn't see it. I told him to set up for dinner." Her voice quivered. Perce's expression was so grim that, helplessly, she asked, "Are you sorry?"

She had lowered her head, but the candlelight glittered on tears in the corners of her eyes. He pulled her hard into his arms. "Yes, I am," he said fiercely, "because I don't know how I'm going to live without you, Brina. Because day and night I'm going to dream of murdering Elvan. Because I don't think I can behave like a gentleman. I'm scared to death I'll ruin you, and you'll hate me for it."

"I won't hate you," Sabrina said softly. She lifted her head and really looked at him and was shocked. "Perce! You look so tired!" She disengaged herself gently and pushed him. "Sit down."

He obeyed promptly as if it were a relief, not waiting for her to take a chair, but he began to laugh. "What the devil do you expect? You look a little heavy-eyed yourself."

"Don't be silly," she replied. "You look as if you haven't slept for a week."

"Not sure I have. When Bennigsen told us about the battles at Jena and Auerstedt and that Boney had taken Berlin . . ." He shuddered. "I was worried about you."

"That's silly, too. The worst that could have happened is that we would have been interned."

"It's not the worst that could have happened," Perce said harshly, his expression bleak and hard. "When troops come into a conquered city, they don't come in like a regiment of guards on parade. They take what they want. And don't talk to me about diplomatic immunity. An apology from one government to another is cheap, but the raped are raped, and the dead are dead. What good would it do you if Boney shot a few troopers after the peace—and probably the wrong ones, too."

She came to the side of the chair and put a hand on his cheek. "It didn't happen, Perce. We're safe here."

"Are you? Can King Frederick William defend this place?"

Sabrina paled a trifle. "No. There's nothing left. Most of Estoque's division is here, but what it amounts to depends upon who tells the story. Estoque says fifteen thousand. I'm sure that's not true. I've heard some say as low as fifteen hundred, but I don't think that's right, either. Sir Robert thinks it's about six thousand. But Boney's in winter quarters, isn't he?"

"Christ!" Perce exclaimed. "It's *worse* than Bennigsen thought. That means doing the thing alone. Oh, Jesus!"

"Are you here to tell King Frederick William that Bonaparte is marching on Königsberg?" Sabrina asked. Her eyes were enormous, but her voice was steady.

"No! Sorry, Brina. I didn't mean to frighten you, but this is no place for you. You must go home."

"And you? Is this a place for you?" Sabrina asked heatedly. "Should you be in the Russian army, which you yourself don't seem to think can 'do it alone'? Anyway, I can't go, Perce."

"What do you mean, you can't go?" Suddenly he remembered the expressions on the faces of the military aides, who had all seemed to know her. "Sabrina, what *have* you been doing?" he thundered.

Sabrina jumped with surprise. "What are you shouting about?" she cried.

"Why does every young attaché at headquarters get a funny look on his face when your name is mentioned?" he snarled.

Sabrina relaxed and burst out laughing. "Oh, that! It's nothing, Perce."

His eyes narrowed. "Your nothing and my nothing might be quite different. What did you do? Out with it!"

"It was nothing," she repeated. "I shot a thief, that's all. It was on the retreat, when we were all running away from Berlin. Part of the road was pretty bad. We didn't realize that a carriage behind us had broken an axle or linchpin. The military escort stopped to guard them while repairs were made. We were at the tail of the group that was still moving, and on a lonely stretch three highwaymen came out. Charlot doesn't like guns, and, of course, they had their eyes on William so he couldn't get at his pistols. So I shot one and wounded another, and the third ran away. I could have shot him, too, but the muff guns are very inaccurate. Well, what's so funny? What are you laughing at?"

"Sorry," Perce gasped, "I should have known your conscience was clear. You never could hide anything you thought was wrong."

The moment he said it, his laughter stopped. The business of shooting highwaymen certainly explained the attitude of the aides, who would neither expect nor approve of any woman handling guns. But Sabrina had been taught to shoot from the time she was strong enough. Leonie had never forgotten the horrors a pistol had saved her from during the French Revolution, and how much more it could have saved her from if she had known how to use it properly. It was also true that Sabrina would regard the shooting of a thief as a perfectly acceptable act of minor importance. She might have been upset at the time, but she would have had no moral qualms about it. Highwaymen were vermin, and vermin were better dead.

What checked Perce's amusement was not the past but the future. Would Sabrina be oppressed by what they had done? She was a very honest person and, as a child, would come weeping to confess her little peccadilloes. And this was not a *little* peccadillo. *I'll have to take her home,* Perce thought. *The hell with the War Office. They'll have to get their information from someone else.*

"Well, of course my conscience is clear," Sabrina had said, and then looked at him questioningly when his mirth dried up so suddenly.

"Is it, Brina?" he asked, starting to get out of his chair again.

She held him still with a hand on his shoulder. "Yes," she said, "if you mean do I feel I've wronged William, I certainly don't. I know it isn't a popular opinion, but to my mind what's sauce for the gander is sauce for the goose, too." She felt Perce wince under her hand, and cried, "Oh, no! That wasn't why. Perce, I love you quite dreadfully. I wouldn't. I couldn't. Not just for spite."

"Of course you wouldn't," he said quickly, smiling up at her. "You aren't spiteful. I'm just too tired to think straight, and—and I can't believe I've got you at last. For years and years I've been hating myself for letting you slip through my fingers. I just can't believe it."

Sabrina sighed, but before she could point out that their situation wasn't quite that simple, they heard Charlot coming up the stairs. He did not enter the sitting room. Presumably he had brought the food up and would be setting the table in the dining room. It wouldn't be safe to talk of personal matters until Sabrina could get rid of him.

"You will eat with me, won't you?" Sabrina asked, seating herself on the sofa across from Perce. "I told Charlot to set a place for you."

"If you can stand me, I will. I must stink like a trooper."

"You do," Sabrina agreed, laughing, but she ran her tongue sensuously across her lower lip. "I don't mind." Their eyes met, and Perce's brows lifted. "But if it bothers *you*," she went on, "I think there must be hot water in the kitchen. Charlot could bring it up for you. Possibly he could do something about your clothing while you eat, too, and you could wear something of William's."

To her surprise Perce flushed and said, "I'd rather not."

She stood and put her hand briefly on his neck. "Don't be silly," she murmured. And before he could think of a way to phrase what he felt so that it could do no harm if overheard, she had opened the door and gone out.

He heard Charlot going downstairs again as Sabrina came back in. "I think I'm borrowing too much," Perce said tightly.

Sabrina stopped and looked at him. "You aren't *borrowing* anything," she snapped. "I gave you something that was my own." And then she asked, "Is *your* conscience bothering *you*?"

"Don't be ridiculous," he snapped back, low and angry, then looked away. "Oh, damn," he sighed. "I'm jealous."

"Jealous?" Sabrina couldn't understand that. "What have you got to be jealous about? You *can't* believe I am promiscuous or that I care for William and would—"

"No, I don't think you're promiscuous," Perce interrupted, his color rising still more, "but you're his wife, damn it! He's got a right—"

"No one has a right!" Sabrina hissed furiously. "Love is an exchange. And I don't sleep with William, if that's what you want to know, because I am *not* promiscuous, and I love you." She came forward a few steps and planted herself squarely in front of her lover. "I'm not a sharing kind of person. I hope you understand that."

Solution to the doubts that had tormented him for months was a pure joy rising in Perce. He looked up at her and grinned. "You needn't be so fierce. I'm not in the petticoat line. You know that. I may not be a saint—"

"No, I guessed that!"

"—but I don't cheat, either," he finished with dignity, ignoring her interruption. He stood up and drew her close. "Brina, performance can be by inspiration as well as by experience," he said softly. "I swear I never loved another woman like that in my life and I never will."

She stared up at him, wide-eyed, and then dropped her head to his breast. In the next instant they had jumped apart in response to the sound of Charlot's footsteps. Perce muttered an oath, and Sabrina bit her lip. This was horrible. Neither of them enjoyed this kind of intrigue, and both realized that the necessity to listen and lie would kill their mutual joy. The footsteps went past and heavily up the second flight of stairs.

"Go up now and bathe," Sabrina said.

When he was gone, she went upstairs also and redid her hair. She tried to think, but her mind kept slipping away from fact to visions of Perce's body, long and lean and naked, and her eyes kept sliding to the bearskin. Instead of thinking about what she could do to convince William that an annulment of their marriage would be desirable, she kept wondering where and how she could be alone with Perce again.

It was her attempt to find a solution to this problem that jerked Sabrina back to reality. The clothing Perce had peeled off so hastily was a uniform. She had been thinking of days and weeks as if Perce's time were his own. He might not be able to stay more than overnight. Her heart sank as she remembered his distress when she told him the Prussian army was decimated. He had said something about doing the thing alone. Surely, then, he expected the Russian army to challenge Bonaparte. But when?

Sabrina finally got her hair into a semblance of order and went downstairs again into the dining room to peer into the serving dishes keeping warm on the sideboard. It was a very simple meal, for they had no cook now. Sabrina jumped when the door opened.

"Lord Kevern, my lady," Charlot said gravely.

"I hope you won't be cross with me for asking you to stay," Sabrina apologized. "I completely forgot that it wasn't going to be much of a meal. Maybe you'd have done better in the inn, or wherever you're staying."

Perce laughed. "I don't even know where I'm staying," he admitted, "and I rather think my fellow aide is having some difficulty finding a place, since Sergei hasn't come to give me the direction. I'll take my chances with you."

His eyes were alight, and his hair was very curly and still damp from toweling, not combed back into its usual smooth waves. Charlot had shaved him, too. Sabrina had to repress an urgent desire to play with his blond curls. She noticed that he had consented to wear William's dressing gown and slippers as well as his shirt and, probably, his smallclothes. He was wearing his own breeches and boots, since he was too tall to fit into William's. Thinking about clothes gave Sabrina the excuse she needed to get rid of Charlot.

"Don't bother serving," she said to the valet. "I'll do that while you do what you can with Lord Kevern's clothing."

"Yes, my lady."

"And let Sergei in when he comes, will you, Charlot?" Perce put in as the servant went out the door.

"Yes, my lord."

The voice was stiff. Charlot did not approve of his mistress doing butler's work, and he disapproved even more of Sergei. He did not think Sergei was a proper gentleman's servant. Katy Petersen didn't seem to approve of Sergei either, Perce thought, his lips twitching with amusement. At least, she spent a lot of time trying to change him. Sergei had complained bitterly that every time he met her she nagged the life out of him—only Perce didn't think Sergei minded at all. There was a hint of pleased pride in his complaints.

Oddly, Katy did not seem to object to Sergei's crudeness or his occasional drunkenness, although she scolded him loud and long about such failings. What Katy really disapproved of was Sergei's acceptance of his role as Perce's serf. Many times while they were still in St. Petersberg, Perce had heard Katy urging Sergei, in her own broken mixture of Scots-accented English, French, and Russian, to demand his freedom, assuring him that Perce would grant it. He smiled again, remembering poor Sergei's horror, his protests, also in a triple mixture of languages, that he would not "belong."

"Perce, how long will you be here?" Sabrina asked as she piled food onto a plate for him.

174

The question pulled his thought to the immediate present, and he sniffed appreciatively. "I had no idea how hungry I was," he remarked as he received the plate, and continued, inelegantly, through a large mouthful, "I don't know how long. Maybe we'll be sent back tomorrow, but I hope not. Possibly a few days."

Sabrina lingered beside him after she set the plate down. He smelled now of soap and shaving soap and, faintly, of himself. He had not used any of William's scents, although Charlot must have offered them. Her hand lifted to touch him but fell away at once. It would be cruel to interrupt his meal. He was hungry. She went back to the sideboard and put a small portion on another plate and sat down.

"Can you tell me why you're here?"

He grinned at her. "Yes, and that will make Bennigsen's suspicions the truth for once. After all, I'm a British agent, first and foremost. But I don't think it's a secret. General Bennigsen wants to know what, if anything, is left of the Prussian army."

"Nothing," Sabrina said. "I told you that." There was hope in her eyes. "Since that's so, won't the tsar order his army to wait until spring? Perhaps by then something can be salvaged of the Prussians."

"I don't know that, either. Alexander was in no rush to get started, and Marshal Kamansky is half-dead already, but it depends on what Bonaparte does, I suppose. If he sits still and talks sweet . . ." He saw Sabrina's expression change. "What is it, Brina?"

"Bonaparte certainly isn't talking sweet. He's loathsome! He seems to have found some letters from Alexander to Queen Louise—just sentimental claptrap, I'm sure. He *published* bits and pieces and . . . and remarks about the queen that were really despicable. She's nice, Perce, a sweet person."

Perce's fork remained suspended halfway to his mouth, and he whistled. "That tears it! Alexander will fight now. He's sentimental, and needs to think of himself as a

175

chivalric hero. Brina, do you know where I can get some reasonably accurate information about military conditions?"

"Yes, I do. Colonel Sir Robert Wilson's with Lord Hutchinson. He's a bit unconventional, but I think he knows his business and he'll tell you the truth, which the Prussians won't."

"Wilson . . . Wilson . . . No, I don't think we are acquainted, Brina."

"It doesn't matter. William will introduce you, or I'll give you a note. You don't want to go tonight, do you? There's a dinner, and I don't know who the guests will be, except that William thought King Frederick William might attend."

Perce thought for a minute or two while he continued to eat, and finally shook his head. "No, I've got to get some sleep. I'm too . . ." His eyes rested on her for a moment, and he moved them down to his plate with an effort. "I can't think—at least, not about the damned war."

There was another silence. Perce reached for the bottle of wine by his glass, poured, and drank. His eyes went to Sabrina again, and his lips tightened. Sleep! What he really wanted was to grab her again. Perce was somewhat surprised by his own reactions. He loved Brina, but he had never thought of himself as a lustful man. He had seldom been interested in joining Philip on his frequent tours of the bawdy houses. On the occasions he had sought sexual adventure, he had been very ready to leave his partner after one passage at arms. Yet he had taken Brina twice less than an hour ago, and he was finding it very hard now to think of anything except a third encounter.

He looked up, hastily averted his eyes, and refilled his wineglass. From Sabrina's expression, she was thinking along the same lines. But it was impossible. It was a miracle they had not been caught. He would not expose Sabrina to such danger again.

176

As if she had been reading his mind, she said, "You could stay here, Perce."

"No!" he exclaimed, then laughed. "I wouldn't care to sleep with Elvan, and I would not be *able* to sleep in your bed."

Sabrina giggled. "Don't be silly. There are extra beds." She blushed when she said it, and lowered her eyes. "The cobbler had five children," she went on quickly. "Charlot could set up a bed in the sitting room, or, perhaps, Sergei could set it up. Poor Charlot is having a very bad time of it, forced into all these tasks that are beneath him."

"I can't, Brina." He cut off the senseless babble. Their eyes met. "It's too crazy, too dangerous."

Sabrina's blush deepened painfully. She had been thinking under all the talk about Charlot that she might be able to slip down in the middle of the night. She hadn't realized her intention was so obvious.

"I'd never sleep a wink," Perce went on wryly. "I'd be too busy trying to pick the best time to sneak upstairs."

He hadn't read her mind; he'd just wanted the same thing. Sabrina looked at him longingly. "Katy sleeps in the other bed," she warned. Then she sighed. "I couldn't get down to you, either, Perce. She has ears like a fox. If I turn over, she hears."

"We must be sensible."

"Yes," she agreed, but in a very small voice.

Perce began to eat again. After a while he said, "You must go home, Brina."

"I can't," she replied. "As soon as Lord Hutchinson arrived, William asked to have me sent back to England, but Hutchinson advised against it."

"Against it?" Perce echoed, his opinion of the British envoy's common sense plummeting to zero.

"Aside from trying to get a settlement on Hanover, Hutchinson is trying to keep King Frederick William in the war. You know, I guess, that all the Prussian ministers and those doddering generals have been urging the king to sue for peace. Hutchinson felt if I were sent home, it would imply that he and William really thought the situation was hopeless. It would turn everything they said into lies."

Perce put down his fork, his appetite suddenly gone. The reasoning was good, but to sacrifice Brina seemed entirely out of order. But perhaps he was doing Hutchinson an injustice; perhaps the situation wasn't as bad as he thought.

"I don't know anything," he told her. "We've been on the march since the middle of October. I didn't learn about the defeats at Jena and Auerstedt until Bennigsen told me and Pëtr Pavlovitch a week ago. It was quite a shock. We all thought the Prussians intended to wait for our army to join theirs or, at least, get close before he gave Bonaparte an excuse to attack."

"Sir Robert has been trying to find out, discreetly, of course. Naturally, everyone blames everyone else, but it seems that the original intent was to declare war and then attack only the French outposts and the relatively small army quartered in Germany. Only, as far as Sir Robert can tell, the Prussian high command got cold feet. This comes mostly from one young general, Scharnhorst, who is very bitter. He begged them to take the offensive, but they just sat there on the banks of the Saale."

"And gave Boney the chance to consolidate his force and get there himself," Perce finished for her with a sigh. "Yes, I see. So he just rolled them up." He picked up his fork and began to eat again. "Even so, I don't understand. The Prussian army was pretty well trained, the numbers weren't too far off. . . . I think I'll take you up on that introduction to Sir Robert."

Sabrina had opened her mouth to answer when they heard the peal of the bell. It was annoying that it rang on the bedroom and living room floors as well as in the shop.

Obviously the cobbler was an ambitious man who did not wish to lose any business, even if he should happen to be eating or in bed. Sabrina had decided not to have the system disconnected, since messages for William came at odd hours, sometimes when neither the cobbler nor Charlot was on the ground floor.

"That must be Sergei," Perce said. He looked at Sabrina for a long moment and then lowered his head. "I think I had better go." His voice cracked, and he cleared his throat. "I'll try to stop by tomorrow, Brina, but I can't say when or even promise that I definitely will come."

Sabrina stood up. "I'll go write that note to Sir Robert. Finish your meal, Perce."

She reached the door just as Charlot opened it to announce in frigid tones that Lord Kevern's servant had arrived. Over his arm he had the remainder of Perce's clothing, restored to an approximation of cleanliness. Looking down his nose, the valet said he would await Lord Kevern's convenience in Lord Elvan's bedchamber, where he would assist him to dress. It was markedly apparent that Charlot felt Sergei's hands would dirty the clothes he had just cleaned, and if Sergei were allowed to help Lord Kevern dress, he would certainly put the garments on backward.

"That's very kind, Charlot," Sabrina said, with only the faintest quiver of mirth in her voice. "Er—what did you do with Sergei?" It was not impossible that Charlot had made the poor man wait out in the cold, and Sabrina could not permit that even if it offended Charlot's sensibilities.

"The person is warming himself and having a slight repast in My Room," Charlot responded.

And it will have to be fumigated afterward. The words, although unspoken, hung in the air. Perce choked over his mouthful, suddenly remembering how Charlot had taken his clothes with an air of being at arm's length and touching them only with long tongs; neither was true, of course. Gentlemen, to Charlot's mind, did not get themselves into the condition in which Perce had appeared—at least, gentlemen who had adequate gentlemen's gentlemen did not.

Perce was not offended; he could have kissed Charlot for breaking the tension and misery of parting that had seized him and Sabrina. From the corner of his eye he could see her. Her face was slightly pink and her body rigid with suppressed laughter.

"Thank you, Charlot," he said. "I won't keep you long."

Sabrina went out, and Charlot followed. As soon as Perce was sure Sabrina was engaged in writing the promised introduction to Sir Robert, he went upstairs. It would be better for them both if there was no further opportunity to be alone. He did not trust either himself or Sabrina just now. It was clear that their lovemaking had only whetted their appetites.

He was successful, managing to take the letter Sabrina had ready for him and say formal thanks for her hospitality under Charlot's eyes and ears. He realized Sabrina must have known the action was deliberate. Since he had not sufficient courage to look directly at her face, he did not know whether she had been angry or reproachful. Her voice conveyed nothing, perhaps a shade more of formality than was usual between them. Plodding through the freezing night with snow stinging his face, Perce tried desperately not to think about the possibility that he had hurt her. Surely Sabrina would understand, surely.

The inn was dreadful, filled with smoke and noise. With typical Russian adaptability, Pëtr Pavlovitch had joined the crowd, singing Russian songs and conversing volubly in French and Russian interspersed with the few German words he knew. He bellowed gaily at Perce to join them, waving a dented and stained tin mug filled with God-alone-knew-what. Perce forced a smile and shook his head, calling back that he was tired. Then he could have kicked himself. Pëtr Pavlovitch burst into obscene laughter, yelling congratulations on Perce's successful visit—fortunately in Russian.

"Don't be a fool!" Perce snarled, suppressing an impulse to take his friend by the neck and dash his brains out against the floor.

But it was too late, and he couldn't think of any way to mend the situation. If it had not been forbidden by his code, Perce would have burst into tears of frustration and fury and fatigue. Fortunately he still had enough sense to say no more and take himself up to the room. He nearly wept again when he saw it. The bed was filthy, marked with blood spots from where previous sleepers had been bitten by the multitude of resident fleas and bedbugs. Nor would he have the bed to himself. Pëtr's bags were in a disorderly heap on the floor.

Shuddering with distaste, Perce began to peel off his outer clothing. He would have been glad to sleep in the stable with Sergei and Pëtr's orderly. At least there he would have had clean straw; but that would be a social solecism that would really offend Pëtr Pavlovitch. Even the floor of the room held charms in comparison with that bed, but that simply was not practical at the end of November. He would take a chill, and this was no time to be sick. A few bites wouldn't hurt him, nor would sleeping in the same bed with Pëtr Pavlovitch, he told himself firmly. Then, as he got into the clammy, icy bed, clenching his jaws to keep his teeth from chattering, he thought wryly he would probably be glad of Pëtr Pavlovitch's warmth before the night was over.

Actually, Perce never knew when his companion joined him, nor was he aware of the gourmet dinner he provided for the bedbugs, fleas, and lice. Physical and emotional fatigue solved all of Perce's problems within minutes. By the time Pëtr Pavlovitch came up to bed, he was so soundly asleep that his companion was able to roll him over like a log to make room for himself.

Sabrina stood on the landing, watching Perce until he disappeared into the darkness of the shop. She knew he would not turn back. Still, she waited until she heard the door close and Charlot shoot the bolts. Then she went into the dining room. It would be stupid to let Charlot find her standing there with tears streaming down her cheeks. It was stupid to cry, stupid! Perce had said he would try to come tomorrow.

She wiped the tears from her face and eyes and began to eat the cold, tasteless food on her plate. It wouldn't be hard to find a reason to cancel any engagements she had for the next day. But even as she decided on the excuse she would use, she knew it was hopeless. Perce wouldn't come. Tears started to her eyes again, but she brushed them away impatiently. Stupid! That wouldn't help. Perce was right. If they found themselves alone, they would end up making love, regardless of the danger. And if they weren't alone, they would betray themselves.

It was impossible! Impossible to live without Perce, equally impossible for them to conduct an affair. Neither of them wanted an affair. It was also impossible to break with William at this moment. She had her duty to her country; just as Perce had his duty. His duty! War! He hadn't agreed that the battles would be put off until spring. In fact, Sabrina had the feeling that Perce thought there would be fighting soon, possibly as soon as Alexander found out what Bonaparte had done with his letters to Queen Louise and could order his forces forward. Sabrina shivered.

Don't be a fool, she told herself. *You'll end up with the vapors, and everyone will think William has passed along some dreadful news.* Sabrina knew that her principal purpose was to attend as many social functions as she could, looking serene and happy and talking with knowledge and hopefulness of the political situation. She couldn't make excuses tomorrow. Her shoulders sagged. She would have to make her usual round of visits and attend the dinner to which she was invited. She might miss Perce! *Don't be a fool,* she repeated to herself. *He won't come.*

CHAPTER TEN

Sabrina was quite correct in her assumption—Perce did not come—but wide of the mark on the reason. Although it was quite true that he trusted neither himself nor Sabrina, his desire was stronger than his caution. He would have come if he could have. He was trapped into a round of meetings and conferences all designed to extract information from him or to push Bennigsen into a particular path of action.

The avidity with which he and Pëtr Pavlovitch were received and passed from person to person bespoke the desperation of the Prussians. Aides-de-camp were high-class messenger boys most of the time. Although there were cases in which officers made confidants of their aides, Bennigsen was definitely not among that grouping.

Between the first meeting, aimed at pumping out information, and the first conference, designed to convince them that one particular military objective was more important than any other, Perce and Pëtr Pavlovitch found time for a hurried consultation of their own. They did not have to decide whether or not to be truthful and admit they knew nothing—their ignorance would soon be obvious—but rather how to admit it. Also, Perce had to arrange a visit to Sir Robert. He did not need to lie to Pëtr Pavlovitch about that, only to tell him half the truth: Sir Robert had been ferreting out information about the Jena-Auerstedt battles and the subsequent condition of the

Prussians, and Sir Robert might be willing to pass some of this information on to a fellow Englishman.

Possibly Perce's evasion to visit Sir Robert planted suspicions in the minds of the Prussian officers; possibly it had nothing to do with Perce's actions, and they had already decided that it was unwise to have two bright-eyed and big-eared young men wandering loose for too long in Königsberg. The Prussians thought it safer to sequester the aides in endless meetings. They were not actually trying to conceal the magnitude of the military disaster. What they did not wish transmitted were the strong efforts being made to push King Frederick William into making peace and abandoning his Russian ally. If Bennigsen knew of that, he might withdraw, leaving them utterly defenseless.

The result, whatever reason the Prussian staff had, was that when Perce returned, he found that he would not be able to get away again. Every moment of the day and evening was arranged, and they were scheduled to leave as soon as it was light enough, with "urgent" letters for General Bennigsen. Perce's countenance gave no evidence of his bitter disappointment. He was surprised himself by the fury he felt at not having used his free time to be with Sabrina rather than Sir Robert. In the next moment he was shocked at such a thought. The hour he had spent with Sir Robert might be of great value to his country. Surely that was more important than making love to Sabrina.

Whatever his mind might dictate, Perce's body did not agree that the British nation preceded Sabrina in importance. He *knew* his duty, but he *felt* he should have gone to Sabrina. At any event, the opportunity was gone. Perce barely found time to scribble a note, which he pressed into Sergei's hand.

"Give it to Lady Elvan," he murmured, "only to her or Katy—Mrs. Petersen—not to Charlot, understand?"

Perce hated to confide even in Sergei, but he had no time to think, no time to phrase a letter of regret that would pass Elvan's scrutiny and still convey meaning to Sabrina. Besides, he felt a desperate need to write what he felt. Thus, although Sabrina could have burst into tears of disappointment when she came home from her visits to dress for dinner and found Sergei waiting in a dark corner of the cobbler's shop, she had some recompense.

"Darling, darling," she read, when she had broken the seal in the privacy of her bedchamber. "I will not be able to come at all. We are held almost prisoners and must return to Bennigsen at dawn tomorrow. I hate the Prussians. I hate my duty. I hate everyone in the world but you. I am not sure letters will get to me, and I am almost certain any letter will be read by others before being delivered in any case, so, although it breaks my heart to write this, do not write to me unless you must. At need, address me care of General Levin August Bennigsen at Pultusk. I beg you to forgive me for taking the soft sweetness of your body, yet I would do it again and still again, knowing it to be wrong and unable to resist. I want you. I need you—and what I have is Pëtr Pavlovitch, who is hard as a rock and not overnice with regard to bathing. Pity me. Love me. Perce."

With tears on her face, Sabrina burst out laughing. How like Perce to add a comic note to a love letter. She read it again, her eyes refilling and spilling over. Fool that she was! Fool! She had had so many love letters from William, far more beautifully phrased, carefully written on rich paper, and she had never felt the falseness in them. She sat back, and the tears dried on her cheeks as a smile twitched her lips. Pieces of a half-remembered sonnet jumped into her mind:

My mistress' eyes are nothing like the sun;
Coral is far more red than her lips' red:
If snow be white, why then her breasts are dun;
If hairs be wires, black wires grow on her head.

186

And then there were verses about loving her as much as those whose charms were vaunted as beyond compare.

Sabrina read Perce's letter once more and sighed. The naked need for her, just raw wanting, leapt out of the page undisguised and as stimulating as a caress. This was no pretty game to Perce. It was not when she denied herself that she became more desirable. What were those other lines from the same poet? No, it was not poetry, it was in a play, *Hamlet*: "As if increase of appetite had grown/By what it fed on." That was right. That was how it should be. Having her, he wanted more.

For how long? The horrid question buzzed into her mind, and she swatted it like a fly. Not Perce. He said he had never been in the petticoat line, and it was true. Sabrina had heard a great deal from Philip about his bits of muslin and the easy delights of a bawdy house compared with the stiff agonies of a formal courtship. But Perce engaged in neither. Philip had teased him, sometimes within Sabrina's hearing, about his lack of enthusiasm for paid female companionship, and Sabrina knew from her own experience at places like Almack's that he did not flirt. He was pleasant and easy with women in general, the result of having a mother and sisters he genuinely liked, but no one could mistake his manner for flirtation or seduction.

Anyhow, it was lunatic to worry about Perce becoming surfeited with her charms when they might not see each other again for months . . . or ever. Sabrina instinctively pressed the letter against her breast as if she could shield Perce in the circle of her arms. The crackle of paper drew her attention to the physical existence of the note. It was dangerously open, a total betrayal of their relationship. She should destroy it at once, but she would sooner have put out her own eyes.

It must be hidden, but where? There was no place private from Katy. Of course, Katy was no danger to her, but it was wrong, Sabrina thought, to burden Katy with this knowledge. She needed time to think, and besides, she could not bear to be parted from her letter. Hastily, she folded it and thrust it down inside her breastband. Sabrina smiled at her own silliness, but nonetheless she felt a square of extra warmth where the letter lay.

That was a comfort. Unfortunately, all else was a misery. No matter how she struggled not to think of it while she dressed, Sabrina could not help fearing that the letter and her memories might be all that would remain for her of Perce. In court circles there were a number of black-clad women whose men had died at Jena or Auerstedt or in the other lost battles and sieges that broke the Prussian army. There was also a pervading aura of failure and melancholy that fed on itself, increasing fear as fear increased.

Until now, Sabrina had been resistant to that miasma. She had been careful not to sparkle, not to flaunt her sense of reliance on a secure island kingdom that had never been beaten. She had, however, tried to counteract the prevailing oppression with sturdy common sense and hope. Many nations had been defeated and had risen again to conquer. This, although quite true, was not in the case of Prussia very practical, since most of the effective means of waging war had been lost as well as the battles. However, there was also the fact that the Russians were coming.

The trouble was that now Sabrina was racked by personal fear. When the Russians had come—at least, the advance units—there was assurance that the remainder of the army would follow as speedily as they could. She should be glowing with assurance, reinforcing hope. But she was quite terrified and ready to sink into despair. While the Russians "were coming," Perce had been safe. The presence of Bennigsen's army guaranteed that Bonaparte could not simply walk into East Prussia and gather it up at will, and thus substantially increase the safety of those in Königsberg. But it exposed Perce to danger.

But did it? Sabrina asked herself. Not every man in an army was on the front line. A ray of hope broke through the gloom enveloping her. The day of the knight who led his own men into battle was gone. Kings and generals tended to sit on a hillside at a safe distance to watch and direct the action through spyglasses. Captains and sergeants led the men, not generals. As a general's aide, Perce probably would be no closer to the action than the general. Or would he? Sabrina realized she would have to discover the duties of an aide, and the way to do it was to get a general to tell her.

Suddenly her interest in the clothing she was putting on, her choice of jewels, the way the coiffure she had chosen framed her face, escalated dramatically. She began to primp with more real interest in her appearance than Katy had seen in months. Yet it was not anticipated pleasure Katy saw in the lovely face reflected in the mirror; it was an excited determination.

"Brina," she said sharply, "I dinna like the look of ye."

"I'm fine," Sabrina said absently, pulling a curl forward, then back, then lifting it higher to see the effect. "I feel fine."

"I dinna doubt that, but yer plannin' some mischief. I see that fine. This isna the time to be runnin' wild."

"Wild?" The word caught Sabrina's attention, and she turned her head. "I promise I won't do anything wild."

Katy pursed her lips, unable to find much consolation in Sabrina's pledge. However, she was clever enough to know that her little girl was now grown up. Katy sighed. Poor Brina was more grown up than anyone had hoped. Katy wished she had been at home when Lord Kevern had paid his visit, but from Charlot's description it had been most innocent. Still, it had made a deep mark on Brina.

"Does Lord Kevern know what yer plannin'?" Katy asked.

It was safe enough to ask that. Such a question would not make Brina defensive or indignant. It had been a common question in childhood. Does Philip know? Does Perce know? Many of Brina's escapades had been attempts to prove her capabilities to her "brother" and his friend. Thus Katy's litany was to initiate caution, for Brina would hesitate to incur her idols' wrath when she would ignore Katy's.

The question did not have its usual effect of bringing guilty consideration to Sabrina's eyes. Her lips softened as warm memories were evoked, and then lifted in a half smile. "No, he doesn't, but I don't think he'd mind. I'm only going to seduce a general or two."

Katy relaxed. It must be that Brina had just figured out how to do some piece of business for Himself. That was all right. Himself might be a bad husband, but he would never set Brina a task that was dangerous or disreputable. Katy did not misunderstand Sabrina's remark. The seduction would stop long before anyone could accept it seriously or be hurt. Katy knew Sabrina merely wished to extract some information painlessly.

But the information Sabrina wanted was not for William's benefit. And in order to obtain a description of the duties of an aide-de-camp in battle, she hardly had to use her charms. Any general she approached was only too willing either to praise or to complain about his aides, depending largely on his own personality. Sabrina could have asked the aides directly, of course, but she was afraid that they would make light of any dangers involved. Accustomed to sifting rumor, Sabrina had no trouble picking out the facts she wanted from the chaff of opinions.

Unfortunately, this left her little better off. An aide-de-camp's duties were multifarious and included duties as widely different as acting as secretary and accountant and escorting female relations on picnics. In battle, however, the principal duty of an aide was as a liaison. Instructions from the general to his subordinate officers and the responses to those orders were carried by the aide. Whether this duty was dangerous depended, Sabrina discovered, on the kind of general and the nature of the battle. Generals who planned every action in advance used aides less than those who preferred vague, overall battle plans. Also, victorious actions, in which the aides moved far behind the lines because the troops were forward of the original positions, were less risky than defeats, in which an aide might find himself riding right through the action or across enemy lines.

None of it sounded safe to Sabrina, but she could understand varying degrees of danger. This seemed to depend a good deal on what kind of general Bennigsen was. Here Sabrina met her first check. Everyone to whom she spoke that night and during the following weeks was just as eager as she to discover what General Bennigsen was likely to do, but no one had better predictions about it than she did.

Certain matters were well known. Bennigsen was a Hanoverian who had been in the Russian army for nearly thirty years. He had been deeply involved in the conspiracy to murder Tsar Paul, Alexander's father. It was said that he had appointed the guards who looked the other way while the murderers entered Paul's chamber and that he had actually led the party that did away with the tsar. This sounded dreadful—the treachery of a trusted officer. But the general agreement that Paul *had* to be removed before thousands or hundreds of thousands died because of his lunacy left it undecided whether Bennigsen was a devil or a saint.

December passed slowly. The negotiations in which Lord Hutchinson and William were involved did not progress at all. Although Sabrina was still kindly received by the queen, she sensed that there was a growing resentment against the British. It was difficult not to sympathize with the Prussians. Sabrina felt that her government *was* being unreasonable. They were asking the Prussians, who had lost so much, to give up the Electorate of Hanover, a territory they had long coveted, and to fight the French, an enemy they had learned to fear greatly; in return, they were being offered encouragement and high-sounding phrases and "possibilities if . . ."; in other words, nothing.

In contrast, the Russians were finally in position. About one hundred and twenty thousand men under the command of Marshal Kamansky were centered in various towns between the Vistula and the Narev rivers. There was tremendous excitement in Königsberg as news of maneuvers and countermaneuvers came in. Sabrina would have been frantic, except that she had received a letter from Perce a week before Christmas that discounted the movements of the army. Since it was sent by a general courier, it was nearly impersonal. In fact, Sabrina was sure it was meant as much for Sir Robert Wilson as for herself.

"I am standing up better to the cold than I had expected," Perce wrote, "partly because Sergei is a genius at finding sheltered corners and food, and partly because I have rapidly cast away all British notions of privacy and propriety. I huddle up with any warm body available. It is indeed fortunate that Russian army officers seem to be chosen more for their size than anything else. Those big bodies generate plenty of heat, and Pëtr Pavlovitch, Matvei Semenovitch, Ivan Petrovitch, and I sleep—when we can sleep—more closely embraced than any newlywed pair."

Sabrina smiled. She didn't believe Perce was really cold and sleeping out in the open. If he had been, she suspected he would never have mentioned it. He was trying to tell her that his nights were accounted for.

"But perhaps," the letter continued, "it is only the supreme command in the Russian army that is currently dependent on addled wits. My companions are not stupid, nor is my general, and they find themselves as puzzled as I by this continual moving around. There does not seem to be any purpose in it. At first I thought we must be probing for the French positions, but this cannot be true. We are rushed forward as if to attack, find nothing, and instead of moving farther forward or right or left, we are commanded to retreat. General Bennigsen is not one to confide in his inferiors, but I believe he is furious. He has several times been to Kamansky's headquarters. The last time I thought he would have an apoplectic fit when he came from speaking to the marshal. Considering this and taking into account various conversations I have had, I would say the movements are merely a result of Kamansky's inability to make up his mind."

When Sabrina transmitted this information to Sir Robert, as she was sure Perce intended, he agreed heartily. "Good head on his shoulders, Kevern has. Remarkable how he picked up military ways. Understand he never trained for it at all."

"Yes, that's true. He's the earl of Moreton's heir. His brother Robert is the military one. He's in India now, serving under Wellesley."

Sir Robert's brows went up. "Arthur Wellesley? Good man, that. Brilliant in defense and has a solid notion of how to get the best out of his men. But there may be some good to come out of Kamansky's dithering. I've had some word from the French side, you know. We have our ways. Boney's staff seems just as confused as the Russians. Seems they can't decide whether Kamansky intends to attack or retreat or even where he's concentrating his forces."

"But what will they do?" Sabrina asked anxiously.

"That, my dear Lady Elvan, is *the* question. If I could answer it, we would be well off. Unfortunately, I cannot even guess. Partly it depends on things we can judge—like how well Boney has been able to resupply his army. That, I fear, has been going well for him, better than we had projected. It is possible that once the men are outfitted, he will attack. However, he isn't predictable. If his attention is drawn away or if he doesn't feel the Russians to be a serious threat, he may do nothing."

Sabrina did not say *I hope so,* which was what she felt. Instead she asked, "What would be best for us, Sir Robert?"

He laughed rather bitterly. "Would you believe I don't even know that? I *think* it would be better if the armies engaged at once. The Russians can better withstand the cold, and the longer the time Boney has between actions, the more chance he has to train reinforcements and gather supplies." He paused when he realized Sabrina had grown quite pale. "Worried about Kevern?" he asked kindly.

"Yes, I am," she admitted. "I've known him since I was eight years old."

"Well, probably you've no need to worry right now," Sir Robert assured her, "not so long as Kamansky's in charge, anyway. I don't think he'll fight. If Boney moves, I'm pretty sure Kamansky will back away. Even Boney won't try to advance far at this time of year. It won't do to outrun your supply lines in winter."

Much cheered by those comforting words, Sabrina went on about her life, happily unaware that Sir Robert's assurances were totally valueless. It was not that Sir Robert had lied to her. He himself did not yet know that Marshal Kamansky had resigned his command and that Bonaparte had decided, weeks earlier, to fight the Russians at the first favorable opportunity.

In support of this intention, Bonaparte roused the Poles against the Russians with vague promises of freedom, which he never intended to fulfill. His generals Davout and Lannes had accompanied him when he marched into Warsaw. The army then turned northward while Bona-

parte remained in the city. Meanwhile Bonaparte's generals
Ney and Bernadotte crossed the Vistula, moving eastward
toward the Russians, while French forces under the command of Soult and Augereau advanced as far as the village
of Golymin, where General Buxhöwden commanded a
division of Russian troops.

Had Marshal Kamansky been in charge, an order for
withdrawal might have been given. However, General
Bennigsen had been left without a commanding officer,
and he knew he might never again have so much freedom
of opportunity. He was well aware that his involvement in
Tsar Paul's death had made an inveterate enemy of the
dowager tsarina, while Alexander himself blew hot and
cold—at one moment hating his father's murderer and at
the next admiring the courage and force of character that
had enabled Bennigsen to act. Marshal Kamansky's retire-
ment was, to Bennigsen, another moment in which to seize
opportunity. Orders went out to all his subordinate commanders to stand fast and repulse the French.

On Christmas Day, Bernadotte launched an attack on
the Russian forces at Moehrungen in an attempt to out-
flank them. The Russians were driven back, but they did
not break and flee as the Prussians had done at Jena and
Auerstedt. In fact, as they retreated they inflicted such
heavy losses on Bernadotte's division that he dared not
pursue. Nor did Bennigsen take fright at this minor rever-
sal. If the French had been defeated and had not attacked
again, the credit for stopping Bonaparte's men would have
gone to others than himself.

Therefore, General Bennigsen was in good spirits when
he summoned his aides at about four o'clock in the morning of December twenty-sixth. All divisions had to be
warned that an attack was imminent. Orders were already
prepared in sealed packets. Bennigsen did not consider it
necessary for his messengers to know too much about
large-scale plans; however, each aide was instructed that

195

the principal order for each officer was to hold fast at all cost.

Perce had plenty of time to ponder the possibilities, since he had the longest ride, to where Buxhöwden's division held Golymin. Perce had been around the military long enough to know that the standard procedure would be to take the most defensible position possible and use artillery and rapid musket-fire to hold off the enemy. But personally, he did not think artillery or rapid-fire technique would work. For one thing, he was very uncertain of the accuracy of Russian shooting; for another, he was not sure there was enough ammunition for the shooting to last very long.

If the firepower failed, there would be a real mess. The French had a fondness for bayonet work. Perce restrained a shudder as he remembered one charge he had survived. Bullets were far less frightening. One knew they could kill, but invisible as bullets were, they were easier to ignore. A man coming toward one with a bayonet mounted on his musket, a wall of men so armed, inspired a most fervent desire to be elsewhere.

Wrenching his mind from too vivid memories, Perce analyzed Bennigsen's decision to stand fast. He felt Bennigsen had judged correctly. It was better to stand and fight now, Perce thought, than to retreat on a possibility. The hopeful sign of preventing Bernadotte's advance at Moehrungen would hearten the officers, reminding them that the French could be held. But Perce felt a victory was needed. Automatically he pulled up his horse's head as the animal stumbled on the rutted road. He looked across the ditch, but he could hardly make out the fields in the dull light of a gray dawn. Also, the uneven ground was covered by a deceptive layer of snow and ice and would offer even more unsafe footing. Mostly it would be the French that were moving, but if they got this far the victory would be theirs, as so often it was.

Why? Was Bonaparte a genius? Perce sighed. The beaten always insisted he was, because it mitigated their defeats, and perhaps it was true. It was the men who did the fighting, after all, the corporals and sergeants who held them to their work. The French, often worse trained and worse equipped than their enemies, had uniformly been more successful. Perce thought of the Prussian troops, as rigid and as useful as wooden soldiers. It was said that every man in the French army felt he had a marshal's baton in his knapsack. Why not? Bonaparte himself had started as a corporal, and promotion from the ranks to officer was reasonably common, although generally not in two steps to marshal, as Boney had done it. Certainly such a hope might motivate a man wishing to distinguish himself.

However, if that was the source of French courage, there was no way of using it to inspire Russian troops. They were not even free men, and if Sergei was any example, they did not *want* promotion and responsibility. With that perspective, Perce wondered why the common soldiers fought at all. He knew why he was here—for king and country, yes, because he had a considerable investment in his country; but the Russian serf had none. No, that wasn't true, he knew it wasn't. He had heard the men talking about the "little father's" wish that they would be brave and strong. Idiotic as it might seem for such ill-treated slaves, they loved the tsar.

Suddenly Perce's eyes narrowed. He remembered Bennigsen sending out instructions to his subordinate officers that each unit was to be read the words of the tsar on the declaration of war, and all the church bells were to be rung before and after the announcement. What pretty words Alexander had used? One bit came back: The war was against "the principal enemy of Mankind, one who worships idols and whores . . . who is bringing together every Judas in the world . . . in order that the Church of God be destroyed."

197

Hot damn! Alexander was no fool when he was jolted out of his indecision. He had given his serf-soldiers something for which to fight. He had started a Holy War. Perce whistled aloud, and his horse twitched his ears. He urged the animal forward at a slightly faster pace. The light was better now. It must be nearly six o'clock. Golymin should not be far.

It was not difficult to find General Buxhöwden. Perce just headed for the largest and least miserable building in the village. His uniform and the packet of dispatches were swift passports to the general's presence. Perce found him dressed and just finishing breakfast, which meant that he must have been warned by movements of the enemy troops. He handed over the packet, gave Buxhöwden Bennigsen's verbal message, and added that if there was time, General Bennigsen thought it might inspire the men to remind them of the "little father's" directive against the Antichrist Bonaparte and his legions of devils.

"What we can, we will do," Buxhöwden said grimly. "We are outnumbered. I do not know how badly, but our position is good, and the cavalry they have will not be of much effect. If I had more men . . ."

"All of the generals are being warned, sir," Perce said. "From that I conclude that General Bennigsen is convinced the attack will be on all fronts. However, I will carry your request most willingly."

Buxhöwden thought a moment, then waved Perce away toward the outer room. "I will have a reply shortly."

Perce was delighted with the delay, since it gave him a chance to warm up and have a glass of tea—in Russian encampments, tea was served in mugs rather than in cups—and something to eat. It was fortunate he had done so. By the time Buxhöwden had handed him a note for Bennigsen, his horse was rested and he made reasonably good time. Nonetheless, when he neared Pultusk, he could hear guns. He spurred his mount to greater speed and then veered sharply east over the fields when he saw figures moving to his left. They were small enough to indicate distance, but he heard the crack of musket fire.

There was little danger from that. Perce wondered how anyone could be fool enough to fire at him at such a distance. Unless there was cavalry . . . A swift glance around assured him on that point; what he saw must be only a small patrol, but he continued to drive his horse as fast as it could go. The road, the only safe path he knew to Pultusk, was bounded by soft, boggy land that had been made nearly impassable by the snow and sleet.

He lost that patrol, but eventually his horse began to tire. When Perce was forced back toward the road at the end of the plowed fields that warned of bog beyond, he was scarcely five hundred yards in advance of the French troops. That he made it at all was owing to the fact that the division sent around to the north was somewhat behind the advancing center. The nearer he came to the town, the louder and more insistent was the noise of gunfire. However, his narrowest escape was from the nervous men of his own forces, one of whom fired at him almost point-blank as he approached the lines.

That the shot missed worried Perce almost as much as it pleased him. If the trooper could not hit him at that range, he was not likely to be very dangerous to the oncoming French, either. The one consolation, Perce thought as he drove his flagging horse along the empty street toward General Bennigsen's headquarters, was that the French would be massed together. He hoped that a bullet directed, even vaguely, at man level would hit someone, provided these idiots didn't fire into the ground or the air.

Sergei came running out to meet him as he slid from his horse, calling out that the general was gone to "that place" east of town. Perce nodded. The aides knew the spot, a rising piece of ground with some trees for shelter, which would provide a better place for observation.

"Saddle Bravo for me," he said, "and follow me with the rest of the horses. You'd better bring poor Major, too. Rub him down and put a blanket on him. Bring some feed along; it may be a long day, and we might not be coming back to Pultusk. You'd better put the extra saddle on Red."

"Is the battle lost?" Sergei asked, his eyes narrowing.

"No! It's barely begun, but I doubt we'll remain here. If the French are thrown back, we'll have to advance. If not, it can't hurt to be prepared."

"Yes. Don't worry. I'll be ready."

Sergei seized Major's bridle, and Perce stamped into the building, trying to bring feeling back to his feet. It was not terribly cold today, but clutching the saddle with thighs and knees tended to numb the feet. Perce eased off his gloves and blew on his fingers. His hands were not too bad, although both little fingers were swollen and cracked with chilblains. Only a frightened clerk remained in the general's office, and he gave Perce the same message as Sergei had. Since Perce knew that no one would have told the serf anything, he marveled anew at his man's ability to pluck useful information out of the air or to put two and two together to find an answer his employer-master might need.

He stayed only long enough to drink another mug of tea, hot and strong, and he made it far too sweet by putting the lumps the Russians sucked into the cup, but the warmth the sugar would give was worth the sickly taste. Outside, Bravo was stamping and tossing his head. Perce ran his hand down the gleaming neck, feeling a tightening in his throat. He hated riding a horse into battle. They were too easy a target. He had had to shoot one of his mounts, which had been badly wounded at Austerlitz.

"You better reprime your pistols," Sergei said.

Perce jerked around, then turned back to soothe the

200

startled horse. Sergei's remark seemed like a horrible presentiment.

"Four or five hours in the damp. You don't want a misfire if you come face-to-face with a Frenchman," Sergei added, looking questioningly at Perce.

"I hope it's only Frenchmen I have to shoot," Perce replied, and then as Sergei looked even more surprised, he said, "I was thinking about Dancer."

Relief came over Sergei's face. "You be careful, little father," he said, smiling indulgently. "There's cold meat and cheese and bread in the saddlebags, and I put the waterproof over the blanket. Weather for lapdogs they have here, so much rain instead of decent snow. I'll watch. If you need another horse, wave your hat."

Sergei turned away to the stable, shaking his head. He had wondered for a minute if the officers feared a rout and expected to have to shoot their own men to keep them from running away, but it was only that crazy English thinking again, worrying about the horses. He was sure his master would rather be shot himself than have one of the horses hurt. Sergei gathered the gear and loaded it on a pack mule, not only feed but Perce's extra clothing, fur coat, and blankets. Then he slung a stolen carbine over his shoulder. Servants were not supposed to be armed, but people got funny ideas in the middle of a battle when it was hard to know who was where.

Actually, Sergei had a certain amount of sympathy for those who would rather steal than fight. He himself didn't mind fighting, but when a man was cold and hungry, stealing did seem like a better idea. It was especially appealing when the chances for getting away with it were so good. Only not *his* master's goods. Sergei had defended Perce's belongings successfully on the retreat from Austerlitz—at least, what was left after his too generous little father had given away everything they could survive without. Sergei sighed, then brightened. This time he had hidden the most essential items. Once more he checked the leading reins. He didn't want the horses bolting when they came closer to the thunder of the big guns.

Perce was up and away before Sergei reached the stable. He was laughing as he rode, amused by Sergei's motherly advice. Nonetheless, it was an enormous advantage to him to have so trustworthy a servant. Then he laughed again. Perhaps trustworthy was the wrong word. It would not surprise him in the least to discover that the food in his saddlebags as well as a great many other items he found of use and comfort were stolen. But Sergei did not steal from him.

He then gave his attention to his horse, who was very lively and was taking exception to the growing noise. Perce allowed Bravo to gallop up the road. The pace was scarcely safe on the rutted surface, but it was better to work off the animal's surplus energy before they arrived at General Bennigsen's command station than to have Bravo bucking and kicking in a crowd. The half-mile distance was just barely enough to accomplish this purpose. Perce was able to present himself and hand over Buxhöwden's note without causing a disaster.

General Bennigsen read it swiftly and shoved it carelessly into a pocket. "Did he say anything to you?" he asked.

Perce repeated Buxhöwden's remarks.

Bennigsen's mouth twisted. "I will pray for him," he said caustically. "That is all the help I *can* send."

While he spoke, his attention had never left the battlefield below them, and now he lifted his spyglass to his eye again. Perce looked out over the field, also. It was interesting from this distance, like watching a very large game with toy soldiers, except that the toys moved around by themselves. A shot from one of their guns struck a group of French infantrymen struggling through the morass, and half a dozen of the little figures threw up their hands, or twisted wildly, dropping their weapons as they fell. Perce felt a vague satisfaction. They were out of the game. There were no individual shrill cries; all the sounds blended into a dull roar punctuated and underlined by the repeated deep throb of the artillery.

"Kevern!" Bennigsen snapped.

"Sir?" Perce kicked Bravo forward. It was his turn. Pëtr Pavlovitch and Ivan Petrovitch had been sent out already with messages for the left wing and center. Matvei Semenovitch must have been sent off earlier, before Perce returned from Golymin; he had not yet returned.

The general pointed his baton down the hill and off to the right. "Tell the colonel of artillery there that I want a heavy barrage of grapeshot laid down ahead of the French. If he can lay the shot right on their front ranks, so much the better, but it is the forward ranks I wish to suffer now."

Perce acknowledged the message and touched the horse with his heel. He discovered five minutes later that the most direct route to the guns was not practicable for a horse, so he rode northward to an easier slope then worked his way around. He had to force Bravo with whip and spur and realized it was not only the French who were suffering the effects of battle. Bodies had been dragged away from one gun lying on its side amid splintered wheels and carriage. Not all were dead. One man was screaming with the shrill regularity of a creaking wheel. The men working the other guns did not even turn their heads.

There was clearly no upper officer here. Perce bellowed a question, got a pointed finger in response. He drove Bravo on, almost lost control of him as a shot crashed into the ground not more than two hundred feet away. A shriek and roar of foul language followed. Perce did not look back to see what had happened, concentrating wholly on getting his horse to move forward. Another shell and then another fell, but both short of the target, possibly from guns farther away. At the next battery of guns, Perce found his colonel and delivered his message, adding the information that there were wounded at the battery he had passed.

He heard orders rapped out to the colonel's aides, but his part was done. Now he was only in the way. A hasty survey of the area showed a rough road, probably the one the guns had come down on from Pultusk. He spurred toward that, Bravo going more readily as the immediate roar of the guns diminished. It seemed to Perce, however, that the overall noise of battle was louder. When he reached the general again, having gone nearly all the way back to town to find a place to climb the hill, it was apparent his perception was correct. The fighting had intensified. A powerful thrust was under way.

Before Perce had even reached Bennigsen's side or could report that he had delivered the orders, the general was roaring further instructions for Perce to carry to Colonel Semorov on the left flank. Perce laid his whip to Bravo's hindquarters and flew off back toward Pultusk and through it. It was like a town of the dead. He alone moved along the street. Those who could, had fled; those less fortunate—or more courageous—were hidden in their houses. Not far from the town another brigade of artillery was at work. There were fewer guns than in the batteries to the north, and Perce did not remember any guns so close to the town when he had come back from Golymin. Also, many of the gunners seemed to be bandaged or bloody.

Then Perce realized that the guns had been pulled back from a more forward position. He raised his whip to bring it down on Bravo's hindquarters again, in an attempt to wring more speed from him, but instead was forced to pull back slightly on the reins. Ahead the road was no longer clear and empty. Men with bloodstained uniforms crawled, limped, dragged others. Beyond them were carts laden with those who could not even crawl. For an instant, sickness rose in Perce's throat as the fear of another rout like Austerlitz seized him. In the next moment that fear was gone. The column of wounded were, in fact, a guarantee that there was no rout. When an army breaks and runs, it is the unscathed who come first; the wounded are left to die.

Perce drove Bravo right and then left, seeking safe ground that would avoid the road. It was essential that Bennigsen's message reach his subordinate. Failure in communications had materially increased the disaster of Austerlitz, if it had not actually caused the disaster. On both sides of the road, however, the ground dropped away sharply, indicating that the land was boggy. It looked smooth and clean under its blanket of snow, but Perce knew better than to try it. The wounded would have to make way for him.

By now he was almost upon them. As far as Perce could see, there was little choice between the sides of the road. He stayed where he was, shouting, "Make way." The walking wounded at the front pressed together, and Perce passed; those farther back tried to move closer to the wagons or get between them; still farther back the screams and groans drowned Perce's voice. He drew the pistol from his left holster, pointed it into the air, and pulled the trigger. The flint sparked, but the priming powder failed to flash. Perce cursed with a fluency and heartfelt sincerity that would have done credit to any trooper—and in five languages. Sergei had reminded him to renew his charges, but he had forgotten.

Leaving Bravo to make his way forward as best he could, Perce fumbled for the small powderhorn and renewed the charges in both guns. The sound of the shot was helpful for a short distance. Those who could move, moved fast, assuming the officer had shot someone impeding his path. Even so, Bravo could barely work up a trot, and a few poor devils were shouldered aside so that they rolled down into the bog. Perce was sorry; he hoped their companions would help them, but his message might mean all their lives and those of many others.

Still the shrieks of fear and pitiful cries for help upset him, and he could hear them in memory long after he had worked free and delivered his message. Coming back by a thin goat-track pointed out by one of the colonel's aides, which would permit him to avoid the column of wounded, Perce ran headlong into a troop of enemy French struggling through the bog. They were spread out all over the place; only two had actually reached the solid ground of the path he was on. Most of the men in the morass were too concerned with their own difficulties to bother about him, but the two on the path raised their muskets. Perce's first shot took the nearest man full in the face, giving him a horrifying split-second view of a mouth open with surprise and a red ruin—eyeless, noseless—above it.

His second shot disconcerted or wounded the other soldier so that the bullet he fired at Perce went wide. Then Bravo reared, screaming with pain as the man's bayonet, aimed to split the horse in the throat, missed and tore his shoulder. Perce had managed to draw his sword, but he had no chance to use it because suddenly Bravo screamed again and bolted forward. Perce had all he could do to keep the animal on the track and save them both from floundering into the bog. The troop of French was behind them now, and it was not until another of them fired at him that Perce connected the crack of a musket with the burst of speed that saved them.

A few minutes later more men appeared. Perce, who had had no time to reload his pistols, could only hope that their speed and his swinging sword would get them through before anyone could shoot him. He had raised the weapon when he realized they wore Russian uniforms. He shouted identification and then warning about the enemy troop as the soldiers jumped off the path to give his horse room. Some sank to their knees in the swamp, but unless they lost their boots, not much harm would be done. Bravo, on the other hand, could break a leg or sink so deep, owing to the great weight and small hooves, that he would have to be abandoned.

Perce came in by the rear of Pultusk. The town was no longer silent. It rang with the cries of the wounded, with the blows of gun butts and other tools breaking doors as houses were forced open to shelter the wounded, with the rumbling of cartwheels as more maimed bodies were brought in. Perce glanced down at Bravo's shoulder. Blood glistened red and wet down the whole leg, but the horse was still going strongly, not even favoring that side, apparently still too frightened to feel much pain. Unable to do more than curse, Perce turned north toward Bennigsen's command post.

Now it seemed quieter again, much as it had been when he first rode out, but he could hear the general's voice as he neared. It was strangely hoarse, as if he had been shouting for a long time. Perce felt that was odd, but he could spare it no thought. Bravo had been stumbling for the last five minutes. Feeling the horse might go down, Perce swung out of the saddle and nearly fell on his face. His legs were numb, his feet totally without feeling, although sweat was trickling down his back and breast.

That, too, was odd, but it was far more important to get Bravo to Sergei and get atop Red before he had to ride out again. Perce closed his eyes and shook his head, trying to remember where they had decided Sergei would wait. The answer had not yet come to him when Bravo's rein was pulled from his hand.

"Did you eat?" Sergei asked.

Perce looked at him blankly. "See what you can do for

207

Bravo," he said. "He may have a bullet in him somewhere in his left haunch."

"The food. The food," Sergei insisted. "Did you eat it?"

"No. You can have it if you're hungry." Perce reached for Red's reins, but Sergei pulled them away.

"You need to eat," he insisted, taking both sets of reins into one hand and fumbling in Bravo's saddlebags.

He thrust the food packet at Perce, who pushed it away, protesting that he was not hungry and he had eaten at General Buxhöwden's headquarters.

"That was six o'clock in the morning," Sergei said slowly and clearly. "It is afternoon now." He pointed to the sun.

Perce looked at it and then toward the town, which he knew to be southeast of where Bennigsen had stationed himself. He could hardly believe what he saw. It must be nearly three o'clock from the position of the sun. He took the package that Sergei was thrusting at him again and reached for the flap, but he could not open it. He heard the shrieks of the wounded, the screaming of injured horses, saw the half face of the man whose head he had shot away.

"Later," he said.

"Later will be worse," Sergei warned. "The French have pulled back, but they will come on again."

"I can eat while I ride," Perce insisted, pulling Red's reins from Sergei's hand.

He pushed the food into Red's saddlebags and transferred his pistols, powderhorn, and bullets. As he did he cursed himself again for failing to take his Ellis repeaters. At the time he left England, it had not seemed appropriate. He had planned to play the part of an army-struck English dandy, stupid and impractical. He certainly had not planned to get mixed up in the war, and the Ellis pistols he had felt would strike too practical and efficient a note. His role had developed along other lines, however; well, it was too late to worry now.

"See if you can find someone to sew up Bravo," Perce ordered.

"There are plenty of horses," Sergei shouted as Perce started to ride away. "Matvei Semenovitch is dead, and Pëtr Pavlovitch too badly wounded to ride. You be careful! You can get killed out there!"

CHAPTER ELEVEN

The month of January was one long nightmare of horror for Sabrina. The news of the battle at Pultusk reached Königsberg on the twenty-seventh of December. First it was heralded as a Prussian victory, but by the end of the year it was plain that the evaluation had been a gross exaggeration. All that could truly be said of Pultusk was that it had not been a defeat. The Russians had stood their ground against everything Bonaparte could send against them; however, they had been hit so hard that even Bennigsen acknowledged it would be suicide to attempt to throw the French back. In fact, he had been unwilling to remain so close to Bonaparte's army and had pulled his own forces back to Preussisch Eylau, twenty-three miles south of Königsberg.

Only twenty-three miles. At first Sabrina had been overjoyed. Perce could come at any time his duties allowed. But Perce had not come, nor a letter, nor Sergei with a message, and as tales of the battle drifted in to Königsberg, a terrified conviction grew in Sabrina that Perce was dead. In her first anxiety she asked about him, saying he was an aide to Bennigsen. No one knew anything specific about Lord Kevern, but it was known that several of the general's aides had been killed and one, badly wounded, had been sent back to Russia. Sabrina ceased to inquire. She believed Perce was dead, but as long as no one confirmed it, she could go on hoping.

It made no difference that hope hurt more than certain knowledge, that once she *knew,* she could try to begin remaking her life. She did not want to remake her life. She would rather endure the constant pricking of the tiny, sharp knife of hope than learn the truth. Thus, she did not approach Sir Robert and ask him to find out about Perce, nor did she write to General Bennigsen himself to ask. She waited, clutching her pain of hope to her, trying to avoid those who discussed the battle and the future moves the Russians and French might make.

The latter was growing quite easy, not because the war was less talked about but because fewer and fewer people seemed to want to talk to Sabrina. Many evenings now she sat at home, working at her embroidery or netting a purse for Leonie. Fewer and fewer invitations came, and the coldness toward the English was growing into something warmer—an active distaste.

The indecisive meeting at Pultusk had generated a fever of hope in the Prussians. If the Russians alone had been able to do so much, surely more might be accomplished with British help. Now was the time to send help, King Frederick William and his ministers insisted; supplies were needed, as were money and trained men. They pointed out angrily that the British had sent twenty-six thousand men to Cuxhaven by the Elbe River and had then withdrawn them without ever using them. Now the strength of the British army had increased from one hundred eighty-five thousand to two hundred thousand, and surely at least twenty-five thousand could be spared to fight Bonaparte directly.

There was little the British emissaries could do beyond make excuses, which were less and less graciously received. The truth was that War Secretary Windham had a dreadful proclivity for dispersing his forces on harebrained missions designed to snatch a pot of gold from places like Egypt or South America. To admit this would not have improved matters in any way. As the anger in the negotiators grew, they respected the confidentiality of the negotiations less and less. Outraged Prussian ministers expressed their feelings to their wives, who in turn grew outraged and expressed themselves to their friends and servants.

Although this tattling had no effect on the negotiations, it had a great effect on Sabrina, who bore the brunt of the women's spite against the English. Thus, she was not invited to the social functions that tried to welcome in the New Year with what cheer could be mustered. In addition, there were incidents at the house and on the street—insults called, a rock thrown. The English were no longer welcome to the nobility or the people. Sabrina knew she was useless and should now go home, that she would be forced to go home as soon as Lord Hutchinson and William had the time to think about her. She made herself small and inconspicuous, staying out of William's sight as much as possible. She could not go home! She could not! Perce was still in East Prussia, his long, pale body, which had brought her such exquisite pleasure, smirched with earth . . . rotting. . . . But she could not leave him alone, all alone.

The days dragged by, the weather grew worse and worse. By the beginning of February, howling storms of sleet during the day were followed by snowstorms at night, so that sheets of ice were deceptively covered with snow, and horse and man slipped and fell. No shipmaster in his right mind set sail, and Sabrina stayed at home, huddling close to the stove in the sitting room. She could not bear to remain in her bedchamber, even though one particular bearskin had been removed from the floor and carefully rolled up in the closet.

In Russian headquarters the weather was regarded with far greater indulgence. The French may have been left to take Pultusk, but General Bennigsen had made sure that it

212

was worthless to them, as was the whole area for miles around. Every animal capable of walking had been driven out, the towns and villages had been stripped, the houses burnt. Reports from the countryside informed the general that the French army was suffering horribly. Bonaparte was accustomed to letting his men live off the land by foraging, but the Russians made certain there was nothing to forage. Conditions were so bad that the supply trains sent out to relieve the needs of the front lines were set upon and robbed by equally starving troops farther back. The French, Bennigsen had heard, were dying like flies. What he had begun at Pultusk was being helped along mightily by the weather.

These reports were quite true, which was not always the case. At the end of January, matters had been so desperate that the French marshal Ney decided to strike at Königsberg in the hope of finding supplies and better winter quarters. Bennigsen was delighted. Estoque's division, about ten thousand Prussians, barred the way, and Bennigsen, with grim joy, marched his whole Russian army of fifty-six thousand out to join him. He hoped to overwhelm Ney's twelve thousand and destroy them completely.

The weather on February eighth was worse, if possible, than it had been all the previous week. The wind was a ravening monster, eating warmth and hurling icy snow. Sabrina was so cold, even wrapped in shawls and sitting so close to the stove that the wool was singeing, that she could not do her needlework. She sat staring stonily out into the driving snow, nursing her painful hope, telling herself that there really was a good chance Perce was alive. Surely if an English aide-de-camp to Bennigsen were dead or missing, word would have filtered back by now to the British envoy.

There could be many reasons why Perce had not written. He might have hurt his hand; he might be too busy. That supposition was very painful. She could not imagine being too busy under the same circumstances, not too busy for a few words just to assure a woman who loved him that he was alive. She blanked her mind on that, saying aloud, "How dreadful the snow and wind are today."

"Yes, luv," Katy answered eagerly. She was painfully eager to make conversation on any subject; she, too, thought Lord Kevern was dead, and his man also, or Sergei would have come to tell them, but she dared not mention either name. "And it's strange weather, too. I keep hearin' thunder, very faint and far away. But this isna the season for thunder."

"Thunder?" Sabrina repeated, gladly seizing on something to think about. "That would be odd."

She listened for a while and heard nothing but the high-pitched howl of the wind. Just as she was about to shake her head negatively, however, a wind blast struck the house from a different direction and, quite clearly, there was a very faint, heavy grumble under the higher-pitched sounds.

"There!" Katy exclaimed, her eyes brightening at having distracted Sabrina for even a few minutes. "Isna that strange?"

Rubbing her icy hands, Sabrina stood up and walked to the window to peer out. It was snowing so hard that one could not see through it any more than one can see through a fog. However, the gusts, changing direction every few minutes, often opened a brief window in the veil of flakes. In one of these Sabrina caught sight of the sky.

"I suppose the weather may be different where the thunder is," she said at last, looking rather puzzled, "but you know, Katy, that isn't the kind of sky thunder comes from."

"Now what can ye mean, luv?" Katy asked.

She was not the least interested. Having left the island where fishing, and therefore weather, was a major part of life, she had abandoned interest in the weather beyond the need to dress Brina appropriately. Now, however, she would have professed an interest in higher mathematics or whether pigs had wings if only Brina were willing to talk about either subject.

"I'm not sure, but thunder always seems to come from a billowy sky. That sounds dreadfully silly. I just can't describe what I mean, only the clouds seem sort of flat and high up, you know, the kind that make a daylong drizzle instead of the kind that make a thunderstorm."

To encourage Brina, Katy also came to stand by the window and watch for a break in the snow during which she could examine the sky. Since there had been a time when she was ardently interested in the weather, Katy did understand what Brina had said when she caught a glimpse of the dull, even cloud cover. Nonetheless, intermittently throughout the day when the wind blew from inland rather than from the ocean, a deep grumble could be barely perceived.

It was something to talk about, and Sabrina mentioned it to William at dinner that evening.

"Thunder!" he exclaimed, "that's not thunder. There's a life-and-death battle going on in Eylau. I was going to warn you to pack a small bag of utter necessities for us in case we must try to escape."

Sabrina turned so pale that her husband told her sharply to drink some wine. Numbly, she obeyed, but it was not fear for herself that had sapped her color.

"I will go back to Lord Hutchinson, but I don't want you to expose yourself to this weather, and anyhow, you're closer to the stable here. Besides, I don't think we will need to run. The news we have had from Eylau so far is not all bad, and even if it should grow worse, we will have adequate warning. Just try to forget about it."

"No. Tell me, please. You must tell me whatever you've heard."

Her eyes were staring wide, the white showing all

215

around the lovely dark ring that edged her iris. William began to utter some soothing remarks, but realized these were only increasing Sabrina's distress. He did not want her hysterical, confusing the servants and causing delays if they did need to escape.

"Now, Sabrina, there's no need for a fit of the vapors," William went on sharply. "I don't know what's come over you recently. You've turned into a watering pot, sniveling all the time. You should be accustomed to diplomatic cold shoulders by now and not take such slights to heart."

"The battle," Sabrina stammered, "the battle . . . Who? Who is in it?"

"Both complete armies, the Russians and Prussians joined against the French, so far as we can tell. Now, I'm sorry to have frightened you," he added hastily, seeing that even her lips were turning white and she was clinging to the table for support. "Actually, I doubt very strongly that there will be any need for us to leave Königsberg."

"I don't care about leaving Königsberg," Sabrina said. "I'll be ready. I want to hear about the battle."

William raised his brows, but he was not really surprised. Some women were dreadfully bloodthirsty; possibly it was excitement that was making Sabrina so pale. "I will tell you what I can, which naturally is not very much. Last night the Russians were surprised by Murat's French cavalry and some of Soult's French mounted forces and driven out of Eylau. However, the Russians counterattacked strongly, took back the town, and set up their artillery and most of the infantry on a ridge. This was an enormous advantage. I understand whole regiments of Saint Hilare's corps were mowed down by grapeshot, and the Twenty-fourth Regiment, thirty-six hundred men, was utterly wiped out."

More bodies, more bodies that women had borne and loved and kissed, to lie rotting under the earth. Sabrina lowered tear-filled eyes. She was quite sure it was not the

216

French alone that had taken such losses. Nonetheless she understood that she had made a mistake. No one could have any information about individuals, and even if such information existed, it would be worthless since the battle had been going on for hours after any news William could have received had come in.

William accepted Sabrina's seemingly restored calm with relief. He left hurriedly before the light failed, not wanting to struggle through dark as well as snow. As soon as he left the room, Sabrina pushed away her untouched food. She went to the sitting room and just sat. Her mind could not have been more blank or her emotions more dead if she had been unconscious. She did not hear the doorbell ring several hours later, nor did she hear the door of the sitting room open. Katy had to shake her before she blinked her staring eyes and turned her head to ask dully what was wanted.

"It's a note from Himself," Katy said. "Ye've got to read it, Brina. Charlot told me we may be in bad trouble."

"Oh, yes, I forgot." She had not packed the bags or told Katy to do so, but it did not seem very important. Not looking at what she was doing, she opened the folded paper. An enclosure dropped out, but she did not see it. Katy shook her again, and she focused her eyes.

A packet of papers was sent over from Prussian headquarters, William wrote. *The enclosed letter was with them. Since I know you have been anxious about Lord Kevern, I thought you should have it immediately. In haste. William.*

Sabrina gaped at the note, literally gaped, her mouth opening in surprise.

"Brina," Katy pleaded, "wake up, baby. What's to do?"

"Enclosed," Sabrina breathed, turning the note over and over in her hands, "but there was nothing enclosed."

"Yes, luv, here it is." Katy picked up the fallen paper

and put it in Sabrina's hand. It was open, without a seal, and had no doubt been read.

"Perce!" Sabrina shrieked as soon as she saw the handwriting. "Oh, my God! Perce!"

For a moment she was so blinded by tears that she could not read, but she rubbed her eyes fiercely. *Seventh of February, Preussisch Eylau,* she made out. *My dear Sabrina. Since you did not answer my note of the thirtieth of January with a refusal, I must assume you are expecting to see me on the tenth of this month. I deeply regret that it may not be possible for me to pay the promised visit. All leaves have been canceled. I do not know the reason, but I beg you will not be concerned. Very likely it is no great matter. Remember me to all with deepest love. Your humble servant, etc., Perce.*

"His note of the thirtieth!" Sabrina exclaimed. "I never got it. He must have written before that, too."

"I told ye not to worrit," Katy cried, her voice almost vicious with relief. "A bad penny is bound to turn up again, I said. And all that worritin! Ye druv me near crazy."

In fact, Katy had not told Sabrina not to worry, but Sabrina made no denial. She was rereading the precious paper that told her Perce was still alive. Its formal tone did not bother her. She guessed that the request for permission to visit her had been phrased just as formally. Then if her husband had read it, she could simply be "at home" and receive him as a visitor, whereas if she had received the note herself and was sure no one else had seen its contents, she could have devised a way for them to be alone. A dreadful pang of regret passed through Sabrina. She *hated* the French, who had interfered with her meeting Perce. Could they not have waited ten days before renewing the fighting?

No sooner was the thought formed than Sabrina broke into hysterical laughter. How ridiculous to be angry because a war between great nations did not wait upon the meeting of two individuals. How ridiculous to be angry at all when she had just been assured that the man she loved was alive rather than dead and rotting. Joy filled her, lifted her so that she felt as if she were floating, flying—and in the instant, terror seized her and crushed her down.

All she really knew was that Perce had been alive yesterday, before the battle began.

Katy could read her Brina and saw the succession of emotions. "Dinna ye start again," she snapped. "It's been enough this month past. Have some sense, girl. He came through the last bloodbath. He's a bad penny, I tell ye. He'll turn up fine. Dinna think other! Ye'll bring it on!"

Sabrina blinked. It was an old superstition of the isles: to think of evil drew evil. She swallowed and tried to smile. The attempt did not quite succeed, but Katy was heartened that Sabrina had tried. She was less troubled by the grief and pain that showed on Brina's face than by the deadness that had been growing worse and worse over the past month. Grief and pain came into every life; she would have saved Brina from them if she could. But if she could not, Brina must fight and live through them.

Katy had been frightened by the way Brina had retreated into herself as if, having been hurt differently each time, she would close out the possibility of love. Katy had loved the husband she had lost, but she had not deliberately rejected the idea of marrying again. There simply had not been another man who attracted her. That Sergei now, if he came alive out of this . . . *No*, Katy told herself. It wouldn't do. A decent woman couldn't accept a man who wanted to be a slave.

"You know that's only superstition," Sabrina said.

"Maybe so," Katy rejoined briskly, "but it doesna hurt to be on the safe side."

That drew a wan smile. It wasn't really true. It did hurt to hope. Sabrina had realized that she really had not

219

hoped all the long month past. Now the tearing alternation of terror and joy were racking her. But resist as she might, Katy's superstition had a hold on her, too. She felt she *must* believe Perce was alive; she must *not* see him as hurt or dead. Still, the images would recur, no matter how firmly she thrust them out of her mind. Abruptly she stood up.

"I think I'll go up to bed," she said to Katy. "I've been cold all day. There isn't any sense in sitting here when my hands are so cold I can't work."

"Do that, luv," Katy agreed. "I'll bring ye a tray for supper. Himself won't be back, and it's easier when all's said than settin' up the dinin' room."

They parted in the corridor, Sabrina climbing up and Katy going down the stairs. Katy knew that there was no sense in trying to keep Sabrina company. Besides, she had her own worries to bury, and the best way to do that was to give the kitchen a good scouring and maybe polish all the furniture. If she had to sit and watch Sabrina, she would soon be just as bad. They would make each other worse.

If Sabrina had known Katy's intentions, she might have helped to polish the furniture. She had seized on a different way to direct her thoughts along positive lines. She hurried up the stairs as fast as she could go and tugged at the bearskin in the closet. After a few minutes she discarded her shawl and went back to work. She had had no conception of how heavy and awkward the rug was. It took a long time and furious effort before she hauled it out, dragged it across the floor, and lifted, shoved, pulled, and twisted it until it lay on her bed.

Sabrina found herself drenched in sweat but grinning with triumph. She pulled off all her clothing, got into the bed, and wrapped herself completely in the pelt. She did not care if Katy thought she was mad, lying naked in a bearskin. The feel of the coarse fur against her body and the warmth it was generating around her would bring memories of Perce pulsating with life. That was how she needed to hold him in her mind, kissing her or scolding her, but all the time, whatever he was doing, alive and loving her.

The device worked very well. Sabrina did not realize how sure she had been that only death could keep Perce from writing to her or visiting her when he was only twenty-three miles away. Now, although terrified of losing him again, she could believe he was alive. A month of broken nights, of lying awake while silent tears rolled, of struggling with grief—topped by the physical effort of getting the bearskin on the bed—brought first exhaustion and very soon oblivion.

When Katy silently looked in an hour and a half later, Sabrina was deeply asleep. She slept right through suppertime, and Katy wisely did not disturb her, although periodically she thought she would burst with curiosity. Surely there were easier and cleaner ways of warming oneself than dragging a heavy bearskin, which had been used as a rug, onto one's bed. Eventually Katy was exhausted also. Never had the living room and sitting room furniture gleamed so brightly; never had the kitchen been so spotlessly clean; Katy, too, slept peacefully.

Charlot did not much care who lived or died, except himself. Nonetheless he found it very difficult to sleep. Residence in Prussia had been growing increasingly uncomfortable, not only because of the demeaning work in a house he considered shameful but also the increasing animosity of the natives.

And if the French took Königsberg, would it be possible, Charlot wondered, to claim to be French? Or would he be accused of being a traitor for serving an English lord? He lay awake, turning over in his mind the various expedients. He was not disloyal to Lord Elvan, who had been a reasonably good master. Among other matters, he even considered whether his French background might be helpful to the family he served.

Suddenly, he stiffened. A horse had trotted down the street. Charlot had not identified the sound at once because the noise of the hooves was muffled by the snow. It was too late to see who the horseman had been. Restlessly, Charlot turned, but his ears were attuned now, and it seemed to him he heard more horses. Hurriedly, he rose from his bed, wrapped himself warmly, and went into the darkened shop to watch the activity on the street.

Charlot had just about decided his fevered imagination had created the sounds, when two more mounted men went by, the horses plodding wearily with hanging heads. Then, after a shorter interval, two more, and then a group. The weather had finally cleared, and the moon, reflected off the snow, gave sufficient light to see that the uniforms were those of Russian officers and that most of them were streaked and spattered with dark stains that Charlot knew without closer examination were blood. He rushed back to his room and threw on his clothes, then up the stairs to pound on Lady Elvan's door, crying of the need to escape.

Startled awake, Katy and Sabrina shouted questions, but Charlot had not remained to answer them. He had run down again to pull on his coat. He intended to run out to question anyone who went by, but he suddenly realized he did not dare ask questions in French. Even though nearly all of the Russian nobility spoke French, their reaction to that language at this moment might not be friendly. By this time Katy had pulled on her shoes and stockings and a heavy dressing gown and was calling questions down the stairwell. Charlot ran up again, halfway, to describe what he had seen. Meanwhile, Sabrina had also found a dressing gown and slippers and came out onto the landing.

"Stop shouting at each other," she ordered. "What the devil do you mean, we must escape?"

Stumbling over his words, all condescending dignity

gone, Charlot described the Russian troops heading northeast through the town. "They are retreating," he cried. "The French will follow. We must escape!"

"To where?" Sabrina snapped. "Don't be a fool! Lord Hutchinson's house is more likely to be attacked than ours, and we might not even be safe in the streets getting there. If Lord Elvan has not taken his pistols, bring them to me. After that, see if you can secure the windows in the shop. Katy, you get my muff guns. We will defend the house if we must."

Cursing his fate, Charlot found the pistols and set about blocking the ground-floor windows. His impulse was still to run, but Lady Elvan's objections made sense to him, and while he was busy he felt better. Still, more and more men straggled down the street, and by the time he had finished securing the windows, about an hour later, many soldiers were on foot, staggering, falling, and picking themselves up to stagger farther. That made Charlot more nervous than ever. That men so exhausted should be desperate enough to struggle on was a very bad sign about what was following them. Charlot again began to think of escape.

Indecisiveness held him for nearly another hour. He had been to the back door several times, but had returned because he knew his job would be forfeit if he left. Still, when the bell pealed, he jumped about a foot in the air and stood panting, undecided whether to run out through the back or answer the door. The bell pealed again, louder and longer. Someone was yanking desperately on the pull.

Clatter of shoes on the stairs and Katy's voice, low and tense, "Who's that? Charlot, who's at the door?"

The bell rang still again. Sabrina, now completely dressed, came halfway down the stairs, a long-nosed pistol in each hand. "Answer the door," she called softly. Then, angrily but still in a low voice, "Charlot, answer the door."

He came from the back reluctantly, more because he realized there was no escape, than out of obedience. It had occurred to him that he could run out the back way, but then he would have to come out on the main street anyway. Sabrina gestured toward the door.

"Open it and get out of the way," she hissed.

Katy was a little farther down the stairs, flattened against the wall so she would not be in the way if Sabrina had to shoot, but able to throw herself between her "baby" and any invader if the guns did not stop them. The lamp Charlot carried picked up a cold glitter by the side of her skirt where the fish-gutting knife was only partially concealed. Charlot shuddered. The bell rang again. This time Sabrina pointed one gun at him.

"I said open the door and step out of the way of my pistol," she ordered, her voice now loud and angry. "If they break the door down, we'll be in worse trouble."

As if in response to hearing Sabrina, a muffled voice called through the door, "Charlot! Katy! Open up."

With answering shrieks of joy, all three made a concerted rush for the door, Sabrina first uncocking her weapons and laying them on a nearby counter. Joy changed to terror on the instant. Perce and Sergei stood wavering in the doorway, both covered with blood. Sabrina's mouth opened to scream, but Katy's work-hardened hand closed on her arm like a vise.

"They walked," she said loudly. "They canna be hurt bad." Katy said "they," but her eyes were on Sergei.

And before her words died away, Perce said in most formally polite tones, "Can you put us up, Brina?" His voice wavered on the last word, and his eyes slid upward under his lids. "I don't think—"

It was impossible to tell whether Sergei was supporting Perce or vice versa. Sabrina jumped to catch her lover; Katy grasped Sergei's arm. Perce tried to rally for a moment.

"There were no more horses," he said softly. "They were dead, all dead. It—it was a long walk."

His voice was very odd, his face stiff, flecked with the dead white of frostbite, but Sabrina didn't care. Katy was right. No one could be badly hurt and walk twenty-three miles. She slid her shoulder under his arm and pulled him toward her, away from Sergei. Simultaneously, Katy pulled Sergei to the side. His knees started to buckle, and she made no attempt to hold his great weight upright, only supporting him enough so that he was eased down to the floor rather than falling hard. Meanwhile, Sabrina had given a sharp order to Charlot that jolted him out of his paralysis.

Between them Sabrina and Charlot half carried Perce up the two flights of stairs. Sabrina had thought of stopping in the sitting room to save a flight of struggle, but there was no place for Perce to lie down, and she had no intention of making him wait until Charlot could find and erect an extra bed. Besides, the bedding would be freezing cold, and Perce didn't need any more cold. She tugged the bearskin to the floor while Charlot held him, then laid him down right on top of the quilts.

"I'll manage here," she said over her shoulder to Charlot. "You go down and help Katy get Sergei into your bed. Then heat water in every pot we've got. Get the dining room and sitting room stoves going and heat water on them, too."

Sabrina had heard Katy shutting and bolting the door while they went upstairs, so there was no need to worry about that. Perce's eyes were already closed. Sabrina shook him hard. He moaned but did not open his eyes. She shook him hard again.

"One question, Perce, only one. Open your eyes. Only one question."

The lids parted slightly. "Wha'?"

"Are the French coming? How long do we have?"

"Dead," he mumbled, his eyes closing again. "All dead
. . . all dead . . . French . . . Russians . . . all dead.
Never saw . . . never saw so many dead . . . dead. . . ."

CHAPTER TWELVE

Sabrina stood still for a moment, frowning. She wondered how much reliance could be placed on what Perce had told her, but then she shrugged and began to tug at his boots. Perce could go no farther in any case, nor could Sergei, and there was no way she, Katy, and Charlot could carry them. To send a message with what Perce had told her to William would surely be carrying coals to Newcastle. William must know the situation better than she. If there had been any immediate danger and a need to escape from Königsberg, he would have sent her word to get the carriage ready.

The boots had come off, although Perce's feet were so swollen it had taken all Sabrina's strength to remove them. His socks were black and stiff with blood, and she carefully cut them off, with a distasteful shudder. Then she rolled him to the side and pulled on the sleeve of his greatcoat. Perce protested querulously, but she paid no attention. Even if they had to leave soon, he would be better off if she could get him warmed and into dry garments. Between the sweat of exertion and the snow and sleet that had melted on him, he was soaked through.

By the time Charlot came laboring up the stairs with a pail of hot water and a pot of cold that could be set on the flat top of the stove that warmed the bedchamber, Sabrina had removed all Perce's clothes, tucked him into the bed, and stirred up the fire. All the valet's cool superiority had been reestablished. He gave a shocked glance at the heap of filthy, discarded clothing as he set the pot on the stove and the pail beside the bed.

"You will be glad to hear, my lady, that we seem to be in no danger from the French. From what we can make out, the withdrawal was planned. The lack of horses was owing to the ferocity of the battle, I understand. Do you wish me to attend to Lord Kevern now?"

Sabrina flashed him a single glance, but there was as much amusement in it as contempt. Just now, everything amused her because she was certain Perce had no serious injury. There was a nasty saber cut on his forearm that had been roughly bandaged and needed to be sewed and dressed, a smaller slash above the knee, and what looked like a bullet graze in the flesh between the neck and shoulder. Sabrina had almost fainted when she saw that. Not that the wound in itself was at all dangerous, but two inches to the left and Perce would have been dead.

"No," she replied dryly. "There is no longer any part of Lord Kevern with which I am unacquainted. Please find some old linen suitable for tearing into bandages and make strips about two or three inches wide. I will also need a sponge, a bowl, some rice powder, lint, and sticking plaster. When you have brought those, you had better find the extra beds and bedding. You can put one in Lord Elvan's chamber and, I suppose, one in the sitting room."

"Then Lord Kevern and his—er—man will be staying."

"I would imagine so. If the whole army has fallen back on Königsberg, every inn and hotel will be full. It will be better to shelter Lord Kevern than to have God-knows-who quartered on us."

"Yes, indeed, my lady."

Although Charlot's expression was properly wooden, Sabrina was sure that what she had said would reconcile him somewhat to Sergei's presence. She was growing a little impatient with Charlot's airs and graces, but this was certainly not the time to reprimand him. That would only turn him sullen and even more disagreeable. And, after all, he was William's servant. Sabrina looked at Perce's sleeping face. If only she could think of a way of freeing herself from William, she would not need to put up with his servant, either. But for now Charlot was necessary.

When he returned with what she had asked for, Sabrina sent him out for a surgeon, but he was soon back with the news that there was not a doctor to be had. Fortunately, William returned soon after nine o'clock to tell Sabrina that all was safe and to get some rest. He sent Charlot out again with a message to Lord Hutchinson, who contrived to lay his hands upon a harried Prussian doctor. He sewed Perce up in short order, extracted a bullet from the fleshy part of Sergei's arm, and left the house, having said hardly a word.

After the doctor left, William courteously stepped in to to ask how Perce was, and found Sabrina carrying out an empty bottle of his best brandy. Having remembered the tale of how Pierre Restoir had washed Megaera's wounded head with brandy and of how it had healed perfectly clean, without suppuration, Sabrina had used William's choicest supply on her patients. William did not, like Sabrina and Philip, think that the Breton pirate was an oracle on any out-of-the-way subject. Actually, he did not even know of Pierre's existence. He took exception to Sabrina's "idiocy." Good French brandy, he protested, was hard to obtain in enemy territory.

Ignoring such pettiness, Sabrina followed him into his bedchamber. "I won't keep you long," she said when William informed her coldly that he had sat up all night and would like to get some sleep. "I know you must be tired, but can you tell me what happened? All Perce kept saying was 'dead, dead.' They walked. Sergei told Katy that Perce's horses were all killed, and he gave the screws they were riding to some medical officer for carts for the wounded."

"I don't know the whole, of course," William replied somewhat more civilly, "but it seems it was a bloodbath on both sides, and totally inconclusive. Bennigsen withdrew his army—what remains of it—so I suppose Bonaparte will claim a victory, but the truth is, he must be much more hurt than the Russians."

" 'Inconclusive' means there will be another battle?" Sabrina asked, horror in her voice.

"I shouldn't think so. At least, not immediately. Probably not until spring. In that sense, it is unfortunate that the Russians were so badly mauled. If they could have attacked again, it is likely the French would have suffered a defeat. However, it will be far more difficult for Bonaparte to replace the men than for Alexander to do so, and the French army is far from home without shelter and supplies."

Sabrina stared blankly for a moment. She could feel tears prickling behind her eyes. Replace the men, he said, but one couldn't replace the men. They were dead, and their mothers, sisters, wives, and sweethearts would suffer. How could one "replace" a man? Could Perce be "replaced" for her if he had died?

"There's nothing to be frightened of now, Sabrina," William said, misreading her expression. "Although Bonaparte took Preussisch Eylau, observers report that the condition of his army makes it impossible that he should even consider advancing on Königsberg. The expectation is that he will pull back, and if he does, it will have to be west of the Vistula, since the Russians have made a desert of the land between here and the river."

"But everyone will starve," Sabrina cried.

William snorted. "There probably isn't anyone left to starve. I imagine those who aren't dead ran away long ago. In any case, it's nothing for you to worry about. We are going back to England as soon as a ship can sail. It's impossible now to negotiate, unless the government will give us something with which to negotiate. Lord Hutchinson desires me to try to convince Windham to commit a force of at least twenty-five thousand."

"Going back to England?" Sabrina nearly glanced over her shoulder at the room across the corridor in which Perce lay sleeping, but she controlled the gesture in time.

"Yes," William said, "and you will remain there. I do not like the temper of the people or the court. And we must have a reckoning also, my dear. I have been too busy and too worried to attend to personal matters, but—"

"Yes, we must," Sabrina agreed, with a tinge of amusement. "Whenever you are at leisure, just let me know. But I'm sure you are too tired now."

"Yes, I am, but I wish to thank you, Sabrina, for being so considerate as not to put Lord Kevern in my bed."

"I never thought of it," Sabrina blurted out, and then had sense enough to add, "I thought he might need nursing, and it would be more convenient if there were two beds in the room."

William smiled at her without replying. She had been an idiot about the brandy, but it was clear to him that she had deliberately sacrificed her comfort to his. The way he looked at her annoyed Sabrina so much she was shaken by the impulse to tell him the truth. She mastered it, knowing a confession would only increase her difficulties, and there could hardly be a less appropriate moment for it. Somewhat flushed with anger, which simply convinced William that his notion was correct, she left the room without another word.

Sabrina stepped back into her own bedroom, but Perce had not even stirred in his sleep. The quilts were as smooth as when she had tucked them around him. Indeed, even the pain of being stitched up had hardly kept his eyes open. She thought briefly of sitting by his bed or even lying down beside it on the bearskin, which was on the floor, then laughed at herself for being a romantic fool. There was nothing really wrong with Perce. When he had slept off his exhaustion, he would be ravenous. In fact, Sabrina realized, she was ravenous herself.

No regular breakfast had been prepared, and Sabrina ran down to the kitchen to snatch some bread and cheese, but Katy said she would bring tea and sandwiches to the sitting room in a few minutes. She stirred up the stove and stoked it, and when Katy came up with the promised provisions, Sabrina fell on them with enthusiasm. She had eaten nothing the previous night and had not eaten terribly well for a long time. Since the house was all at sixes and sevens, Katy broke her usual rule not to seem to be other than a trusted servant except when privacy was assured, and sat down to eat with Sabrina.

"How's Sergei?" Sabrina asked through her chewing.

"Ye canna hurt an ox like that wi' a bullet or two," Katy replied dryly. "He's asleep again, after nearly cleanin' out the larder. Will Himself be home for dinner? And how about Lord Kevern? Will he be wantin' an invalid diet?"

"I think he'll be wanting a roasted ox—whole," Sabrina said. "I can't see that there's much wrong with him either. The worst is his feet. Riding boots aren't the best footwear for long walks in deep snow. He'll be lame for a while. Oh, damn! I should have asked William for slippers, but he'll probably wake before Perce does. I don't know whether he'll be in for dinner. Don't bother with a real meal. Can you make a stew that can be hotted up a few times?"

"Surely. And I'll do a roast, too. Them that eats when it's ready will have it hot. Later it can be served cold."

"Whatever you like, so long as you aren't too tired. Can I help?"

232

"Ye can stay out of my kitchen. That'll be my best help," Katy warned, laughing.

"It's just as well," Sabrina agreed. "I'll begin packing. William just told me that we'll go back to England on the first ship that sails."

Katy flashed a swift glance at Sabrina, but there was little to be read from her expression; it was simply thoughtful. *She doesna know yet,* Katy thought, *she doesna know whether Kevern will be goin' back to England, too. But whatever he does, she must go. It isna safe here.*

Oddly enough, those were the first words Perce said when he opened his eyes. They fell on Sabrina, kneeling beside a trunk into which she was packing her ball gowns.

"Thank God you're going home," he said, levering himself up on an elbow. "It isn't safe here."

Sabrina jumped to her feet. "You aren't supposed to say that," she protested, smiling at him. "You're supposed to say, 'Where am I?' Or groan dramatically to draw the nurse's attention."

For answer, Perce held out the arm that was not supporting him and drew her close when she placed herself within it. "I know where I am," he sighed after their lips parted. "I'm in heaven, being greeted by an angel."

Sabrina drew back a little to look at him suspiciously. In the throes of passion Perce might murmur sweet nothings, but such an exaggeration—heaven, angel—was most likely teasing. However, there was no laughter in his face. His eyes were dark with remembered horror, and he was trembling a little. She clutched him tight momentarily and then pulled away gently and said, as prosaically as she could, "You must be very hungry. Do you think you could walk if I fetched you a pair of slippers, or would you rather have a tray in bed?" As she spoke she reached under the bed and drew out the chamber pot, which she handed to him, turning her back politely while he used it.

He groaned as he shoved it back under the bed, after which he asked, "What day is this, and what time?"

"It's the ninth, about four o'clock."

"I have to let General Bennigsen know where I am," he said.

"I can send Charlot with a note," Sabrina offered. "Or perhaps it would be better to send the note to William. He's gone back to Lord Hutchinson. They could send a German servant from there. Charlot is afraid to wander around the city because of being French."

"I don't care who takes it, but it will have to go to Prussian headquarters. I don't know where Bennigsen is. I can only hope they'll know there. Bennigsen didn't decide to withdraw until it was dark. He thought . . . right up to the end, he thought we would take back Eylau."

Perce shuddered, reached for Sabrina, and pulled her tightly against him. Then he kissed her again and pushed himself more upright to a sitting position. Sabrina sat down beside him on the edge of the bed.

"What are you going to say?" she asked. "Are you going to resign? Perce . . . please. It's a miracle you're alive."

"It's a miracle any of us are alive," he said harshly, and then, more gently, "No, I'm not going to resign. This was the most horrible thing I've ever lived through, but the worst of it is that it was all for *nothing*. Nothing was decided by this battle. There are thousands dead, tens of thousands, and I don't know how many more are maimed and will die—and we're right back where we started."

"It isn't your war," Sabrina cried.

"Don't be a fool. If Boney beats Russia, England will be all alone against him. If I can read the handwriting on the wall, it may help."

Sabrina swallowed. "You expect Bonaparte to win."

Perce looked out past her, his eyes still heavy after twelve hours of sleep. "Bonaparte will beat Bennigsen," he said flatly. "I wasn't sure after Pultusk. There we held a great advantage on the ground, but they had more men. This time we had most of the advantages. Our men were better fed, more rested, and far more accustomed to the weather. We had the advantage of higher ground. Everything else was about even. The men——" He clenched his teeth, swallowed, and began again. "I've never seen such dogged courage, such heroism . . . on both sides. Still, we should have rolled over them. Boney just outmaneuvered Bennigsen. Of course, his generals are better, too, or more eager."

"But William was saying that Bonaparte was hurt worse because he's short of manpower and far from his base."

"That's true enough, but we weren't in any shape to go after him. The advantage will evaporate with time. There's another problem. Bennigsen's going to play up Boney's losses and play down our own. That's his way, and also he doesn't want to be superseded by another general. That will make double trouble. We'll get fewer replacements, more slowly—and Bennigsen will stay in command."

"But I don't see what it has to do with you," Sabrina protested desperately. "It seems to me that if you're so sure Bonaparte will win the next battle, it's a better reason to resign now. Boney doesn't like the English. If you get captured—"

"Sabrina."

The one word, sad, touched with a longing that was already being denied, stopped her.

"Bennigsen doesn't trust anyone," Perce went on quietly, "but he has come nearest to trust with me. He knows I don't wish to be a general in the Russian army, and my rank isn't high enough for me to steal any of his glory, so he doesn't need to worry about me stabbing him in the back to gain promotion. He thinks I'm an English spy, which is true, I suppose, but he doesn't care about that right now because he understands that British aims and his

235

aims are pretty much the same—to beat Boney. After Pultusk he even talked to me a little about his plans and used me almost exclusively as a liaison with the other generals."

"But—"

"Sabrina, surely you must see that this places me in an advantageous position for gathering information. Now, if Bennigsen retains command and is defeated in the next major battle, it will be very important to discover whether Alexander will continue to fight or will make terms. And if he makes terms, what terms. It is crucial for the English to have the inside information that I can provide for them."

"I'm sorry, Perce," Sabrina whispered. "I'm frightened. I didn't get any of your letters after the battle of Pultusk, except the one you wrote on the seventh. I thought you were dead. It hurt so much. I can't . . . I'm afraid."

He pulled her close and kissed her again. "If it's any consolation," he said, smiling, after their lips parted, "I'm scared nearly witless myself. I don't want to see another battle like this. But I have to stay with it, Brina." He hugged her once more, fiercely, then grinned at her. "Where's this dinner I've been promised?"

"I'm thinking of withdrawing the offer," she said, blinking back tears. "Any man who talks politics instead of answering my thoughtful question about where he wants dinner served isn't hungry."

Perce was looking at her fixedly, and he brought a hand up to trace the line of her cheek with his finger. Then he ran it down her throat, along the edge of her spencer where it lay open to expose the front of her low-cut gown.

"Maybe I'm not so hungry," he murmured.

Sabrina made a wordless sound, whether of invitation or protest she did not know herself as Perce bent forward to kiss the cleft between her breasts. She thought guiltily that he must be starved, but such practical considerations were already fading from her mind. He pushed the spencer off her shoulder, and then pulled at the sleeve. When that arm was bare, Sabrina used the hand to play with Perce's hair and touch his ear. He pulled the sleeve off her other arm, dropped the spencer to the floor, and plucked at the tie that held Sabrina's gown in under her breasts. That was easily undone, but when he began to tug the dress off her shoulder, Sabrina lifted her head.

"Don't. You'll tear it," she whispered.

That would be impossible to explain. Perce desisted. "Take it off, then," he said thickly.

It was crazy. Katy might walk in on them. Sabrina stood up and pulled the dress off over her head. She didn't care if the whole Grande Armée walked in on them. She would have to go back to England, and Perce would have to stay. God alone knew when she would see him and touch him again. She was not leaving because William was going, not because of conventionality. At this moment Sabrina would gladly have offered to remain openly as Perce's mistress, but she knew she would be a burden and a danger to him.

"You are so beautiful," Perce murmured, watching as she removed her underclothes, "all of you. It's quite dreadful. I can't even look at the snow without thinking of you. Your skin has the same silvery shine. Sometimes I would reach out and touch a drift. The wind carves them into shapes—a shoulder, a hip—and I would be surprised because they were cold."

His voice was a low monotone, like that of a man mesmerized, but Sabrina felt as if it were touching her. And when he reached out and ran a hand caressingly over her shoulder and hip, the sensation seemed part of the vocal caress. She stood quite still, aware of the need to hurry, that delay might mean detection, but she was quite indifferent to the danger. It was more important to enjoy and be enjoyed than to be safe.

"Now I'm surprised that you are warm," Perce said.

"Am I dying in that hell out there, dreaming of my snow maiden?"

He pulled her close suddenly, fiercely, burrowing his face between her breasts so hard he hurt her. Sabrina stroked his hair, still speckled with blood that was not his own, which she had not been able to wash out, mute evidence of agony or death that had brushed close by him. Her other hand stroked his back, feeling the play of hard muscle, the shoulder blades and ribs too prominent from loss of weight.

The feel of her body seemed, at least for this moment, to block ugly memory. Perce relaxed his grip somewhat and began to kiss her, then leaned back slowly, drawing her with him until the edge of the bed touched her thighs. He released her completely then and slid down, lifting the quilts at the same time so she could slip in beside him. As soon as she was in the bed, he clutched her close again, as if the brief loss of contact had unleashed the horrors that plagued him. And, for all his eagerness, he was not ready.

Sabrina had no difficulty connecting the fearful words *Am I dying in that hell out there, dreaming* . . . with Perce's impotence. *Dreaming*. When a man dreams, she assumed, he is the aggressor. All she could think of was that she must make herself real to him, and she began to caress him more actively, more intimately, copying his own actions the last time they had made love. He uttered a soft exclamation of surprise as she began to run her lips down his body, but the sound soon changed to incoherent murmurs of pleasure.

The warm, wet mouth, the tiny scrape of teeth, worked a near-immediate miracle of resurrection. Perce moaned, tried to heave his hips upward, and desisted with a gasp as pain lanced through his abused feet. He had to lie still, and for some reason that made what Sabrina was doing more exciting. He pulled at her, kissing and sucking whatever part presented itself to his mouth.

Meanwhile, Sabrina found she was as much stimulated by her activities as was her lover, and his nearly drove her wild. She yielded when Perce pulled her up urgently and helped her mount him. She had been so excited by readying him, that she came to climax at once, with his first few thrusts, but he was not nearly finished and succeeded in arousing her again so that she found herself convulsed with pleasure a second time, not quite so violently, but sweetly all the same.

They were quiet for a while, simply lying together in warm comfort, until Perce said softly, "Sorry to seem so unromantic, Brina, but I've got to have something to eat."

It was not true. He was hungry but would gladly have starved to keep the delight of lying warm and loving beside Sabrina. Only there was no delight. Perce was horribly aware of the stupidity of what he had done and the danger of discovery. He simply used the best excuse that would not hurt or frighten Sabrina to get her to leave the bed.

"Oh, goodness," she cried, getting up at once. "I forgot all about it. I'll run down and tell Katy."

"Not like that, in God's name," he laughed.

Sabrina made a "don't be silly" gesture and began to dress, making for the door as soon as her clothes were on. Perce stopped her with a hissed, "Your hair!" and she turned back and stooped by the mirror to pin up some strands that had fallen down altogether; however, she did not trouble to redo it, explaining that some disorder would be expected when she was in and out of closets and drawers to do the packing. The word brought them both up short, staring at each other. Perce started to speak, and then closed his mouth firmly. Sabrina waited a moment but then moved toward the door.

With her hand on the latch she said, "Stay in bed. I'll bring up a tray for you." And when it looked as if he would protest, "It's really easier than setting up the dining room, and it will be easier to talk, too. If you come down, Charlot will insist on serving."

"No gruel," Perce called after her as she went out, and he heard her laughing as she went down.

He slid down under the covers again, annoyed with himself for not reminding Sabrina to bring some clothing, but she had not forgotten. Charlot came in soon after she left with a shirt and smallclothes and a dressing gown. As Perce was inserted tenderly into the garments, Charlot explained that his breeches had not been salvageable; new nether garments were being made, using the old as a pattern, by a local tailor. They would be ready, hopefully, by the next morning.

Perce assumed the exquisite care in dressing him and the efficiency about the breeches were Charlot's attempts to demonstrate to him what he was missing by employing a boor like Sergei. Perce jerked his mind away from Sergei's finding him after that last bloody attempt to take back Eylau. They had all been in the fighting that time, even the general's aides, but there were only Ivan Petrovitch and himself left, and he wouldn't have been alive if not for Sergei. He couldn't think about it. If he did, he would begin to shake, and he would *not* shake in front of Charlot. He fixed his mind on Charlot's delicate drawing up over his legs of Elvan's smalls, and his lips twisted wryly. How unfortunate that he couldn't slip into Elvan's role with as little fuss as he slipped into his clothing.

Obviously, Sabrina was concerned with the same subject, but she was approaching it from a more practical angle. She allowed Perce to eat, which he did with considerable concentration, while she went on with her packing until he looked up from the plate of his own accord. Then Sabrina turned to face him.

"This morning when William came home to sleep for a few hours, he said we must have a reckoning. I'm going to tell him I want to end the marriage."

"No!" Perce exclaimed.

The color faded from Sabrina's face. "You want me to stay married to William?"

"Don't be a fool, Brina," he snapped. "There's nothing I want more than your freedom. That's why I don't want you to say anything to Elvan. Stall! Cry! Have hysterics or the vapors! Do anything you like, but *don't* discuss the matter with him until you talk to Roger. You're bound to say just the wrong thing."

There was good sense in that, but Sabrina felt a flicker of unease. Perce had said he wanted her to be free, but he hadn't said he wanted to marry her himself. She told herself she was a fool and called to memory the way he had clutched at her, not only for sex but for comfort.

"I'm not so sure it will be so easy to wait until I can speak with Roger," she said.

"Is William giving you trouble?" Perce asked tightly.

"No. He's been too busy. Diplomatically, the situation is a mess. But once we're on the ship, I don't know how we'll travel or what the accommodations will be."

Perce looked down at the remaining food on his tray as if he no longer recognized what it was. "I'll try to get leave," he said. "I'll come with you, and—"

Almost all the doubt Sabrina had felt dissipated. "No." She came up to the bed and put a hand on his. With her other hand she pulled his face toward her. "If I thought I could make you stay in England, I'd lie and say that would help. But I know you'll just turn around and come back here. By that time your precious general will have found a new favorite or will have decided there was some dreadful anti-Bennigsen motive for the trip. So, no. It wouldn't help, Perce."

"I could make him stay away from you," he said.

"I suppose you could, but that would be a disaster. You're a fine one to tell me I'd say the wrong thing. I'll manage." She let go of him. "Finish your dinner."

He began to eat again, more slowly, and Sabrina went back to her packing. After several more mouthfuls Perce said, "Would you get me something to write with, Sabrina?"

He wanted her out of the room for a few minutes because he was drowning in a flood of jealousy so violent that a lifetime of masking his expression would not be enough to hide this emotion. It was utterly ridiculous for him to be jealous. He knew it was ridiculous. Hadn't Sabrina just told him she intended to dissolve her marriage? And hadn't she made love to him in a way that . . . Where the devil had she learned *that*? Perce felt himself flush and thanked God Sabrina had left the room. He called himself an ungrateful idiot. He had needed it, and, out of love, she had given him what he needed. How dared he be jealous.

There was no sense to it. Perce knew why Sabrina had rejected his offer to travel with her. She was quite right. And Sabrina was not the kind to use people, at least not knowingly. The cold rage of jealousy caught him again. He thought of the dead on the battlefield, and each one of them had Lord Elvan's face.

The door opened, and Sabrina came in. She removed the empty soup bowl and set a small basket of bread down on the quilt so there was room on his tray for a sheet of paper and the inkwell. Perce wrote the few lines necessary to give his address and describe his condition to his senior officer, then folded the sheet, wrote Bennigsen's name on the flat surface, and took off his seal ring, which he handed to Sabrina.

"Will you seal it for me, please? Send it the best way to Prussian headquarters. Someone there will surely know where Bennigsen is by now."

"Perce, what's wrong?" she asked anxiously.

She knows me too well, he thought. "Nothing. Reaction, I suppose. I'm angry at the whole world."

242

It was the best he could do, and to his mingled shame and relief Sabrina accepted it. She was distressed because she knew she could not understand or share what he had suffered, but she was respectful of such pain, unlikely to prod at it. Perce was ashamed of playing on her feelings, but he comforted himself with the knowledge that the worry in her eyes held no personal hurt. Nonetheless he found he could not eat any more when Sabrina left to seal his letter, and he put the tray aside and swung his legs out of bed, frowning as he saw the condition of his feet. Served him right, he thought, for never setting a foot to the ground when a horse was available.

Then he passed a hand over his face. He would have to buy horses and saddles. No, maybe not saddles; Sergei had cached those when they gave up the horses—no, mules. He closed his eyes. By then there were no horses. They were all dead, poor beasts. Bravo, Major, Red. It wasn't fair that such beautiful, innocent creatures should die in a man's war. Tears burned behind his eyes, and he fought them back. He wouldn't think about it. He wouldn't.

Money . . . well, he had some. He and Sergei had carried the gold in money belts, but it wouldn't be enough to buy three or four good horses. And he had to live, too. That didn't matter. Either Elvan or Hutchinson would advance him what he needed, and he could give them a draft on his bank in London. He had a banker in St. Petersburg, too, but there wasn't time to write to him.

A more immediate problem was where to stay. It was courting disaster to remain here. He knew he would not be able to keep his hands off Sabrina, and she no longer seemed to care whether or not they were discovered. But that was stupid. There was some chance that Roger would be able to arrange an annulment. Then he would be able to marry her, which would be impossible if Elvan divorced her. There might be a few cold shoulders turned toward her after an annulment, but he hoped not many or for long. In any case, their children would be legitimate. It was all his own fault, too. How could he have been so stupid as not to know he loved her until she was beyond his reach?

Sabrina found him sitting on the edge of the bed with his head in his hands. "Perce, stop," she said. "Thinking about it can't help."

He straightened up. "It wasn't the battle, Brina. It's us. We've been lucky, but I'd better not stay here."

"I don't think you have much choice," she said. "I think every place is full." Her voice trembled a little on the words.

At first he didn't answer, just staring at her face, but then he shook his head. "It's no good, Brina. If I stay here, I'll have you in that bed again in no time. I don't know what's wrong with me. I want you all the time."

She blushed faintly, but didn't look displeased; in fact, she looked much happier. The passive attitude was very provocative, and Perce limped over to her and took her in his arms.

"You have to stay," she said softly. "If you don't, they'll quarter troops on us. Charlot told me that someone had been here already. Luckily, Sergei went to the door and said we were full. It will only be a few days." Her voice trembled again.

Perce tilted down the face raised so invitingly to his and pressed his lips to her hair. "We must be sensible then," he sighed, "at least until you talk with Roger. There just isn't any sense in losing whatever chance you have for an annulment."

"All right," she conceded. "We can go down to the sitting room. I'll get you some socks and slippers, but what you'll do for nether garments I don't know. Your breeches haven't come yet, and anyway, you can't wear breeches because you can't get those feet into boots. You can't wear William's pantaloons; they'd be too short."

"For right now it doesn't matter if they're short," he interrupted sharply, moving away from her.

Sabrina looked at him and giggled.

"Go and get me those goddamned pantaloons!" Perce roared.

Sabrina fled, laughing.

Once established in the sitting room where Charlot seemed to be popping in and out every few minutes with questions about how, where, and what was to be packed, the sexual tension between them diminished. A visit by Sir Robert in the evening to discuss the military situation as Perce understood it further eased the tension by directing their minds to other matters of great importance. Although Sir Robert was not as pessimistic as Perce, he agreed most heartily that Lord Kevern *must* remain with General Bennigsen.

Sabrina did not protest. She was accustomed to accepting what Perce said as wisdom and was already resigned to the separation. All she wanted to be reassured of was that there would be no more fighting, and in this she obtained satisfaction. There might be some small skirmishing, Sir Robert said, but the general's staff would not be involved in that. He did not believe that there would be a major action again until spring. That would be two or three months, Sabrina told herself, and anything might happen before then to keep Perce safe.

CHAPTER THIRTEEN

When Sabrina told Perce that she intended to end her marriage, she had not considered that she would be returning home at the beginning of the London social season. She had managed with effort to resist telling William on the ship that she desired an annulment. There had been a mild confrontation; William had requested one cabin to be shared, and Sabrina had made it plain that she and Katy would exchange accommodation if he insisted on that arrangement. When she convinced him she was serious, he had secured another cabin for himself, but he was furious.

Fortunately a ship was no place to try to tame one's wife, and William's stay in London was going to be brief. There was no sense in trying to cancel the rental of his own house. Instead, they stayed with Roger and Leonie. Naturally, William would not dare try any form of coercion in the vicinity of Sabrina's doting foster parents, and from Sabrina's point of view the situation had the additional advantage of making her estrangement from her husband nakedly apparent. Leonie knew already, of course, and Roger was not much surprised, having observed William's behavior when last the Elvans were in England. He knew Sabrina's character and upbringing; he knew she would not accept such behavior in a husband any more than Leonie would. His only doubt was what Sabrina wanted to do about it.

This doubt was not resolved immediately. William was

absorbed by his duties and in continual conferences between the War Office and the Foreign Office, which had
differing views of the situation. Sabrina was too good an
Englishwoman to intrude her personal affairs into a national problem. Besides that, she was instantly snatched up
into the social-diplomatic whirl. The very day after she arrived, footmen appeared in veritable droves bearing notes
that included her in invitations to every fashionable affair
of the Season.

William set out for Königsberg again at the end of the
first week in March, in an angry and dissatisfied frame of
mind that had little to do with his wife. He had scarcely
given Sabrina a thought since they arrived in England.
What troubled him was that he had very little more to offer the Prussians than what Lord Hutchinson had
originally been enpowered to suggest. Despite his strongest representations and Lord Hutchinson's vigorously
worded letters and reports, Windham would not be moved.
He had committed his forces to schemes dear to his heart,
and he insisted that the few men England could send
would be useless because Russia had more than sufficient
manpower. Moreover, he claimed, British troops might be
misused because of animosity. William's explanation that
the need was one of morale, that the Russians and Prussians needed to be assured that the English were doing their
fair share, was summarily dismissed.

Although she longed to be nearer Perce, Sabrina was
not so foolish as to propose going with her husband. She
would be a danger to him and a worrisome distraction to
Perce, who had already told her more than once that she
should on no account return. She had had a letter from
him, written immediately after the battle of Ostrolenka, to
assure her he had not been involved in the conflict, and
two more pages with general news. A month after William
left, there was another letter. The first had been directed
to William's house and sent over to Leonie's by the cur-

rent tenants, the next two had been simply addressed to Sabrina at her cousin's, but the last had been addressed to Leonie under a separate cover that requested it be given to Sabrina privately and personally.

It was apparent from the first words why the letter was directed where there was no chance of William seeing it. There was no news in it, no reason for writing, only a passionate outpouring of love and longing. Sabrina looked up at Leonie who, after passing her the letter, was paying more than the usual strict attention to her own correspondence.

"Do you think it will be possible for Roger to obtain an annulment of my marriage?" Sabrina asked.

"Perce?" Leonie responded. "It is Perce?" She had suspected as much when Sabrina had last been home, but had felt it imperative not to intrude into her cousin's life.

"Yes," Sabrina admitted calmly. She had not intended to involve Perce if it were possible, but by sending a letter to Leonie in that manner, he had betrayed himself. "It's quite dreadful that neither of us should have realized it before I met William, but I suppose we were too accustomed to each other."

"*Dieu! Bon Dieu!*" Leonie breathed. "I do not know, *petite*. Is William willing?"

"I have no idea. I was going to speak to him about it on the ship coming home, but Perce said not to do so until I could discuss the matter with Roger. Leonie, do you think he will be very angry?"

Leonie felt startled. "Do you care whether William is angry? If you do—"

"Not William," Sabrina interrupted. "I don't care if he has an apoplexy, so long as he'll grant me the annulment. I meant Roger. Will he think . . . I'm . . . bad?"

"I am more worried that he will call William out than that he will think ill of you, *petite*," Leonie assured her. "Last year, oh, he was *furieux*. He talked of horsewhipping to mend William's manners. It was only that I talked and talked and told him that William was *nécessaire,* that he was one of the few who still believed in the war."

"I don't want William's manners mended," Sabrina said firmly. "I want Perce. But if I can't get an annulment, I won't know what to do. Oh, Leonie, he's Moreton's heir. He *must* have a legitimate son. I could divorce William for adultery. It wouldn't be hard to get evidence, but then I wouldn't be able to marry Perce."

Leonie shook her head. "Let us not begin to imagine difficulties. I do not know what can be done; Roger may not know either, but he will know to whom to speak. Somehow we will arrange." Tears came to her eyes. "Ah, *petite, petite,* it is our fault—no, mine, all mine—"

Sabrina cut short Leonie's self-blame with the sharp remark that it was useless to worry about that and that they had been over it all before. "You must believe that I'm not leaving William because he hurt me," she insisted. "If I wanted him, I would fight for him. I just don't love him anymore. I realized that in Russia when I saw him starting an affair that I could have stopped, but it wasn't worth the effort to me."

Leonie began to ask another question and bit it back. Sabrina smiled at her.

"No," she said, knowing what Leonie had resisted asking. "It wasn't Perce then. I didn't even know he was in Russia when I decided I didn't want William any longer."

That was clear enough, but when the matter was presented to Roger, he seized on the pertinent problem at once. The question was, he remarked wryly, whether William wanted her. Sabrina had to reply honestly that, at the moment, he probably did not; however, the instant she said she wanted her freedom, there was a good chance William's mind would change.

"God knows I could get you a divorce—*a mensa et thoro*—with no trouble at all. It would even be to your advantage if he contested, but that wouldn't do you any good. You wouldn't be able to marry."

Roger had not been told about Perce. Both Leonie and Sabrina, although for different reasons, felt it was better he should not know there was already another man. Neither was concerned that he would overlook the need of a healthy twenty-year-old to remarry, and of course he had not.

"And a dissolution act by Parliament . . . I don't know, Brina. I don't think they've ever given one to a woman. . . ."

"I'm sure that's true," Sabrina said bitterly. "Women aren't supposed to notice their men whoring around. And if they do, they're supposed to be polite about it. You're allowed to cry in the privacy of your bedchamber or whisper to your friends, but make a scandal—never!"

"It is true, my love," Leonie said, "but maintain your reason, do. Many women do not mind. They think it is something men do. Some are even glad."

"But those who are not glad have no recourse."

"They can make their husband's lives miserable," Roger said dryly. "The theory is that marriage is a sacred tie and cannot be dissolved."

"Regardless of the variety of hell that sacred tie causes one to inhabit," Sabrina snapped, and then cried, "Oh, Roger, I'm sorry."

He smiled and touched his wife's hand. "My dear, the particular hell I inhabited makes me more sympathetic than most men might be, although I must admit Solange never gave me any cause to suspect her of adultery. However, if Solange had not died and all else happened as it did, I don't know what I would have done."

"I know what I would have done," Leonie put in.

"Yes." Roger's smile turned wry. "I fear I know also, but then both of us . . . No. Thank God there was no problem. But that is why I am not willing simply to go out

250

and find evidence against William. Perhaps it *is* unfair, Sabrina, but we alone cannot change the law. Tomorrow I will consult a man I know who specializes in canon law. If we can find cause to void the marriage and can bring William to agree . . ."

"That means waiting until William returns," Sabrina said.

Suddenly Roger looked anxious, his eyes flickering for just a moment to Sabrina's slender waist. "Is there some reason to hurry?" he asked tensely.

"No," Sabrina replied, innocently unconscious of what he had thought, although Leonie had stiffened. "I just want it to be over." She shuddered. "It will be so horrid."

Roger rose, put his arm around her shoulders, and hugged her. "An annulment will be quite private. Only a few questions to answer, and no spectators, which is another reason to avoid a divorce if possible. In any case, it would be better not to act at once. Thank God that peculiarly untalented Ministry of All Talents has finally fallen apart. But the new government is just getting organized. I have a good many friends in this administration. Just let them catch their breath."

"Yes, and also to arrange an annulment during the Season is to invite attention, *petite*," Leonie pointed out.

"There's no hurry," Sabrina repeated.

As far as she was concerned, it was true. Until Perce came home, she was content to let matters move at any pace Roger thought best. He was not likely to neglect her affairs. The only trouble was, she did not know what to write to Perce. She shrank from replying to his passionate letter with one equally passionate. Not that she could not or would not write such words, but he had told her he believed his mail was opened, and she remembered that his letter to her had been opened and read. And she could not, after what he had written, reply in the light, friendly way she had previously written to him. Day after day she put off answering, and each day it grew harder to decide what to say.

She had one hope, and that was to write about the status of her marriage, but she had nothing to say about that just at this moment, either. The All Talents Ministry had fallen on March 24, 1807, and was replaced by one headed by the duke of Portland. Roger had groaned at the choice of a man both dull and ill, but he understood it. The two most brilliant and most forceful politicians of the day, Mr. Canning and Viscount Castlereagh, loathed each other. Both were sufficiently patriotic, or ambitious, to serve in the same administration, but neither would accept orders from the other. Thus, poor Portland had been pushed into the prime minister's position.

For Roger, personally, this was an advantage. Lord Hawkesbury was now home secretary. Unaware of Roger's earlier doubts about his competence and good sense, he was sincerely attached to the St. Eyres, father and son. Since it was the home secretary who would deal with divorce, and who could apply pressure to the Church if that were necessary, Roger was delighted with this appointment. Moreover, Portland's inertness would guarantee no interference from that end.

Politically, Roger was less sure he was satisfied. Castlereagh as secretary of war was fine. He was a real workhorse who would give that passionate attention to detail that was necessary for dealing with the endless intricacies of war. If anyone could salvage anything from the wreck Windham had left, it was Castlereagh. Canning at the Foreign Office was something else again. The man was absolutely brilliant, but he was reckless, ill-bred, and contemptuous of others in a way that earned and kept enemies. He was passionately in favor of the war but impatient with receiving advice, and was wildly erratic in action.

By mid-April the effects of Canning's restlessness were

being felt. He was recalling ambassadors, changing the staffs of the embassies, and in general shaking up the entire administration of the Foreign Office. To speak the truth, there was not enough in foreign affairs to keep him busy. So many nations were dominated by Bonaparte, and thus had no relations with England, that there was little room to maneuver politically.

Naturally one of the first matters to seize Canning's attention was William's plea for military aid to Russia and Prussia. William was recalled and arrived in London toward the end of April. There had been, as yet, no military action to speak of, William reported, but that was because Tsar Alexander was conferring with Prussia's King Frederick William. However, the action must come soon, and, William insisted, whether the Russians won or lost, England would lose unless there was a substantial British contingent in the next military action.

Canning grasped this without difficulty and agreed heartily. A paper was prepared on the subject and sent off to Castlereagh. The answer lacked the minister of war's usual suavity. It did not matter, Castlereagh responded, what was expedient or right. There were no British forces available, and if there had been, there were no transports to carry them. Canning fretted and fumed, spreading abroad the contention that in his desire to flout Canning's foreign policy, Castlereagh was prepared to ruin the country.

Unfortunately, Canning's suspicions were not the truth. The previous ministry, having dispersed regiments to Egypt, Italy, and South America—to produce in Egypt one disastrous defeat; in Italy, a pointless victory that brought enormous suffering and lingering horror to the native forces that supported the British action; and a thus far unknown result in South America—had left Castlereagh with twelve thousand men and Lord Mulgrave at the Admiralty without ships for transport.

Needless to say, Castlereagh was not going to sit back quietly and allow truth to refute for him Canning's calumnies. Recriminations flew thick and fast, the antagonists seeming to have forgotten the cause in the enthusiasm with which they joined combat. Lord Hawkesbury, alerted by Roger, who had been warned by William, acted as mediator to calm the tantrums of his fellow ministers, and achieved a compromise. The German Legion, about eight thousand men, would be sent to Sweden to resist the French invasion of Swedish Pomerania. This must draw men from other French campaigns and thus, indirectly, assist Russia.

William was horrified. Sweden was the traditional enemy of Russia, and this was a case in which "the enemy of my enemy is my friend" would not work. William stated flatly to Canning that the arrangement would not be sufficient. If only eight thousand men could be spared, he would try to explain the situation, but the men should be sent to East Prussia and not to Sweden.

Had William gone to Castlereagh, he might have received an impartial hearing; however, protocol made it necessary that William address his objections to his own superior, and *Mr.* Canning took offense at *Lord* Elvan's disapproval of a brilliant plan of his devising. For his pains, William was withdrawn from the East Prussian mission. He was, said Canning, beginning to identify himself too closely with the Prussian-Russian cause rather than with the best interests of England. This left William, who did not even like the Prussians or Russians, in a state of near shock.

Naturally, in the midst of such activity and anxiety, Sabrina did not feel it fair to add the threat of an annulment or divorce proceedings to William's other problems. He was deeply distressed over what appeared to be the failure of a most promising diplomatic career. Once a man gets a reputation for being susceptible to foreign influence, he is finished. Angry as Roger was at William for the pain he had inflicted on Sabrina, he was not prepared to endure this injustice. He made the strongest representations to Canning supporting William's patriotism, and Lord Hawkesbury backed him up with all the power he had.

Enamored of his own opinion, Canning would not back down completely. However, he realized that it would be a mistake to damn Lord Elvan. If events should fall out so that Elvan appeared to have given the correct advice—which was possible even if the advice were prejudiced—it would be very embarrassing. Canning compromised. William was recalled and offered a new mission.

After the fall of Berlin, following the Jena-Auerstedt disaster, Bonaparte had issued decrees ordering the confiscation of all British goods, the imprisonment of all British citizens, and the seizure of any ship of any nation that traded with England. Few such nations remained in Europe. One of them was Portugal, but stronger and stronger pressure was being exerted on Prince Regent João to close his country's ports to England. Thus far he had resisted, but strength of character was not one of Prince João's notable virtues. It would be necessary to increase the British mission in Portugal and, by combined persuasion and threat, keep the influential nobility convinced of the advantages of continued alliance with England.

William accepted the compromise with joy. Since he was convinced that the Prussian mission was hopeless, he was only too glad to be dissociated from it. Let Lord Hutchinson try to explain to Canning that Hanover was lost to England whether the Russians won or lost. The only way Hanover could have been returned to British domination was if England had furnished the driving force for a decisive victory over Bonaparte, and then that force had sat down to occupy Hanover. As it was, both Alexander and Frederick would laugh in the face of an emissary who demanded the return of Hanover.

Pleased with Lord Elvan's easy and, indeed, grateful acceptance, Canning made some polite remarks about Sabrina, whom he had met at a number of social functions. He commented on how fortunate William was to have a wife at one and the same time beautiful and politically astute. She would be the greatest help to him on the Portuguese mission, Canning remarked. It was idle conversation really, a gracious gesture toward someone who had, in Canning's opinion, smoothly swallowed reprimand and insult. However, since such gestures were sufficiently rare on Canning's part, William took the comment quite seriously.

William returned to Leonie's house full of the new mission, delighted to find Roger having tea with Leonie and Sabrina. He related what little he knew about the situation—he was to be briefed more thoroughly over the next few weeks—and mentioned how much Sabrina would enjoy Portugal, which was said to be a very beautiful country. These enthusiastic remarks were met by an embarrassed silence, which Sabrina broke.

"I will not be going with you, William," she said. "I'm sorry if I have led you into a misunderstanding by saying nothing about it before, but I wish to dissolve our marriage."

He looked at her for a moment, then laughed. "Come now, Sabrina, you are being ridiculous."

"Very likely in your opinion I am," she said steadily, "but I told you when I first discovered your infidelities that I was not prepared to take other women's leavings."

"Sabrina!" William exclaimed. "You are indelicate!"

"I am more interested in the truth than in delicacy," Sabrina snapped. "The first time I was willing to admit you were deceiving me, you said you had misunderstood and promised you would give me no further cause for complaint. I felt that to be possible and reasonable and agreed to forget what had happened. However, I discovered you never had any intention of keeping that promise."

William stood up. "You are being childish and ridiculous. One does make promises to silly girls to stop their squealing, but no woman has a right to demand—"

"Right or not—" Leonie began angrily.

Roger's glance silenced her. "Whatever custom has permitted," he said coldly, "the law actually applies equally to husband and wife. Both canon law and civil law imply that chastity is required of each partner."

William looked at Roger as if he had suddenly sprouted two extra purple heads. "You—you intend to support Sabrina in this lunacy?"

"It is not lunacy to desire a happy marriage," Leonie said, rising to her feet, her golden eyes nearly shooting sparks. "It is not lunacy to desire a husband whose love is only yours. It—"

"Leonie!" Again she was silenced, and Roger turned his attention to William. "To answer your question, yes, I intend to support Sabrina. I also happen to agree with my wife."

"I cannot believe this!" William exclaimed. "I have been patient and understanding far beyond the ordinary, and this is my reward. Do you realize that Sabrina has denied me my conjugal rights for more than a year?"

"I didn't think you had noticed," Sabrina remarked sardonically. "I'm sure you suffered no deprivation, although in bad weather it might have been an inconvenience to have to go out of the house."

"Sabrina! That was unnecessary," Roger snapped. "I suggest we suspend this discussion before it degenerates into a shouting of insults totally irrelevant to the basic problem. From what Sabrina has told me, this is not a new or sudden decision. She has been considering the matter since January 1806, roughly when she closed her door to you, William. No doubt this is a shock to you, and you will need time—"

"I don't need time. I'll never agree. This is a silly whim of a silly girl. Moreover, it's ridiculous. I do love my wife. I married for love, as you well know, St. Eyre, since her fortune is tied up out of my hands. My amusements are none of her business."

"You don't know what love is, William," Sabrina said quietly, sad now rather than angry. "Love's first act is to set the joy of the beloved before any light diversion. I don't say before anything. A man has duties that are more important than his beloved's pleasure or happiness, but no *amusement* can be more important."

"I haven't noticed you setting *my* happiness first," William retorted caustically.

"I did at first," Sabrina replied. "I may not have succeeded, but I tried with all my heart to do and be what you wanted. I don't now for a very good reason. I *don't* love you. Your happiness has only as much influence on my actions as that of any other common acquaintance."

William stared, then laughed. "I don't believe you. You're insane with jealousy, but no matter how crazy you are, I will not bind myself to your stupid prejudices. You are my wife. I will always honor you as such. You have no right to ask more of me than any other woman would ask."

"I didn't wish to go this far just now," Roger interposed, "but you must understand that it's impossible to dismiss the situation in this way. Sabrina is resolved to dissolve this marriage whatever the cost. It might be possible to do it quietly and privately if you will agree to an annulment. Sabrina is willing to bear the blame, or it might be possible to put the onus on me—a forced marriage."

"Who the devil would believe that?" William sneered.

"No one, but bishops and ecclesiastical courts are scarcely incorruptible. The truth will be known, of course,

258

but, as you yourself said, it will be Sabrina who will be thought ridiculous."

"Even so," William argued, "I don't want an annulment. I love Sabrina. Eventually she will realize that she must accept life as it is and not as a silly child dreams it."

"Unfortunately I have no intentions of doing that." Sabrina's voice was as cold now as her ice-blue eyes. "I will never live with you again under any circumstances, and if I must take my freedom the hard way, I will obtain a divorce. There is more than sufficient evidence of your adultery available."

"You're mad!" William turned to Roger. "Will you permit this?"

"There is no way for me to stop it, even if I wished," Roger pointed out. "Sabrina is mistress of her own fortune and can do as she pleases. I can't deny that I would prefer she did *not* engage in an action that would doubtless ruin you both—"

"Both! I can't see how it would ruin me," William snarled. "She would be laughed out of court."

"No, she would not," Roger retorted coldly. "You may be sure that however little the judges approve of her suit, it will be so presented that they have no choice but to rule in her favor. And, however valuable you are to the Foreign Office, it will not be in their power to ignore what the court must decree."

There was a period of dead silence. William was aware that it was largely through Roger's efforts that he had retained his diplomatic position. At first he felt furious at the reminder. Almost at once he realized that Roger was not being snide, that he meant exactly what he said. If Roger had not believed him valuable to the Foreign Office, he would not have supported him.

Diplomacy for William was a labor of love. It provided the interest in his life. He had never had the slightest desire to be a country gentleman. His estates were well managed by his younger brother, who loved the land and bucolic pleasures. Until William had met Sabrina, he had no intention of marrying, even though he recognized that the right wife was a great diplomatic asset. He had always planned to allow his brother and his already numerous progeny to inherit Elvan. When Sabrina had conceived, William had rather regretted it. He had felt he was cheating his brother, of whom he was very fond.

"William, please try not to be so angry." Sabrina broke the tense silence. "I am ready to acknowledge that my demands are extraordinary, but I can't help it. It's the way I am. Call me different. Call me mad, if you like, but I cannot and will not share my man with either common or highborn whores. Perhaps you are right, and my nature is jealous. For me, the condition is so acute—"

"That it's a mania," William interrupted.

"Yes, if you wish," she replied meekly, suddenly realizing that William's pride must be salved if she were ever to get him to agree to an annulment. "But the condition is incurable, I assure you. It grows worse, not better. I don't hate you, yet. I sincerely appreciate your good qualities, your great ability in your work, your kindness, your generosity. Be generous to me. Give me back my freedom before I learn to hate, before I learn to desire your hurt before my own good."

The sop to his pride, the plea—and the veiled threat under it—made William reconsider. He had experience of Sabrina when she turned vicious. It was true that she did not seem to feel pain of mind or body but attacked like a berserk thing, only intent on injuring her opponent regardless of cost to herself. He understood she was not speaking of physical injury now, but he thought her quite capable of destroying herself without a regret so long as she dragged him down with her.

He cast not Sabrina but Roger a glance of venomous dislike. This was what came of permitting women the right to use their own fortunes. They became totally ungovernable. If he had controlled Sabrina's money, she would not have the power to make both of them ridiculous. She would simply have recovered from her jealousy. But it was his own fault for agreeing. Only there had been no way around it. St. Eyre had tied up the money so that it would have taken an act of Parliament to untie it when the girl became his ward. The legalities, William knew, had been directed as much against St. Eyre himself, as her guardian, as against any future husband who might wish to take advantage of Sabrina. And there were controls on Sabrina, too. An honest man, St. Eyre.

That thought struck William forcefully as he connected it with the fact that Roger had stood up to Canning for him although it was certain he already knew that Sabrina intended to dissolve her marriage. With Canning's name a double-headed possibility arose. Sabrina had to come to Portugal; Canning had implied her presence was necessary, possibly because of social conditions in the Portuguese court. If she refused, Canning would doubtless say the mission had to go to a married man and use that as a more acceptable excuse to shut William out.

On the other hand, he could use the political lever to move Sabrina. She really was a patriotic Englishwoman and, in addition, loved the diplomatic life as much as he did. Once she agreed to go, he might be able to change her mind. Perhaps this separation was not even Sabrina's idea. Everyone knew that Lady Leonie was jealous as a cat, and St. Eyre did not dare take a night out on the town for fear of her. Away from Leonie's influence, Sabrina might be more reasonable. Even if she were not, the Portuguese mission might take some time. The longer he had to reason with Sabrina, the greater the chances he would find a solution that would satisfy him and still avoid an embarrassing rupture.

"You ask me to be generous," he said to Sabrina. "I

might be willing to be generous at another time, but just now you are not asking for a gift, you are asking me to cut my own throat."

"What do you mean?"

Sabrina was plainly startled—and concerned. William felt a flicker of satisfaction. She did care for him, no matter how she denied it. If he could find a way to convince her to admit her affections and allow him his pleasures . . . But he must get her to Portugal first. William described his conversation with Canning.

"That *is* an odd start," Roger admitted. "If it were any other man, I would say he was making polite conversation, but Canning doesn't make small talk. I suppose he can be as courteous as another man when he desires, but it's not his way."

"That was what I thought," William agreed. "Now I'm afraid he has got wind of this lunacy of Sabrina's and felt it would be a good way to deprive me of what he offered without political overtones."

"That isn't possible," Sabrina cried. "I swear I haven't said a word to anyone except Leonie and Roger—not even Katy." Perce knew, of course, Sabrina's guilty mind pointed out, but Perce wouldn't talk—not Perce. Besides, he was in East Prussia.

"Don't be naive, Sabrina," William snapped. "Can your maid or my man fail to know I have not been in your bedchamber for over a year? Who knows what rumors they've started."

"Not Katy!" Sabrina exclaimed.

"It makes no difference to me which one spread the word. Once such a rumor reached that grapevine of information servants seem to cultivate, it would soon start drifting upward."

"Oh, heaven," Sabrina said, "I want to be free, but I don't want to hurt you, William—not unless you force me to do it."

262

"Force you? I can't protect myself!" William remarked bitterly. "After all, I can't *make* you go to Portugal. Even if I were so mad as to think of abducting you, which I assure you I am not, that would scarcely serve Canning's purpose. And if you refuse . . ."

"But I could be ill, or——"

"If Canning's purpose requires a married diplomat with an active wife, it will scarcely make a difference what excuse is given," William pointed out.

That was true. Sabrina stared at her husband, her sense of duty warring with suspicion. But he had mentioned the expectation that she would accompany him before the subject of dissolving the marriage had come up. Also, it was not likely anyone would believe she was sick when for weeks she had been attending balls, Venetian breakfasts, the theater, and the opera with indefatigable energy and enjoyment. And she did not dare use the excuse that she was breeding, because it was possible the application for annulment would claim her incapable of bearing children.

"If you will go with me," William said into the anxious silence that had fallen over the group, "I will consider the subject of an annulment."

"Do not do it, *petite*," Leonie cried. "When you are far away——"

"Leonie!" Roger warned. "William is not a monster. There is no question of cruelty or ill-treatment."

Sabrina thought fleetingly of the two violent episodes there had been, but she had won both of those battles and it was obvious that William had not enjoyed them. Besides, with Katy on the watch now, there really was no danger that William could mistreat her.

"No, indeed, William is not a monster," she agreed.

"You have asked me to be generous," William remarked. "Does that work only one way?"

"Just a moment," Roger interposed, "this is undue influence."

"No," Sabrina said, "William has a perfect right to fight for his career, as I have a right to fight for my—my mania."

She was thinking that Perce was in East Prussia and that there was absolutely no chance that she could get there. London's Season was nearly over. If she had nothing to keep her occupied but the idle pastimes of summer in the country or at a watering place, she would go mad worrying about him. Would it not be better to go to Portugal, where she would be occupied? If Perce came home, Leonie would let her know and she could return to England at once. There was no way William could hold her. Perhaps she could even convince William that the dissolution of their marriage would be best for both of them. Now that her intention was out in the open, they could talk about it. And he would be under obligation to her for accompanying him at his request.

"Brina!" Leonie cried.

"I assure you, Lady Leonie," William said coldly, "that I have no intention of trying to beat your cousin into submission or locking her up and starving her if she agrees to come. In fact, you should realize that the situation itself would preclude such behavior, if my character did not. Sabrina must be willing and cheerful to be of use to me, and she could destroy me if she wished to make a scandal. Besides," he added bitterly, "there is no way I could keep her in Portugal if she wished to leave the country. I assume she will make her own banking arrangements, as usual."

Roger looked worried, but he said nothing. If Elvan could convince Sabrina to try again to make the marriage work and get her pregnant, the problem would be enormously complicated. Probably then Sabrina would have to settle for a half-life as his wife. But she had resisted him for more than a year already. Still, he might not have been trying to pacify her, since he believed she was either trapped or content. There was no need to raise the question immediately, however. Roger knew he would have time to warn Sabrina of that trap, and he was convinced Elvan would not try to force her.

"It's all right, Leonie," Sabrina said. "If I agree . . . no, let's not be silly. Obviously I am considering seriously going to Portugal, but I will want assurances, William."

"Oh, God," he said with disgust, "for all I care, you can hire ten lusty footmen and have them surround you whenever we are in private. Surely you don't believe I would attack you in public?"

Sabrina could not help smiling. "I don't mean assurances that you won't be violent, William. I want assurances that you won't use my agreement to come with you against me in the matter of dissolving our marriage and that you will really, very seriously, consider the advantages of a quiet annulment, for which I am ready to bear the blame, over a vile exposure of our private lives in a divorce suit."

"Of course I will consider it. I have said so already," William replied, far too readily.

"It will have to be a formal agreement," Roger said dryly. "I cannot prevent Sabrina from doing what she thinks best, but I will advise her *most strongly* not to go without a written statement of intention. You understand, this will not bind her, or you for that matter, to any particular action. It will merely protect Sabrina if you should wish to deny this conversation."

William was really furious. For one moment it almost looked as if he might attack Roger physically; however, that would have been futile in every sense. Although Roger was at least ten years older, he was stronger and more fit. With an effort, William recovered his temper. He realized that the formal statement could do him little harm. After all, St. Eyre and his wife were already witnesses that the conversation had taken place. In any case, his purpose was to convince Sabrina she would be better off remaining married to him, not trapping her into a situation that would make her desperate and dangerous.

"Very well," he said, "if Sabrina will come to Portugal and behave in public as my wife, fulfilling the duties necessary, I will sign your formal agreement."

CHAPTER FOURTEEN

The weather was dreadful, which was unfortunate both for William's dignity and for his plans to use the voyage from England to Portugal to convince Sabrina that she was being foolish. Unthinkingly, William had explained arranging separate cabins for them by saying that Sabrina was afflicted by sickness at sea. He had forgotten that Sabrina had never been seasick. She had extensive experience with pitching and rolling boats, having been for some years a "fisherman's child" and sailing on Philip's yacht.

Since William was not equally resistant, the high seas encountered during the passage inconvenienced him more than his wife. The captain of the ship made no remark of this, of course, but it amused him to see Sabrina, bright-eyed and pink-cheeked, her silver-gilt hair charmingly windblown, appear for every meal no matter what antics the ship played.

There were a number of others unaffected by the playful behavior of the ship and the sea. Two were Portuguese merchants, who made the passage to England so frequently that they could almost have sailed the vessel themselves. Sabrina found them delightful and useful companions. They taught her enough Portuguese to communicate simply and told her some rather astonishing facts about Portuguese history, such as the practice of marrying niece to uncle when the male line failed in the royal family.

Although Sabrina made no comment, she privately

thought it was not very surprising that Queen Maria was quite mad and that her son, the Prince Regent João, was neither remarkably intelligent nor capable of clinging to his own opinions. No matter that she disapproved, Sabrina was sincerely interested, and her absorbed attention was an irresistible inducement to the gentlemen to enlarge on their reminiscences. Both bewailed the days of the Marquês de Pombal, the favorite of the preceding monarch, Maria's father, who, they sighed, had done more than enrich himself by taking full advantage of his position.

Admittedly, Sabrina thought, as she listened, the Marquês de Pombal seemed to have been an excellent choice for a favorite. When Lisbon had been destroyed in 1755 by a severe earthquake—half the city turned to rubble and thirty thousand dead—he had seized the opportunity not only to restore Lisbon but to remake Portugal. The city had been rebuilt completely, all except for one old section that had survived intact. In addition, the paralyzing power of the Inquisition was broken, the Jesuits driven out of the country, and the administration of the country reformed along more liberal and less corrupt lines. Pombal had not stopped there. He had fostered agriculture, built new roads, improved communications, and encouraged industries and trade. Everything was done that could make the country self-sufficient.

Unfortunately this renaissance did not long survive. When his patron died, Pombal was cast aside by Queen Maria (also married to her uncle), who was a religious fanatic and already slightly unbalanced. Before long the death of her husband and her eldest son had driven her incurably insane, but she had ruled long enough to permit the Church to reestablish its hold in Portugal. The accession of Prince João as regent had prevented a total return to the stranglehold of the Inquisition on all life, but matters were now tending more and more in that direction. Dom João was strongly influenced by his wife, Carlota

Joaquina, who was almost as much of a religious fanatic as his mother.

The merchants were particularly explicit about this point because personal worries were involved. They feared for their business, which was largely with Britain—a country of heretics. Sabrina blinked at that and uttered a mild protest. England had no love for Papists; in fact, it was the question of liberalizing the restrictive laws against Catholics that had brought down the previous government. However, religion had nothing to do with business. In recent times, at least, trade was pursued with total impartiality and enthusiasm whether the partners were Papist, Protestant, or pagan.

There was more to it than that, Sabrina realized when she thought over the various conversations. Without being specific the two kind gentlemen seemed to be delivering a word of warning. She would not be a favorite at court this time, Sabrina knew. Also, William had not instructed her regarding what or whom he expected her to cultivate.

This was a disturbing thought, but she put it aside. It was really quite natural for William to avoid any discussion with her that was not absolutely necessary. When he had become more adjusted to the idea that she wanted an annulment, life would be easier. Besides, the poor man had not expected to be so seasick. Could the sickness be a device to avoid her? If so, for what reason? Sabrina shrugged her shapely shoulders. She would be on guard and so would Katy, but she couldn't imagine what William might intend.

Actually, he intended nothing dire. Although his original purpose of using romantic, moonlit nights on shipboard to soften Sabrina's heart had been foiled by the weather and by bouts with seasickness, the reason William had not instructed Sabrina was that there was nothing for her to do. He had found, once his own briefing started, that Canning's remark *had* been mere casual pleasantry, and in fact, the foreign minister either had not really been considering what he was saying or had not been in possession of all the facts of the case. Carlota Joaquina had a strong influence on her husband, it was true. Ordinarily such a situation was a natural for Sabrina, who would ingratiate herself with the regent's wife or her ladies or both. This time, however, Carlota Joaquina's unnaturally intense religious prejudice would probably preclude all but a formal relationship.

William had said nothing about this discovery because he had no intention of leaving Sabrina behind. In England, supported by her doting foster parents, her intentions of dissolving their marriage would only harden as she slipped back into the role of a single girl. William considered Sabrina an almost ideal wife. Even if she persisted in the lunacy of refusing to sleep with him, he did not mind. Bodies were two a penny, but women with Sabrina's ability in the diplomatic sphere combined with great beauty were few and far between. She would be, as she grew older, and more experienced, even more valuable, and William intended to use every device he could discover to keep her.

One plan came to his mind immediately when he learned Sabrina was not likely to be warmly received. He remembered how depressed she had become in Prussia when she was excluded from the court and its entertainments. There he had neglected her. He regretted it now, although he had not really had much choice, but possibly that was what had decided her on the idea of an annulment. In Portugal she would be in a similar situation, but he would be able to spend more time with her. Also, she would not be invited to social functions on her own due to the rigid conditions of Portugal. She would be dependent on him, and he would win her back on his own terms.

They landed in Lisbon in the middle of May. The passage up the Tagus was lovely, the hills clothed with the fresh green of late spring and the white city climbing upward on them. For the first two weeks they were housed in the British embassy. It was more convenient for William, who had a good deal to discuss with his superior, Lord Strangford. Naturally, Sabrina was not present at the diplomatic conferences, but the problems were so serious that it was impossible for Lord Strangford or William to dismiss them from mind. Thus, since Sabrina was as interested as the men in the political situation, it was soon discussed as eagerly at the dinner table and tea table as in the offices.

It was unfortunate for Sabrina's peace of mind that the Portuguese situation was tied so closely to the war in East Prussia. As early as 1802, Bonaparte had decided to dismember Portugal. First he tried to force the small country into war by sending as emissary Marshal Lannes, the crudest and least educated of his generals. Although Lannes deliberately offended and humiliated the Portuguese, they did not fall into the trap of pitting their puny strength against Bonaparte's temporarily idle legions. Prince João simply complied with Bonaparte's demands to dismiss the anti-French members of his council.

By 1804, Bonaparte had replaced Lannes with Junot and was demanding that Portugal declare war on England. This, however, the prince regent was unwilling to do. England was the market for most of Portugal's grain and wine, and the long coastline of Portugal was dreadfully vulnerable to attack by a sea power. Fortunately for Portugal, through 1805 and 1806, Bonaparte was so deeply embroiled in his campaigns in Germany and Austria that he did not push his demands.

Now, however, Portugal's safety hung on Russia's ability to resist the French. If the war continued in East Prussia and Poland, no more pressure would fall on Portugal. There would be no need for William and Lord Strangford to do anything except wait. If the Russians defeated Bonaparte, it might be worthwhile for England to encourage Portugal, and Spain, too, to attack France. If Bonaparte defeated the Russians, the situation would become critical. Almost certainly, Bonaparte's attention would return to the Peninsula as soon as Russia ceased to oppose him. However, if enough time had elapsed for Castlereagh to have reorganized the armed forces, Britain might be able to send help.

The defense of Portugal was not impossible. With the British navy to protect the coastline and to land forces if necessary, the major cities could be defended. The northern portion of the country was so mountainous, native troops would have a marked advantage against foreign invaders. The terrain in the south was more suitable to Bonaparte's type of war, but it was strategically far less important and was vulnerable to attack from the English-held base of Gibraltar.

The problem Lord Strangford and William discussed most frequently was not how to defend Portugal, but how to make the prince regent willing to defend it. At the present time he was doing his best to ignore both the threat from France and the threat from England. He was too terrified of the British navy and his own merchant class to yield to the urgings of the French and close his ports to England, confiscate English goods, and imprison all British citizens. On the other hand, he was too terrified of the French to set his generals to readying the army for defense, which the British envoys kept pressing him to do.

Three days after arrival Sabrina had been presented at court. The reception she received was cold and formal. Sabrina could not be certain whether this was owing to the disfavor of the pro-French advisors, whether it was Carlota Joaquina's particular feeling against heretics, or whether it was simply Portuguese manners to which she was not yet accustomed. In the next week the fact that the icy reception was intended, not an accident of manner, was confirmed. Instead of the rush of private invitations and cards that were customary when a new face appeared on the diplomatic scene, Sabrina received but two invitations to court functions, and only one visiting card was left.

Having left Sabrina to stew in idleness for a week, William suddenly became as attentive as when he had first courted her. He accompanied her on her hunt for a house; he took her to the theater and for rides to examine the astonishingly beautiful scenery; at court functions he remained by her side, including her carefully in the stiff conversations. While they were still resident in the British embassy, Sabrina had little choice but to accept these attentions. When they were alone, she tried to explain to William the fixity of her purpose, but he laughed and would not listen.

There are none so deaf as those who will not hear, Sabrina thought exasperatedly. Even after they were settled in their own house, and Sabrina was free to refuse her husband's escort, he persisted. He merely smiled indulgently at her and told her she was childishly cutting off her nose to spite her face, punishing herself rather than him by moping alone. It was useless to say again that she had rather read a book alone than go to an entertainment with him; he would not listen.

Sabrina continued to be surprised by the amount of time William seemed able to devote to courting her. Usually in a tense diplomatic situation he was far too busy, at least during the day, to woo a woman. Even when chasing most desperately, William usually confined his romancing to the evening hours. Eventually she reasoned that out, too. Although the situation was poised on a knife edge, the British could not do much until they had news of the way the war was going in East Prussia. The actions necessary in response to victory, defeat, or stalemate were so different that it was not even possible to "pave the way."

Having talked over the possibilities and settled their plans of action for each eventuality, William and Lord Strangford could only wait.

Despite the hostile climate of the court itself, William was not excluded totally from Portuguese society. Those who had been put out of favor by Bonaparte's pressure were willing to receive the British envoys. Lord Strangford himself could not accept these invitations because such acceptance might betoken a conspiracy against the government or an insult, but a lesser personage like William could accept and did quite eagerly. The prince regent might have bowed before Bonaparte's pressure, but he did not have to like doing it or feel any great attachment for the men he had been forced to appoint. It was thus entirely possible that those now out of favor had more unofficial influence on Dom João than his ministers.

The situation between William and Sabrina remained static for the next two weeks, although William began to show resentment at Sabrina's steadfast indifference to him. However, toward the end of June there were two significant changes: William suddenly acquired the sleek, satisfied look of a tomcat that is the accepted suitor, and the weather turned very hot. The first change Sabrina accepted with real pleasure, knowing that William was on the hunt again. The second she was only marginally aware of because she hardly left the cool, thick-walled house during the day until William changed his polite invitations to angry and insistent demands. He now needed his wife as a cover for his seduction.

Actually, Sabrina was not at all averse to assisting him. She was not spiteful and, now that she no longer believed herself in love with him, had no objection to her husband's philandering. She knew he would not be taking advantage of innocent maidens, that it was most likely that the woman he pursued was as hard and cynical as he was inconstant. It was rather amusing to watch. However, willingness to assist her husband fix his attention elsewhere was not all that was needed. When Sabrina agreed to accompany William to an al fresco party, she found the weather had become her enemy. In spite of a parasol and a large, shady hat, the southern sun struck at her. She could barely see in the brilliant light, and the heat turned her sick and dizzy.

She tried to explain this to William when he remonstrated with her angrily for being sullenly silent, but he did not believe her. He insisted she was only making an excuse to spite him. Although Sabrina knew the accusation was untrue, she was not certain that it was entirely the heat that had affected her. She had been in her period of flux. This did not usually inconvenience her, but it was not impossible that it was her condition rather than the sun that was at fault. She had little experience with real heat. Most of her childhood had been spent in Ireland and on the island off Scotland, both notably cool and rainy. England, too, seldom suffered high temperatures, and there everyone hid from the heat on dog days.

Thus, when William insisted she go on a picnic on the twentieth of June, Sabrina agreed without much protest. She took what precautions she could, the hat and parasol again and also lavender water to dab on her temples and wrists and a vinaigrette holding smelling salts in the event she felt faint. And, although she was an excellent horsewoman, she suggested that she go in the carriage, to which William agreed with such enthusiasm that Sabrina guessed his inamorata was going to ride. In spite of all precautions, Sabrina had all she could do not to faint on the way. On arrival, however, she collapsed and gave everyone a dreadful fright because she could not be revived for a long time.

William's new light of love was both shrewd and practical. Sabrina's collapse played right into her hands, which was very fortunate for Sabrina. Donna Francisca Maria da

Silviera de Brito promptly directed the party to an inn with a cool, dark parlor and attended Sabrina herself until she revived. They would stay until the cool evening breeze began, she assured Sabrina, and settled her to sleep off her weakness. And when William whispered in her ear that Sabrina was acting up because she was jealous, Donna Francisca shook her head.

"It is the whiteness," she said. "She is not fair as our women from the Minho are fair. They are blond, yes, but their skin is more golden. Lady Elvan is white, all white, even her hair, all pale, like silver."

William's forehead creased. He was really annoyed with Sabrina. Deliberately or not, she was causing more trouble than she was worth. If she were going to faint every time she stepped out of the house, she would be utterly useless.

"I will have to send her home," he said.

Donna Francisca cast him a flickering glance from under long black lashes. Her large, almond-shaped brown eyes were hard but beautiful. Sending Sabrina home would not fit in with her plans at all.

"Ah, no!" she exclaimed. "How cruel you are to send so fragile and delicate a woman on so long a journey all alone."

Instantly alerted by the tone of Donna Francisca's voice, William glanced across the room to where Sabrina was slowly recovering, lying on a sofa. "But she cannot endure the heat. You saw that she was ill at the party last week. This time it was worse. However little love there is between us"—he lowered his voice seductively over those words—"for she is as cold as her ice-maiden appearance, she is my wife. I could not permit harm to come to her."

"No, indeed," Donna Francisca purred. "It is the last thing I should wish. But there is no need to send Lady Elvan home. It would be . . . uncomfortable for a man to send away his wife. . . . It would be . . . remarked upon.

It would be far better to take her to the mountains. There it is cool and pleasant."

William looked sidelong at the ripe and beautiful woman sitting across from him. "But I do not know your country. I would not know where to take her."

"That is easy. Poor Lady Elvan. My sympathy is engaged for her. There is a house, small but well appointed—it was built for my grandmother when my own mother came to La Casa des Ermidas. I am sure it could be arranged that Lady Elvan spend the summer there. It is cool, quite high, and it is no great distance from Coimbra, so that a good physician could be fetched from the university should she be ill."

William stared into the dark eyes. "But will it be too lonely for Sabrina? There will be times when I must be in Lisbon on business."

"Ah, no! How could you think I would suggest such a thing? So delicate a lady, all alone. The town of Lousa, a lovely little town, is no more than a half-hour walk, a fifteen-minute drive or ride. Lady Elvan rides, does she not?"

"Yes, very well."

"And for little things, a few moments' chat perhaps, La Casa des Ermidas is only a mile up the hill by road or a quarter mile by the path behind the house. I will be there, at des Ermidas. Of course, the path is somewhat overgrown but it could be cleared."

"I would not think of putting you to the trouble of clearing it," William said with a significant glance. "The hill would be too steep for Sabrina, and walking is not a favorite activity of hers." That was a flat lie, but William uttered it without a blink. "Naturally I will look over the path, and if she insists, I will have it cleared. Surely that must be my responsibility."

"Certainly. I will be happy to leave it to your judgment."

Donna Francisca's smile was brilliant. William's answering smile was caressing. If it held a glint of triumph, the lady who received it did not mind. She was willing to allow her pursuer to think he had won a victory. She had a use for this Englishman.

Both were very pleased with themselves, and when eventually Sabrina stirred and sat up, William found he was very pleased with her, also. Her weakness, instead of being detrimental, had provided the opportunity for which he had been searching. In addition, she had remained asleep for just the right amount of time—enough for hints and suggestions, for an "accidental" touch or two—and wakened before it became embarrassing to go no further. Her awakening, moreover, invested the conversation with a spicy aura of wrongdoing.

William knelt beside Sabrina to ask tenderly whether she felt well enough to come to the table if he supported her. Donna Francisca came also, extending a hand to touch Sabrina's forehead and exclaim that she was better, since the clammy sweat was gone. Sabrina smiled seraphically on both of them, begging pardon for being such a trouble. She had not been asleep nearly as long as they thought, and she was almost as pleased as they were with the arrangements. It would have been dreadfully dull to be imprisoned in the house all summer.

Arrangements were made with remarkable rapidity. That was not surprising when tenant and landlord outdid each other in courtesy and willingness to please. Donna Francisca's husband, Dom José, was very sorry for the lovely *blanca*, the so fair English lady who could not endure the heat. He was also glad to please the English milord. The court might be stupidly cold, but Dom José knew it was the British who bought his wine. France and Austria made their own; Germany drank beer. It was the English, whose taste favored the sweet sherries and rich

278

dark ports and whose climate would not permit the grapes to grow properly, who made his father a rich man and him still richer.

Thus, Dom José was well pleased and complimented his wife on her wisdom in first considering his business. He was not at all surprised; Donna Francisca had a nice discernment about what was best for the business. Dom José smiled, although he was alone in his office. Everyone had warned him against marriage with her. Everyone said she was prouder of her lineage than the royal family, that she would treat him like dirt, that all she wanted was his money to save her family estates.

It was true about the money, of course, but Dom José did not mind at all. It was the estates he wanted. Now they were his and would be his sons' after him. And most of the other warnings had not been fulfilled. Although she was cold and most reluctant to couple with him, she did not treat him with contempt. In fact, she took a most lively interest in the business, eagerly studying every aspect of its management. Dom José smiled again. Perhaps he should have taken her as a partner instead of a wife. In six months she had learned so well and so quickly that he almost thought she could take his place as head of the firm if he should die.

On the other hand, she had not yet conceived. The smile disappeared. Nor was it likely she would if she continued to refuse him constantly. Well, that was partly his fault. Dom José was aware that he was not exactly a girl's dream suitor. She had been repelled by him in the beginning, he knew. He had been willing to allow her to grow accustomed slowly, since she was so frigid. Also, he had been very busy.

The handwriting on the wall had been plain to Dom José for months. Unless a miracle occurred, trade would be disrupted. Dom José had needed his time and energy to dispose of his stock and secure his wealth as best he could. He was no boy who could work all day and play all night. He needed his rest and had not pressed his wife about sexual congress. Soon there would be little business to attend to. Francisca probably knew that, Dom José thought wryly, and had decided to go to La Casa des Ermidas to escape him. He laughed.

It suited him very well that she had decided to go and to take the Englishwoman as company. The English would make no trouble and might be out of the country soon. When his business was all settled in a few weeks, he would go up to La Casa des Ermidas himself. Then he would stand no nonsense from Francisca and do his duty until he got her with child. A good beating or two in the privacy of des Ermidas, where her bruises would heal unremarked, would quickly make her receptive if not enthusiastic.

It was important that his sons would be what he could never be. Dom José knew he was barely tolerated among the nobility for his wealth. His own land was nothing, a few vineyards. There was no ancient castle on it; there was no tomb in which ancestors lay with legs crossed to show they had gone on crusade. But his sons would come down from La Casa des Ermidas knowing their forefathers had owned the land for six hundred years, had fought the Moors from the ruined keep on the river below. His family's financial success joined with his wife's regal lineage would create sons with the advantages of both backgrounds.

Oddly enough, at the same moment Donna Francisca was also thinking about Dom José's sons. She was not speaking of that subject; in fact, she was inquiring civilly but coolly of William when she should send a servant to the dower house to have it opened, cleaned, and stocked with food. However, whenever she spoke to William, she thought of Dom José's sons. She thought this Englishman would be ideal for her purpose. He was not some jumped-up diplomatic lackey. One could tell his breeding in the beautifully shaped head, the long, slender hands and feet. The employment at the embassy, that was noblesse oblige, the duty a man owes his country—a man of honor, then. To take him—yes. It would be better if Lord Elvan fathered the son she must provide than that crude, common toad of a merchant she had been forced to marry for his wealth. Once she had the child, she could be rid of Dom José; the money and business would be the child's—and, thus, hers.

She had understood her husband far better than he guessed. She knew for what purpose he had bought her; she knew that she herself—beautiful, educated, intelligent, and nobly born—meant nothing to him. He would have taken a mewling idiot, coarse and deformed, to have sons of a noble line. He made her nothing! Less than nothing! How she hated him! She could not refuse when he had offered, but she would have her revenge. Sweet, full, and sure, she would first have her revenge—and then everything.

First, the son she bore would not be José's. That was most important. It would be tricky, too. He had not the pride of a grandee, who might well keep silent to save his own face. José would tell the world and repudiate her and the child if he suspected. She would need to sleep with him several times after she missed the first flux, but she would manage that somehow. Perhaps she could say she had had special prayers for conception and felt they would be answered at that particular time.

"As for me," William said, startling Donna Francisca, who had forgotten that she had asked when she should open the house, "immediately would not be too soon, but"—his smile caressing, suggestive—"I would not wish to hurry you in any way."

Donna Francisca managed to control her faint start when William's voice woke her from her thoughts. She found she was staring into his eyes, and lowered her lids slowly while she made sense of what he had said.

"I assure you," William murmured, "I wish we could all be whisked away there by magic at this moment."

"Oh, I agree," Francisca said with a slow smile. "It is so dreadfully hot. Even I feel it. Poor Lady Elvan must be prostrate."

William's eyes held hers for a moment while a flicker of laughter crossed his face. Francisca read it clearly enough and blushed. His expression had implied that, shame though it might be, William was not interested in Sabrina, even prostrate. That was flattering, but for practical reasons Francisca wanted to leave as soon as possible. José was still tied to urgent business matters and would be unable to make the trip to des Ermidas for several weeks. After that, he might have more time free to come up, and at des Ermidas José always demanded his conjugal rights. Francisca disguised a shudder under a soft laugh.

"Then I will send a man out today, and if Lady Elvan can be readied, you could start the day after tomorrow. There will be no need to bring anything more than clothing. Everything else will be there and ready."

This news was as welcome to Sabrina as to William. Although she had not collapsed again, the growing heat was beginning to affect her even in the house during the hottest hours of the day. Katy was frantic, begging her to go home to England, but Sabrina did not wish to return. One of her reasons for agreeing to accompany William had been to dull her fear for Perce, and in that sense the journey had been relatively successful.

Although Sabrina had not been occupied by diplomatic

282

duties as she believed she would be, there had been the distractions of learning a little of a new language, setting up a new household, and seeing a new city. The distance, too, lent a kind of calm. Because Sabrina knew it would be several weeks before news from East Prussia could come to Lisbon, something inside her blocked the black, sick, unreasoning fear that had darkened every day after the battle of Pultusk. She thought of Perce all the time, but with patient eagerness.

Thus, she was looking forward to her trip to the mountains. Lord Strangford also hoped the cooler and purer air would enable her to stay. He had been annoyed with William for having brought his wife, but—quite aside from having grown rather fond of Sabrina—he did not wish her to leave. It would look entirely too much like a retreat in the face of Carlota Joaquina's hostility if Sabrina returned to England. Therefore, Lord Strangford gave William several weeks' leave to take Sabrina to the mountains and to settle her there comfortably.

Two days after the Elvans left Lisbon, Lord Strangford received a dispatch reporting that there had been a major battle at Friedland. The Russians had been defeated by the French; they had lost ten thousand men and eighty guns and had retreated in some disorder. But they had inflicted twelve thousand casualties on the French. The news was bad, but not bad enough for Strangford to recall William. The Russians were far closer to their home territory than were the French. They could replace men and guns more easily than could Bonaparte.

There was one hopeful aspect to the news. The defeat had been owing to a disastrous mistake on the part of General Bennigsen, the commanding general on the Russian side. He had allowed himself to be trapped in an untenable position, his troops outnumbered two to one. Even at these odds the Russians had apparently outfought the French, inflicting more casualties than they received.

Had numbers and ground been more equal, it was possible the Russians would have won. If only this idea could be presented compellingly enough to the tsar, the war would continue.

CHAPTER FIFTEEN

Some days after the battle, General Bennigsen had been trying to accomplish just that. He had assured Tsar Alexander passionately that he could defeat Bonaparte. He had come near doing it twice, he averred. This defeat was owing only to bad information. Their men had fought better than the French. They had been tricked, tired, unfed, and still had stood their ground. If reinforcements could have reached them, they would have won. But Alexander was not listening. He did not even say, which he could have done with justification, that Bennigsen had been a fool and had fallen into a deliberately laid trap. Alexander was again in the grip of a deep depression.

Early on the eighteenth of June the tsar had heard without apparent emotion that Königsberg had been taken by the French marshal Soult on the sixteenth, but the next day he told Bennigsen that he had already sent Prince Dimitri Lobanov-Rostovsky, a lieutenant general under Bennigsen's own command, to ask for an armistice. Bennigsen was furious. This was the end of his dream of glory, his obsessive hope of being the man who conquered Bonaparte. Instead of being the most powerful and important general in Europe, he would sink into obscurity—one more name on the list of those whom Bonaparte had destroyed. In fact, his fate would be worse than others' because he would be the scapegoat.

The tsar would be willing to sacrifice him. Alexander

knew he owed Bennigsen a debt of gratitude. Very likely the general had saved Alexander's life by removing Tsar Paul from the throne; otherwise, Paul would have killed his son. But, of course, the dowager empress hated Bennigsen. She called what he had done murder, and never allowed her son to forget his own or Bennigsen's guilt.

The fury and frustration Bennigsen felt had to be expressed. Nor were his fears diminished by the fact that Prince Lobanov-Rostovsky was handling the negotiations. To Bennigsen the use of his subordinate instead of himself was a sure sign that he was in disfavor. Worse yet, all the other officers seemed in perfect sympathy with the tsar, delighted that peace would be made. Even his own aides-de-camp had no enthusiasm for continuing the fight. Although not to his face, they said—all except Lord Kevern—it was not Russian business what Bonaparte did in Germany.

Bennigsen knew that Kevern's desire to continue the war sprang from his belief that it was best for England, and not from any special sympathy for him. Kevern had never denied that. However, in a way, Kevern was a symbol for another scapegoat. It was well known that the tsar now loudly blamed the English for dragging him into a war he had not wanted, then abandoning him. Alexander claimed the British had not paid the subsidies that they had promised him, but he was far more bitter about what he called their cowardice. He had been promised a diversion that would draw off some of Bonaparte's troops to another front, and it had not materialized.

There was no danger in telling Kevern what he thought. Bennigsen was sure he was a safe confidant. He was not Russian and owed no loyalty to the tsar. How could he, when Alexander's first words on meeting Bonaparte were, "I hate the English as much as you do and am ready to assist you in any undertaking against them." Bennigsen, who had been present at the meeting, informed Perce of this remark himself. There was a moment of silence, after which Perce had offered to resign if his presence would cause his superior any more problems.

"Nothing can make my situation worse," Bennigsen snarled. "Alexander might blame the English now, but as soon as he returns to St. Petersburg, the dowager empress will make sure the blame falls upon me."

Perce had already been the recipient of several heated defenses of Bennigsen's conduct. In his personal opinion the general had been a fool. He had allowed his eagerness to obtain one clear victory to deceive him into accepting unconfirmed and suspicious reports. Perce felt that the defeat at Friedland had been Bennigsen's fault; however, it was useless to worry about that now. Considering what Alexander had said and Bonaparte's mania on the subject of the British, it was clear that part of the peace treaty would affect England. Perce's duty to his homeland was to discover what was planned for England by France and Russia in the terms of their treaty. His only key was Bennigsen, and he must do his best to hold on to it.

He said what was expedient, trying to insert in Bennigsen's consciousness that a final end to the war with all of Europe and England, too, under the heel of the French would be a final end for him.

"Doubtless my country should have contributed more," Perce commented somewhat later, "but I am convinced that their failure was a mistake owing to a lack of understanding. Of one thing I am certain, England is unalterably opposed to Bonaparte's ambitions. What I fear is that the tsar will agree to conditions that will lead to the conquest of England."

Bennigsen laughed. "That is a most reasonable fear. It would not suit you at all."

"It would not suit you, either, sir," Perce said soberly. "When England's resistance is over, do you believe Bonaparte will stop? There will be one nation and one nation alone that has not been conquered—Russia. Do you *really* believe Bonaparte will permit *two* emperors to exist?"

"That may be true," Bennigsen remarked cynically, "but for all the good England did us, we might as well have fought alone."

That was the wrong tack. Perce raised one eyebrow. "I doubt, if England is conquered, you will have a chance to fight. You know there was no need to end the war over one lost battle that was not even fought on Russian soil. The tsar has lost the will to fight. It is in his mind that he was defeated, not on the battlefield. England's destruction will only confirm that conviction of helplessness. So, when Bonaparte encroaches and makes more and more demands, Alexander will yield each time. And whom do you think will be blamed each time—England?"

Bennigsen said nothing for a long few minutes. Kevern had stated what he himself feared—that his name would be synonymous with ultimate defeat. His one chance would be a resumption of the war, during which he could redeem himself.

Shortly afterward Bennigsen roused himself to dismiss Perce. For several days he was not summoned, and the general barely acknowledged his presence when they met accidentally. However, on the evening of July fifth, Perce was approached rather secretively by a personal servant of General Bennigsen, who asked him to report to the general's quarters. There Perce found Bennigsen standing rigidly and looking out of the window. Without turning, he gestured Perce toward the desk and told him to write out his resignation, adding that England and Russia would be at war within a few months.

"You have done good service, Lord Kevern," he said stiffly, "and I am sorry to lose you, but you must understand that it is not reasonable for me to have as an aide a national of a country with which we are at war."

"Yes, sir. Thank you, sir," Perce replied formally.

He sat down to write what was required, but his eyes examined the desk minutely. He wondered whether he had been told to sit in order to find the information he wanted concealed somewhere. There was nothing. Perce's heart sank. Bennigsen had decided against helping England, he feared. And yet, that could not be. There could be no other reason for a servant to approach him quietly. Then, to his dismay, as if reading his mind, Bennigsen answered that.

"I asked you to come here privately," he said, "to allow you the choice of leaving with or without good-byes to your fellow officers. It makes no difference to me, of course."

"Thank you, sir. That is kind."

Although it was reasonable to leave the resignation on the desk, Perce stood up with it in his hand. It was clear enough that Bennigsen wanted to be rid of him as quickly as possible. He approached the general, wondering whether it would be worthwhile to render him unconscious and search him and the desk. Just before he was close enough to strike, Bennigsen turned and drew a folded sheaf of papers from his pocket.

"I have here a letter stating that your service was satisfactory and honorable, plus a passport, which will enable you to cross into Russia. From there you can take ship for England or wherever else you like."

"Thank you, sir."

There was nothing else Perce could say, but he was furious. It seemed that he had misjudged Bennigsen, until he took the sheaf of papers in his hand. It seemed far thicker to him than a single letter and passport should be. His eyes flashed from the papers to Bennigsen, but the general had turned away again. Perce strangled the far more grateful "thank you" that rose in his throat, stowed the papers casually in his pocket, saluted smartly, and left the room without further ado.

In the street he hesitated. The first thing he had to do was look at those papers. A private room at the nearest inn satisfied all the requirements. Perce ordered a bottle of brandy. He actually had two drinks while he examined what he had, after which he emptied half the bottle into the fireplace. Bennigsen had not disappointed him. There in the packet, along with the passport and report of service, were the clauses of the Treaty of Tilsit. Perce's eyes widened as he quickly scanned the pertinent passages. Bad! It was very bad. If the information Bennigsen had given him was true, the general had urged his speedy departure for good reason. Bonaparte, with Russia's compliance, intended to seize the navies of Denmark, Spain, and Portugal. Good God, that would give Boney superior numbers to the British navy.

Perce did not expect any trouble in leaving and did not have any. To be on the safe side, he committed the articles of the treaty to memory and concealed the papers between the outer shell and inner lining of his portmanteau, but no one ever examined his effects. Nor was there any surprise when he gathered his friends that night and told them he was leaving.

The young men with whom he had served were sorry, but they were not surprised by his haste. They assumed it was bitterness—hurt that his long, honest service was set at naught—and they offered fervent assurances of their trust and undying friendship no matter what the future relations between their countries should be. Perce returned these with sincerity, even when they embraced him and kissed him and wept over him—displays he never got used to and that embarrassed him very much.

Before dawn, when all others were abed sleeping off the farewell party, Perce rode northeast out of Tilsit with Sergei and two extra horses carrying baggage. They were in

Riga two days later, and the next morning Perce found several British ships hastily loading cargo and preparing to leave. The news of Friedland and the meeting of Bonaparte and Alexander was known all over the city, and every merchant with British connections was trying to send and receive all the merchandise he could before the expected order ended trading.

Having arranged his passage on a ship that would leave the next day, Perce had at last confronted the problem of Sergei. He had grown deeply attached to the man and believed the attachment to be mutual, but he could not believe Sergei would be happy in England. He took the man up to his bedchamber, appalled at the scene he feared would ensue.

"I must leave for my country tomorrow, Sergei," he began.

"Yes. What do you want me to do with the horses?"

"There's something more important than that," Perce said. "I don't believe I will ever return to Russia."

"That's bad," Sergei remarked calmly. "It's a good country. You have friends here, too."

"Yes. I suppose you want to stay here—or, rather, go back to wherever—er . . . Well, you can keep the horses, and—"

"Stay here? Go back? Go back where?" Sergei interrupted with an expression of astonishment. "How can I stay or go anywhere if you don't go? I belong to you. Where you go, I must go."

"Now you know that isn't true," Perce said, avoiding the question of belonging. "Not every serf goes with his master."

"Of course," Sergei replied, "but they stay on their master's land. That's the same thing. You don't own any land in Russia, so I go with you."

Perce sat a moment in silence. What Sergei said could have betokened ignorance or even stupidity, but Perce knew perfectly well that neither was true. In fact, he was being put in his place. Sergei's expression showed he understood quite well what Perce was suggesting—that Perce did not intend to sell him but was offering him his freedom. Sergei's answers had been characteristic—a sly and extremely shrewd deliberate act of refusal, a deliberate reminder that Perce had accepted responsibility for him and was stuck with it!

"Don't be a fool, Sergei," Perce exclaimed. "I've paid you well, and you've saved a great deal of your salary. I'll give you all the money I can now, and I'll send you more. You can buy a piece of land and even marry. I don't think you'll like England. It's even wetter and warmer than Prussia. Besides, you can't belong to me in England. By law, any serf or slave who touches English soil becomes a free man at once."

"I know that. *She* told me often enough. Nag, nag, nag. Be a man. Men aren't slaves." Sergei shrugged dyspeptically. "I probably *won't* like England. It's full of crazy people, so far as I can tell, but I can get used to it. You'll take 'my lady,' "—his tone altered on the two words to one of profound respect—"soon, I guess, and I'll take *her*. It will be best that way. We can all stay together."

Perce was again silent, but this time because he had been stricken mute with shock. When he finally managed to say, "Her? Katy?" his voice squeaked like a rusty hinge.

Sergei nodded sadly. "I belong in England, I think. Would a sane man take such a woman? Nag, nag, nag. Your shirt is dirty. You stink. You drink too much." He turned reproachful eyes on Perce. "It's all your fault."

Perce took his head in his hands, carefully, as if he were afraid it would burst or fall off. He didn't know to which shocking statement to apply himself first. How could any of this be his fault? Should he deny he would soon "take" Sabrina? How could he deny it? He certainly intended to take her as soon as he could. But how did Sergei know? Did Katy know too? Had they planned this together?

Katy? And Sergei? Prim, proper, neat-as-a-pin Katy and Sergei? Perce looked at his man, patiently squatting on his heels. Take away the current hangdog expression and Sergei was quite a man. His dark hair was slightly touched with gray, but still thick and curly; his dark eyes were expressive, bright with shrewd intelligence. His body was like the trunk of an old tree, thick and strong. Perce wondered what Katy's first husband had been like. Fishermen didn't always smell too sweet either.

"You are agreed on this?" Perce asked, his voice still creaking with shock. "I mean, does Katy—Mrs. Petersen—has she accepted you?"

"We never talked about it," Sergei replied, "but she'll take me."

"Now wait, Sergei." Perce was suddenly fearful of hurt for this man of whom he was very fond. Sergei was shrewd, but after a life in the army, what could he know about women? "Are you sure you aren't believing what you want to believe? Don't forget, you and Mrs. Petersen don't really speak the same language. You could have misunderstood her. Also, customs differ in different countries. Maybe she didn't mean what you thought she meant. It's a long way to England if there's nothing but disappointment at the end of the road."

Stubbornly, Sergei shook his head. "I'll have less trouble getting mine than you'll have getting yours. It's *later* I'll have the trouble. Nag, nag, nag."

Perce opened his mouth, shut it, then got out, "Lady Elvan is married."

Sergei didn't answer that beyond a single glance. What he said was, "What do you want me to do with the horses?"

They were back where they started. Perce shrugged. If it didn't work out, he could always send Sergei back to

Russia. If it did work out . . . A surge of desire washed over him. He had rarely allowed himself to think of Sabrina since their parting in February. It was not the physical frustration he minded but the feeling of helplessness, knowing he had no right to prod her to leave her husband, knowing he had no way to protect her if she did, until she was free. Any hint that there was more than casual friendship between them could do her infinite harm.

Sergei stood up, interrupting Perce's thoughts. "The horses?" he repeated.

"Sell them," Perce said, "privately, if you can. Otherwise look over the stock of the dealer to see that the animals are decently cared for."

After the battle of Eylau, Perce had not had the heart to buy fine animals again, but he did not want even the dull creatures he owned to be mistreated. As Sergei left, his mind came back to Sabrina. He had had letters, of course, but they had been purely friendly; he had warned her that his mail would probably be examined. Nonetheless, it was the receipt of such a letter that had caused him to forget himself and write what he had no right to put on paper. He could not remember exactly what he had said in the letter he had sent through Lady Leonie, but he had been drunk and aching with longing, and like a fool had given it to Sergei to put in the post bag.

He was not afraid the letter could have caused any trouble. Lady Leonie would have seen that it got to Brina in private. Only he had not had an answer; he had not had *any* letter from Sabrina since that one must have arrived. Perce gnawed his lip. It was ridiculous to think Sabrina might have been offended. Or was she? Could she have thought such a letter implied contempt on his part? Could she believe he thought she was soiled, lowered by their relationship?

It would do him no good to speculate. As soon as he saw Sabrina, he could clear up any misunderstanding. The first business was to return to the ship and book passage for Sergei. That done, he wandered restlessly around the city until it was time for dinner, seeing nothing no matter where he looked, except some very fair women. It was infuriating that there should be so many blondes. Perce's heart lurched every time a fair creature stepped out of a shop or into a carriage.

He ate slowly, trying to kill time, trying to think only of his food, but it did not work. The fear that Sabrina had withdrawn kept nagging at him. He walked around again, trying to tire himself enough to sleep, but the exertion seemed only to make him more tense. Finally he came back to the inn and began to drink. Eventually that must have worked, because Perce did not remember going to bed; however, for a long time he remembered being wakened the next morning. Seldom had he had so excruciating a hangover—and so futile a one. Physical misery only seemed to intensify the conviction that he had lost Sabrina.

The trouble with an uncomfortable idea is that the harder one tries to push it out of one's mind, the more one actually thinks about it. And there was no external relief. The voyage to England was peaceful and tedious. Perce tried to read and talk to his fellow passengers, but he could not shake off his fears.

Arrival in London did not ease matters. Perce had been agonizingly tempted to make for Stour Castle from the port at which he arrived, but he knew that the information he carried was urgent. To his dismay he found he had to follow Foreign Secretary Canning to his country seat. The news was too important for deputies. All he could do was write to Sabrina at Stour with an attached note to the housekeeper to send the letter on to Lady Elvan or to Lady Leonie if they were not in residence. It was not much of a satisfaction because he could give no return address except his own chambers in London; he had no idea how long Canning would keep him or whether they would return to London.

The latter actually occurred, and Perce found a message from Leonie that she was at Stour but that Sabrina had gone to Portugal with William. This information was followed by an urgent request that Perce come to Stour as soon as possible. Perce nearly had a fit. There was a note of urgency and anxiety in Leonie's brief letter that sent his heart right up into his throat, but it was impossible for him to leave London now. Minister of War Castlereagh and First Lord of the Admiralty Mulgrave were on their way and insisted on speaking to him personally; neither of them trusted Canning. The welfare of all England might hang on the discussions forthcoming, because if Canning put up the backs of the War Office and the Admiralty, action to subvert the special clauses in the Treaty of Tilsit might be delayed.

Logic and patriotism notwithstanding, Perce decided he could post up to Stour this afternoon. True, he would arrive about ten o'clock and might have to wake Leonie, but she would not mind. Having heard what she had to tell him, he could travel back during the night. He realized he might not be very wide awake at the conference the next day, but he would be no better able to function if he could not stop worrying about Sabrina for a single minute. He was just about to shout for Sergei to call his groom when Roger walked into his sitting room.

"I understand," he said, "that you are the savior of the nation. I have all but been kissed on both cheeks by Portland because he had been told you were sent out to Russia on my recommendation. How the devil did you convince—"

"Never mind that," Perce interrupted harshly. "Why the hell did you let Sabrina go to Portugal with Elvan? Don't you know—"

296

"Sabrina?" Roger echoed, baffled by the deep anxiety displayed on Perce's face.

Roger opened his mouth again, but nothing came out and an expression of mingled anger and revelation appeared on his face. Perce bit his lip, repressing a strong desire to burst into tears. Altogether, he thought, he was behaving as if he were ten years old, when he first met Roger. Clearly Roger was not aware of Leonie's letter to him.

"I beg your pardon," Perce got out. "Won't you sit down? Wine?" Roger being still speechless, Perce turned his head and shouted, "Sergei!"

"What now?" Sergei asked, sticking his head in from Perce's bedroom.

"Bring up some sherry and some claret," Perce said, then turned to Roger. "Will that be all right, sir?"

"Better add some brandy," Roger said in French, since that was the language in which Perce had addressed Sergei. "I think I might need it." He watched Sergei until he went down the stairs and then said, "Are you the reason Sabrina decided to leave William?"

"Yes. . . . No. . . . I don't know how to answer that," Perce said, sitting down rather hard.

Roger stared at him, his face impassive now because so many different emotions seethed behind it that no expression was able to dominate long enough to register. Then, slowly, he also sat down. The worst part of his shock, oddly enough, had little to do with Perce's relationship with Sabrina. It was the need to come to grips with the realization that Perce was a man rather than a mischievous boy. It was the shock of seeing Perce's face, bare of its masking, the face of a man. The mouth was hard, marked by lines of pain, and the eyes had seen far, far too much.

"I think," Roger said slowly, "that I have a right to ask for a better explanation than that."

"You have the right," Perce agreed, "but is there ever an explanation for something like this? I can only tell you what happened."

He did so as briefly as possible, without embroidery, beginning with his own awakening when Elvan's courtship of Sabrina began and Sabrina's response after they had met at Czartoryski's ball.

"Maybe I shouldn't have done it," Perce finished angrily, "but I'm glad I did. I love her, and I want her—"

"How?" Roger asked pointedly.

"There's no need to insult me, sir," Perce said quietly, flushing again. "I want to marry her, but—but I'll take her and care for her any way at all."

"If a breath of this gets out, I'll never get an annulment," Roger remarked. "You realize that, don't you?"

There was a pause while Perce digested the implications. Roger was telling him that he must avoid Sabrina until she was free. He turned his head to stare out the window, unaware that Sergei had come up from the cellar.

Roger watched with considerable astonishment. He had been considerably shocked by Sergei's tone and manner when he replied to Perce. Now that he thought of it, he realized he should have been shocked by the way Perce shouted instead of ringing a bell. Now his eyes opened wide as Sergei set two glasses on the table and drew the corks from the bottles with his teeth! Roger opened his mouth to protest, but Sergei did not notice, having turned his head toward Perce to ask in a casual tone, "You want me to pour?"

"No, go away," Perce responded automatically.

Sergei went back into the bedroom, and Roger said mildly, "Your man's method of uncorking wine is original. His style and manner are also not just in the common mode."

Perce looked at him, then at the bottles of wine and glasses standing on the table: no tray, no decanter, and tooth marks on the corks. He began to laugh. "He isn't my servant, he's my serf, or slave—at least he insists he is, and nothing I can say will dissuade him. But, you know, he's saved my life I don't know how many times, and besides, he expects to marry Katy."

"*What?*" Roger exploded.

Laughing even harder, Perce recounted the conversation in the inn at Riga. By the end of that story Roger was laughing, too. The tension between them evaporated, leaving them looking soberly at each other when the mirth was over.

"I'll do my damnedest to make Brina happy," Perce said. "I'll never forgive myself for not realizing in time what she meant to me. Perhaps I could have spared her all this unhappiness."

"Don't," Roger interrupted. "It was our fault, Leonie's and mine, but really all mine. I should have known better, but I was sure Elvan was ripe to settle down."

Perce shrugged. "It's no use flogging a dead horse, sir. We're all to blame. Brina, too. She's stubborn. It might have happened no matter what we did. The course now is to get her out of it."

"Yes, well, that's one of the reasons we all agreed that she should go to Portugal."

That statement left Perce with his mouth hanging open. Roger took advantage of his surprise to explain the scene that had taken place with William. One big weight toppled off Perce. If Brina had actually asked that an annulment of her marriage be procured, she must not have been angered or hurt by his letter.

"But I don't understand, if an annulment was being discussed, why Brina agreed to accompany William to Portugal."

"He agreed to consider the annulment only if she would go," Roger said. "Elvan claimed Canning would give the assignment to someone else if Sabrina refused to accompany him, because a hostess was necessary." Roger's face grew bleak. "It wasn't true, in fact, but I only learned about that a few weeks ago."

Perce jumped to his feet. "Then why? Why did he say—"

"Sit down and don't imagine horrors. You're as bad as Leonie. We've had letters from Brina all along. And don't say that Elvan may be forcing her to write. I'm not sure he could, but quite aside from my opinion, the housekeeper at Stour has had letters from Katy. You know damned well Elvan wouldn't have thought of that. I think he planned to court Brina again. He can't believe she isn't still in love with him. He seems to think she wants to dissolve the marriage because she's jealous. In any case, the only thing Katy seemed worried about was the heat making Brina weak and dizzy."

"Then is Brina coming home?" Perce asked eagerly.

Roger looked at him sadly and shook his head. "Once, just once, let Lady Jersey or any of those other society gossips get a look at your face with that expression on it, and any chance I might have to get Brina free without a scandal would be gone. Anyway, she isn't coming home. Elvan has taken a house for her in the mountains where it's cool."

"You needn't worry about *my* face," Perce replied, immediately assuming his village-idiot expression.

Roger had to laugh, but he shook his head again. "You know it isn't so easy. If you came across her unexpectedly . . ."

"Well, there isn't much chance of that now, is there?" Perce began to pace the room. Rather than easing his tension, this discussion seemed to have increased it. He had the feeling that he had to go to Sabrina at once, but he could not say that outright after what Roger had been telling him. After one turn he stopped in front of Roger. "Sir,

Portugal isn't safe. Brina must come home immediately. Didn't Portland tell you what was in those articles?"

Roger stood up too, his brow wrinkling. "No, he didn't, and I didn't ask. For God's sake, I thought it must be another invasion scheme, perhaps using the Russian navy."

"No. Oh, it's invasion in the long run, but Boney's no fool. He must have guessed right off that he couldn't touch Russian troops or ships, not without Alexander interfering constantly and probably taking offense and withdrawing the troops and ships at the last moment. Instead, the navies of Denmark, Holland, Spain, and Portugal are to be loaned to France until the end of the war. The end being, of course, the conquest of England."

Roger whistled. "Denmark must yield, of course. She is completely surrounded and has no power to resist. However, Spain will fight if invaded. There's a British fleet at Gibraltar. There will be plenty of time to take out our nationals."

"No, there will be no time. You haven't heard it all. Spain will not be invaded. At least, Spain won't realize it's being invaded until it's too late. You remember back in 1801, Boney proposed a treaty with Spain that would divide Portugal? He's going to propose the same again and ask permission to march his armies across Spain for the purpose of subduing Portugal."

Roger spat an obscenity. That would work. The Spanish hated the Portuguese because Portugal had won its freedom from Spain twice. The Spanish would jump at any chance to regain power over their erstwhile territory. Besides, the government of Spain was violently divided. Between the factions, Bonaparte would surely get agreement for any scheme he suggested. None of the fools, all of whom would be busy trying to destroy each other, would stop to realize that when Bonaparte's armies were in Spain, he would pick them all off like ripe plums, swallow them, and set whomever he wanted on the throne.

"If he stops to take over Spain—" Roger began.

"He can do both at the same time, you know," Perce said sharply, and then, looking away again, "I'm going to get Brina as soon as Canning is through with me. I'll leave her at whatever port we touch in England. She can travel safely with Katy, or I can send Sergei with them, but I'm going to Portugal."

"Don't be a fool," Roger protested. "You'll probably miss her. She isn't really of any diplomatic use. I'm sure Elvan will send her home as soon as he hears about the Russian defeat at Friedland. He'll realize—"

"Maybe, and maybe he won't. It won't matter if I miss her. If she's on her way home, so much the better. I won't be around to make a nuisance of myself for a few weeks. I'm sorry if you don't like it, sir, but I've got an ugly feeling. I don't know whether it's about Brina or about the situation in Portugal, but I must go."

"Superstition, Perce?" Roger had meant to tease, but his voice sounded worried and he found himself agreeing. "Yes, go. If there's any way I can help you, let me know. Superstition or not, I'd rather have you bring her home than trust her safety to Elvan. His work comes first to him. He should have sent Brina home from Prussia two months before he did. It worked out that time, but this time we may not be so fortunate. Yes, go."

CHAPTER SIXTEEN

Whatever feelings of doom or danger Roger and Perce suffered, Sabrina felt none. She was delighted with the house on the mountainside above the town of Lousa. The town itself, although small, was a retreat from the heat of summer for many families of the minor nobility. Thus, there were shops that catered to expensive tastes and amusements suitable for a lady. Not many families were yet in residence, but those that were had little sympathy for the notions of Carlota Joaquina. They might have ignored the heretic Englishwoman at court under orders, but here they welcomed her cheerfully.

Nearly two weeks passed pleasantly. The only difficulty Sabrina faced was explaining why she would not accept evening engagements. This was, of course, because William would not accompany her. Now that he was reverting to his old habits, William usually did not accompany her during the day, either, but this did not matter, because her visits were to the ladies. Evening engagements were different; they were events for couples. She could not come unaccompanied to those, not while her husband was known to be in residence.

Sometimes it was very difficult to think of reasons for refusing. Sabrina noticed a few odd expressions. There had also been odd expressions when she was asked about how she came to rent the dower house on the da Silviera estate. She had told the truth, insofar as it concerned herself, that

303

she could not endure the heat in Lisbon, and Donna Francisca had very kindly offered the house out of sympathy for her affliction.

Later she realized this was a mistake. From certain hints and warm, protective acts, Sabrina came to understand that the ladies of Lousa had guessed Donna Francisca was attracted to her husband. Donna Francisca, it seemed, did not make a practice of extending sympathy to beautiful women. All that was needed to confirm the idea of an affair between William and a high-and-mighty lady they did not like in the gossip-hungry minds of the ladies of Lousa was William himself. A few meetings fixed in their minds his superb good looks, his obvious high breeding, and his caressing manners, all of which were a violent contrast to Donna Francisca's elderly, unattractive, common-born husband.

But Sabrina did not give the matter much thought. Frankly she was annoyed with William for his carelessness. It would have done him no harm, she felt, if he gave up two or three evenings of his mistress's company to go to a dinner or musical party in Lousa. Had he done so, Sabrina could have found more logical excuses for other refusals. She had done her best, and if he would not cooperate even a little and her excuses were not believed, she could do no more.

Sabrina was looking forward to her husband's departure back to Lisbon once his leave expired. Then she would be known to be without escort, and an extra man would be found to make numbers even. Actually, this departure took place somewhat sooner than Sabrina had expected. On July twenty-fifth a letter arrived from Lord Strangford summoning William back to the embassy at once. Although there was a sense of urgency about the message, it said nothing about Sabrina. William gave the matter only a few minutes' consideration. If he took Sabrina back with him, he would have no excuse to return to des Ermidas.

William's conscience twinged, but he soothed it with the idea that if the situation had been critical, Strangford, who doted on Sabrina, would have mentioned specifically that she must go home.

Although William's interest in Donna Francisca was already waning—she was entirely too eager and far less interested in delicate innuendo than in copulation—the interest was not dead. Also, William rather relished the idea of a romantic parting, one in which he could play the role of a heartbroken lover torn by political forces, rather than surfeit, from his lady. It would be a novelty to part with tears rather than recriminations.

His conscience smote him again when he discovered the full facts, but Lord Strangford assured him that there was, as yet, no emergency. Although Russia had made peace and agreed to certain secret clauses directed against Britain, the government was preparing countermeasures. Ships would be gathered and readied to take aboard all English nationals with their families and personal property, and certain Portuguese who had close connections in England if they wished to go. William had been summoned back partly to sound out the Portuguese and partly to warn longtime British residents in Portugal in such a way as to avoid any panic. Those who intended to leave, should it be necessary to do so, were to collect their valuables, sell what they could, and discreetly transfer as much of their funds as possible, a little at a time.

On August first the Portuguese foreign secretary, Antônio de Araujo, summoned Lord Strangford and told him he had received an ultimatum from the French demanding the closure of all ports to British ships, and even neutral ships that had stopped at any British port, by September first. William again raised the question with Lord Strangford of warning Sabrina. The ambassador agreed that he should write her to be prepared to leave at a day's

305

notice, but promised he would send William to fetch his wife in good time.

William felt very ill-used as he wrote his letter. It had been a dreadful waste of time, energy, and money to bring Sabrina to Portugal, and it was going to be a great bother to get her back home. That stupid little chit was as ice cold, as resolved as ever, to dissolve their marriage. Even if the marriage were annulled quietly, it would be very bad for him, and nothing that smooth-tongued St. Eyre could say would change his mind. God alone knew what depravity would be credited to him. Who would dream that the chit would be so insane as to object to a little flirtation now and then?

Suddenly he thought how convenient it would be if events moved so fast that he could not go to fetch Sabrina. If she missed the ships that were to leave Portugal in a convoy, she might be detained in the country. There was little chance she would come to any harm, he told himself, ignoring the likelihood that troops might get to her before any high-level officer recognized her quality. She could take refuge with the friends she had made in Lousa, he decided. The idea had only been born of irritation, but as William surveyed it again he saw possibilities in it. The main problem would be to avoid blame for abandoning his wife.

Pursing his lips, William tore up what he had written and began again. He made only casual mention of the French threat, but he could not avoid mentioning it, because Sabrina's acquaintances in Lousa might have heard. Nor had he any fixed decision on what he would do. It might be possible to say she had gone off somewhere and he could not find her, or that she had been captured by bandits. Would it be expected of him to stay and look for her? William sent off his much abbreviated letter and sat back to think more seriously of reasons for leaving her behind.

It was just as well he never came up with a ploy that he believed he could carry off successfully, because Strangford's arrangements gave him more than enough time to bring Sabrina to Lisbon. On the tenth of August the ambassador gave him three weeks' leave for that purpose. He said there was little more for William to do until France made another move. The British arguments why Portugal should not yield were being made clear enough by the English ships that sailed past Tagus Bay at regular intervals. Their gunports were now closed, but the prince regent did not need any reminders that every major city in his country was a seaport that could be reduced to rubble by the guns behind the ports.

On the other hand, it was not possible for Portugal to resist the French. Where the combined might of Russia and Prussia and Austria had failed, it was not likely that tiny Portugal could succeed. Lord Strangford did not expect it. He was merely holding off the inevitable as long as possible. Also, the British government desired that Portugal be invaded rather than capitulate and invite the French into the country. If there were no armed resistance, it would make little difference to the inhabitants. Bonaparte was as rapacious with his helpless allies as with his enemies.

To the English, however, there was a difference. A country prostrate under a conqueror was morally open to invasion by a country wishing to rescue the vanquished. To attack a Portugal that had made arrangements with France would be less acceptable. There was a plan to produce such a condition, but Lord Strangford knew it was impossible to put it into effect until the Portuguese court saw imminent capture or destruction staring at them. That could not be before the ultimatum date of September first, and would probably be weeks or months later. Thus, William had three weeks clear before Lord Strangford would need him to help convince Prince João to escape

the French by fleeing to Brazil under the protection of the
British fleet.

With the collection of ships for the transport of people
and property to England, Dom José's efforts to sell stock
were ended. He did not really mind. He had been warned
in good time and had been quite successful in his efforts.
A great deal of other business, matters of the estate that
had been his wife's plus the vineyards and farms that were
his, had been put aside while he concentrated on trade.
Now he turned his attention to this.

He had received two polite letters from Francisca, the
first assuring him that the weather was fine and that both
houses had been in good order. In the second, aside from
more comments on the weather, Francisca stated that
Lord and Lady Elvan were no trouble at all. The cold and
formal tone of the epistles did not bother Dom José, but
he wrinkled his brow deeply as he read that Francisca
hardly saw either of her tenants.

That was odd. When she had asked him to rent the
house to the Elvans, Francisca had claimed that Lady Elvan was a friend. Moreover, she had gone up to the house
with them so that the delicate Lady Elvan should not be
completely alone in a strange place—or so she had told
him at the time. Dom José shrugged. Perhaps Francisca
had already quarreled with the lady, or possibly she had
used the excuse to get away from him. He had noticed
that her interest in the business had been waning for two
or three weeks before she left. He smiled none too
pleasantly as he absently put her brief letter in his pocket.
There was little business to attend to in any case. He
would soon give Francisca a new interest.

He tied up the few loose ends that remained, having told
his servants to close the house, all except his bedchamber,
and to pack his clothing for a stay at La Casa des Ermidas.
His last real duty was to have dinner with the man who

had been Francisca's guardian and had arranged their marriage. Their relationship was pleasant but formal, and Dom José was considerably surprised when, after they had eaten, Dom Pedro invited him to a private conversation.

"You should not leave Francisca alone without a duenna," Dom Pedro said when they were in his study.

"A duenna," Dom José echoed. "But she is a married woman, and her behavior has always been just as it should be. What do you mean?"

"I am not blaming Francisca for anything," Dom Pedro replied distastefully. "She was properly raised and has always been modest and discreet. However, no matter how innocent the woman, people will smear filth if there is the smallest spot exposed. Dom Miguel de Andrade wrote to me a few days ago—a matter of a horse—but he mentioned that the tongues of the ladies of Lousa are clacking like castanets."

"About Francisca? But why? What do they say?"

"It seems the English lady is very well liked."

"Lady Elvan speaks against Francisca?" Dom José's angry astonishment brought him to his feet.

Dom Pedro gestured him back to his seat. "Not at all. That is why the tale is so ridiculous, and I began by saying I do not believe Francisca to be in any way at fault. The Englishwoman has told everyone of Francisca's kindness in arranging that she have the house. But you know that Francisca is reckoned proud and ungenerous by those women because she does not court their company. Thus, they have decided there must be another reason for renting the house to the Elvans."

"I am surprised they do not say I am bankrupt and we need the money," Dom José remarked dryly.

"No, it is Francisca they wish to injure. They have put together the rental with the fact that Lord Elvan does not wish to attend the evening parties and entertainments in Lousa."

Dom José laughed. "I do not blame him."

"Nor do I," Dom Pedro continued, "and from what Dom Miguel says about Lady Elvan's beauty, I should think no one would be surprised that her husband wishes to spend his evenings alone with her when his business in Lisbon draws him so often away. However, from these two small, silly bricks—Francisca's kindness and Elvan's uxoriousness—the idle, light-minded dames have built a castle of infidelity and deception. It is, they say, Francisca with whom Elvan spends his evenings—and his nights, too."

Dom José made no reply, but his expression made Dom Pedro rise and put a hand on his shoulder.

"José," Dom Pedro said, "do not be so angry. There is nothing one can do to silence the tongues of women. You are about to go to La Casa des Ermidas anyway. As soon as it is seen that you are on good terms and go about as usual together, and that you are friendly with the Elvans, the gossip will stop. However, in the future when you are not with Francisca, be sure there is an elderly companion, perhaps an aunt of yours, or . . . ah . . . oh . . . if there is no one . . . er . . . available from your family, I have indigent cousins by the dozen."

By the time Dom Pedro had finished and walked back to sit down again, Dom José had his face and feelings well under control. He made some acceptable reply in an even voice, which did not betray his fury. Like Dom Pedro, he did not believe Francisca was unfaithful. Unlike him, he was not convinced that the gossip was directed against Francisca at all. He saw it directed against himself. The women gossiped about Francisca, he believed, not because of her pride but because she had married a common merchant rather than her own kind.

Rage, more furious because he was helpless to defend himself against those who offended him, ate at him. He was furious with Francisca, too. The fact that she had no way to control the behavior of Lord Elvan only made him angrier. She should have known better than to ask him to rent the house to such people. The additional fact that he had heartily approved her choice of tenants added fuel to the flames that were burning his insides.

But the capping insult, the words that threw oil on the flames instead of water, was that remark about the duenna. Dom Pedro had spoken first without really thinking, as if to a man of his own class, suggesting an aunt. Then Dom Pedro had realized that the company of Dom José's aunt would be no more regarded than that of a maid, so he had offered his own cousin, whose blood was pure enough that her chaperoning would be of value.

Had Dom Pedro known what was seething under Dom José's now placid exterior, he could have extinguished the worst of the rage. His hesitation after mentioning Dom José's aunt had nothing to do with the commonness of her blood. It had occurred to Dom Pedro that any aunt Dom José had was either too old to act as a duenna or else was dead. He did not wish to make a point of the difference in ages between Dom José and his wife; that was all that had caused his slight embarrassment.

Soon after, Dom José had taken his leave, having found several more causes for insult where none was intended. Dom Pedro did not try to keep him, innocently accepting the excuse that he had much to do before his departure for des Ermidas. Naturally, Dom José took this as a further, more blatant, insult. Instead of going home to sleep, quite beyond reason now, he left that night. It was actually a good night to travel, cool, with a brilliant three-quarter moon, and the road from Lisbon to Leiria was excellent. Still, travel at night was less safe than during the day. Dom José took the precaution of arming himself and his servants with pistols and swords.

There was no need for the weapons or any other hindrance to travel, but it was impossible to move as fast by

311

moonlight as in the daytime. The frustration Dom José suffered was merely increased by the inadequate distance covered by the time the moon set. He ordered that the horses be changed and that they continue. The stars were so bright and clear that it was possible to do so, but by no means possible to avoid ruts and rocks in the road, which might have been bypassed in daylight. The bruising and fatigue did nothing at all to improve Dom José's temper. He began to remember slights and snubs long past to add to the new lacerations on his pride, and his fury multiplied.

Then disaster struck. The carriage hit a rock, bounced into a rut, veered to the side of the road, and tipped. An ominous crack gave warning that serious damage had occurred. Because the horses were moving fairly slowly, no accident took place, but they could go no farther. Dom José was forced to sit by the side of the road while one of the servants unhitched the horses and rode to the next town. It was ten o'clock the following morning before repairs were made and the carriage could go forward. Although he did not curse or strike his servants, Dom José was no longer rational.

Daylight made the ride smoother, and exhaustion overwhelmed Dom José. He slept intermittently, waking to a stiff misery that dampened the heat of his rage without assuaging it. While he was twisting to find comfort, a crackle of paper drew his attention to Francisca's letter. He drew it from his pocket and reread it. For the first time a doubt of her virtue and honesty came into his mind. Why should she say Lady Elvan was her friend before they took the house and now say she never saw the woman? Lord Elvan was young and very handsome. Perhaps the ladies of Lousa were not so far from the truth in their gossip.

He tried to take hold of his careening mind, telling himself that Lord Elvan was not even at the dower house. He himself had spoken to Elvan on the twenty-eighth of July.

The man had been very pleasant, not self-conscious or embarrassed. He had called on purpose to say how much better his wife was feeling in the cool mountain climate.

The road grew worse as they drove farther and farther from the capital. They changed horses again, but even the fresh animals could not make much speed up the hills. Dom José's frustration grew and rationality had less and less grip on him. When they turned off the main highway onto the narrower, rougher road that went to Lousa, the speed of their progress diminished further.

Instead of feeling relief that he was so close, Dom José found his rage building again. He grew more and more sure that Francisca and Elvan were lovers. While he struggled to control an imagination run wild, he suddenly remembered that Dom Pedro had never implied that Francisca was virtuous or faithful. All Dom Pedro had said was that she was discreet and that he did not blame her. Well, Dom José raged, naturally he would not blame her for betraying a common creature like her husband. Perhaps Dom Pedro would even think that was a laudable act.

In some sane corner of his mind Dom José knew none of these accusations was true, knew that when he reached des Ermidas he would find his wife innocently embroidering or reading. He also knew that when he said he wished to come to her bed, she would refuse him. Then he would allow this rage and jealousy to boil over. It would give him the strength and the will to beat her and in the end to break her. But the sane corner was a small, cool spot far withdrawn from the inferno of hatred that burned within him.

The carriage turned into the steep track that climbed in a zigzag up from the road to La Casa des Ermidas. The tired horses barely crawled along in the rapidly failing twilight. At that slow pace the wheels and hooves made little sound on the dry earth of the track, which had been pounded into a thick dust. The carriage passed the dower house, set back a little from the road, where soft lights could be seen through carelessly drawn curtains on several windows. Here the track curved away for almost half a mile, turned, and came back to make the slope to the gate of the main house negotiable for horses.

Even more impatient for a relief from his frustration, Dom José remembered there was a direct path between the houses. Probably it was dreadfully overgrown, but he was certain he would be able to find his way far more quickly than the exhausted beasts could trudge the last steep mile uphill. He called out to stop the carriage, told the servants he would walk because he was stiff and wished to exercise, and made his way around the dower house to the back where the path started.

There was still sufficient light to find the path without difficulty, and at first he thought it had been cleared. As it grew steeper, however, he realized that this was not the case. Branches whipped his face and caught at his clothing. Nonetheless, even though it was almost completely dark under the trees, it was surprisingly easy to find his way. His feet seemed able to pick out the path. The climb was steep, and Dom José soon paused for breath. While he was standing there, aware that he could hardly make out the faintest glimmer of light from the sky any longer, the answer came to him. The path had not been cleared, but someone had passed over it several times very recently.

Fire burst in Dom José's brain. *Elvan is her lover,* he thought. Strength flowed through his limbs and he began to climb the path in leaps. Sanity screamed at him that Elvan was in Lisbon, that a servant must have trodden down the weeds and grass when fetching something from the main house or delivering the messages women were forever sending each other. Sanity and breathlessness had nearly won when, as he thrust forward, a branch caught at

314

his coat. He grasped at the cloth to yank it free, and his hand touched the heavy bulge in the pocket where lay one of the pistols he had prepared to repel highwaymen.

There was another in the other pocket. Dom José's mouth twisted, and he climbed more slowly. He was not living in some bad melodrama. When he got to the house, he told himself, he would find the small gate locked. Then he would be angry all over again because he would have to walk around to the main gate.

Only, the small gate was not locked. Dom José stood just inside it and stared at the house. The back, the kitchens and sculleries, were lit up, and here and there a dim lamp burned in the servants' quarters, but Francisca's—no, *his*—wing was dark, all dark. Not a glimmer showed from the reception rooms or in Francisca's suite. Then she is out or the curtains are properly drawn for once, sanity told him. But the voice was very faint. Even when rage set his hand on a pistol butt and urged him through a scullery door and into a dark side corridor, sanity hardly protested at all.

Once out of the servants' section and into the grand corridors, there was no chance of meeting anyone. Dom José walked along, not even hurrying. The dark had not all been owing to curtains. There were no lights. It did not matter. His dark-adjusted eyes could see well enough not to bump into anything, and he knew the way. He paused for just one heartbeat with his hand on the latch of Francisca's sitting room. Sanity uttered a tiny whimper. *It is better not to know. They will still be your sons and bear your name.*

Only they would not be his sons, or, even if they were, he would never be sure. Quietly he opened the latch and stepped in, shutting the heavy door just as quietly behind him. A soft murmur of voices drifted from the bedchamber beyond. They had not even bothered to close the door. Dom José pulled both pistols from his pockets and cocked them. Sanity breathed a dying gasp of *no,* but it was too late.

In his private office Foreign Secretary Canning thanked Perce once more for his remarkable coup and, with marked sarcasm, for his patience in answering questions about the Russian and Prussian attitudes toward Bonaparte. The sarcastic tone was not unmerited. Over the past ten days Perce's face had grown more like that of a graven image, his voice colder, and his answers briefer and more painfully pointed. However, there was considerable reason for Perce's attitude of impatience, also. Well aware of what he had been sent to do, his information had been neatly summarized in his head and had been related in organized units with remarkable clarity.

Perce really had no more to tell, but Canning did not seem to believe it. He was accustomed to dealing with bureaucratic fools, and he did not trust the nobility. Actually, after a few days of questioning and probing, Canning had realized that Lord Kevern had not forgotten anything and had not told only what *he* thought was relevant. However, a highly secret operation was already being organized to blunt the effect of the special clauses in the Treaty of Tilsit, and Canning did not trust Lord Kevern's discretion. Young noblemen had a weakness for the bottle and for women of doubtful reputation, and under the influence of either or both, tongues were known to flap. He could not quite put Lord Kevern under arrest, but he made sure, until it was too late for incautious talk to do much harm, that Perce had barely enough time to eat and sleep away from the Foreign Office or its personnel.

Having concluded his remarks, Canning fired a parting shot. With a self-satisfied smile he informed Perce that Lord Mulgrave, first lord of the Admiralty, also wished to thank him and that he expected to see Lord Kevern at eleven o'clock.

"I feel that I have received quite sufficient marks of the government's gratitude," Perce said stiffly. "And I know nothing about the navy of any country—and not much about sailing."

"Be that as it may, you have an appointment at eleven o'clock with Lord Mulgrave," Canning repeated sharply, making a gesture of dismissal and looking rudely down at some papers on his desk.

Perce stood still because he knew if he allowed himself to move, he would step forward and hit Canning. That would be unpardonable on several accounts, like age, strength, skill, and propriety. Moreover, it was Canning's usual manner toward everyone; no particular insult was intended. Impulse conquered, he left the Foreign Office and pulled out his watch. Barely time to get to the Admiralty. Perce sighed. He was not at all stupid. It had dawned on him some time earlier that all the appointments so carefully arranged had to be to prevent him from seeing anyone not a trusted government employee.

"I wonder what's up?" he muttered as he signaled a cab.

Inside the vehicle he dismissed the question. It was none of his business, and, in a sense, Perce realized, there was some justification for Canning's suspicions. He had told Roger about the articles the day he had returned from Canning's country house. Was that why? Possibly, but if it were, Canning was a fool. Roger was safe. Perce had told Philip about the special articles in the treaty, too, but Philip was one of their own spies.

In any case the period of detention seemed about over. There was no mistaking the dismissal in Canning's manner this morning. Now Perce would be free to leave for Portugal and not a moment too soon, either. Philip had been over in France again to attempt to discover the effect of the Berlin Decree—issued by Napoleon, ordering a blockade of Great Britain and the closure of the Continent to British trade—on the French economy. He had come back earlier than expected because there was no need for subtle investigation. France was being hurt by Bonaparte's blockade far worse than England.

However, Philip had also brought back a report that Bonaparte had sent or was about to send an ultimatum to the Portuguese. Roger had told Philip not to pass that information along to Perce, but it was too late. Discussion had calmed Perce's immediate panic, but Philip's news had hardened his resolve to go after Sabrina—a decision Philip endorsed heartily. He had been no slower to pick up the significance behind Perce's interest in Sabrina's welfare and had welcomed it more quickly and more enthusiastically than Roger. He had never really been comfortable with William, who was considerably older and more sophisticated. And, with typical careless optimism, he could skate over the difficulties and rhapsodize on the pleasure of the foursome they would make.

Perce was not nearly as sanguine as his friend, but at the moment he was concentrating on the first step in that direction, which was bringing Sabrina back to England. Nothing showed in his expression when he was ushered into Lord Mulgrave's presence, but the tenseness of his body when he took the seat proffered was not lost on his host.

"I will not keep you long," Mulgrave said. "I imagine you know by now how great a service you have rendered your country."

"I did what I had been sent to do, my lord," Perce replied with stiff impatience. "The magnitude of the service was a chance no one could have foreseen and entailed no extra effort on my part."

Mulgrave smiled. "I cannot accept that, but it's rather foolish to discuss it at any length. Whatever you think, we are grateful to you, to your father, who approved your mission with great reluctance, and, most particularly, to

Roger St. Eyre, who brought you to the attention of the Foreign Office."

A muscle jumped in Perce's jaw, and Mulgrave laughed aloud. "You are wishing all our thanks and me personally at the bottom of a well, I believe," he went on, "but I must ask you to be patient only a few minutes longer. There has been considerable discussion of a suitable reward, since no public—"

"Please!" Perce interrupted, losing his temper. "If I have been of service, I am glad. If you wish to reward me, give me back my freedom."

"Ah, yes, you have been rather hedged about by civil servants. You deserve an explanation of that. A fleet of ships under Admiral Lord Gambier is sailing for Denmark. The Danish fleet will not fall into Bonaparte's hands."

"I am delighted to know," Perce said bleakly, "how evenly your thanks accord with your faith in my intelligence and discretion."

"It wasn't my idea," Mulgrave said defensively. He found himself quite disconcerted by the cold rage that somehow emanated from the blank mask turned on him, and he hurried on. "Let the matter of reward stand aside. It can be discussed at a more suitable time. However, what made me think of it is that Mr. St. Eyre has asked a favor of me. Directives are going out tomorrow evening concerning the Portuguese fleet. It was suggested to me that you might be willing to go along on the cutter that will take them."

"Go along?" Perce echoed, interrupting again.

"I assure you," Mulgrave hastened to add, "that this is no further attempt to keep you from your friends and normal activities."

That was not true. Canning had realized he could not hold Perce any longer and had requested help in keeping him out of circulation; however, Lord Mulgrave had no intention of confessing.

"Mr. St. Eyre," he went on quickly, "is very much concerned for the safety of his wife's cousin, Lady Elvan, who is currently in Portugal. He asked me whether it would be possible to bring her home on a naval vessel. Ordinarily I would have had to refuse. In time of war, you know . . . However, I find it difficult to refuse Mr. St. Eyre any reasonable request, and the cutter, you know, has instructions to avoid all action until message and reply are delivered."

Perce sat mute, his mouth a little open, his brain whirring and clicking as pieces fell into place. Vaguely he heard Mulgrave still talking, but it was about how little naval officers liked the responsibility of a female passenger. All he heard was that Roger had suggested that Perce, a family friend acquainted with Sabrina from childhood, might be willing to escort her home.

This Perce translated without difficulty as meaning that Roger had seized the opportunity created by Canning's suspicions to kill two birds with one stone. Suggesting that Perce go to Portugal would calm Canning and get Perce out of the way until all actions to render the secret clauses ineffective were under way or even completed, and bring Sabrina home safely. Perce lowered his eyelids to hide the unholy glee he felt and let Lord Mulgrave run down.

When the explanations were finished, Perce was well in control of himself. He accepted the duty rather grudgingly and said he wished to take his valet along. Mulgrave assured him that would be possible; probably, Perce thought, Mulgrave would have agreed that an elephant go along to get rid of him. However, Perce knew it would not be a surprising request to Mulgrave's way of thinking. Many aristocratic young men were far more attached to their valets than to their wives. *Someday,* Perce thought with amusement, *I must let him meet my "valet."*

Perce traveled to Portsmouth with the young naval lieu-

320

tenant who commanded the cutter. He was glad to share the comfort of Perce's post chaise, and soon relaxed the formality with which he had acknowledged their introduction. It was plain that he resented and feared the use of his ship to carry home a privileged lady.

Far from relieving Perce's worries, the fortunate turn of events seemed to intensify them. No matter how irrational he knew it to be, Perce grew more and more sure that he would arrive too late. That he had no idea what he could possibly be too late for was irrelevant, and each day of the voyage seemed the longest in his life. By the time he went ashore in Lisbon with the lieutenant, his gently vacuous expression was masking violent emotions.

At the British embassy Perce inquired for Lord Elvan's direction. Having forgotten at that moment that Lord Elvan had left for La Casa des Ermidas on the tenth of August, the clerk gave the address of the house in the city. Perce went out at once with Sergei, thinking that if Sabrina were not at home, he could at least talk to Katy and get the packing under way. He was not at all certain how long the lieutenant would be able to wait for his passengers. It would depend on the urgency of the reply Lord Strangford must make. It might also depend on private instructions given to the lieutenant, Perce thought. He was now so suspicious that he wondered whether Mulgrave had instructed the lieutenant to strand him in Portugal.

Naturally, Perce's emotional state was not improved by finding the house empty except for a few servants. Nor did his attempts to communicate with them—they understood only a few words of English, but no other language he spoke—calm him. He came back to the embassy fit to commit murder. Fortunately for all concerned, the moment he stepped into the building, the clerk greeted him with cries of apology and explanation and asked him to speak to Lord Strangford.

The conversation that ensued put an end to Perce's most

lurid imaginings. The ambassador gave him clear instructions on how to reach Lord Elvan's house near Lousa. In addition, he said it was not necessary for Sabrina to come back in time to sail on the cutter. Lord Mulgrave had given permission for her to sail on any naval vessel going directly to England. It would be best, of course, if she could return in time to sail with the cutter, but it was not essential.

Perce considered this information in the light of what he knew and suspected and promptly excused himself. Lord Strangford seemed a little surprised at his eagerness to leave, but was not sorry. There was a pile of material that he had not yet examined that had come with the cutter. Out of the private office, Perce found the clerk who had misled him, correctly judging that a guilty conscience would make him, at least temporarily, more efficient, and arranged to change English money for Portuguese coinage and to have an embassy groom rent horses and equipment for Sergei and himself.

Obviously, Canning and Lord Mulgrave had not had the nerve to order he be detained at the risk of Sabrina's safety, but they had done their best to avoid any pressing need to hurry. Partly out of pure spite and partly out of the irrational fear that he would be too late, Perce decided to get Sabrina on that cutter if it was humanly possible. As soon as all the arrangements had been completed, he and Sergei set out north.

CHAPTER SEVENTEEN

Dom José stepped forward softly, avoiding furniture without difficulty. The floor creaked once, but he did not pause and neither did the soft voices. So sure, he thought bitterly, so very sure that he was a fool, a dupe. Just as he crossed the threshold into the bedchamber, Francisca laughed.

"Oh, but I am delighted," she said. "You need not worry. I will make sure he thinks the child is his. I have had prayers said and a medal blessed. All I need do is say I am sure I will conceive. He is so eager for it, he will know it is God's will."

Dom José jerked to a halt. His eyes widened and his mouth opened, but his agony was too intense for sound. He was paralyzed by pain just long enough to hear the male voice murmur silkily something about being very happy to be of service. Then Dom José moved again, swiftly. It was only six long strides to the bed, and he leaned in through the bed-curtain, put a pistol to each head, and pulled the triggers. He had been so quick and they so much at ease and unsuspecting, that they continued to face each other in death. Neither Francisca nor William had had time to look at the intruder.

The two shots going off together had deafened Dom José, but when he pulled the pistols away and put them back in his pockets, he could hear again. He listened intently for several minutes, but there was no indication that the servants on the floor below at the other end of the house had heard anything. Dom José then looked again at his handiwork, only it was too dark to see much. The pale blurs of the two faces were unmarred. The black bullet holes were masked by black hair on the entry side, and the gaping exit holes, from which blood gushed, were hidden by the pillows on which the heads rested.

Suddenly Dom José began to weep. He was not regretting what he had done or even the lost opportunity of founding a great noble line. He wept because the guilty had not suffered. They had died laughing at him, far too swiftly to feel pain or fear. He looked at them, still gazing into each other's faces, Francisca's hand on her lover's shoulder. Under the thin cover he could see that their legs were still intertwined. Sobs of renewed rage and frustration tore him as he remembered the pang of agony he had endured, the pain he was now enduring. He, the innocent, was suffering, while they, the guilty, still lay at peace, laughing.

The sobs broke into howls, and he seized the bodies and tried to wrench them apart. He would literally have torn them, except that he was not strong enough. In the end the limp weight defeated him. Instead of separating them, he merely tumbled them closer together so that they looked as if they were making love. And, in flopping over, William's limp arm struck Dom José as if to push him away. Insanely, he punched and pummeled the corpses, but the blows only pressed them more tightly to each other.

They did not care! Only he suffered! It was not just! From the maelstrom in Dom José's mind a fact was cast up. The seducer's wife had spoken too well of Francisca and had made excuses for her husband. She must have known! Guilty! Lady Elvan was as guilty as her man, filthy whore, pandering to her husband's lewdness. Surely that noble-born bitch also laughed at his pretensions and gladly lent her husband so that no common seed should contaminate a pure line of aristocrats. She must suffer for her complicity.

Without another glance at the corpses, Dom José left the room and then the house, unbolting and unlocking the front door on his way out. No one heard, and it was very unlikely that any servant would check the door once it was locked for the night. In the yard he stopped. The arrival of the carriage would wake everyone. The dead pair would be discovered. Everyone would pity him aloud and laugh privately. Again his brain whirled, and again an unpalatable fact came uppermost. Lady Elvan was well liked by the noble families in Lousa. They would not think of her as guilty. They would sympathize, support her.

But she *must* suffer. Someone must suffer. Yet no one would help him. Very well, then, no one must hinder him, either. No one must know until all the guilty were punished.

Now that his resolution was made, Dom José felt his mind clear. It was a shrewd mind, and it came to grips with the problem quite easily. Dom José slipped around the house and walked in the back door, raising his voice to shout the butler's name as he came in. A chaos of welcome broke out at once, although Dom José knew that he was not really welcome. He silenced the servants quickly and heard what he expected to hear—that Donna Francisca had felt unwell, retired to bed early, and left orders not to be disturbed. Dom José seconded those orders firmly, bidding the housekeeper to make up a room for him for the night well away from his wife's apartment.

Strangely, now that he was sure of what he wished to do, he felt quite calm. He allowed the servants to go about their work without impatience, gave directions when the carriage arrived that it should not be unloaded until the next day so as not to disturb his wife, and sat quietly in a parlor where he reloaded his pistols and refined his plans until his room was ready. Then he dismissed the servants to bed, warning them to keep away from his and his wife's rooms in the morning until they were specifically summoned.

When the house was quiet, he went out the front door again, through the back gate, and down the path he had climbed less than an hour before. Oddly, it was harder to go down the path than to come up it. He fell twice, which made him very angry.

There were fewer lights in the dower house now than when he had driven by earlier. That was right. The house was small, and most of the servants came in by the day and left at dusk. Dom José walked boldly up to the front door and rang the bell. Through the glazing he could see a light approaching. The door opened. The servant began to step back, as if to allow an expected arrival to pass. The movement convinced Dom José of the collective guilt of the entire household. All of them knew where their master had gone. All of them had been laughing at him.

In an instant the servant realized the man at the door was not whom he had expected. He checked his welcoming gesture and moved to block the doorway, his eyes widening in alarm.

"Who the devil are you?" Charlot snapped at the wild-eyed apparition covered with dirt, leaves, and twigs.

"I am your landlord, Dom José," the madman replied, reaching into his pocket and cocking one pistol.

Charlot laughed and began to swing the door shut. He assumed the creature was the local idiot, who believed he was the great landholder of the district. Charlot was no hero, but he was not afraid of this pathetic-looking creature, twenty years older and four inches shorter than himself, who obviously had no place better to sleep than a thicket.

"Shoo!" he said contemptuously. "Go away, you silly

creature, before I call the men from the stables to drive you—"

The words caught in his throat and his mouth opened wider, but the scream was never uttered. The pistol had come out of Dom José's pocket, his arm extended so that the gun in his hand was no more than a foot from Charlot's face, and he fired. Charlot toppled backward. From somewhere farther back in the house and from a room above, women's voices cried questions. Dom José pushed the pistol he had fired back into his pocket and drew out the other. He ran up the curving staircase and reached the head just as Sabrina came out of the open door of her sitting room, calling, "Charlot, what was that?"

Then her eyes fell on the intruder. "Dom José," she cried. "What's happened? Are you hurt?"

There was so much concern in her lovely face and voice, in the hands outstretched to support him if necessary, that for one moment Dom José's insane purpose wavered.

"Your husband," he croaked.

Sabrina's hand drew back and lifted to cover her mouth, and there was horror in her eyes. From this Dom José drew the conclusion that Sabrina was aware he had caught and killed William and his reason for it. He was much mistaken. The wild look on his face, the scratches and twigs on him, and the gun in his hand made her think of bandits or of a French invasion. Nonetheless, the seeming proof of her guilt drove Dom José back into his madness. He gestured with the gun.

"Go down," he ordered.

"Wait, Dom José," Sabrina cried, "let me—"

She was about to tell him she would get William's pistols and help him defend them, when Katy's sharp cry of distress cut off her speech. Sabrina still had no suspicion of Dom José because she could not see the floor near the front door or Charlot's corpse from where she stood. At

Katy's cry she ran forward. Dom José met her and, with the strength of madness, pushed her so hard that she flew backward and fell, striking her head on the wainscoting of the corridor wall.

Partially stunned, Sabrina lay for a moment gasping with shock and pain. She lifted her head just in time to see Dom José whirl about and strike viciously at Katy, who had run up the stairs. Her scream and any cry Katy might have uttered as she arched over mingled too closely to be distinguished. Sabrina screamed again when she heard the banister give way and the thud as Katy struck the floor of the lower hall. Desperately she scrambled to get to her feet, calling, "Katy! Katy!" but there was no answer.

She was on her knees, hands extended like claws, but the gun was pointed at her, and the face above it was totally insane. Fear of death checked Sabrina's impulse to attack for a moment. In the next, reason of a sort reasserted itself. This madman had killed Katy, and he would surely kill her if she attacked him now. She remembered his only words to her and understood that William was almost certainly dead, too. Dom José must have learned of his wife's infidelity. Sabrina uttered a hopeless sob.

The gun gestured toward the stairs. Sabrina climbed slowly to her feet, holding to the wall for support. She thought of pushing Dom José down, as he had pushed Katy, but his insanity was not of that careless kind. He moved back out of the way where Sabrina could not reach him.

"Go down," he ordered.

Sabrina wet her lips to try to speak, but the pistol lifted significantly, and she sobbed again and started down the stairs, clinging to the wall. When she reached the bottom, she turned her head, hoping against her desolated fear that she would see Katy stir. The whole body was not visible, but what she could see was utterly still and one leg was horribly and unnaturally twisted. Sabrina moaned softly, feeling the underpinning of her whole life slipping away.

"Out," Dom José ordered.

A shudder so violent that it almost shook Sabrina off her feet passed over her. She balked, and Dom José stepped forward swiftly and struck her across the face with his left hand. She hardly felt it. Just at that moment her eyes had fallen on Charlot—what was left of Charlot. Most of his face had been torn away. Sabrina whimpered and stumbled forward toward the open door.

Blinded by the relative darkness, Sabrina tripped on the steps and fell, saving herself from real injury by instinct. Dom José kicked her, not terribly hard but indicating that worse would follow if she did not get up. As she dragged herself upright it occurred to Sabrina that Dom José did not mean to kill her, at least not immediately. If he had, she reasoned, he would have done so at once. Why bother making her leave the house if all he meant to do was to shoot her?

As her immediate terror receded a cold hatred took its place. It was true that William was guilty, that he had cuckolded Dom José. Sabrina did not like unfaithfulness, either, but she did not think it so great a crime as to deserve death. Still, she would not have hated Dom José for avenging himself; she knew some men felt differently than she did. It was the killing of Charlot and—her heart lurched—Katy. That was senseless. And what did the lunatic want with her? She pushed that out of her mind. Whatever it was could not be good. But for the others, for her Katy, her darling Katy, and for poor Charlot with his silly pride, for them she would somehow be avenged.

Hardly realizing what she did, Sabrina had staggered around the house to the back under Dom José's orders. Her eyes had adjusted, and it was not really dark on the lawn. The moon was just rising. She stumbled again when she entered the pathway, but recovered without falling. Various ideas flicked through her mind—seizing a stick and striking the gun from Dom José's hand, falling and snatching up a rock to throw at him. However, the pathway itself was clear of loose branches, and it was too dark to see anything on either side of it.

Sabrina felt desperately with her feet for loose stones and with her hands, too, when she could use them on the steeper sections. She found no stone large enough in the brief contacts with the ground that Dom José permitted. When she hesitated a few seconds longer than his impatience thought necessary, he kicked her again. She struggled ahead, sobbing more with frustration than with fear.

Suddenly she was out in the open again on the wide lawns of La Casa des Ermidas, and whatever chance she had had on the path was gone. She thought of screaming, but she would be dead long before anyone could come—if they would come. The house was all dark, except for a dim light coming through the fanlight above the back door. Besides, she was not sure Dom José's servants would be able or willing to interfere, and none might be in the house. They might all have run away, if they knew he had killed his wife and William. Wildly trying to think of a new expedient for escaping him, Sabrina was driven forward, around the front of the house.

"Open the door and go up the right-hand branch of the stairs," he said. "You can scream if you like," he added, laughing. "No one will hear."

"What do you want?" Sabrina whispered. "I have done you no harm. Why are you doing this?"

"Done me no harm?" Dom José snarled. "You panderer! You whore-mistress! You knew your filthy lecher of a husband was lying with my wife, and you lied for him. You helped him!"

330

"Oh, my God," Sabrina breathed. "What could I do? How could I stop him?"

But there was little hope or conviction in her protest. She certainly was guilty in that sense; she had even been glad of William's affair, found it amusing because it took his attention away from her. Then she remembered Katy and Charlot. They had been completely innocent. Sabrina's trembling knees stiffened. She would not give up. Somehow she would get away and see that Dom José paid for destroying those who had never done him, or anyone else, any harm.

She fumbled with the door, wondering whether she could turn swiftly and knock his arm aside so that he would miss if he fired. A quick glance backward showed he was too far behind her for that. Could she grapple with him if she refused to open the door and he came closer to strike her? Then Sabrina remembered the force with which he had thrown her backward in the house. He was far stronger than he looked. Her best chance, she decided, was to go in, letting him think she was terrified and helpless. In the house there would be weapons—candlesticks, chairs, tables, ornaments. But why had he brought her to his house?

Her hopes were all disappointed. The hall was only dimly lit by a few candles, but it was far too light to consider hiding: the candles were in sconces on the walls; the furniture was too heavy for Sabrina to contemplate moving it, and there was nothing to throw. As she started up the stairs Sabrina realized he must be taking her to the bedchambers. Suddenly she felt cold and sick. Could this madman want to revenge himself on William by raping her?

Sabrina gathered herself together to turn swiftly and throw herself down the stairs at Dom José. There was a chance that, if she were quick enough, he would miss his shot and that, falling on top of him, she would stun him.

And if she failed, she would rather be dead than let him ... But why bring her here to do that?

To shame William in front of his face? But that would mean that William was *not* dead. What if Dom José had caught him and only wounded him or tied him up? Then there would be two of them. William was no fool. No matter how helpless he was, he would try to make a sound or movement that would distract Dom José so that she could attack him. And even if William could not help, there would be endless ways to make Dom José expend his one shot if he tried to rape her with a gun in his hand. If only he did not knock her unconscious.

With that last fear in mind, Sabrina turned around to face him when she came to the top of the stairs. He gestured impatiently toward the right with the gun, but made no comment when she backed slowly down the corridor.

"Stop," Dom José said. "Open the door at your right and go in."

He was staring at her. Sabrina began to tremble uncontrollably. Even in the dim light she could see the whites of his eyes all around the dark irises. He was mad!

"What are you going to do?" Sabrina gasped, less able than she had thought to face a sexual assault.

Since Dom José really had no idea what he was going to do, only that he must bring Sabrina face to face with her guilt so that she would suffer as he had suffered, he did not answer. However, through the madness he sensed that Sabrina was growing desperate enough to challenge him. He knew he could kill her, but it was too soon for that. She had not perceived the depth of her sin. She had not suffered enough. He stepped back and around to face her more directly and lifted the gun in threat.

"It is only my wife's sitting room," he said. "There is nothing to be afraid of."

Sabrina hardly heard the words. The staring eyes had driven her back a pace before he moved or spoke, and her

332

hand, feeling for support, had fallen on the door latch as she asked her question. The latch turned down; the door opened a hair—opened inward! Before the thought had even formed clearly in her mind, Sabrina had leapt into the room and slammed the door behind her in Dom José's face. She dropped to her knees at once, expecting a bullet to fly through the wood, but even as she went down her hand fumbled below the latch and found the key and turned it.

She was barely in time. Just as the lock seated, the latch went down and there was a meaty thud as Dom José threw his weight against the door. Sabrina scuttled sideways on her hands and knees, still fearing a gunshot. Once out of line she sat back on her heels to catch her breath and think. The doors in the dower house were strong and solid. These should be no less resistant. Until Dom José brought help, the door should hold—unless he shot the lock away.

Sabrina glanced around, but what she could see of the furniture in the dim light seemed too fragile to block the door. Beyond was the rectangular shadow of another open doorway. That had to be the bedchamber. Sabrina looked from that very questionable refuge around the room. The quiet beyond the door to the corridor was unnerving. After that first rattle of the latch and thud, there had been no sign from her captor.

Probably he had gone for help, Sabrina told herself. It would be useless to appeal to anyone Dom José brought, so it was up to her to save herself in the next few minutes. A wave of despair flooded over her. There was no time! And Katy was dead!

Again rage pushed out despair. There were the windows. She could jump. She went quickly across the room and pulled back the drapes. The distance to the lawn seemed dreadfully far, and below was an expanse of stone portico rather than shrubs or soft flower beds, which could

333

have broken her fall. It would be impossible to escape injury altogether, which would only make her more helpless.

Again Sabrina looked around the room, this time seeing it more clearly in the moonlight. Quickly she drew the other drape. She was disappointed to find that her first guess had been correct. There was no piece of furniture heavy enough to block the door. Even the sofas were spindly. If she piled one on top of the other . . . Sabrina sighed. She was no weakling, but she did not think she could lift even a light sofa so high.

There were, however, plenty of things she could use for weapons. If Dom José came in alone, she could brain him from behind the door. A warm flush of satisfaction filled Sabrina at the thought, but it faded quickly. There was little chance he would be alone. Again her eyes strayed to the dark rectangle of the bedchamber door. Perhaps the bedchamber was on a corner and had windows that did not overlook the portico.

Sabrina glanced at the outer door of the sitting room, but all was still silent. After a few steps toward the bedchamber she hesitated. Was there an entrance from the corridor directly into the bedchamber? Was Dom José waiting there for her in the dark? She shuddered, but reason soon asserted itself over fear. If there had been another entrance, surely he would already have come in that way. And why should he wait in the dark? The pistol was a far more useful threat in the light.

Although she hated to leave the security she had, however false, Sabrina told herself that the bedchamber would be safer. There would be heavier furnishings with which she could block the door. Seizing a candelabra so that she would have something with which to strike or to throw, she darted through the door opening. Inside, she fumbled along the door, then breathed a sigh of relief when she found a key in that lock, also. There was just enough light from the silvery glow in the sitting room to make out the black bulk of the bed and several other pieces of furniture. Ears cocked for any sound from the sitting room, Sabrina crossed to where two long shadows marked draped windows.

When the drapes were drawn, Sabrina looked around while she tried to steady her breathing. Now that she could see, she realized that the bedchamber was a better place to defend herself than the sitting room. There were closets, bulky furniture to hide behind, large pieces of cloth with which to try to envelop or trip her attacker. She went to the door and locked it, then began to shove a heavy dressing table with a tall mirror across the door. If that were battered away from the door, the mirror would crash and provide many sharp missiles to throw. If she wrapped her hand in a cloth, the fragments would provide a dagger of sorts.

Moving the dressing table so that the mirror would not fall took some time. When she was finished, Sabrina rested for a few minutes, listening intently for sounds in the adjoining room. It was still silent, and she assumed that Dom José had not yet unlocked or forced the door. He probably would have cried out on not seeing her. If not, he was cleverer than she thought. Then she sighed. He could not surprise her in here. She would have time to think and plan for an escape.

The first move was to find a tinderbox. If she lit all the candles in the room with the drapes drawn back, someone might see the light and wonder. It was not much of a chance. La Casa des Ermidas was very isolated. Nonetheless, there was a chance, and the light would give her courage. Sabrina found the tinderbox in its usual place in the drawer of a small table beside the bed. She struck her flame, lit one candle, and used that to set all the others ablaze.

The next step must be to escape. Again Sabrina looked out the long window. There was a small metal balcony outside that blocked her view of the ground below. Would that make it easier or harder to jump? Then Sabrina laughed shakily. Why jump at all? She had read enough romances where the silly heroine eloped by climbing down a rope of knotted sheets. Sabrina had laughed at that, wondering how one could knot a sheet. Now she began to think of it seriously.

If she could find a scissor, it would be possible to slit the sheets into thirds. That should be narrow enough to knot together and still wide enough not to tear under her weight because of the raw edges. Yes. Then she could fasten the rope to the bars of the balcony. They should be strong enough, and even if they gave way after a while, she would be closer to the ground and not have so far to fall. She cocked her head. There was still no sound from the sitting room. That was odd rather than frightening, but Sabrina would not let herself think about it. She concentrated on looking in all the places where a pair of scissors might be found.

In the corridor, Dom José stood quite still, staring at the locked door. Although he had thrown himself against it instinctively when Sabrina escaped him, he had drawn back in the next instant with a sense of relief. He really did not want to go in there. He did not fight the feeling, nor did he think about it. In fact, his mind was curiously blank, as if everything had come to a full stop when the sitting room door was locked. He simply stood and waited, exactly for what, he did not know.

Once he heard a dull scraping very faint and far away. He did not connect the sound with a heavy object being pushed across the floor in the bedchamber. It held no meaning for him at all and did not induce in him any concern or desire to move or do anything else. He continued to stand for a long time, watching the door dully, the now useless pistol hanging from his hand. Then, faintly, he heard a woman scream, and scream, and scream.

Like an ill-managed marionette, Dom José jerked into life. That was what he was waiting for! With each of Sabrina's shrieks a paralyzing thorn of agony was extracted from his mind, and when the screams stopped abruptly, Dom José smiled. Now he was avenged. Now there had been terror and pain to match his own shame and suffering. He listened, but without anxiety, not for more screams but for sounds of the servants stirring. There were none. It was not surprising. If they had not heard the shots while they were awake, it was not likely they would have heard the woman screaming after he had sent them to bed in the servant's wing.

For one moment, in the peace revenge had brought him, Dom José became rational again. He suddenly realized what he had done—everything he had done. His mouth dried, and the breath strangled in his throat. God in Heaven, he had killed four people! Four! Francisca and her lover did not matter. Had he stopped there, he could simply have reported the matter. No one would have blamed him. But the two servants! That was murder. And his abduction of Lady Elvan . . .

Thoughts of Sabrina tipped Dom José into madness again, but it was a lucid madness fixed on one idea. Everything that had happened was Sabrina's fault. If she had not ignored, even encouraged, her husband's lecheries, none of this would have happened. She was to blame for all four murders, and the punishment for them must fall upon her. But how? How? But of course! She *was* guilty of the murders. She, not he, had killed them all out of jealousy. But why tonight? Because she had not known until tonight. He had stopped at the dower house to warn her of the rumors regarding her husband and his wife. How fortunate that he had bidden his coachman set him down at the dower house. They could not have seen him go around to the back. In any case, Carlo, Pedro, Pablo, and Manuelo would not contradict him, whatever he said.

337

Suddenly Dom José realized he was covered with dirt and twigs. He gave one last glance at the door and smiled again as he walked slowly away to the room that had been prepared for him. It did not matter what Lady Elvan did, whether she stayed locked in the bedchamber or came out and escaped. When he was in his bedclothes, he would ring for the servants and rush to his wife's door, crying that he had heard shots. But she had no gun. Ah!

Dom José hurried down the stairs and out the front door again, unloading as he went the one pistol that still carried a charge. He laughed silently with pleasure when he saw the light from the window of Francisca's bedchamber. It was as if Lady Elvan accepted her guilt and was trying to help him. The light showed just where he should throw down the guns.

Then his brow wrinkled. How had she got his pistols? Ah, of course. When he stepped in to speak to her, he had laid them on the hall table. One does not, after all, go to visit a lady with pistols in one's pockets. And then, when she became so hysterical, had made such dreadful, shameless threats, he had called her servants to care for her and had gone away quickly, forgetting all about the guns. His lips turned down in a parody of grief and concern over his carelessness. How he would sigh when he said he regretted it and that had he not forgotten, the deaths might not have occurred.

When Dom José entered the house this time, he bolted the front door, went into the long drawing room, broke a pane on one of the French doors, and unbolted it. Then he went up to his bedchamber, where he took off his clothes, shook them hard out of the window, beat them with his hands, and brushed them by rubbing his dark socks over them. There were still a few mud stains, but that would be easily explained by a stumble on the dark path. Then he washed his face and hands carefully, throwing the first lot of water out the window and washing again in a second basinful.

His hand went out to the bellpull as soon as he had his nightclothes on, and then jerked back as if the pull were hot. He had not rumpled the bed. It would be necessary to lie in it. But when he climbed in, he stretched and groaned with exhaustion and the ache of muscles forced to unaccustomed exertion. How long should he wait, he wondered, and then the question in his mind changed to how long dare he wait. He was so tired. Would it matter if he slept for an hour? No, he assured himself as he slid into an engulfing blackness, whether she was in the room or had run away made no difference; she would be adjudged guilty.

As Dom José slipped asleep Sabrina was sitting on the floor trying to pick up the pieces of her shattered strength and courage. She had revived from the faint that had cut off her hysterical screams about ten minutes ago. When her eyes had first opened, she was completely confused. It seemed so odd to find herself lying on the floor of a room she had never seen before. She was all bruised, too, and her palms were sore, as if she had fallen. Raising her hands to look at them, she felt something fall from one and lifted herself to examine it. It was the pair of scissors.

As soon as she saw it, memory returned. Screams rose in Sabrina's throat again, but she choked them back and then had to struggle to keep from vomiting. She dared not turn her head or raise her eyes for fear she would see again the horror she had uncovered when she drew back the bed-curtains to get at the sheets. Whimpering, Sabrina covered her face with her hands. She wanted to crawl to the farthest corner of the room and hide, but she did not dare move for fear the movement would take her closer to that bed with its burden of death.

The horror had been all the more intense for being so unexpected. In the instant that she had pulled back the bed-curtain, she had gasped in embarrassment at seeing a couple seemingly locked in lovemaking. Then the gory grotesqueries that had been the backs of their heads struck her eyes together with the blood-soaked pillows, and the mindless shrieks of hysteria burst from her until fear piled on fear had been too much and she had found safety in unconsciousness.

Only now had she realized that it was William and Donna Francisca in the bed, that Dom José had brought her here to—to what? She knew he thought her guilty for doing nothing when she knew of the affair. Had he wished only to punish her by terrifying her and exposing her to the result of her indifference? But he had killed Charlot and—and Katy. Sabrina sobbed more bitterly in heartbroken desolation. She was guilty, but Katy had died for it.

When the spasm of grief had passed, her mind returned to Dom José's purpose. A long time had passed, and there still had been no attempt to open the door. Could he have meant to lock her in here all along? Leave her to die of hunger and thirst in the presence of her dead husband and his lover? Long shudders shook Sabrina, but she bit her lips and fought them. She must escape and report what had happened.

The thought of escape brought her mind right back to the bed and its contents. She had found a pair of scissors and had gone to the bed to get sheets to tear up so she could climb down from the balcony, and she had seen . . . No! Sabrina pressed her hand against her mouth. She would not think of it, but that meant no sheets. She would have to find something else.

Sabrina shuddered again, but she picked up the scissors, turned her back to the bed, and got to her feet looking determinedly in the opposite direction. With her face turned away, she went crabwise around the room to the windows and began to yank as hard as she could on the heavy draperies. The cloth was new and strong; the interiors had

340

been refurbished when Francisca married enough money. Sabrina had considerable trouble tearing the drapes down and cutting each panel roughly in half, but that gave her confidence that the cloth would not tear when she climbed down.

It occurred to Sabrina as she knotted the strips together, automatically using the knots Philip and Perce had taught her on the yacht, that if the purpose had been to keep her in the room, there would be a guard outside. She opened the window very softly and stepped out, half expecting a shout of warning. There was no sound besides the sigh of the breeze and the singing of the night insects. She examined as much as she could see of the lawn, but there was no movement, no shadow that was not readily accountable as a tree, bush, or ornament.

Sabrina trembled and sobbed once. It was too easy. It must be a trick. Somewhere below her that lunatic must be waiting for her, waiting to seize her again and drag her back to the room. He must be playing some horrible game with her—or was he mad enough to have been distracted and forgotten all about her? Sabrina did not believe that, but it made no difference. She could not stay in that room with what lay in the bed.

During the time she had been busy preparing for escape, the horror had only been a dark shadow on her mind. If she remained there, however, the horror would take on color, a dreadful kind of life. No. She could fight recapture. She went back into the room, cut another strip of drape, and tied a heavy candlestick around her waist. Then, after a few deep and tremulous breaths, Sabrina went back out on the balcony, lugging her heavy rope. She tied it to the bars quickly, threw it over, again expecting to hear a cry of alarm. Nothing. Before she could think any more and frighten herself further, she stepped over the rail to climb down.

CHAPTER EIGHTEEN

Perce and Sergei kept a good pace, stopping only briefly to change horses and eat. When it was time to find a place to sleep for the second night, Perce could not bear the thought. If they rode straight through at the best pace the horses could give, changing when the animals began to flag, they could make the distance in several hours more. They would arrive about ten or eleven o'clock, rather late for a visit, but Perce thought it would not be unreasonable or really untruthful to say that it would be best to sail with the cutter, if possible, so he had wished to arrive that night.

"We'll ride straight through," he said to Sergei as they approached the posting house. "We should be there in a few hours."

The Russian turned his head and looked at his master with a frown. Then he nodded curtly. "The moon will rise soon and be bright enough, but we have no guns. What will we do if we are stopped?"

"We won't stop," Perce replied. "If you see anyone on the road, lay on with your whip and ride like hell. Chances are they'll be so surprised they won't fire or will miss if they do."

Sergei laughed. "Back in the wars again, eh? I thought I was through galloping into the mouths of guns."

"With any luck there won't be any," Perce remarked indifferently.

In this estimate he was quite correct. They were not set upon by highwaymen or bandits, and the road was clear and reasonably visible in the moonlight. However, Perce found he had been somewhat oversanguine in his estimate of the time it would take to cover the distance. They were slowed by the dark until the moon rose, and in many places the grades were steeper than he had expected. It would have been cruel to try to make the horses gallop up them, and it would have been dangerous to go faster than a trot on the way down. They would be far longer delayed if an animal should stumble and be injured than by the slower pace.

Thus, it was well after midnight before they saw the entrance to the dower house, even though they had been fortunate in finding without difficulty the turnoff to Lousa and then the even narrower track that went up the mountain. Everything was very quiet, and Perce felt a complete fool. He was thinking of turning back to Lousa rather than disturbing the household. There had been a man pounding on an inn door across the square as they rode through the town. If they went back immediately, the place would probably still be stirring, and the innkeeper would be pleased to have two extra customers to pay for his broken rest.

Then Sergei said, "Someone's awake," and pointed.

Surely enough, there was a light-streak between the curtains on the upper floor. It was probably Elvan, who wouldn't be best pleased with his visitors, Perce thought, smiling nastily. Anyway, if Elvan were awake, Charlot would be awake too, and would answer the door. Perce and Sergei dismounted, Sergei to hold the horses and Perce to climb the steps and knock on the door.

For nearly an hour Dom José slept the deep, dreamless sleep of exhaustion. However, too much violent emotion had exploded within him for even exhaustion to dull his

343

mind for long. Soon the dreams came, and they were such that Dom José screamed and bolted upright, his hand automatically yanking the bellpull that would summon his servant. As he came awake he released the bell for a moment, but his plan came back fully into his mind and he began to pull the bell again hysterically, allowing his fear and hate to show openly.

The frantic summons brought Pablo running in his nightshirt, hopping now on one leg and then on the other as he tried to draw up his breeches. As he came up the back stairs he heard his master shouting his name and screaming something about shots. Just as he reached the top he saw Dom José running out of the room barefoot and also in his nightshirt.

"Wake the other men," Dom José cried. "Look to the doors, the windows. I heard shots."

"Not outside, senhor," Pablo gasped. "I heard nothing."

"Oh, my God," Dom José shrieked, "could that woman have . . ."

He rushed along the corridor to Donna Francisca's room and tried to open the door. He was not sure whether he was more relieved or disappointed when he found it still locked. That meant Lady Elvan was still inside. However, he was not much worried about her ability to deny the crime of which he would accuse her. From her screams, she had been completely hysterical. Perhaps she had lost her mind entirely or had died of fright. That would be convenient. As the thoughts passed through his mind, Dom José pounded on the door and screamed his wife's name with a superb rendering of a man nearly out of his mind with anxiety.

Pablo meanwhile had raced down the back stairs into the menservants' quarters, shouting for the men to rise, to look through the house for thieves and for some to come upstairs and help open the door to Donna Francisca's apartment. The butler, dazed and stupid with sleep, mumbled that he would look for the keys. When Pablo again ran up the stairs, his master was no longer at the door, but light streamed from the room in which he had been sleeping, and he followed there. Dom José was searching wildly through his clothing, crying, "My guns, my guns, where are they? We must break the lock. Where are my guns?"

"Senhor," Pablo protested, "the butler will bring the extra keys. Do not—"

"My God! Oh, God!" Dom José shouted as soon as he was sure he had an audience. "I left them at the dower house. I left them on the table there. Oh, my God!"

"Be calm, senhor," Pablo begged. "I will fetch them tomorrow. There is no need for guns. The butler—"

"You stupid fool!" Dom José screamed. "The woman—Elvan's wife—was enraged, hysterical, perhaps mad! If she seized the guns . . . No!"

"But senhor, why should the lady take your guns?"

"Imbecile! It was because I had to tell her . . . No! Why am I wasting time speaking to you?"

He rushed out of the room again, to find a knot of menservants around the door of Francisca's room. Without abating his frantic manner, he ordered them to open the door. The butler stepped forward with the keys in his hand, but he was terrified. He had served Francisca's family all his life. To him Dom José was no one, yet he had to obey him because his money paid for all. Yet Donna Francisca had ordered him not to disturb her. The keys trembled so in his hand that he could scarcely find the keyhole, and Dom José screamed at him, and screamed Francisca's name.

The same procedure recurred at the bedchamber door, and by now Dom José was wondering why Lady Elvan had not reacted in any way to all the noise. Perhaps she had killed herself. How delightful that would be. But the bedroom door did not open at once. When pushed, it was brought up short against the dressing table Sabrina had dragged in front of it. Dom José was stunned. It had never occurred to him that Lady Elvan would have the strength.

It must have taken a long time to move that, Dom José thought while he continued alternately urging the men to push away the obstruction and calling his wife to answer him. How was he going to explain it? Insanity, he decided. He must stick to that. The insane were known to have superhuman strength. A quiver of fear passed over him as he remembered what he himself had done, so far beyond his ordinary strength and agility. Perhaps he had been mad for a short time, but he was sane now.

Finally the dressing table yielded, the mirror collapsing forward with a crash. A shout of horror went up from the men who had broken through, for the bed-curtains were open as Sabrina had left them and the intertwined bodies with their mangled heads on the bloody pillows were plainly visible. The scream that was wrenched from Dom José when he pushed aside his servants and saw his handiwork was quite genuine. He had carried out his execution in the dark and had no idea of the ghastly effect of his bullets.

It was really as if this were all new to him, as if he had never seen those tangled bodies before, as if he had never even suspected that Francisca was betraying him. He wept and exclaimed in a frenzy of grief and shame, expressing all that had been shocked into murderous rage when the proof of her infidelity had first burst upon him. But through it all he remembered that the servants must not go near the bodies, lest they realize that the blood was clotted and turning brown, that the bodies were already cold and might be turning stiff, that Francisca and her lover had been dead for hours.

Weeping and wailing, Dom José staggered to the bed and drew the curtains closed. The *regador* of the parish would have to be told, he sobbed, and then he drew himself up and ordered the room searched. The open window with its trailing rope of tied draperies was soon discovered, as were the broken window and unlocked door on the lower floor. By this time Dom José had regained control of himself. He ordered the doors closed and one servant to stand guard so that nothing would be touched. He then had a horse saddled for himself so that he could ride to Lousa and report what had happened, and he bade the rest of the servants search the house and grounds for Lady Elvan. If they did not find her, two men should go to the dower house and guard it, not to enter but watch to see that she did not escape.

Half an hour before Dom José woke from his nightmare, Sabrina let her feet slip off the balcony, clutching at her rope of drapes and sobbing softly with fear. The generalized terror of being recaptured and of the dreadful spectacle lying in the room she was leaving soon crystallized into a real fear of falling. The novels she had read had never indicated how terribly difficult it was to let oneself down on a rope.

Within thirty seconds Sabrina's arms felt as if they would be pulled from her shoulder sockets, and her hands simply would not close tightly enough to hold her. Fear lent her a momentary spurt of strength, and her flailing feet caught on a knot, which gave her a few seconds' support. This was of no particular benefit, as she was too frightened to move. An instant later, both hands and feet slipped. Too terrified even to scream, Sabrina slid down another three feet to where a second knot briefly halted her progress.

This time she had sense enough to rest and then deliberately loosen her grip so that she would slide down to the next knot. Unfortunately, her strength failed so that she could not tighten her grasp enough again. She slid right past that knot, and past the next, to land with a jarring thump on the ground. There she remained, shaking with mingled sobs and laughter because it had not been very far down after all, and no one was on guard, no one had cried out or grabbed her. *Could* Dom José be so insane that he had forgotten all about her? That hope was a little stronger than the first time the idea crossed her mind, but she still could not believe it. It was far more likely, her fears insisted, that he had allowed her escape to increase her torment in some way that she could not even conceive.

Sabrina did have one real hope: that in his complex plan Dom José had outmaneuvered himself, and that if she were careful enough, she could somehow elude him. If she could get down to Lousa and report what had happened, she would be safe. But Lousa was several miles away. Frightened and very tired, Sabrina simply could not face walking those miles down the dark road through the silent woods, and the road was the place most likely for him to look for her. She glanced around the lawn. It was as still and silent as when she had examined it from the balcony. Sabrina rose to her feet. She would not find safety by crouching under the window from which she had escaped. She fought the instinctive reluctance to expose herself, and moved softly around to the back of the house.

Midway, she stopped in a deep patch of shadow, paralyzed by the thought that the path back to the house was an even more likely place for Dom José to wait for her, but she *had* to get back to the house. She needed money and a horse and a better weapon with which to defend herself than the candlestick she had untied from her waist and now carried in her hand. Eventually she forced herself forward, telling herself that Dom José would surely think she would be too afraid to retrace her coming to the house. Also, there would be less chance for anyone to creep up behind her on the path, because twigs would crackle and branches would swish.

Having found courage to cross the open lawn and enter

the dark opening, Sabrina wanted to run. However, like Dom José, she found the downward trip harder than the climb. With the light of the moon dimmed to a bare, occasional glimmer and fear turning every shadow into a leaping enemy, she advanced one slow, blind step at a time, pausing to stand frozen and breathless to listen for pursuit every few minutes.

Even with the care she took, Sabrina fell several times. She was near fainting with fear and exhaustion when she reached the back lawn of the dower house. Farther down the hill to the right stood the stable. Sabrina glanced toward it, but to reach it she would have to go out past the house and down the road. Then she would have to wake the grooms. Softly, Sabrina began to weep. She could not. She simply could not, not without a little rest. She was so tired and hurt and afraid—and Katy was dead.

The return of that memory drove Sabrina out of the mouth of the path and up to the back door in a rush. The house was all dark, the candles burnt out. Sabrina stopped just outside the door. Of all places to set a trap, this was the best; but now desperation, rage, and grief drove her, and she raised the candlestick to strike, pushed the door open, and jumped to the side. No shot was fired; there was no sound at all beside her own harsh breathing.

The sound steadied her and, after drawing another deep breath, she held it. Surely she would hear the breathing of any attacker waiting for her. She remembered how Dom José had panted as he drove her up the path to the house. But there was no sound of breathing inside the door. Sabrina entered. The scullery was dimmer than the lawn outside, but she could see well enough to determine that no one else was in the room.

By the time Sabrina found candles and the flint and tinder with which to light them, she had begun to believe Dom José had forgotten about her. Now she trembled with exhaustion, and simple grief overwhelmed her. She could not bear to look at the two still bodies lying in the front hall. Crying softly, she crept up the back stairs. She must find her guns or William's and load them and then rouse the men in the stable. But when she came into her own room, so normal, so untouched by the incredible events that had taken place, Sabrina set down her branch of candles and sank down on the bed, unable to drive her body further. She only meant to rest for a few minutes, but sleep came in a huge velvety black wave that she could not resist.

As Perce set his foot on the first step he became aware that the door of the house was open. He shouted to Sergei that something was wrong, and leapt up the remainder of the steps. Sergei called for him to wait and looked for a place to tether the horses. By the time he had wound the reins around an ornamental bush a few feet away, he heard Perce cry out again in surprise and then shout a warning to stop in the doorway because someone was lying on the floor. Sergei hurried up the steps, arriving just as Perce exclaimed, "Katy! My God, it's Katy! Sergei, get us some light."

In turning to obey his master, well away from where Perce knelt, Sergei's foot struck something soft. He bent, felt, withdrew his hand hastily. "The manservant," he growled, "he is dead."

Perce's first shout of alarm had wakened Sabrina, and she jerked upright, panting with fear. His second inarticulate cry of surprise as he tripped over Katy, who had managed to drag herself right to the door, brought Sabrina off the bed, looking wildly for a place to hide. When she heard the name Sergei and recognized Perce's voice, she put her hands to her head, fearing that need, desire, and terror had driven her insane. But she had not thought of Perce, not once during the terrible hours of that night.

Why should she imagine he was here now? And then she heard Sergei's shocked exclamations—in Russian!

Sabrina clapped her hands over her lips to hold back a shriek of joy. It must be true, yet it could not be. She must be mad, yet she did not feel mad. She remembered everything, and when she looked down at herself, there was evidence that she had not dreamed a nightmare or made up the horrors. Her dress was torn and stained with earth and grass; the palms of her hands were scored with her falls; she ached with bruises. Sabrina crept out into the upper hall and across to where she could look down the stairs.

As she reached the edge a candle flickered to life. Sabrina saw quite clearly Perce's golden head bent over a still form and Sergei's bulk going down on his knees with the candle in his hand. To the side, Charlot's body lay. Sabrina averted her eyes and her mouth opened to call out, just as Perce's initial shock passed enough for his mind really to grasp the situation. He leapt to his feet, bellowing, "Sabrina! Sabrina!"

"Here," she cried.

Her voice was faint, thin as a child's cry. It was impossible to tell whether Perce heard her, but he was already running up the stairs and she staggered forward a few steps and fell into his arms. For the first few minutes nothing intelligible was said on either side. Perce held Sabrina to him, alternately assuring her she was now safe and asking what had happened. And she alternately tried to tell him what had happened and asked reassurance that he was really there, that she was not dreaming or mad.

Convinced at last of his presence, Sabrina's grief broke over her. "Katy's dead," she sobbed. "Katy's dead."

"No, love, no, she isn't," Perce told her. "Stop crying and listen. Katy—"

But there was more convincing proof than Perce's words. Katy's own voice crying Sabrina's name interrupted him. And Sergei's followed, admonishing Katy to lie still. Fool of a woman that she was, he told her, she had broken her leg and her head, too, and could not get up.

Sabrina flew down the stairs, now weeping with joy, and confusion reigned for some minutes more. While the women wept and kissed each other, Perce closed the door and had a hasty consultation with Sergei. He was very uneasy over the situation. He did not like the necessity of explaining a murder so far from the British embassy in a country in which he could speak no more than a few words of the language.

Worse yet, he had heard the official attitude was anti-British. True, he had seen nothing of that among the people, who seemed uniformly pleasant and open to strangers. Nonetheless, the notion of explaining what had happened to the legal authorities made him decidedly uncomfortable. But Katy had to have a doctor to set her leg. Sergei had straightened it while she was still in a faint, but it was grossly swollen and neither Perce nor Sergei wished to try to set it. On the other hand, with a dead man on the floor next to Katy, it was impossible for them to leave the women unprotected.

At this point Sabrina interrupted the discussion by saying, "I'll go to the stable. One of the grooms must ride for a doctor and to tell the *regador* about this at once."

"Of course," Perce exclaimed with relief.

"But had we better move Katy to a sofa first? The floor is all blood, and Charlot . . ." Sabrina swallowed hard, but she was in complete possession of herself now. Sure of Katy's safety, she could bear the other horrors. She was sorry for Charlot and would truly grieve for William when she had time, but it was most important to see to Katy's comfort.

Sergei grunted approval of this plan and went to the scullery to wrench a light closet door off its hinges. They moved Katy onto this and then to a sofa in the drawing room. As gentle as they tried to be, Katy very nearly fainted again, explaining in a thread of a voice as Sabrina lifted her head and held a glass of wine to her lips, that the loss of consciousness had happened again and again.

"When I came to meself under the stair, I tried to get up, and I went off. And every time I tried to move, I wanted to go to the stable to get the men, but I'd only move a few inches and go off again. How did ye get away from him, luv?"

"From whom? What happened?" Perce asked.

"Doctor first," Sabrina said.

"Yes, you can tell me on the way," Perce agreed, assuming from Sabrina's willingness to go outside that there was no danger.

However, no sooner had she stepped out of the door than a man shouted a single word and rushed toward her. Sabrina shrank back with a cry of fear, and Perce stepped around her and struck the oncoming man heavily on the jaw. Hearing the noise, Sergei rushed out and hauled the half-dazed man to his feet, securing his arms behind him. A torrent of Portuguese poured from him, in which the first word he had said was repeated frequently.

Everyone's attention was on the captured man. No one noticed Dom José's second servant, who had come around from the back at his companion's shout in time to see him seized. He would have run back to des Ermidas, except he knew there was no one there who could do anything. And although Dom José was not a bad master, he could be very severe when his instructions were not obeyed.

Pablo shrank back into the shadows and watched. He had been told to prevent the lady from escaping. He could no longer do so if the two men accompanied her, but he could watch and tell his master which road she took. That would be better than nothing. He found a place off to the side where he could watch the paths from both front and

...ere was no need to be close now, since he
...er trying to guard the doors.

...re of the watcher, Perce, Sabrina, and Sergei
... at their captive. "What did he say?" Perce asked Sa-
b...na, rubbing his knuckles.

She stared, wide-eyed. "I think he is calling me a murderess," she replied in a shocked voice, and then, "Oh, he's
mad, but—"

"Who?" Perce roared. "Not this creature. Whom the
devil are you talking about?"

"Dom José. The man who rented us the house. Didn't
you hear what I said? He—he shot William and his
wife—in bed." She shuddered. "I—I saw them. I
thought—for a moment I thought they were m-making
love. I—I told you."

He put his arms around her. "Maybe you did, darling,
but you were crying so hard I guess I didn't understand
you. But who the devil is this?" He gestured to the man
they had captured. "And why call *you* a murderess?"

Sabrina put a hand to her head. "I don't know who he
is, and it's such a long story. But we must get a doctor for
Katy first."

"Take him into the house and tie him up," Perce said to
Sergei. Looking then to Sabrina, he continued, "We can
ride my horses to the stables. I left them just outside. Can
you ride astride? I'd go myself, but your men don't know
me, and I haven't more than two or three words of Portuguese."

She nodded wordlessly, her mind busy assembling all
the peculiarities of what Dom José had done. Perce lifted
her to the saddle. She had to raise her narrow skirt above
her thighs, but did not give it a thought. Perce had seen
her legs before, and she was quite unaware of Pablo, who
gasped and cursed when he saw Perce put her up on the
horse. The best he could do was run out to the road and
across it into the shadow of the trees. Pablo's haste de-

prived him of a sight he would have found most titillating
had he not been so worried.

The white thighs might not be new, but they were a
devilish distraction in spite of the urgency of the situation.
Perce could not resist kissing the one nearest him. Sabrina
quivered and put a hand on his head. He turned his check
against her leg and sighed, fumbling behind the saddle to
unstrap his cloak. Then he kissed her again before he flung
the cloak around her to preserve the decencies.

There was no great difficulty in waking the grooms; explaining what had happened was harder. Sabrina was able
to speak Portuguese, but words like "attacked" and
"killed" were not part of the everyday vocabulary one
used with servants or in polite conversation during a visit.
Sabrina compromised and used the word of which she was
sure. There had been an accident. A doctor was urgently
needed. She saw she was understood. One groom ran off
to dress himself while another went to saddle a horse for
him to ride.

"It's just too hard to explain," she said to Perce. "The
doctor may speak English, and anyway he'll see Charlot.
He can explain to a groom and send for the *regador*. I
can't believe another hour would matter. If Dom José intended to run away, he's likely to have done so already."

"Yes. I'm glad you didn't tell him to fetch the law. Let's
get back to the house."

A third groom accompanied them to take the animals
they were riding back to the stable. They had other company, too. Pablo offered many a prayer of thanksgiving
when he saw the lady and her companion going back to
the house.

Inside, Perce and Sabrina found Sergei had brought the
captive into the drawing room so the Russian could watch
him and Katy at the same time. It was she who recognized
the man as Dom José's servant. She had learned about as
much Portuguese as Sabrina, but from dealing with the

maids on a more personal level, Katy had obtained a different vocabulary. Thus, she was better able to understand what Manuelo said. At first she was so indignant that she nearly told Sergei to throttle him. Fury, reduction in her pain, the relief of knowing that Brina was safe, and—surprisingly important—the security that Sergei's presence gave her, had restored much of Katy's strength. When Sabrina and Perce came in, she knew the whole story except one important piece: There was another watcher.

"He says Dom José has gone to Lousa to be accusin' ye of murder," Katy raged. "He told this man that he left his guns here, that ye were ravin' mad because he hinted to ye that Himself was unfaithful. How did I fall down the stair, then, I ask? Oh, says he, I must have been tryin' to stop ye from goin' to murder the pair of them, so ye pushed me, then grabbed the guns and shot poor Charlot. Then ye ran to the house, breakin' a pane in the door—the servants found one broke—then shot the two. When ye heard Dom José yellin' for help, ye locked the doors and climbed out the window."

"But I *didn't* have the guns!" Sabrina said.

"Oh, they found those, too. Right under the window," Katy said bitterly.

"It's ridiculous!" Sabrina cried. "How could I have had time to move the dressing table and slit the drapes and tie them up—"

"Of course it's ridiculous," Perce agreed, but he was frowning. "Still, I don't like it, not at all. Dom José is a wealthy landholder around here, and this *regador* you mentioned is going to be very reluctant to displease him. Add to that the fact that his servants will swear he never left the house, plus the disadvantage that none of us can really speak Portuguese. Sergei, take this man and dump him in the cellar."

Sabrina turned frightened eyes to her lover. "You don't think the *regador* will believe him!"

"I don't know," Perce replied thoughtfully. "And anyhow, 'believing' isn't what I'm worried about. Boney's going to take over Portugal, and English influence will disappear. I think everyone must know that. From the *regador*'s point of view, it might not be worth stirring up a local hornet's nest for an Englishwoman. He can assume you're guilty and insane and send you back to Lisbon for Strangford to deal with."

"I won't stand for it!" Sabrina exclaimed, her eyes blazing. "Katy will back me up."

"And a whole house full of servants will back up Dom José."

"Are you saying I should allow him to accuse me of murder and not defend myself?" Sabrina shrieked.

"No," Perce replied, pulling her toward him. "I'm saying it would be best for you if we went back to Lisbon and told your story to Strangford before any accusations are made. I don't think this *regador* will do much if he knows you're gone. He'll probably be relieved."

"But Dom José shot Charlot and almost killed Katy," Sabrina exclaimed. "I won't let him get away with it and blame me!"

"No, of course not," Perce soothed, "but the way to deal with it is through Portuguese lawyers in Lisbon. You'll accuse him from there."

"Won't it look as if I've run away?" Sabrina asked, and then said, "But we can't go. Katy can't go."

"No. Katy stays here. That's proof you haven't run away. Also, if the *regador* asks about what happened here, Dom José will probably say, or imply, that Katy is an innocent victim of your lunacy." He raised a questioning brow toward Katy, and she nodded. "He can't go back on that without making the rest of his story look fishy."

"I won't leave Katy alone," Sabrina said.

"No, neither would I. Sergei will stay and accompany her to Lisbon as soon as the doctor says she can travel.

Since she will be questioned, your side of the story will go on record here too."

"Yes," Katy said at once, "ye go, Brina. If ye dinna go, like as not we'll all end up in the soup. Ye'll lose yer temper, and then I'll lose mine. Then we'll both say things that will make the *regador* mad, and that canna help."

"If I stay and take her south alone," Sergei put in, "should I marry her now?"

The question was obviously addressed to Perce and Sabrina, and Sergei looked from one to the other. Perce opened his mouth, but nothing came out. Sabrina, who had been kneeling near Katy, sat back on her heels, overbalanced, and landed with a thump on her behind. Katy gasped and flushed rosily, suddenly looking quite young and pretty.

"Ye dirty ox," she said, in the broken mixture of languages in which she and Sergei communicated, "I'm no slave, whatever ye are. It's me ye ask if ye want me."

Sergei turned his eyes to her. "This is no time to play games," he replied. "In the end we marry. This is true— no? So I ask which time is best for my little father and for the great lady."

This time it was Katy who opened her mouth without producing any response. Sabrina had clapped a hand across her own lips to smother near-hysterical giggles. Katy and Sergei! It was ridiculous! And yet it was not at all ridiculous, Sabrina realized in a flash of insight. She had never known Katy's husband, but Katy's father had been much like Sergei—big, quiet, patient—only Sergei was much cleverer. The realization only made Sabrina giggle more. The stretching silence was a perfectly clear indication that Katy did intend to accept Sergei, and that she had no answer to his astute remark.

"Not in Portugal," Perce said at last in so wooden a tone that Sabrina did not dare look at him. If she did, she knew his control might disintegrate, and for him to whoop with laughter would be unkind. Sabrina herself nearly strangled subduing her mirth. "However," Perce went on more easily as he concentrated on the meaning of Sergei's question and did not find that in the least funny, "if you have to go back to England on a ship other than the one Sabrina and I take, ask the captain to marry you. That will make the voyage safer and easier for Katy, since the ship might be very crowded."

"Go back on a different ship!" Katy exclaimed. "But why?"

"It may be a week or two before you are fit to travel," Perce replied, "and the trip to Lisbon will be slow for you, too. Lord Strangford might want Brina to leave at once. I have permission for her to go on a naval vessel. We might have to sail before you arrive in Lisbon."

"No!" Sabrina cried.

"Yes!" Katy contradicted with considerable force. "Dinna ye be a stubborn fool, Brina. If ye willna go, I'll have to travel before I'm ready for it. Ye know I'll do it if ye willna go without me, so dinna force it on me. Sergei will see me safe. Do ye doubt he can?"

"No, of course he can," Sabrina said uncertainly. "And you mustn't travel before you're quite well."

"At least not before the doctor says it's safe," Perce amended, "but as soon as you can, Katy. Now, Sergei, you have your own papers and money. Do you have enough?"

"There's money in William's strongbox and all my jewels," Sabrina said. "You use what you need, Katy."

"Good. I have more than enough for Sabrina and myself," Perce said approvingly. "Sergei, go into the kitchen and put together enough food for a couple of days. We probably won't need it, but just in case things go wrong and we have to spend a night on the road, I don't want to starve. Brina, get traveling clothes on, and take a heavy cloak and a couple of blankets. I'll walk down to the stable again and get a pair of horses saddled. And Brina, if you hear anyone coming, go out the back door and hide. I'll find you."

The man Perce had seen pounding on the door in Lousa was not, of course, a traveler seeking a bed. It was Dom José, and he was trying to wake the *regador*, not an innkeeper. Before Perce had turned off on the road that led to La Casa des Ermidas and the dower house, Dom José had gained entrance and had begun to tell his story. Needless to say, the tale was received with considerable shock, and Dom José had to repeat it more than once. Since his excitement and frustration increased in proportion to what he considered the stupidity of his auditor, it was more than half an hour before the *regador*, Senhor de Sousa, was able to take in what he said. More time elapsed as two of the town's guards were summoned. Lousa was a quiet town, and there was no reason to keep men on duty at night.

Dom José fretted and fumed, making the *regador* look sideways at him. There were aspects of Dom José's story that stuck in his throat. One peculiarity he simply could not imagine was a woman invading someone else's house to do what Dom José had said. In the second place, he had met Sabrina, and nothing in her manner or appearance had prepared him for the raging virago of Dom José's story. A third consideration was the use of the guns. Most women hated and feared firearms and would not touch them. Last and most puzzling of all was the blockading of the bedroom and the escape through the window. Surely a murderess would have left the chamber in a more facile manner. Strange was not a strong enough word for that!

During the ride out of town the *regador* had little chance to think over the problem, because he was engaged in insisting that he would first go to des Ermidas to examine the dead. Dom José objected to this, arguing that he should first secure Lady Elvan and confront her with those she had slain. If he did not, Dom José insisted, she would escape.

"To where?" the *regador* asked. "Where could a woman go all alone in the middle of the night? Did you not say her servants were trying to calm her? If they believed her hysterical, would they agree to rush away from the house at this hour?"

"She is a sly, clever woman," Dom José replied desperately. "Who knows what she could have told them."

"She does not seem to have acted with either slyness or cleverness," the *regador* responded dryly. "Perhaps to break in and shoot them is possible, but what would stop her from instantly running down the stairs—she knew where they were already—and out the way she came? Why should she barricade the door? And to cut the drapes and tie them? That could not be the work of a few minutes."

"How do I know what a madwoman will do?"

"I hesitate to add to your grief," de Sousa interrupted quickly, but his voice was gentle. "Could Donna Francisca have had . . . er . . . another . . . ah . . . friend? One who became jealous over Lord Elvan's attentions?"

"No! No! Impossible!" Dom José shouted, startling the horses.

The *regador* made a noncommittal, soothing remark, but Dom José continued to insist frantically that Francisca had been a good woman, seduced by Lord Elvan. He could not afford the introduction of the idea of a second lover. Although he did not mention it to the *regador*, he knew such a person would certainly have no reason to involve Lady Elvan or to hurt her servants. Although Senhor de Sousa interjected soothing noises from time to time, the tone and manner in which Dom José spoke was definitely disturbing him.

He was about to urge again that Dom José try to compose himself, when the sound of a swiftly moving horse warned them of someone coming down the road. The men set up a shout of warning so that the rider coming down the hill would have time to slow his horse. Dom José snarled viciously to Senhor de Sousa that it was Lady Elvan escaping, and perhaps in the future he would be believed more readily when he spoke. The *regador* did not reply, but when the rider appeared and was quite apparently a man, he made it obvious that he was *not* looking at Dom José.

A few questions extracted all the facts: The man was a groom from the dower house. His lady had come to the stable with a tall, blond companion and told the grooms that there had been an accident. Her maid had broken her leg. Yes, his lady certainly looked as if there had been bad trouble. Her dress was dirty and torn and her face all bruised. He had been sent to summon the doctor as quickly as possible. The *regador* waved the groom on, urging him to hurry but not so fast that he did not arrive. Finally he turned to Dom José.

"I think now that you were right," he said. "We had better stop at the dower house first. If Lady Elvan and her maid were hurt, this may be the work of bandits, or other intruders. Do you know who this tall, blond companion could be?"

Dom José shook his head. He was stricken dumb by this double disaster. If Lady Elvan was calmly sending for a doctor rather than running away or hiding, and the maid was alive, he was finished. *What can I do?* Dom José wondered desperately.

"Perhaps I have been a fool from the beginning," Dom José said in a choked voice. "Perhaps there was another, or more than one. If so, the servants may have known of it. I will go up to the house and question them. You will come there as soon as you are finished at the dower house?"

The *regador* was pleased by Dom José's acceptance of his logic. A crazed lover could have tried to attack Lord Elvan at home and, when he found he was not there, have gone on to La Casa des Ermidas and killed his unfaithful mistress and her lover there. Of course the blocked door and the rope from the window were still puzzling, but at least Dom José was no longer trying to blame Lady Elvan. Ladies wept when they learned of a husband's infidelity— or smiled—but they did not break into people's houses and shoot the offenders.

It never occurred to the *regador* to suspect Dom José. If Dom José had shot his wife and her lover, there would be no need to lie about it. No one would blame him. The priest would absolve him with a minor penance, and the civil court would declare justifiable homicide in a private session. Thus, Senhor de Sousa agreed instantly with Dom José's suggestion and with considerable relief watched him ride away.

Questioning the servants would keep Dom José occupied and might ease his anguish. Meanwhile, perhaps the identity of the attacker, or a description of him, could be obtained from the servants or Lady Elvan. It would also be necessary to inform the poor lady of her erring husband's fate. Now it would be possible to give her the sad news with decency and sympathy. And if the blond stranger were a countryman, perhaps even a relative, of Lady Elvan's, he would be able to assist her. That would take a great weight off Senhor de Sousa's mind and conscience. Sure that Dom José was well ahead and would not complicate the distressing revelation he must make at the dower house, Senhor de Sousa increased his horse's pace.

CHAPTER NINETEEN

Dom José drove his horse up the road as fast as he could. He would have to escape. Escape to where? To what? For what? The last question was the bitterest of all. His life had had many goals: to please his father, to run his business so that he would be both respected and rich, to found a noble line. Now all were gone. A whole lifetime destroyed by a lecherous woman and a man he could not describe in words sufficiently filthy and degrading. They were dead and beyond his reach. He cursed himself for the speed and directness of his actions, not for the outcome. They should have suffered for what they had done.

The thought hammered and hammered in his head with the beat of his horse's hooves. Then he saw the dim lights around the curtains in two windows of the dower house. Again the boil of hatred swelled, and pain lanced through him. It was her fault as much as her husband's. "What could I do?" she had whined. She could have fought him, complained. If she had not made excuses for him, smiling so pleasantly at him when they were together, perhaps warning would have come in time to prevent a consummation. She was as guilty as the other two, and she would get off unscathed, wrapped in sympathy and concern.

No, she would not! Oh, no, she would not. Dom José knew he was ruined in any case. He would not be deprived of the last flicker of his revenge. But how to achieve it? As soon as the *regador* heard Lady Elvan's story, he would come to des Ermidas. Whether or not he believed her, de Sousa would have to take care that all persons who might be connected with the shootings remained within his reach until the matter was thrashed out. But would he leave a guard at the dower house? Perhaps not, definitely not if he believed Lady Elvan's tale. And the blond visitor? Dom José shrugged. Some fool of a diplomat, no doubt. He could be dealt with.

In his mind Dom José reviewed the servants who would obey him unquestioningly even if what he demanded seemed wrong. Pablo and Manuelo were at the house already and could be picked up there. The coachman, Carlo, and the coach guard, Pedro, would also do as he told them. With him, that would make five. Dom José smiled viciously. Even if the *regador* had left one man, they could overpower him and get that conniving bitch out of the house. He felt quite pleased as he rode up to the stable of des Ermidas. He would have his revenge. After that—who cared!

Perce heard Dom José's horse as he neared the stable. He held his breath, but the sound continued without hesitation past the short drive of the dower house and diminished on the long curve that continued up to La Casa des Ermidas. As soon as he was sure the noise would not reach the rider, Perce called the grooms. They responded at once, not yet having gone back to bed, and two fresh horses were saddled very quickly, but not quickly enough. Before they were quite ready, the *regador*'s party was heard on the road.

Praying that whoever had gone by would go on up to the big house, Perce led the horses out and paused to listen when the party had passed. He could not hear them, and that was not good. If they had gone on up the road, he should still be able to hear something. Cursing fluently if silently in several languages, Perce went slowly toward the house, keeping in the shadows along the side of the road. At the turn into the drive, he stopped. They were there, and one man was holding the three horses outside.

A quick look at the ground told Perce he would never get the horses around to the back except across the lawn. The ground on which the dower house stood had either been cut out of the mountain or built up to make it level. The stable was down a very steep drop. He led the horses back a little way and then across the road into the wooded area where he was able to conceal them.

To make his own way along the shadowed edge of the lawn was not difficult. Obviously the guard who remained outside was not watching for anything; he was just holding the horses. Perce did not worry about his casual assurance to Sabrina that he would find her until he almost ran into her. It was a lot darker, even in this lightly wooded area, than it had been on the lawn and on the road. They clutched at each other, teetering uncertainly on the uneven ground.

"The horses are across the road," Perce murmured into Sabrina's ear. "And there's a man out in front of the house."

Sabrina nodded without speaking and drew him back along the way she had come. Her eyes were on her feet, picking out the path, and she was ridiculously, shamefully happy. Ever since Sergei's crazy announcement, she had been bubbling over with joy and laughter. She knew it was indecent to feel this way when poor William was lying dead, murdered only a few hours earlier, but she could not help it. She did not notice a darker shadow move suddenly to the side and blend into those cast by trees and bushes.

The telltale movement escaped Perce's attention, too. He was watching the way the small patches of moonlight that came between the leaves gleamed on Sabrina's silver-gilt hair. Rightfully, Perce knew he should be worried sick. He should be seriously concerned about this wild plan to evade a legal investigation. What Sabrina had said was true. Running away would certainly increase the chance that the *regador* would presume her guilty without investigating. The truth was that Perce did not care what the *regador* presumed. If he could get Sabrina to Lisbon and aboard that naval cutter, they could make any assumptions they wanted in Portugal. Brina would be safe—and his.

Every time he remembered that Elvan was dead, his heart leapt. No annulment. No divorce. Not only could he have Brina, but he could go into the diplomatic service as he had intended originally and she would have the life she loved. He almost hoped the *regador* would assume Sabrina was guilty and let Dom José get away with it. Of course, it was dreadful that he had killed Charlot and hurt Katy, but that was temporary insanity. The man had done him and Sabrina, too, an enormous favor. If he could get Brina away safely, Perce would gladly call it quits with Dom José.

Pablo cursed silently. He had missed his chance. This time the lady would escape, but there was nothing he could do about it. She had come out with the big dark man who had held Manuelo prisoner with as little effort as if he were holding a small child. Pablo had no intention of engaging in any physical contest with him. He had tried to get at the woman when the big man went back into the house, but first the horsemen had arrived and then the blond man had come. Pablo did not intend to challenge him, either, not after he had seen him fell Manuelo with a single blow.

He watched as Sabrina led Perce to a pile of equipment. She took her cloak, one blanket, and a long coil of rope. Perce pointed at it, and Sabrina raised her hands in mute puzzlement, murmuring, "Sergei." Perce shrugged, but he had considerable respect for Sergei's survival instincts. He merely picked up the food bag, grunting with surprise at how heavy it was, the other blanket, and another small bag, which presumably held a change of clothing and other necessities for Sabrina. Then they retraced their steps.

Pablo followed, far enough back so that they would not hear him if he took a misstep. This made his quarry barely visible. Several times they did disappear. Then Pablo hurried, all his attention on finding them without allowing them to notice him. He did not wish whatever had happened to Manuelo to happen to him. Thus, he did not notice that there was a man holding the three horses that had arrived until his quarry had turned into the main road. When he saw the horse holder, his mouth opened, then shut. It was Dom José he must tell that the lady was escaping, but if this was a guard, his master must be in the house.

Pablo stepped boldly out of the trees and walked along the lawn to hail the guard. "Is Dom José within?" he asked.

"No, he rode back to La Casa des Ermidas," the guard answered.

Pablo stopped, again on the horns of a dilemma. If he ran up to the main house, the lady would have more time to escape. If he told the *regador*'s guard that she was out of the house, there would be a better chance to take her, but that might not be what his master wanted. One good thing, she and the man had been on foot, probably headed for the stables. Pablo decided he could climb the path and tell Dom José what had happened in just about the same time it would take to saddle and load the horses. There was only one road down the mountain. There could be no doubt where they would go. His master could overtake them if he wished. Pablo waved at the guard and ran toward the path behind the house.

Meanwhile, Perce and Sabrina had reached the horses, loaded them, and mounted. They made their way diagonally toward the road so that they would come out as far as possible from the dower house drive. It would have been better if they had been able to ride through the woods, but that was impossible because there was another very sharp drop-off. The actual distance gained was not much, but it seemed to be enough since there were no sounds of alarm or of pursuit.

Just as they came out into the open, a man's voice called aloud. Sabrina lifted her quirt, but Perce shook his head and kept to a walk at the very side of the road where the dust was thickest. No second cry followed the first, and they went on down toward Lousa for about ten minutes in almost complete silence. It wasn't until they were well on their way and Perce realized they couldn't stay in Lousa or in any nearby inn that he began to regret what he had done. Brina must be totally exhausted. How much longer could she ride?

"Are you unbearably tired, Brina?" he asked softly.

Her head turned toward him alertly. "No, I'm not." She laughed quietly. "I know I should be, but I'm not. Do you think we've got away? I suppose when the excitement wears off, I'll fall flat on my face and notice all my black and blue marks, but now I'm fine."

"Maybe, but I'm not sure we shouldn't go back, not because of the legalities, but—but I must have been crazy! You can't sleep out in the woods."

"Why not?" she asked, laughing again. "I did it often enough when I was a child. Do you think I've gotten so decrepit that I'll melt in the rain? Besides, it won't rain, and it will be warm enough because we'll sleep during the day. Anyhow, I don't want to go back. Oh, Perce, I know it's wrong, but I'm quite dreadfully happy. I want to escape."

He turned his head to look at her fully. The moon was very low, nearly ready to set, and it shone directly into her face. Perce's breath caught. Her hair was a rat's nest and her face was bruised and filthy, streaked with dirt and tears, but he had never seen her look more beautiful. Her pale eyes were brilliant, and her skin seemed translucent, glowing from within instead of lit from outside. But Perce had neither a chance to tell her that nor to answer her remarks. Both flew out of his head as he heard a faint thunder behind them.

Horses, more than one or two, and coming fast, he decided, faster than dictated by safety. That meant pursuit. Sabrina's head turned farther to look over her shoulder. She heard them too, but to Perce's amazement, she laughed aloud. The expression on her face was the same mischievous delight that he had seen on it all through the years when she engaged in some harebrained and often dangerous adventure.

"Brina!" he exclaimed.

But she had already struck her mare with her quirt and was flying down the road, the loosened strands of her hair streaming behind her like concentrated beams of moonlight. Perce took off after her without even needing to touch William's powerful gelding. Both animals were fresh, the road was still well lit in the last light of the moon, and best of all it was leveling off. However, their pursuers had obviously heard the quickened pace. There were shouts from the road above and behind them.

Perce pulled even with Sabrina. "This is crazy," he shouted as they came into the short, straight stretch of track that preceded the junction with the road to Lousa. "We don't have to run away. We can just tell them exactly what happened."

From the road above, where an opening in the trees on one of the curves showed the fugitives, a shot rang out and then another.

"They don't sound friendly," Sabrina shouted back to Perce, slapping her mare with the quirt again.

Logic told Perce that the shots were probably warnings. Nonetheless, every instinct screamed that the shots were a bad sign. The pursuers could just as well have called threats or warnings. Shooting implied that Sabrina had already been adjudged guilty. Perhaps Dom José had convinced the *regador* that if she could be caught and killed, the whole situation could be hushed up completely.

If Sabrina were dead, it might be thought that no one would believe Katy's story. Certainly no one in Portugal would bother to listen to a maid's defense of her mistress if the *regador* would not. As soon as the ugly idea came into Perce's mind, he found evidence to support it. Why send a whole party of men to stop a woman with one unarmed escort? Party? Where did the party come from, Perce asked himself with startled realization. There had been only three horses on the lawn. There were certainly more than three horses in the group following them. Sabrina was right. They didn't sound friendly. Not at all.

There was another shout—this time ahead of them from the road that led to Lousa. Without volition, Perce's head turned left in the direction of the sound, and in the same instant he heard the scrape and rattle of carriage wheels.

"Right!" he called to Sabrina. "Go right!"

Five seconds later they burst out into the road, veering right and narrowly missing the groom from the dower house, who was riding just ahead of the doctor's carriage and had shouted the warning Perce had heard. Well into their stride, the horses thundered on.

Two minutes later the groom was shouting another warning as he heard Dom José and his men coming down. This time his voice was more frantic, and he roared that there was a carriage on the road. Perforce, Dom José came to a halt. It was impossible, he knew, for horses to get by a carriage on the narrow track without great care. Then he took offense because the doctor did not move aside quickly enough. A shouting match ensued, which caused more delay because the doctor also took offense

ROBERTA GELLIS

and would not move his vehicle at all. By the time they
were past and had reached the main road, all sight and
sound of Perce and Sabrina were gone.

When Pablo had rushed out of the path between the
houses and told him what he had seen, Dom José had
been overjoyed. It would be far easier to kill Sabrina out
in the open than to invade her house, and pursuing her
would raise fewer doubts in his men. They already believed her a murderess. They would believe that the
regador had told him to capture her alive or dead. They
only needed to saddle four horses and find weapons, and
while this was being done, Pablo told Dom José that Manuelo had been captured and dragged into the house.

Dom José's mood began to darken with that information and slipped further into discontent as they rode down
the track. As fast as they went, it seemed to him that they
were barely moving. After they passed the dower house
stables and could not see horses ahead on any of the
straight stretches, he began to fear his quarry had a longer
lead than he had expected. A sense of desperation began
to torment him. Catching Lady Elvan might not be so easy
as he had first thought.

It was that feeling of desperation that caused him to fire
his pistol at the fleeing pair when he caught sight of them
far below. He realized immediately that it was a stupid
thing to do. The chance of hitting anything, even a horse,
at that distance was nil. As soon as he recognized the futil-
ity of his action, he ordered his men to save their shots,
but the order came a second too late to stop Pedro from
firing also. At the meeting of the roads Dom José was
faced with a bitter choice. To the left was Lousa, to the
right nothing but small mountain villages. But would the
woman know that? If he went the wrong way, his prey
would escape and his revenge would be incomplete. He
would have salvaged nothing from the wreck of his life.

* * *

Some distance down the road, Perce and Sabrina had pulled their horses to a canter to ease them a little. They expected that their pursuers would soon be on their heels again, since they believed that both the groom and the doctor had seen them go right. Sabrina raised the question of whether it would be worth going back and said she had brought William's pistols.

"I think we'd run right into them," Perce replied. Then, hesitantly, he asked, "Do you want me to try to disable Dom José? I don't think the men would be dangerous once he was out of action."

Sabrina hesitated also. "No," she said thoughtfully. "No, I don't want you to hurt him. It was wrong of him to kill poor Charlot, but William . . . I'm sorry he's dead, Perce. I never wanted harm to come to him. I never hated him . . . except for a few days when I first realized what he really was. Then I got over it. I wanted to be free, but not for him to be dead. Still, if it hadn't been Dom José, it probably would have been another husband. He was getting . . . I don't know . . . careless. I can't blame Dom José for William's death."

"Well, I'm glad about that because, to tell you the truth, Brina, I'm grateful to the man. It's no use my pretending. I did want Elvan dead. I would have killed him myself, except I knew he wouldn't challenge me, and if I had forced it on him, you would never have forgiven me."

"No, I wouldn't have," Sabrina replied seriously. "I would have been his murderer, even if you pulled the trigger, Perce. I couldn't have lived with that. As for Dom José, I guess it was his right, and anyway I'm as much to blame as he is."

"Don't be a fool!" Perce snapped, his voice harsh. "You had nothing to do with Elvan's chasing."

"Yes," she insisted bleakly. "I could have stopped him, but I didn't care enough. That's why Dom José dragged me off to his house."

"Dom José is quite obviously insane," Perce interrupted, even more angrily. "Are you trying to tell me that Charlot should have tried to stop Elvan too? Or Katy? Don't you start beating your breast over him. He was no child and no fool—at least, in a general way. And I'll say this, too, Brina. I don't mean to hurt you. You're more beautiful than any other woman I know, but you couldn't have stopped him forever. Sooner or later you would have run out of ploys to keep him interested."

"I suppose so."

Her voice was low but not tearful. Sabrina would always blame herself, whatever anyone said, but Perce was right in that it was no use beating her breast over it. What was really important was that she had never wished her husband dead, not even after she began to love Perce. She had always wanted William to be safe and happy. Thus, she felt free to be glad she was alive, glad to be with Perce, quite able to enjoy this crazy adventure on which they were embarking.

"Where are we going?" Sabrina asked curiously.

"Back to Lisbon, as soon as we can shake whoever is on our tail. I'm sorry, Brina. Now I think you were right. It must be because I convinced you to run that they assume you're guilty."

"I'm not sorry." Her voice was light and full of mischief again. "I'd rather be here than trying to explain what happened over and over again. The *regador* is no fool. The minute he stops to think—"

"You know him?" Perce interrupted.

"I've met him several times at the homes of acquaintances in Lousa. He's a very good *regador*, from everything I've heard."

"But if he knows you, how could he think you would be involved in a triple murder?"

Sabrina giggled. "Not everyone is as convinced as you are that I'm an angel."

374

"I *never* thought you were an angel," Perce riposted with dignity, "and extended acquaintance has convinced me that you are more likely to have come from the nether regions. However, on first sight, if he *didn't* know you, the *regador* might feel it unlikely that you would blow off three people's heads."

It was necessary for Sabrina to hold back a shudder. Perce's teasing remark came too close to the horror she had seen in the bed and in the dower house, but she didn't wish to hurt him by letting him see the reminder still frightened her. To shut out the memory, she concentrated on what she knew of Senhor de Sousa. She remembered him grave and courteous, rather slow of speech, and conservative in ideas and manners. A frown wrinkled her broad forehead.

"All joking aside," she said, "I don't think the *regador* is the kind to shoot at anyone. Well, maybe at a crowd of bandits, but he couldn't have thought that. And I'm sure he wouldn't shoot at a woman without warning, no matter what Dom José told him."

"Then it isn't the *regador* behind us. There were only three horses at the house. I'm pretty sure no law officer would leave Sergei and Katy alone under the circumstances, so that leaves two to chase us once they knew you were gone. But there were more than two horses."

"It could be Dom José. He has servants who would obey him." Sabrina repressed another shudder, remembering how she had screamed when she saw the bodies, but no one had come. It did not occur to her that no one had heard her.

"Even in something like this?"

"Wouldn't Sergei obey *you*?"

"Oh, certainly," Perce replied, smiling. "But only after arguing for so long that anyone I was pursuing would have escaped hours before."

But he didn't feel much like smiling. If it was Dom

José behind them, then those shots took on a really ugly connotation. An officer of the law might fire a shot in warning if he thought his voice would not carry. When a triple murderer—quadruple in intent—fires, the purpose is not likely to be warning. Perce listened intently but could hear nothing. Near Lousa the harder surface of the road and the noise of his and Sabrina's mounts had masked all other sound. Now the road was little better than the track that went up to La Casa des Ermidas, but he still heard nothing.

"Do you know where this road goes?" Perce asked.

The horses had dropped into a trot, and it was obvious that they were climbing.

"No. There must be a village or a few villages somewhere ahead, but I can't think of any large town in this direction. Not that that means anything, because I haven't been here long, and my Portuguese isn't good enough to have learned much geography. No one really wanted to talk about anything except what Boney would do, and whether they should try to fight him or accept their fate and try to enjoy it."

"Then I think we'd better try to circle around and get back to the road we know. The whole damned country is only about one hundred and twenty miles wide, and I think Lousa is near the middle. The last mistake I'd want would be to ride into Spain unknowingly." Perce pulled his horse to a stop, and Sabrina's mare halted also.

She laughed. "We'd be very welcome, but I think the invitation to stay might be more pressing than we would like."

Then she fell silent, and both listened intently. Aside from the song of the night insects and the chuckle of a small stream nearby, all was silent.

"Perhaps they've gone on to Lousa or given up," Perce said.

"I don't think Dom José would give up," Sabrina replied. "The *regador* would, but the more I think of it, the less I can believe that he would shoot at me even if he believed I was a murderess. Why should he? He only has to send word down to Lisbon."

Perce knew there were reasons why an official might prefer to have a "criminal" safely dead rather than to report the escape of that person. However, from what Sabrina had said, the *regador* did not seem to be that type of official. Then it was the madman who was pursuing them. It did not seem to Perce, under the circumstances, that they should take the risk of turning back along the road. He looked around, but he could hardly see a few yards in any direction. The moon had finally set, and it was very dark.

"Yes, it might be Dom José," he replied to Sabrina's remarks, "and I think it would be best to get off the road here. We'll have to lead the horses, but the moon's set now and we don't have to go far into the woods. There won't be any way to tell at what point we left the road—I hope—or whether we left it at all. Now, do you know whether it would be better to go north or south?"

They were speaking very quietly, listening between phrases for the sound of oncoming horses. Perce dismounted, looped the reins of his gelding over his arm, and helped Sabrina down. She was frowning thoughtfully, trying to remember anything anyone had told her about the region. At last she shook her head.

"I'm not sure of anything, but if we go south, I think we'll come up against the mountains. Also, it seems to me that someone said there's a road that runs to Coimbra to the north. There was something, though . . . no, I don't remember, but I think it isn't easy to reach that road from here."

"More mountains, I suppose," Perce said. "Do you want to decide, or shall I flip a coin?"

"Dom José would guess we would go toward Lisbon.

377

That's south. Why don't we go north. I know the slopes of the Sierra de Lousa are too steep for horses in this area. Perhaps it's only foothills to the north."

"Right," Perce agreed without hesitation. "It doesn't matter much anyway. We won't go very far. Maybe we'll be able to see something in the morning."

They moved together to the left of the road and walked slowly, looking for a break in the brush. There was nothing completely cleared, but in one spot the trees were particularly large and dense, so that the undergrowth was somewhat more sparse. Perce led the way in, aware that they were leaving a trail but unable to do anything about it. He and Sabrina could have been careful not to break and crush the weeds and low bushes, but there was no way to explain stealth to a horse. Even if there had been, Perce thought, amused by the concept, the horses were just too big to avoid all the obstacles.

Farther in under the trees there was even less undergrowth, but here they could not avoid what little there was. As the canopy of leaves above them grew thicker, it cut off all light from the sky. Even the slight visibility provided by the starshine to their dark-adjusted eyes was gone; it was pitch black. Perce felt his way with one outstretched hand and his feet, calling soft warnings to Sabrina. In spite of this help, she was little better off. Although she did not need to worry about running into trees, Sabrina promptly bumped into the rear end of Perce's horse.

Having thought of the way to solve this problem by seizing the gelding's tail, Sabrina became overconfident and tripped into a hole. She had forgotten that Perce could not detail every irregularity in the ground. Her cry of surprise brought him back at once to fumble around for her. When he found her, she was already getting to her feet. Nonetheless, he held her tight, inquiring anxiously whether she was hurt.

378

Sabrina did not answer directly. Except for their initial embrace, which was caused more by fear than passion, and the brief touch of Perce's lips on her thigh before they had gone to the stable to send a groom for the doctor, there had not been a personal touch between them. Now she clung fiercely.

"There's nothing to be afraid of," Perce assured her, blaming himself for leaving her alone.

"I'm not frightened," she murmured. "I still can't believe you're here."

Perce looked back in the direction from which they had come—at least, he thought that was the direction—but he could see nothing, not even the slightest reduction of the darkness that surrounded them. He looked all around, in case he had turned and was mistaken in the way he thought they had come. Nothing. No difference, no sign of darker trunks against the lighter background. Sabrina was warm and soft in the circle of his arms. The desire he had subdued several times rose in him again. He dropped his head, seeking Sabrina's lips, and found them reaching for his.

"God, how I've wanted you," he sighed.

"And I you. But I didn't let myself think about you. I couldn't bear it. I was so worried about the war."

"I told you not to worry."

He kissed her again, but this time briefly because the gelding decided that he might as well have a bite to eat if they were going to stand still. His reaching for a tidbit yanked at the reins Perce held and almost pulled him off balance. Perce looked around again and realized he had lost all sense of direction. If they moved now, he might be leading them back toward the road as easily as away from it. He cursed himself for being a fool, but Sabrina only snuggled closer into the arm that held her.

"If we can't see out, no one could possibly see in, Perce. It's harder to see from light into dark than from dark to light. And even if they found the place we came in, it's so dark they could never follow us. Anyway, we'd hear them. We might as well stay here as anywhere else."

"Right," he agreed with indecent haste, then chuckled. "If I can find a place flat enough to sit down."

"Find one flat enough to lie down," Sabrina suggested softly.

"Darling, are you faint?" Perce asked, tightening his grip.

There was a little silence, then a little laugh, and teeth nibbled Perce's chin gently.

"I'm sorry," Perce whispered, his voice shaken between desire and laughter. "I didn't mean to be obtuse, but if I let go of the horses, we'll be in trouble. And if I don't let go, we can't . . ."

"Tie them up," Sabrina urged. "Talk about foresight, there's that rope that Sergei sent along. If you pass the reins through it and tie a long loop around a tree, that will leave them free to graze but they won't be able to get away."

It was a good idea and sounded simple, but in the dark even simple tasks became terribly complicated. First they had to find the rope. Each searched the same horse by mistake, and if their hands had not met by accident, both would have been convinced that the rope had been lost. Then Perce found the rope but lost Sabrina and the other horse. That was even more ridiculous. Each spoke to the other and tried to move toward the sound, but they passed just out of reach of outstretched arms. Fortunately Sabrina walked into a tree before they wandered far apart.

Having stopped, she realized the advantages of her position and stayed there. Perce soon found her, which gave him both horses and a tree to which to tie them. But the rope had got itself into a seemingly inextricable tangle, and when that unwound itself as mysteriously as it had appeared, Perce nearly got lost walking around the tree. By then, both he and Sabrina were laughing helplessly, which did not speed the activities of tying the rope and securing the horses.

Even then their troubles were not at an end. Perce had to loosen the saddle girths to make the horses more comfortable. He decided not to take the saddles off. If, against all likelihood, Dom José found them, tightening two girths would be quicker than resaddling. In a real emergency they could lead the horses without mounting. While Perce was fumbling with the horses, Sabrina had managed to unstrap the blankets and their cloaks, passing in front of the horses as Perce passed behind them, afraid to touch him by accident.

She had done that instinctively, because instead of quenching desire, every delay, every ridiculous mistake and awkward accident had increased her passion. Her breasts were hard and painful against the restrictions of her blouse and tight riding coat, and her loins throbbed. That, too, was utterly ridiculous. Sabrina shivered with desire and giggled at the same time. She could hear Perce's voice, although not the words that he was saying, and she knew it was best she should not hear those. The soft singsong intonation told her he was mouthing the worst obscenities he knew—and that excited her, too.

"Where are you?" he asked at last, the words soft and slurred.

"Holding the stirrup of the far-side horse," Sabrina replied.

Her giggles checked abruptly as she wondered whether the events since their kiss might have had an opposite effect on Perce than on her. He must be much more tired than she. He had probably ridden all the way from Lisbon without a real rest, and she had slept for at least a little while. Disappointment brought tears to her eyes but did not substantially quench her desire. The horses moved uneasily. Perce was coming around them. She could not see him but reached out, and her hand came in contact with his sleeve. His arm jerked.

"Don't touch me," he said.

He sounded drunk, his voice coarse and ugly. Sabrina drew in on herself with the shock of rejection. "What?" she gasped.

"I'll spend." He choked on laughter. "You'd think all this fumbling around with horses in the dark would have cooled me off, but you have a terrible effect on me, Sabrina. Here, take the rope and walk out as far as it reaches. Otherwise the horses may step on us."

Sabrina began to grope for the end of the rope, which Perce was holding toward her. Almost immediately she brushed his chest. He drew in his breath with a hiss, and thrust the rope into her hand.

"The blankets are by my feet," she said, her voice shaking uncontrollably.

The rope jerked slightly in her hands, and she knew Perce was bending to pick up the blankets. Sabrina let go of the stirrup, turned her back to the horses, and began to walk, stretching one hand ahead of her, feeling with her feet. A bush tore at her pleated safeguard and she drew in her hand to undo the buttons, flinging it aside as the last came free. Her steps were slow, but she tried to make them as long as possible. At about ten, her shoulder brushed the trunk of a tree. Behind it, they would be safe. She reached out to it, and Perce, coming behind her holding the rope, walked into her arm.

He dropped the blankets; she dropped the rope. Their mouths met as if they were going to eat each other rather than make love. Sabrina could not tell whether she was laughing or crying. Her need was so violent, it was closer to pain than to pleasure. She clutched Perce with one arm and struggled with her clothing with the other while Perce did the same.

Buttons undone, Sabrina's skirt dropped around her

ankles. She pulled her petticoat free of it, kicked it away, and fumbled underneath for the button of her pantalettes. Perce had been quicker. There was no hope at all of his ridding himself of his breeches, since he could not get his boots off. He knew he should let Sabrina go and spread the blankets, but he could not do it. He pulled her down with him, feeling her twist and wriggle as she tried to step out of the pantalettes. He did not know what she was doing but understood that she was not trying to free herself from him because her lips clung to his and she held him tightly all the time.

Behind their locked mouths, Sabrina moaned as he entered her, thrusting up violently. Perce tried to contain himself, but it was impossible. It was apparently needless, also. Sabrina was jerking and writhing under him, despite his weight, in a climax as violent as his own. In less than a minute they were finished, their kiss broken by the need for more air. Two seconds later Perce was biting his lips to hold back more laughter, afraid Sabrina would not think what had happened was funny. He felt her quivering under him and rolled off.

"S-sorry," he choked.

Sabrina gurgled. "You're a hero," she gasped. "I didn't think we would make it. Poor Perce. You must be near dead for sleep."

"Sleep? Was that what you thought my problem was?"

She gurgled again. "Not your immediate problem, no. But you must be very tired."

"Probably I am," he agreed, "but I've been too busy to notice. I don't feel tired. You remember, you said the same thing."

He had lifted his head to talk, but dropped it again, seizing her lower lip gently in his teeth, then nibbling her chin. Sabrina ran a finger around the outside of his ear. He advanced teeth and lips along her jawline, down under her chin. Sabrina lifted her head to give him more freedom and tried to stroke his body but only found heavy clothing. Perce was having a similar experience when he attempted to run his mouth down her throat to her breasts.

"Wait," she whispered, "let me take off this jacket."

He hesitated, then kissed her lips lightly and moved away. "Let's be comfortable," he said, and felt around for the blankets and cloaks they had discarded.

While Sabrina undid her garments, Perce spread the blankets, sat down, and began to tug at his boots. He took one off with considerable effort. Sabrina knelt naked on the blanket to help with the other. It was then that Perce realized he could see, or, at least, dimly perceive things around him. Perhaps the sky was lightening with false dawn, or perhaps they had found a spot where the leaves were not so dense overhead. He could see a pale glimmer that was Sabrina's bare skin. Having her pull off his boots in that condition was almost unbearably erotic. He reached for her, but she bent aside, undoing the knee buttons on his breeches. Perce looked away, pulled off his coat, undid his waistcoat and shirt, and cast them aside.

This time when he held out his arms, Sabrina came into them, but the wave of urgency he had felt was gone. He was aware of Sabrina, not a body, and he murmured endearments. She responded with a litany of praise, love words of adoration. They petted and kissed, slow to rouse now because of the fatigue that neither would acknowledge for the sake of the loving both desired. This union was as gentle as the first had been violent, but it was sweeter.

When they came apart at last, after lying locked together long after their passion was spent, Perce drew over them the cloaks he had laid ready. He was hardly conscious of what he did, and Sabrina was already deeply asleep. A distant awareness of danger flickered deep in Perce's mind, but fatigue swamped it. He had had no sleep in forty-eight hours and had been violently active and emotionally keyed up all of that time. Immediate need might have spurred him to further effort, but a vague uneasiness could not.

CHAPTER TWENTY

At the meeting of the Lousa road and the mountain track, Dom José had to make a choice. He knew that to the right the road passed through some very wild mountain country and led nowhere beyond a few small villages. In that direction there was no road that led directly south to Lisbon, although eventually one could get to Castelo Branco. Thus, Dom José rode into Lousa instead of to the east.

The mistake was not as costly as it might have been. Because of his noisy awakening of the *regador* and the groom's rousing of the doctor, a number of people were still stirring and popped their heads out of windows to call questions when they heard more horses pounding through the town. Dom José seized the opportunity to ask in turn whether two fugitives had ridden through. No one had seen or heard anything, he was told.

Then his quarry had gone the other way. It seemed stupid, but it was possible the shots had frightened out of her silly head the little wits Lady Elvan had. Dom José had no choice but to try the eastern route. Despite the delay he could not believe he would not catch her. God could not be so cruel as to take everything from him, his pride, his dreams, even his freedom or life, without some recompense. He knew the commandment *Thou shalt not kill,* but there was also one that said *Thou shalt not covet thy neighbor's wife.* He had always been a good and faithful son of the Church. Surely God would not permit that blond bitch to escape. She was a heretic as well as an adulteress because she had assisted her husband's lechery.

He rode back along the road, alternately cursing and praying. Soon the moon set, and the curses predominated. They could continue only slowly, and the men began to murmur among themselves that it was not sensible to continue. None of them said anything to Dom José, however. Then the false dawn came and they went faster, all of them yawning and clinging to their saddles except Dom José, who seemed quite impervious to fatigue. The men were surprised. He was old and not used to such exertion.

It was true dawn when they saw the village of Góis around a bend in the road. Dom José could find no sign to indicate that Lady Elvan and her escort had preceded them. He felt helpless and simultaneously powerful, for the rage inside him gave him an explosive energy. He was filled with a conviction that if he could find the woman, he could brush aside her escort and punish her as she deserved. But he had to find her. His eyes roamed the village desperately and then fixed on a house in which a dim light burned.

His knock and question brought disappointment. A priest answered the door. He told Dom José that the householder's mother was dying, and he and the son had sat awake all night waiting for the spirit to pass. There had been no travelers through the village, unless they passed on foot after dark. Even that was unlikely, the priest said. He had been looking out the window much of the time. Although Dom José contained himself sufficiently to be polite, he was again bursting with rage. Where had the devil woman gone?

When he turned away from the door, the sky was much lighter. Very soon the sun would rise. Two other doors had opened; people had heard horses and wakened. At one door a man called an offer of refreshment. Dom José was about to refuse, driven by the need to *do* something, but he had nowhere to hurry to now, and he dared not go home. He needed time to think. He gave thanks, instead of refusing, and told his men to dismount and take what was offered.

The years Perce had spent with the Russian army had marked him, particularly the last six months, when there had been much maneuvering and more than one small surprise attack in addition to the major battles. His body was accustomed to lack of sleep, and any sense of danger or anxiety made him unusually alert and easy to waken even when he was tired. Thus, the sound of Dom José and his men riding hard had brought him upright, reaching for his gun and sword. His hand had fallen, naturally, on Sabrina, and her yielding warmth had surprised him into complete awareness.

Although Perce could no longer actually hear the horses that had passed, he was quite sure something outside a dream had awakened him. He was also reasonably sure that it must be the men who were pursuing them. He wanted desperately to close his eyes and go back to sleep, but that would be stupid and dangerous. He and Sabrina had left a well-marked trail, he feared. The pursuers had passed, but they might return, and it was impossible to guess how soon or whether they would notice the broken underbrush where he and Sabrina had entered the forest.

Even if the sounds that had wakened him were not their pursuers, Perce thought it would be wise to move on. He could already see moderately well. As soon as it was light, they could better avoid leaving so clear a trail. He groaned softly and forced his tired body upright. Sabrina had stirred when he touched her but slipped back asleep at once. He leaned lower, intending to wake her with a kiss, but drew back before he touched her. Already there was a stirring in his loins. He was almost too tired to keep his eyes open, yet he wanted her again. It would be stupid to make love now, he told himself firmly. They had their whole lives to make love in peace and safety.

Perce slipped out from under the cloak, shivering slightly. It was not really cold, but he was weary and sluggish, and lying still on the damp ground had chilled him. He collected his clothes and Sabrina's, smiling and repressing another urge to lie down and take her in his arms when he saw her apparel strewn around even more wildly than his. As well as he could, he straightened her clothing and laid it alongside her, hoping it would pick up a little warmth. Then he went off a little way to relieve his bladder and bowels. When he returned, he knelt beside Sabrina and kissed her.

"Perce?" she murmured sleepily.

"It's dawn, darling," he replied. "We must move on."

She opened her eyes reluctantly and began to stretch, but desisted with a little cry. "Good Lord, I feel as if every inch of me is black and blue."

"What an ass I am," Perce sighed. "I should never have dragged you out into the woods."

Sabrina raised her brows and smiled. "Yes, and it wasn't too bright to make love to me on a thorn bush, either." She moved slightly and touched herself with care. "Whatever isn't black and blue is scratched to pieces. And I think there are splinters. . . ."

"Shall I look?" Perce asked, his face idiotically blank, his spirits soaring in spite of his weariness. He should have known Sabrina wouldn't make a faradiddle over a few bruises as most other women would. "I could kiss them and make them well."

Sabrina considered the fish-eyed stare bent on her and shook her head. "Oh, no. I know that look. You're more likely to try to remove those splinters with your teeth to get me on my feet. I'd rather get up on my own."

The glazed blankness crumbled as Perce shook his head and lowered his eyes. "It wasn't my teeth I was planning to use," he said softly, "and I'm afraid I'd be more hindrance than help in getting you on your feet." Then, as Sabrina stretched a hand to him, he sighed. "We'll have the world and time enough. It's not safe, my darling."

"No, you're right," Sabrina agreed with regret.

The scratches were from twigs and other debris on the forest floor that she had rolled on or been pressed against by Perce's weight, but the bruises and aching muscles were from falls and the blows Dom José had dealt her. And if last night's guesses were right, he was still looking for her. Sabrina shivered, remembering the terrors of La Casa des Ermidas, and bent to pick up her clothes. It was better to pretend she was cold, better to try to forget than to talk about that horror. Perce helped her dress; he said nothing, but he no longer felt so grateful to Dom José. Sabrina looked as if she had been beaten, and when she went off to relieve herself, she walked stiffly.

They ate a little, but they were too tired and too thirsty to relish the bread and cheese, which were the first provisions Sabrina's hand fell upon, or to try anything else in the bag. Perce remembered he had heard water when he was on the road. If they could find it, they could drink and finish their meal when their thirst was quenched. He untied the horses and coiled the rope, slinging that and the food bag over his shoulder. The blankets they just threw over the horses, and Sabrina left off the heavy safeguard of her riding dress. They went slowly, picking their way carefully now to avoid breaking or crushing the undergrowth. It was not too difficult since the crowns of the trees met overhead and there was little sunlight to encourage shrubs.

In about fifteen minutes they found a stream. Sabrina

sank down beside it with a sigh. Now that fear and passion were both gone, she ached, and the hour or two she had slept seemed to increase her tiredness rather than relieve it. She looked anxiously at Perce, who was watering the horses before he drank himself. He had looked worse—that time he had walked in after the battle of Eylau—but he was clearly not much better off than she. He was clumsy with fatigue, fumbling as he looped the reins around a bush on the bank of the stream. There was grass there, tall and rank, and the animals began to graze peacefully.

The reins were not secure; they slid up along the stem of the bush as Sabrina's mare reached toward a spot that seemed more lush to her. Perce shook his head slightly as if to clear it and reached for the rein.

"Leave it, Perce," Sabrina said. "They won't go anywhere. Have a drink and sit down."

He hesitated, looked vaguely at the horses, which were indeed quite quiet, and came upstream toward Sabrina. The slight glaze in his eyes was no pretense now. He shook his head again, knelt, and began to scoop water into his mouth, then rubbed it over his face and his hair. It was bitterly cold and woke him up. He became aware that the knees of his breeches were getting soaked. The ground near the stream was very soggy.

"Don't sit there, Brina," he said. "You'll get all wet."

As he spoke he stood up and held out a hand to help Sabrina to her feet. He was aware by the pull that she needed the assistance. Usually her hand would only lie on his out of politeness. She had made no complaint, but he thought she was in pain. Did they really need to struggle on farther? Perce looked back along the way they had come. He could see no obvious signs of their passage, although he knew the marks of the horses' hooves would show in the leaf mold. There was no way to avoid that, unless they abandoned the horses. Sabrina leaned against him and sighed.

If they could ride through the woods without returning to the road . . . Perce looked at the trees and abandoned the idea. It would be necessary to weave and bend continually to dodge the low-growing branches. Tired as they were, one of them would surely miss and take a bad blow. Also, there would be no way to stop the horses from stepping on low weeds. All in all, it would be less effort and strain to walk. But was it necessary? If Dom José was as determined as Brina believed, wouldn't he follow no matter how far they went?

"Do we have to go on just now?" Sabrina asked, echoing Perce's thoughts. "There's a nice place just across the brook."

She pointed, and Perce looked. The opposite bank was higher, and a tree had fallen so that there was a small clear area, somewhat screened by the brush that grew along the bank. It would not be difficult to cross. The stream bed was full of large rocks around which the water gurgled and hissed as it hurried downhill. Those would make convenient stepping-stones, but getting the horses across was another matter. Horses hated an uneven, rocky footing that slid and rolled, and getting them up the bank just here would be a struggle.

"The horses—" he began.

"Leave them where they are," Sabrina pleaded, knowing as well as he that it would take more effort than either of them wanted to expend to bring the horses over. "They won't be out of sight."

That was true enough, and Perce felt sure he could catch either of the animals if one began to wander away. They were friendly, placid beasts. He nodded and went to get a blanket and the bag of food. A quick glance at the reins showed them still looped around the bush, caught lightly under the thin but numerous side branches of the main stem. That would hold, he thought dully, turning up-stream to the best set of stepping-stones.

Sabrina was already across, and she reached out for the blanket and food bag so he could make the last jump unhindered. Together they spread the blanket and dropped heavily onto it. Sabrina opened the food bag, but Perce shook his head.

"I'm not hungry either," she said with a faint smile, "but chewing will keep us awake."

Perce's eyes opened wider for a moment. "How the devil do you know that?" he asked. "I'm the one who should have remembered it. God knows, I've done it often enough when I had night duty."

"Not as often as I have," Sabrina replied. "*I* have sat through hundreds of diplomatic dinners." While she spoke she was searching through the bag for a particularly chewy item. "Oh," she exclaimed, pulling a box from the bottom of the bag, "here are William's pistols."

Perce was laughing at her remark about diplomatic dinners, but he reached eagerly for the box and opened it. While Sabrina broke the legs from a capon, which she decided would best serve their purpose, he loaded the guns and set the box aside. He shoved a pistol into each pocket and reached for the chicken leg Sabrina was holding out to him. Chewing hard did help clear his head a little. The wood was very peaceful, although it was not quiet sitting by the lively brook, which hissed and gurgled quite loudly. He looked across at Sabrina, who was chewing slowly on the other leg and staring around. Aside from a bruise on her cheek, several scratches, and her less than perfect coiffure, they might have been having a picnic. It seemed almost impossible that the events of the preceding day had really taken place.

"Brina," Perce said, "we must both have been crazy last night—me for suggesting this lunacy and you for agreeing to it."

She brought her eyes away from the forest, which she had been examining with glazed weariness, and smiled. "I don't think you were crazy, Perce. I think you were giving me what I needed. Even if you didn't know it, I think you felt my need to be away from there, and to love you. I don't know what would have happened if I had to stay, but I'm sure I would have done something stupid and maybe even dangerous." She touched his hand. "I *had* to run away."

"I wish I knew whether you think that's the truth or whether you're trying to cover up my idiocy," Perce said.

"It's the truth for me," Sabrina pointed out seriously. "Katy knew it, too. She said it. Don't you remember she said if I didn't go, we'd all end up in the soup. Perce, I'm pretty sure Senhor de Sousa wouldn't take the easy way out, but last night I wouldn't—couldn't—say it. I had to get away from there, away from the whole ordeal."

Perce took another bite of his capon leg. "Well, maybe it was necessary. Anyway, it's too late to worry about that now. The question is, what do we do next? Go on to Lisbon, or go back?"

Sabrina did not answer at once. Finally she sighed, "I'm so tired. I can't think."

"Sleep awhile," Perce suggested.

"Is that safe?" she asked. "I have this feeling that we haven't seen the last of Dom José."

"I'll watch," he assured her.

"No, that's not fair," she protested. "You're just as tired as I am."

"I'm used to it, Brina," he said, "but I'll take a turn, I promise. You sleep first, and then you can watch while I sleep. You can think over whether you can bear to go back and answer questions."

Sabrina felt that it was wrong to stay. There was a sense of threat hanging over them, even in the peaceful woods, but she was so tired and aching that tears rose to her eyes at the mere thought of trying to go on. She turned away and straightened an edge of the blanket so Perce would not see how near she was to crying. To pull the corner smooth, she had to lean over. Her elbow gave and somehow she was lying down, knowing she should not but no longer caring.

Perce leaned back against the bole of the fallen tree and chewed slowly and deliberately. Once he checked on the horses. The bush was bending as the gelding reached for a patch of grass, but the reins seemed well caught. He looked at Sabrina. It was very pleasant to watch her but it brought a strong urge to lie down beside her, so he turned to watch the tumbling brook instead. It ran so swiftly that the water broke into foam in places, and the bubbles danced a short way downstream before they broke. Perce's eyes followed them, returned to the source of the foam. It was quite bright now, he thought dully. The sun must be up.

When the sun peeped over the horizon, Dom José called his men. The villagers were reluctant to let them leave. They felt well repaid by the coarse wine, cheese, and bread they had expended for the news they had gleaned about Lisbon and the world. Dom José was impatient. If Lady Elvan had not passed through either Lousã or Góis, she must have turned off somewhere into the woods. Dom José had needed to bite his lips to keep his rage in check when he thought of that. She could have waited in shelter until they rode by, then come out and escaped back to Lousã.

Instead of accepting defeat when that idea came to his mind, Dom José merely cast it aside. It could not have happened that way, because his revenge, and thus his life, was not complete. He had to conclude that the woman and her escort had gone into the forest, because they had passed neither Lousã nor Góis, but he chose to believe they planned to hide there until daylight. Yes, that was it. If he rode back toward Lousa very slowly, he would catch them on the road.

It was good to ride slowly. As he mounted Dom José was aware of a pain in his chest and left arm. He must have pulled some muscle scrambling up and down that path, he thought. His breathing was oppressed also, but he often had a little trouble breathing when he was excited, and for some reason he was very eager now, more even than when they were riding toward Góis. He *knew* he would find his quarry.

The early sun, just fully above the horizon, was behind them as they rode west toward Lousa. It cast long, distorted shadows on the road ahead of them and lit the low brush by the sides of the road with a queer one-sided illumination that showed up any unevenness in the growth as black shadows. Three times Dom José directed his horse to one side or the other with a gasp of expectation, only to curse and continue as he found the irregularity to be natural or marked by dead leaves that proved it to be old.

The fourth time, he uttered a cry of mingled joy and pain. When he saw the fresh breakage, even the marks of horses' hooves, his heart had leapt and a horrible cramp had passed down his arm. It passed, but he felt queer and breathless. No matter. Here was what he had sought and here was proof that his vengeance was ordained by God. The guilty would first be punished, then he would send his men back to des Ermidas and he would ride to Lisbon. From there, his future was in God's hands. To Dom José, it made no matter.

They rode in, but within a few yards it was clear that it was not safe to ride. Low branches slapped their faces and caught in their clothing. Once dismounted, Dom José had no trouble following the path of broken bushes and trampled weeds and churned leaf-mold where the horses' hooves had disturbed it. In a little while they came to a larger area of disturbance. Dom José stopped and looked around. He felt calm and peaceful now, sure of success, and his breathing eased. It was easy to identify the place where the horses had been tied and had grazed on the few thin blades of grass and the leaves of bushes, and the spot where the blanket had been spread. So they had slept here. They could not be far ahead.

Dom José's eyes flew around, but he could perceive no clearly marked exit from the area. The men were also looking around, and the three pairs of eyes met with the same hope in each—that those they sought had gone out the same way they had come in, that they were long gone on the road back to Lousã. Their enthusiasm for the chase had long since evaporated.

It had occurred to each of the men that the escape of Lady Elvan was none of his business. There were guards to attend to such matters. None had the courage to argue with Dom José, but they had discussed the matter quietly in Góis. If their master could induce the fugitives to return to the dower house of des Ermidas or Lousã without violence, they would help guard them. They would even help him by firing warning shots aimed well away from the people. However, they would not shoot at the man or woman or strike either of them, and they would bear witness for each other that this was so.

Unaware of his men's reluctance, Dom José moved on purposefully. He spotted disturbed ground bearing the mark of a horse's shod hoof, darted forward to make sure there were further marks, then ran back and told Carlo to stay with the horses. He was sure that those they sought were not far ahead. That they had made no obvious trail showed that it had been light when they moved. He did not want the sound of the horses, or any other sound, to warn them; the men were to be careful not to blunder into bushes, but to look where they put their feet and not to talk.

In spite of the care Perce and Sabrina had taken, it was not hard to follow their trail. A horse can be guided around moderately large obstacles, but anything low-growing will be trod on if a hoof happens to fall in that place. However, their attempt to avoid damaging the undergrowth produced a sinuous track. Dom José did not even see the horses until one whinnied. Then he ran quickly forward toward the sound.

Although his eyes were still open, Perce was close to being asleep, somewhat mesmerized by the bubbles he had been watching. Between that and the noise of the stream, he did not hear the men until they began to run. Even then, it took his dulled wits a moment to connect the noise with himself. Thus, by the time he shook Sabrina, called to her to wake up, and sprang to his feet, their pursuers were in sight.

"Shoot them," Dom José shrieked.

Pedro and Pablo, startled, promptly loosed off shots, one well to the left and the other well to the right of the targets. Unfortunately, in his anxiety not to hit the humans at whom he was looking, Pablo fired directly at the horses. The carelessly aimed bullet barely touched the gelding's rump, but the double explosion, combined with the sharp pain and the scream, panicked the horse. He neighed and lunged away from pain and noise, striking sharply against the already startled and nervous mare. Involuntarily, Perce shouted, which merely added to the animals' terror and confusion.

The careless looping of the reins around the shrub had been meant to discourage the animals from wandering away, not to hold them firmly against an attempt to bolt. With the first powerful lunge the reins came loose, and the mare and gelding took off, bumping and dodging trees. Perce cursed and drew William's pistols from his pockets.

"Perce! Don't," Sabrina shrieked. "Don't hurt them. Don't! I didn't kill William or Donna Francisca. Let the law—"

Her voice cut off as Dom José leveled his pistol at her. She dropped to her knees as he fired, although he was so poor a shot she could just as well have stood still. Infuriated, Perce fired also, but not at Dom José. Mindful of Sabrina's warning, he aimed at the madman's gun. His shot was no more successful than Dom José's, not for any lack of proficiency in Perce but because Dom José had surprised him. Instead of waiting a second to see the result of his shot, Dom José had dropped to his knee as soon as he released the trigger, as if to reload. Indeed, he took out a cartridge and lifted it to his teeth, but then he remembered his men. They should do his dirty work.

"Reload, you fools," he screamed at them, and then at Sabrina, "I may have shot them, but you are the one who is guilty. You—"

But Sabrina had not waited to listen. As soon as the shot was fired, she seized the food bag and her riding dress, leapt to her feet, and began to run. As she moved Perce realized the wisdom of her action. It was apparent to him that all three men were very bad marksmen. If they could keep a fair distance between them and their pursuers, there was little chance that they would be hurt. He swept up the blanket, his eyes still on Dom José, who was now ineptly reloading his guns.

Behind him Perce heard another violent spate of Portuguese. He had not understood any of it except, by implication, the orders to fire and load. He wished he had a chance to reload the fired pistol himself, but that might come. Now was not the time. Either fear or determination had lent Sabrina new strength. She was running like a deer, her brown riding dress blending with the tree trunks and the dead leaves on the ground so that from time to time she was nearly invisible.

There was a wordless bellow of rage and then the splash of water as someone charged through the stream without trying to find crossing steps. Just as the thought that it was a mistake formed in Perce's mind, he heard a crash of water and laughed as he ran. The loose stones of the stream bed had turned under someone's feet and dumped him in the water. Perce increased his speed to overtake Sabrina. With luck this delay should give them time to find a hiding place.

He was surprised at how long it took him to catch up with Sabrina. The sounds of pursuit became quite dim, but Perce was afraid to call out. Voices might travel far better than the thud of feet or the sound of harsh breathing. Finally, he was able to lay a hand on her shoulder. She stopped immediately, gasping from her effort. Terror might give her another spurt of strength, Perce thought, but she was nearly done up. He must find a place to hide her. Now he could hear Dom José's voice, but he could not see any of the men, which meant they, too, were invisible for the moment. Sabrina was leaning against him.

"Those horrid branches," she gasped softly. "One nearly pulled out my hair, and another caught on the food bag and—"

"Branches," Perce breathed. "Brina, if I lifted you up, could you climb higher in a tree?" Even as he spoke, he was cramming the pistols back in his pockets and was lifting her. Sabrina had begun to protest that this was no time for climbing trees, but when she saw he was serious, she let the food bag drop and reached for higher branches without argument. Perce always knew what was best. He watched for a moment, whispering upward, "Sit down and be quiet."

Then he hung the food bag around his neck and jumped for a relatively low crotch in a neighboring tree. It was the devil to climb in boots and with only one hand, since he was clutching the blanket in the other, but he managed to go up about fifteen feet. Neither he nor Sabrina had been silent while climbing, but Perce was not worried about the noise. Dom José was shouting, actually screaming hysterically. All Perce could hear was a thin, distant high-pitched shrieking. He assumed the other men answered but that all three were at some distance, so only the high-pitched sound carried.

Then the screaming stopped, very abruptly. Apparently Dom José was listening. Perce listened, too, and was disturbed by the fact that he could not hear the brook. It seemed odd that they had come so far so quickly. Or was it quickly? How long had they been running? He had no sense of time. One way it seemed as if he had run forever; another, as if no time at all had passed between the moment he had heard their pursuers so close and this very instant.

Pablo and Pedro had nearly been struck into stone when they heard their master confess the murder of his wife and her lover. Both would gladly have turned and run, except that Dom José, having loaded his gun, waved it threateningly at them and commanded them to take up the chase. It was then that Pablo and Pedro realized their master was crazed. Their realization, combined with his waving gun, created panic.

Both charged headlong into the stream. It was Pedro's fall Perce had heard. Dom José had the energy and physical control that uphold the insane and made his way without a slip. He drove his henchmen forward with shouts, and when Pablo lagged, struck him with the barrel of his gun. Neither lagged after that, but neither did they have any notion of where they were running since they were too frightened to look for signs of Perce and Sabrina's passing, and Dom José was too busy watching them to seek the fugitives.

He screamed at them that he would continue until they

caught their quarry, that he would kill them both if they did not soon find the devil woman. He demanded that they go faster, faster, weaving crazily this way and that. Then suddenly the demands and orders stopped, and were replaced by wordless, high-pitched shrieks of agony. For a minute or two Pablo and Pedro ran on, not realizing that their master had collapsed. They would have continued to run even longer, except that in his convulsions of agony, Dom José fired the pistol.

This brought the men to an abrupt stop. Both understood that their only safety lay in overpowering Dom José before he had a chance to load the gun again. They ran back with frantic haste, only to find their master limp on the ground. Pablo darted forward and seized the gun. Then both stood still, gasping with shock. After another minute Pablo called his master's name softly. There was no response.

Although both knew from his stertorous breathing that Dom José was alive, he was clearly unconscious. Pedro suggested timidly that they leave him. Pablo called him a fool. If they did not bring Dom José back and prove there was no wound on him, he pointed out, they might be accused of murder. This way, dead or alive, they would be blameless. They secured all the empty pistols in case Dom José should suddenly revive, then one took his shoulders, the other his feet, and they began to carry him away.

Pedro was completely lost and even Pablo had no idea where they were, but he was not worried. He knew the road was south of them, and he could judge direction well enough. Somewhere they would come out on the road that ran between Lousa and Góis. They could then lay Dom José by the side of the road, and one of them could quest east and west until he found the break through which they had entered. Once Carlo brought the horses out, they could consider whether to send for help or try to bring Dom José back to La Casa des Ermidas.

Perce nearly fell out of the tree when the shot sounded seconds after the screaming stopped. He dragged the one loaded pistol out of his pocket and looked wildly around, but there was no sign of the men, no sound of running or brush tearing. After that, he listened for what seemed hours and hours without hearing another unnatural sound. He was aware again of his inability to judge time and felt in his waistcoat for his watch. That was little help; he had forgotten to wind it since he last went to bed aboard the naval cutter. It had stopped sometime near when he had reached the dower house the previous night.

After what seemed an interminable period of utter silence, Perce heard a bird twitter, then another. Little birds were nice, he thought with the maudlin sentimentality of the utterly exhausted. His eyes closed involuntarily while he thought of how nice little birds were, how sweet, how shy, how reassuring their peeping voices were. He jerked up, and his eyes shot open. Birds only peeped gently where everything was peaceful and quiet.

Perce's brain stuck on that for a while, because it seemed to him that Dom José was madder than a rabid dog and would not be easily dissuaded from the chase. The word "chase" made Perce think of horses, and he remembered how the gelding had neighed, like a scream. The horse would not have made that sound unless he was hurt. But he could only have been hurt by a bullet, because none of the men had been close enough to strike him. So the gun had been aimed deliberately wide of the targets, Sabrina and himself. Then Perce recalled that Dom José had shouted at his men before they fired, probably he had ordered them to shoot. Could that mean they had not wished to shoot? Perce closed his eyes again, but not because he was sleepy now. He was trying to visualize what he had seen but not really absorbed because his attention had been fixed on Dom José. After a time he had become relatively sure that both men had been standing still, that they had done nothing even after Dom José had shouted that second order, almost certainly to reload.

Perce put the facts together with the surmises, and added in the hysterical shouting and the single shot, which was clearly not directed at Sabrina or himself. Then he considered the sudden and protracted silence, the return of natural sounds to the woods. After that, he went over the whole scenario in his mind for fear his exhaustion was addling his wits. Finally he heaved a sigh and dropped the blanket and food bag to the ground.

A few musical and startled squawks were followed by silence. No more happy peeps. It seemed to prove that there had been no intrusion into the area during the time he could hear the birdcalls. In that case, it was possible that his guess was right. Losing their taste for hunting an innocent woman, Dom José's men had turned on their master and overpowered him. Perhaps that was when he had screamed so oddly. Perce wondered briefly whether he had been hurt or killed when the gun went off, but he did not care. He needed all his attention to get to the ground.

Sabrina's condition was worse than Perce's because she was less accustomed to extreme physical exertion, and the emotional shocks she had suffered had been greater. She had jerked to attention when the single shot was fired and peered fearfully around through the pine needles that surrounded her. The quiet that followed the shot had no particular meaning to her. Indeed, she was only semiconscious, barely aware enough to cling to her perch.

The double thud when the food bag and blanket landed startled her into full awareness. It took a couple of minutes for Sabrina to realize what had woken her from her half sleep. By the time she perceived the objects on the ground, there was a violent agitation of the tree next to hers.

404

"Perce," she cried in panic, thinking he had fallen asleep, "don't fall."

"I hope not," he wheezed, pausing to rest. "It seems ridiculous that it's harder to get down unencumbered than up carrying those bundles."

Sabrina instantly concluded that if Perce was climbing down and speaking to her loudly enough to be heard, the danger was over. She could not guess what had brought him to this decision, but she was perfectly willing to trust him. The wave of relief that swept her lifted her out of the dullness of exhaustion into a febrile euphoria.

"Perhaps it's because no one is chasing you with a gun," she suggested, giggling.

The branches began to wave again immediately, and Perce's legs appeared, followed by his body. When he was set in the lowest crotch, he turned his head toward the tree that held Sabrina. "That was an unfair hit," he remarked severely. "It was true, but unkind. However, I am about to get my revenge. It's your turn to come down next."

On the words, he jumped from the crotch, sprawling forward when he landed but rising quickly enough to assure Sabrina he was unhurt. Then he went to the bottom of the tree and looked up, and a wave of cold fear passed over him. From this angle she was quite visible, much, much too far up the forest giant.

Perce swallowed, and his face went blank. "Well?" he urged.

Sabrina was sitting on a branch with one leg on each side and her back against the trunk of the tree. She thought carefully, but she could not remember how she had achieved the position. First she lifted one leg in an attempt to place her foot on the branch, but she tipped dangerously, saving herself by clasping the trunk behind her. She looked down at her lover through a net of branches.

"Monster," she said. "You pushed me up here. Don't you dare stand there looking like a fish. Get me down."

He scratched his head and looked around. "What we need is a ladder," he remarked. "A lady shouldn't climb trees at all, but a ladder would simplify the situation immeasurably."

"You idiot," Sabrina gasped, enraged by the London-dandy tone of voice and gently bemused expression, which implied that a servant would come hurrying up with the requested article any moment. "Where are you going to get a ladder in the middle of a forest?"

"I don't know," Perce drawled, now looking up and down the tree in which Sabrina seemed to be trapped, "but a little ingenuity . . . a little positive thought . . ."

Sabrina reached out, tore off a small branch, and threw it down at Perce. He moved his head just enough to avoid it.

"*Tsk, tsk.* How very unmaidenly."

"It's a long time since I was a maiden, as you should know," Sabrina rejoined. "And you and Philip made sure I was never maidenly."

"Ah, well, if you can't resist the impulse, there's a much better branch on the limb above you."

Instinctively Sabrina looked up. The branches, a little offset from each other, marched upward like—Perce's remarks gave her the simile immediately—like the rungs of a ladder. She looked down again, this time not at Perce himself but at the branches. Downward, they were also well spaced for climbing until about six feet from the ground, but that was no problem; Perce would lift her down. She transferred her eyes to his face. It was still as blank as a bad painting, giving no indication of the thoughts behind.

She was very annoyed with Perce. Philip had always been quick to extricate her when she had called for help, whereas Perce made her find her own solution. Often when she emerged scratched or bruised or half drowned and knew she would have to explain her condition to Leonie and Katy, Sabrina felt furious with him. Then her irritation faded. Yes, but she had also always felt a rich satisfaction in having saved herself—and the need for explanations certainly sharpened her wits. Then she grinned. At least she wouldn't have to explain this to Leonie.

Her cloak caught at one arm, and she took it off and dropped it. Then, with a good grip on the limb above to steady her, she found she was able to lift first one foot and then, twisting, the other to the branch she had been sitting on. Pulling herself up was another problem. She was stiff and sore, every muscle screamed with pain. Sabrina glanced down, tempted to forgo the satisfaction of independence, but Perce was watching with just a touch of a smile. Sabrina set her small, determined jaw and hauled herself up to a standing position and began her descent.

An entirely new problem presented itself when she began to climb down. After a few branches her skirt caught on a small side twig. Sabrina used several *very* unmaidenly epithets as she tried to kick it loose, and glanced down briefly. From the lines around Perce's mouth she assumed he was trying not to laugh.

"Don't you dare laugh at me," she exclaimed. "I'd like to see you do any better wearing a skirt."

"Can you take it off?" he suggested, his voice as flat as his expression.

The suggestion struck Sabrina as inordinately funny. She had a vision of herself, as from below, crawling down the tree in her lace-edged pantalettes. Now that was something she would never be able to explain to Leonie, she thought, giggling helplessly.

"Don't laugh," Perce shouted. "Come down here at once!"

Some movement of her shaking body had freed her skirt, and she descended another two levels, but the giggles continued to rack her. It was so silly, Perce sounding as if she were a naughty kitten deliberately lingering in the tree.

She was convulsed by a sudden mental image of a kitten in lace-edged pantalettes.

"Stop that!" Perce roared.

But it was too late. Sabrina's foot slipped from one branch while she was reaching down for another. For one second she hung, then her tired hands could support her no longer and she fell.

CHAPTER TWENTY-ONE

Sabrina did not realize that she had been hysterical until she found herself sitting on Perce's abdomen on the ground. She did not remember the fall, except that there was a sharper ache near her right shoulder blade, which, she assumed, had been caused by hitting a branch. Immediately after the new pain, the sounds Perce was making forced themselves on her, and she rolled off him, realizing he was whooping in an effort to catch his breath. He had broken her fall, and she had knocked the air out of him.

"It serves you right," she said. "Why did you make me laugh?"

There could be no immediate reply, of course, but after a while Perce stopped wheezing and turned to his side. "I didn't intend to make you laugh, you nitwit," he sighed. "There was nothing I could do to help you down, and I had to give you something to think about so you wouldn't decide you were stuck in the tree and get paralyzed or so scared that you fell. What the hell *were* you laughing about?"

She told him, and he shook his head. "I thought you were teasing me." She paused for a moment and then added, "I don't think I can go on any farther, Perce."

"We don't have to." He told her then what he had deduced about Dom José from the sounds he heard. "I can't believe there's anyone within hearing distance," he concluded. "The noise we've been making would surely have brought them. We've both got to sleep ourselves out. Then we'll decide what to do next."

Sabrina promptly closed her eyes, which had only been half-open anyway. Perce was strongly tempted to follow her example, but he knew they would suffer for it later. It was quite warm now and, he thought, might well get hot as the day advanced. However, if they slept as long as he thought they might, it would be better to prepare against chill. He levered himself up, looked around, and decided they could stay where they were. Years of fallen needles carpeted the ground under the pine tree where they had ended up.

Biting back a groan of protest, Perce got to his feet, gathered their scattered possessions, hung the food bag from a branch above their heads, and spread the blanket near Sabrina. He was so tired, he actually considered rolling her over onto it, but his better nature prevailed and he lifted her and set her down gently. She did not stir then or even when he pulled off her coat and drew her cloak over her. He did not remember pulling off his boots, taking off his coat, and lying down.

When Sabrina woke, she stared up into the branches of the pine tree above her unbelievingly for a few minutes. It was just barely light enough to see, and she was aware of surprise and of thirst and hunger. Then memory returned together with the aches and pains of bruises, scratches, and muscles protesting unaccustomed exercise. None of that mattered. If the pain was there, then Perce was there too, and she was safe. She turned her head, smiling, and found him looking down at her.

"I didn't mean to wake you," he said softly.

"You didn't. I'm thirsty."

He nodded. "I am, too, but we have a problem. I don't know where the brook is. I can't hear a thing. It will be dark soon, I think. I don't know whether it's better to blunder around in the dark or stay put until morning. If we could see, maybe we could find our footprints and follow them back."

Sabrina held out a hand, and Perce pulled her up. "Let's see what's in the food bag," she suggested. "I think there were apples and oranges. I felt them when I was looking for something to chew this morning—was it this morning?"

"I think so. We'll know pretty soon. If it gets lighter, it was yesterday morning. If it gets darker, it was this morning—unless we slept thirty-six hours, which is possible considering the way I felt when I lay down."

While he was speaking, Sabrina had emptied the food bag completely. Sergei had done them well. He must have gathered up all the food he came across and thrown it into the bag. There were two whole loaves of bread and one that they had broken, large chunks of cheese, the remains of the capon whose legs they had eaten and part of another, a part of a ham, six apples, four oranges, and a mashed and bruised mess that Sabrina realized had been bunches of grapes and apricots.

It was this she suggested they begin on, and although some of the juice had leaked away, enough remained to quench their thirst. Then each went off to relieve nature. When Sabrina returned, Perce was comfortably settled, chewing on a strip torn from the capon's breast. She stood over him and glared down until he looked up with an inquiring lift of his brow.

"I hope Eve shoved that apple down Adam's throat," she remarked.

"That sounds like a very reasonable desire," Perce agreed amiably. "It does seem hard that she should be blamed because her man was stupid and weak-willed. But why the sudden passion about an event that, after all, was some time ago."

"Because of all the inequities visited on the female, needing to remove a drawerful of clothing and squat just to piss seems the outside of enough," Sabrina said heatedly.

Perce stared up at her, fish-faced, eyes blank, mouth open. "But that happened before the apple business."

His voice was perfectly grave. Not even Sabrina, who knew him so well, could detect the smallest trace of laughter in it. Sabrina sighed slightly. It was her Perce, just the same in the middle of a forest or a fashionable drawing room. She came down on her knees beside him, feeling warmed and comforted out of the little thrill of fear that had touched her when she went off alone and he was out of sight.

It had seemed to take forever to lift her clothing and unbutton and button her pantalettes. There had been sounds for which she could see no cause. Very likely she had been making the sounds herself—her feet crackling dead leaves and twigs as she shifted position, her skirt brushing against bushes as she lifted it. Sabrina smiled a bit at her own silliness and reached toward the capon.

"That inequity, if it is one, was not devised as a punishment," Perce said, putting his hand on hers.

Sabrina looked at him, startled, and noticed that he had swallowed what he had been chewing, put down the remainder, and wiped his fingers. Although the vacuity was gone from his face, his expression was still unreadable to Sabrina. The remark about the "inequity" could only refer to the difference in construction of male and female genitals, but Sabrina was puzzled by the oblique sexual reference and the touch on her hand. She was quite close enough for Perce to have pulled her over to kiss if he wanted to make love. He had always been very direct, quite forceful about it in the past.

A second sidelong glance at his face gave her nothing more to work on, and an old fear she had buried suddenly surfaced. Did Perce really want to marry her? She didn't doubt he loved her; he had loved her when she was a little girl, and in that sense he would always love her. *Don't be a fool,* she told herself, *it isn't only that kind of love.* He'd grasped at every opportunity to behave like a lover rather than a friend. Or had he? Sabrina tried to think back. Hadn't she invited him each time, if not in words, by clear implication? In the forest last night, she had taken off her safeguard long before Perce touched her. He couldn't ignore an invitation like that, could he? Was this delicate invitation something he hoped she *would* ignore? An attempt to discover whether she still wished to claim him?

Fear and resentment sharpened her voice. "What does that mean?"

The hesitation before Sabrina responded to his invitation struck Perce like a blow in the face. She had always been as eager as he, even the previous night when she was terrified and exhausted. But perhaps that was why. Perhaps last night she had not yet absorbed the fact that she was really and truly free now and could have any man she wanted. Had she taken him as a lover only because she knew she could trust him? No! Not Brina.

"It was meant as a subtle invitation," Perce said without inflection, but he could not meet Sabrina's eyes. If there was refusal, contempt, in them, he could not bear to see it.

"I'm not stupid. I know that," she replied. "Why suddenly bother with subtle invitations?"

"It wouldn't have been very tactful to ask you before," Perce said dryly. "Legally and morally you should have refused me. If I didn't ask, you didn't have to consider that. The situation is different now."

The pressure of his hand on hers lightened infinitesimally. Sabrina knew he was about to lift it. Was he hoping she would refuse so he could escape from the relationship? A sense of loss swept her, and she turned her hand and seized his fingers. Muddled bits of thoughts flicked through her mind—that she loved him, that she could be so good a wife he would learn to be glad of the marriage, that if he did not want her, she could not trap him in his own goodness, that the kindness he had offered was more cruel than unkindness would have been. But blanketing over all her thoughts was a rush of desire, a need to have him before she had to renounce him. She would never force Perce to do anything, because his happiness was more important to her than her own.

The thoughts were so swift that they were in and out of Sabrina's brain even as Perce was returning the pressure of her fingers and leaning forward to murmur, "Please, Brina."

She made no answer to that except to turn more toward him and put her free arm around his neck. That was answer enough, of course. His lips met hers eagerly. It was eagerly, she assured herself. It was! Nor was there the smallest sign of reluctance or hesitation in the remainder of Perce's program. True enough, he was in no hurry, although he had pulled off his own clothes very quickly after they broke the kiss. However, when she started to unbutton her blouse, he had told her sharply to stop.

The small chill generated by that rather harsh order had been warmed away quickly, when it became apparent that Perce intended to use the removal of her clothing as a form of foreplay. It was a completely delightful notion, Sabrina came to think as Perce's lips followed his fingers wherever buttons were loosened and skin revealed. She shivered as what should have tickled and produced giggles—and did—also generated a violent sensuality.

When the blouse was gone and had been followed by breastband and petticoat, Perce caught Sabrina to him, eased her to the ground, and knelt beside her. All the while he proceeded with what he was doing, kissing her midriff and breasts as he unbuttoned her pantalettes. He pushed them down, using the suggestive upward thrusts of Sabrina's hips, which lifted her buttocks from the ground. She freed herself of the final impediment, by kicking the garment off her feet while Perce nuzzled and licked her abdomen.

Sabrina was uttering wordless cries of mingled frustration and excitement, and Perce did not mute her. There was no one to hear, no need to be silent or hurry for fear of discovery. Coherent thought was not really possible in the midst of the powerful sexual arousal, but in some deep recess of Perce's mind there was the fixed intention of proving himself so desirable a lover that Sabrina would be unable to resist the memory.

Using one hand to steady her hips, Perce positioned himself with the other. His own craving bade him thrust deep and hard, but he resisted it, merely inserting the head of his shaft teasingly and moving it so that the rod brushed the tenderest and most sensitive spot in her body. Sabrina was beside herself. She tried to heave against him, but he held her firm. Her hands fluttered over him, unable to grip because she could not decide where she needed the greater pressure most. The feather-light touch of Perce's tongue and lips on her breasts heightened excruciatingly the sensation produced by his shaft. Both tickled and titillated until the pleasure was piercingly near agony, and she shrieked in climax, scoring her lover's back and thighs with her nails.

As the convulsions died away Perce slid himself into her completely and lay still. When Sabrina sighed and put up a hand to brush involuntary tears from her eyes, he began to move slowly. Sabrina moved in rhythm, assuming that he would now satisfy himself. She offered her lips in mute thanks, but Perce accepted them with other intentions, and soon his hands were busy too, stroking and tickling, seeking out areas already sensitized by handling.

After the violence of her preceding orgasm, Sabrina had not thought her body was capable of responding to further stimulation. To her surprise the steady, slow thrusts, the kisses and touches, the suggestive whispers broken by sighs

ROBERTA GELLIS

and tremors indicative of Perce's own pleasure, began to build a second heat in her. As her desire increased Perce slowed his movements, then stopped. Sabrina protested wordlessly, already caught up in the rhythm, but Perce slid a hand under her hips, pushed with his other arm, and lifted her on top of him. Surprise checked Sabrina's building passion, then Perce thrust upward and she moved in response.

Instinct and desire are excellent teachers. In seconds Sabrina discovered the joys of free movement. She lifted herself on her elbows to free her breasts for Perce's caresses while her hips plunged and ground. Her eyes opened. Perce was moaning, "Oh, my God. Oh, my God," over and over, his neck stretched back and his head rolling from side to side. Catching sight of his extremity pitched Sabrina right into a second climax almost as violent as her first, and she collapsed on him, shaking and sobbing.

She was so stunned and exhausted that she hardly realized Perce had turned them again. He was lying quietly, but Sabrina opened her eyes wide at the realization that he was still full and hard inside her. His head was beside hers, his lips mumbling at the lobe of her ear. Sabrina pulled away as far as she could to focus her eyes on him. His were closed, and he was breathing heavily. He licked his lips and then reached blindly to kiss her throat.

"Don't you dare," Sabrina whispered shakily, and stretched down to run her fingernails very gently over his genitals and thighs.

Perce jerked. "No, don't," he begged.

His assaults on her had been so clever and her response so intense that she had not yet caressed him. "Two can play at that game," Sabrina murmured, laughing and continuing to tease him.

"Don't. Don't," Perce pleaded, his voice quivering between desperation and the edge of laughter, but his body was moving.

Sabrina thrust her tongue into his ear and drew her legs up around his back, simultaneously twisting so she could tickle the base of his shaft. His protests became incoherent, his thrusting stronger and more regular. She lifted to meet him, one hand toying with him in front, the other behind. His movements became frantic, jarring her with his ferocity before he went rigid, then heaved and cried out in release.

There was a long silence. In fact, when Sabrina opened her eyes again it was pitch black around them and she realized they had both fallen asleep immediately. She was warm enough, since Perce was still lying atop her, but she could feel him shivering in his sleep. She felt around for the cloaks as carefully as she could, but the movement wakened him, and he rolled off her at once, apologizing thickly for crushing her.

"I'm sturdier than you think," Sabrina replied, and then, after they had found the cloaks, which were close behind the blanket, and wrapped themselves, she added, "Perce, what were you trying to do—kill me in a peculiarly improbable way?"

Perce briefly considered telling her the truth, that he had wanted to prove himself a better lover than her husband or any other man she was likely to look at now that she was free.

"I wanted it to last forever," he said, and that was not a lie either. "Each time you climaxed I could feel it, and it was like heaven. Even making myself wait was wonderful."

Jealousy pricked her. Perce always said he was not much of one for women. If that were so, where had he learned so much? Surely not from the casual whores he paid to relieve his body's need from time to time. William had lied most convincingly. Was Perce a liar, too? On the other hand, the heroic effort he had made could only have been to please her, although he had phrased his answer in

417

terms of his own pleasure. Surely he intended to make her permanently his. Yet he said nothing.

"What are we going to do now?" Sabrina asked.

Perce chuckled. "You'd be horrified to know what came immediately to my mind. You are a terrible influence on me, Sabrina. If you don't want to be 'killed' again, you'd better stay well away from me."

Tears flooded into Sabrina's eyes. Because of what she had been thinking, her question—in her mind—had related to their personal future. She had hoped Perce would say, "Get married as soon as we can." Logic was not operating in any rational fashion in her, and for the moment Sabrina's very lively sense of humor was dead. Both distortions of her reasoning combined to twist what Perce meant as teasing flattery into a rejection. Unfortunately Perce could not see her face, and he took the little sniff she made in fighting back her tears as a wordless comment on his humor and his suggestion.

His mind moved on to practical things. "I had no idea how dark it would be in here. You must be starving, and very thirsty, too, Brina, and—oh, God! I didn't close the food bag or hang it up. It must be crawling with ants."

Sabrina tried to get a grip on herself. That previous remark had sounded like a warning, but what was it supposed to mean? There was a crudity in such a direct warning off that was not at all like Perce. It was cruel, and he would not be deliberately cruel to her. Or would he? If he realized his kindness had led them both astray, would he believe that a brief, sharp pain of severance would be better than a slow wrenching away? She should ask for a plain, clear explanation, Sabrina knew, but she did not want to hear the answer.

"The apples and oranges should be all right," she said in response to Perce's remark about the food bag.

"If they haven't rolled to kingdom come. Do you remember where the food bag was?"

As they crawled around, feeling for it, getting in each other's way and finding extraneous things like boots and oddments of clothing, Sabrina realized how silly she had been in the last few minutes. It was ridiculous to think that Perce was going to make lifelong decisions in the middle of a forest where they might be lost. Obviously he was concentrating on immediate concerns, and if she were not an idiot, she would be, too. Eventually they found two apples and an orange.

Sabrina sat back on her heels, munching her apple while Perce tried to make holes in the orange so it could be sucked. "Could we make a fire?"

"I don't know. This is a carpet of dry pine needles and dead leaves. I'm afraid the forest could catch fire."

Sabrina reached to the edge of the blanket and dug her fingers into the pine needles, pushing them aside. Not far down she found what seemed to be solid, and damp, earth. "We could scrape away the pine needles," she suggested, "except for a little pile in the middle. If you could light those, we could see whether the area around them would catch fire, too. If it did, we could put the blanket on it and step on it. That should put the fire out."

Perce reached over, found her, drew her close, and kissed her. "You've more sense in your hair, Brina, than I have in my head," he said admiringly.

Soon, using the spark from the unloaded pistol and a pinch of powder from the one he had not fired, Perce had a tiny fire going. By its light they cleared the area round it better so they could feed it twigs, more pine needles, and eventually larger dead branches. It was nice to have a fire, comforting, even though they did not need the warmth. If a shadow of doubt about the future remained in either of them, it was buried temporarily. A simple joy in each other's company and in the success of their joint effort overlaid everything else.

When they had partially dressed, eaten part of what

could be salvaged from the ants, and done their best to quench their thirst with another orange and apple each, Sabrina said, "We've been through a lot since last night—was it only last night?—but I can still hardly believe you're here. How did you manage to pop up in Portugal just when I needed you most?"

"You can damn and blast that suspicious son of a cit Canning that I wasn't here a week or two ago. Then none of this would have happened," Perce replied bitterly, and told her how Bennigsen had secretly given him copies of the secret clauses in the Treaty of Tilsit and the action being taken to prevent them from hurting Britain. "He arranged to keep me nearly under house arrest until Lord Gambier sailed. Well, it was politer than that, but it amounted to the same thing."

"But how did you get to Portugal?" Sabrina persisted.

Perce laughed. "That was Roger's idea. Leave it to Roger to kill 'seven with one blow' whenever he can. I suppose Canning realized I was on the edge of telling him where to get off, and he knew he couldn't really keep me bottled up any longer. He must have asked Roger, and Roger suggested that I be sent to fetch you home. But it was all part of the same ploy—Canning wanting to be rid of me because he thought my tongue would wag." He paused a moment, then said coldly, "He's no gentleman."

So it hadn't been Perce's idea to come and get her, Sabrina thought, but hurriedly fixed her mind on what he had said. "No, Canning isn't a gentleman," she agreed. But Perce was. He would never fail to do and say what was right, the niceties that made life easy for others, even it if killed him. There must have been something funny in her voice, because he turned his head quickly to look at her. "He makes the most dreadful mistakes because of it," Sabrina continued hastily. "He's only clever about books and words and plans. I think he's stupid about people. He accused William of being pro-Russian and wouldn't listen at all when William begged that troops be sent to help the Russians. And *now* look what's happened."

Perce looked back at the fire. It seemed to him that Sabrina had been more disturbed by her late husband's problems with Canning than was reasonable if she hadn't cared for him. Yet she spoke of him easily, without any catch in her voice. It makes no difference what she felt, Perce told himself. He's dead. And if it were the diplomatic post she was worried about, I can get into the service easily enough. He felt a temptation to ask outright for a commitment, but subdued it. It wasn't fair.

"It's just as well the British troops weren't sent to Prussia," Perce said, clinging to the impersonal topic. "They would have been slaughtered. Perhaps Alexander wouldn't have been as bitter against us, but it's hard to tell with him. He's more a man of mood than of reason, I'm afraid."

Sabrina nodded acceptance. She was familiar with Alexander's personality. "Is there no hope for Portugal?" she asked. "The people are so nice. The court's dreadful; the queen is mad, the regent can't make up his mind what day it is, not to mention anything else, and his wife is a religious fanatic. But the—well, we could call them squires—they're brave. They'd fight if they had a leader or any help."

Perce sighed. "There isn't any help we can give them just now. That idiot Windham had embarked on all kinds of stupid ventures. I understand we lost eight thousand men in Egypt, and Howick, who should have known better, paid off most of the transports in the interest of 'economy.' Mulgrave's doing his best with the navy, but there are still virtually no ships to move troops, and Castlereagh's got about twelve thousand men available under arms. You know, Brina, this business with Spain and Portugal may be a feint."

"You mean you think Boney's planning an invasion of England again? But he can't. He doesn't have the ships."

"Don't be so sure. Philip says the French never stopped building transport barges, and if Gambier doesn't take the Danish fleet and the Portuguese vessels fall into his hands, then Boney will have about three naval vessels for our two. Admittedly our men are better, but with Nelson dead and some of the senior admirals incompetent, those are bad odds."

"I don't think he'll get the Portuguese fleet," Sabrina said. "If Boney took it, it would never get out of harbor, but I hope it won't come to that. William told me that Strangford is trying to convince the prince regent to flee to Brazil and take his entire fleet with him."

"Flee to Brazil?" Perce echoed. "Leave his people?"

"They'll be better off without him," Sabrina said with a shrug. "I think he means well, but that wife of his pulls him one way, shrieking eternal damnation if he deals with the English heretics, and the business interests pull him another, saying Portugal will be ruined if he abandons the British trade, and he's frightened to death of the French—"

"So am I," Perce interrupted.

Sabrina smiled at him in the last of the fire's light. "Not too frightened to fight them."

Perce laughed shortly. "Too frightened *not* to fight them. Boney's a vampire. He talks of unity and friendship, but he drains the blood out of any nation that makes terms with him."

There was a brief silence while both considered this statement. Then Sabrina asked, "Perce, what will happen to us?" There was a tiny tremor in her voice.

Startled, Perce said, "Nothing, darling. We'll find our way to the road tomorrow. Don't worry."

"I didn't mean that." Sabrina shook her head. Her eyes

were very wide. "I mean England. We can't stay bottled up forever. Can we beat Boney all alone?"

"No, but I don't think we will be all alone for very long. He's growing more and more hated as he grows more and more arrogant and demanding. He'll make a mistake that will turn Alexander against him soon enough. Time's on our side, Brina."

"I hope so," she sighed. "But I'm sorry for all the people who will suffer while time ripens. What do you think he'll do to Portugal if the prince regent goes to Brazil?"

"I can't be sure, but I suspect nothing worse than if Prince João stayed and yielded. Boney will take the best of the army out of the country and send it to Prussia or Austria—anywhere—so that the Portuguese are crippled and can't fight him. And then he'll tax the people to death. But they'd be taxed anyway. If they fight, the money he demands is called reparations; if they don't fight, it's called assistance. He'll quarter his troops on the people, and Boney never buys supplies to feed troops. They forage and live off the land, so they often take more than they need as well as whatever forbidden items they can grab. Some women will be mistreated. It would be worse if they fought."

He fell silent. There were no more flames in their small fire, since Perce had stopped feeding it about half an hour earlier, but a few red embers glowed. He watched those, and Sabrina watched him. She could not make out his features, only the outline of his body. Still, there was something in the way he held his head and hunched his shoulders that called out for comfort. Sabrina moved closer and put an arm around him. He sighed, and leaned his head against hers.

"Something is broken, Brina," he said sadly.

"Are you hurt?" she cried, wondering how he could have concealed it so long.

423

She felt his head shake and his lips against her cheek. "Not in me, just . . . I don't know. We'll win the war with Boney partly because his blind hatred of England will ruin the countries that otherwise would find it easier not to resist him. Last time Austria and Prussia and Russia fought, it was mostly because of pride and greed and fear. Next time it will be utter desperation. But nothing will be the same, Brina."

"Who would want it to be?" Sabrina asked, much surprised by this reaction. "The world must move forward or we'd still be living in caves and painting ourselves blue." Then she had a revelation of what Perce had meant, and her voice sharpened. "And if you're thinking that all the romance and glory have gone out of war, I'll tell you plainly I don't believe there ever was any. The Black Prince might have invited the king of France to dinner after the battle of Poitiers, but I think the screams of the wounded were just as loud and the tears the women shed for the dead just as bitter."

Perce kissed her hair. "You're a clever witch. It *is* partly the loss of the shining armor—"

"With fleas under it," Sabrina put in wickedly.

Perce shuddered. "Don't remind me," he said in a horrified voice. "I was crawling with them from Pultusk until Eylau. And mostly I had so many layers on because of the cold, I couldn't even get my hand in to scratch. Still, I could move the clothes around and rub them against me." He broke into chuckles. "It must have been hell to wear armor. I think I'd better give up this Weltschmerz after the finer days of high honor. There must have been cit-types that tried to eat the world before Boney."

"Think of Attila the Hun!" Sabrina offered.

"I don't think he was a cit," Perce replied with spurious gravity. "Fine old Hun family."

"Carrying only the best blue-blooded fleas." Sabrina

424

giggled, then sighed. "I'm beginning to feel as if I'm carrying a few myself. I'll be glad to get back to the house no matter how many questions I have to answer. What are we going to say about why we ran away?"

"If you don't mind, Brina, I think I'll put the blame on you and say you were afraid of Dom José. I know it was my fault, not yours, and it isn't fair to blame you, but we want to get through this as easily as possible. It wouldn't be very tactful to admit that I thought the *regador* might be corrupt."

"No, of course not, poor Senhor de Sousa would be so shocked. You can exaggerate as much as you like. I won't mind playing the helpless little woman, only . . . will that fit my escape from des Ermidas?"

"Desperation and hysteria make people do strange things. By the way, why did you go out the window?"

Sabrina shuddered. "I thought he was waiting outside the door."

Perce took her in his arms. "Sorry. I shouldn't have brought that back into your mind."

"It isn't that part that bothers me," she whispered, burrowing her head into the warmth of his neck. "It's the . . . They were lying embraced and—and their heads . . ." Her voice faltered into silence.

"Dreadful for you, darling," Perce comforted, holding her with one arm and running his hand soothingly up and down her shoulder, "but better for them. If Dom José shot them in the head while they were—er—coupled, they must have died without the slightest pain or fear."

"Oh, Perce, is that true?" Sabrina asked hopefully.

"Yes, it is. I've seen enough men shot in the head. Their faces hold whatever expression they had before they were hit. Death is so quick, there's no time for thinking or for suffering."

It wasn't always true, of course. It depended on where

425

the wound was and how massive the injury, but Perce had heard the utter relief in Sabrina's voice when she asked her question. He would maintain instantaneous, happy death had taken place no matter what the truth was.

"But wouldn't they have known if he held guns to their heads?" Sabrina persisted, wanting to believe him but seeking further reassurance.

Perce made himself laugh softly. "Darling, if someone had come up very quietly while we were making love a while ago, do you think you would have noticed?"

"No," Sabrina breathed happily, "no, I wouldn't." Then she giggled. "I don't think I *could* have noticed if a whole army had walked right over. Maybe if someone actually stepped on——" Her voice checked.

"Dom José wouldn't even have had to touch them. He probably didn't. With their heads so close together, he just had to bring both hands up and pull both triggers. Truly, Brina, they couldn't have known he was there. They would have jerked apart if they had heard him. Believe me, darling, there was no pain, no fear. Just pleasure one moment and a merciful and forgiving God the next."

She sighed and relaxed against him. "Oh, thank you, Perce, thank you. It was so horrible to think William had died in agony, and it was my fault."

"It wasn't your fault!"

"No, perhaps not, but if he didn't know . . . that's good, Perce. William was afraid of death. I guess everyone is, but if he was spared knowing and was spared any pain, that makes it less dreadful, almost a mercy—except for the years he lost."

She sighed again, but not sorrowfully, in relief. The last little spark of ember winked out. They sat silently in the dark for some time, then Perce hugged Sabrina hard and relaxed his grip. She sat up straighter without protest, and he let her go and began to feel around where the fire had been. The ashes were still warm, but there was no hot spot, and after a careful investigation Perce decided the fire was safely out. He felt his way back to the blanket, and they lay down quietly side by side.

CHAPTER TWENTY-TWO

It was again thirst that wakened Sabrina. She had drifted toward consciousness several times during the night but had managed to fall asleep again. This time, however, there was light enough to see. She turned her head cautiously, unwilling to disturb Perce if he was not yet aware of discomfort. As soon as she moved, however, he sat up. He was smiling, but his mouth was as dry as hers and there was no more fruit. What food remained in the bag could not even be considered until they found water.

The need was now so acute that neither mentioned it. Sabrina did not even feel an urgent need to relieve her bladder, although Perce moved off to do so. Perce rolled the blanket and threw it over his shoulder. He reached for the food bag, too, but Sabrina shook her head and took it. It was depleted and not heavy. There was a brief hesitation before they looked at each other.

"You know, I haven't the faintest notion of where we are or which way to go," Perce remarked, his voice scratchy.

Sabrina took his arm and hugged it. She wasn't frightened. Perce would find a way; he always did. She waited patiently while he stared around, not thinking about their problem but about how she could have been so stupid as to have found William attractive and overlooked Perce. But Perce had never seemed the least interested in her, either—at least, not the way William was interested.

Just as that unpalatable idea crossed her mind, Perce gently disengaged her fingers from his arm.

"You stay here. I'm going to look around," he said.

Sabrina froze. Could she say, *William didn't want me and you don't want me, either*? She would sound like a petulant, idiotic child. He had come all the way to Portugal to take her home. No, he hadn't. Canning had wanted him out of England, and it had been Roger's idea to bring her home. *Stop it*, she told herself, and made herself smile. Perce smiled back readily and started off. His mind was essentially on the practical problem of how to find the stream again. He would have settled for any stream. It would be easier to think when he was not so worried about Sabrina suffering from thirst. She was the most angelic, uncomplaining woman, but that only made him feel more responsible for seeing that she had nothing about which to complain. What an idiot he was to get them lost, and a worse idiot to tell Brina. But she hadn't seemed alarmed, just looked at him the way she used to when she was a little girl, sure he could make everything right.

The memory caused a horrible sinking feeling in Perce's midsection. She had always come to him when she was in trouble if Philip wasn't available. She had come to him when her marriage had gone bad, and he had offered love. She had accepted it eagerly—as eagerly as she had accepted the kitten he had rescued from a tree, the repaired dolls, the bandage around skinned knees, the kisses to salve hurt feelings or wounded pride. Did she love him as a man or as a brother?

That had been worked out during their courtship in Russia, he reminded himself, but he glanced back at Sabrina. She was standing where he had left her, very much as the little girl had stood where she was told while he and Philip did something with which she might have interfered, and that disturbed him. As his eyes searched the ground for footmarks or broken undergrowth, he asked himself if what he was doing to Sabrina was fair—and whether he cared if it was fair. The answer to that was that he didn't, except for one thing. Would Brina wake up some day and resent the advantage he had taken of her?

He stared unseeingly at the ground, realized what he was doing, and focused his eyes. Not now, he told himself. There will be time enough to worry. Now find a way out. He turned back to look at the area he had just passed over without, he feared, proper attention. The light was better. The sun must be up. And then his head came up sharply. It sounded to him as if there had been a human shout, faint and distant but not a bird call or a fox's bark.

"Perce!" Sabrina cried.

"Did you hear that, too?" he called back.

"It sounded like someone shouting," she replied.

"I thought so, too," he agreed. "Can you scream, Brina? I think your voice will carry better than mine." He ran back toward her.

"Do you think it's safe?" she asked.

"We'd better take the chance," he said. "Dom José's servants heard him say he committed the murders. I'm virtually certain they forced him to abandon his search for us. If that's him shouting, he's alone, and I can handle him alone. Go ahead, Brina, yell."

She did, an ear-tingling, high-pitched "Here! We're here!" And then, after a deep breath, she repeated her effort.

There was a response almost overlapping her second cry so that they nearly missed hearing it. But that, too, was repeated. The sound was clearer, as if whoever was shouting had come closer, and Perce was able to determine the general direction from which the voice came. He pulled the loaded pistol from his pocket. It probably would not fire, since he had used most of the priming powder to help start the campfire, but it was the only threat he had.

Sabrina called out again, cupping her hands around her

mouth to direct the sound. Perce put his left arm around her, and they began to make their way cautiously in the direction of the answering cries. After a few minutes, Perce realized there was more than one voice answering Sabrina's shouts, and in another minute he and Sabrina laughed and began to run forward more quickly, Perce stuffing the gun back in his pocket. One of the voices was shouting "Where are you?" in Russian!

They were so intent on reaching their rescuers that they almost fell into the stream. Perce shouted while Sabrina drank. It seemed to be a different part of the stream—or a different stream, as far as either of them knew—but the water was fresh and sweet, and they both laughed and kissed each other with moist, refreshed lips. Then, oddly, they stood on the bank, hesitating to cross although there were plenty of stepping-stones. Both felt the strangest reluctance to leave the forest and return to the world. Sabrina went so far as to look over her shoulder, back the way they had come, and then look up at Perce.

But it was too late. Before Perce could respond in any way to that unspoken question, one and then another of the grooms from the dower house came into view. Sabrina waved and started across the stream. As she tested the second stone for security, Sergei came bursting through the brush lower down, rushed up through the water, and carried her over. He would have handed her to one of the other men to be carried all the way back had she not insisted on being put on her feet. Then he rushed to help Perce, who laughed at him. Meanwhile, everyone was asking questions, which no one bothered to answer, and two more men converged on the party, also talking excitedly.

"Quiet!" Perce bellowed.

The tone if not the word, which only Sergei and Sabrina understood, brought instant results.

"Yes," Sabrina agreed in Portuguese. "Let's go back to

431

the house first. That will be the time to answer questions."

"I am glad we found you so soon," Sergei remarked as they made their way back toward the road. "I hope it is soon enough."

"Is Katy worse?" Sabrina cried fearfully.

"It is impossible for that woman to be worse," Sergei replied. "She is already more unreasonable than any other woman alive."

Sabrina could not help smiling, but she was still worried. "What did you mean, you hope it is soon enough?"

"I mean that she wanted me to go out to look for you last night. It was already dark. The man who brought the horses—"

"What horses? Ours?" Perce interrupted.

"Yes, yours. Who else's would *she* care about?"

"Who brought them?"

"Pavlo, no, Pablo. It seems the horses followed their party when they brought their master home. He is dead now—of the heart, the man said. Then *she* became quite mad, and—"

"Katy was worried about us," Sabrina explained.

"And you think I was not?" Sergei exploded. "But what was the good of going out at night? The man Pablo swore he could not find the place in the dark. He said he would come again at dawn. *She* would not believe him. I had to keep him there, and she questioned him and talked at him until he wept."

Sabrina laughed. Katy could wield her tongue like a lash when necessary, but it seemed quite a feat to have done it in Portuguese. "She's been like a mother to me," she said placatingly to Sergei.

"And would I not be like a dead man without my little father?" Sergei asked heatedly. "Would I neglect his good, on which mine depends? Did I not say this a hundred times? A thousand? Mad! She is quite mad!" Then he

432

shrugged, and a smile illuminated his harsh features and dark eyes. "She is a worse slave than I, for I can recognize what is reasonable, and she cannot."

The smug satisfaction in his voice made Perce and Sabrina choke, but conversation was suspended when they came to the road and then went toward the horses. Nor did they talk on the road, since all were intent on getting back as soon as possible. Nonetheless, it was not until about noon that the whole muddle was straightened out. Arrival back at the dower house was punctuated at first by kisses and tears rather than by explanations, and then by a deeply desired and heavenly bath. Breakfast followed, and although there was enough for two, Perce did not come to share it. Sabrina knew he would not, that it would be stupid to display so much intimacy, especially before the matter of William's murder was settled. Still, she felt she had lost something, and with sudden tears in her eyes remembered the shared greasy, awkward meals in the forest.

At least she did not need to hide or explain the tears. Katy was in a makeshift bed in the parlor. The break in her leg had been worse than they expected, and she was forbidden to move more than the absolutely necessary minimum for at least one week on pain of being permanently crippled. That was why Sergei had been so worried, and the worry was for Katy, not for himself having a crippled wife. Sabrina had seen that in the look he gave Katy when they entered the room. And Katy's "Ye brought them back. God be thanked for ye, Sergei" had warmed Sabrina's heart.

After all, as soon as Katy saw they were unhurt, she must have realized they would have found their way home. That was sweet. Sabrina sighed romantically. She could afford to be sentimental about Katy's coming marriage. It was very pleasant to think about when she dared not think about her own.

While she was combing her hair—that was a long and

painful process; it took her nearly an hour to get the tangles out, and she had to snip several strands that were matted with tree sap—Sabrina decided to take time to shop in Lisbon, naval vessel or no naval vessel. Katy had to have different underthings now, and—and different nightgowns, yes, and a more revealing peignoir or two—or three, even. Portugal had beautiful lace and exquisite embroideries, and everything was very inexpensive. Not that the price mattered to Sabrina, but Katy would be angry and embarrassed if she thought Sabrina was giving her too costly a gift.

And now that the matter of William's death was settled—or would be . . . Sabrina's thoughts paused, and she considered William's death. Her mind no longer shied away. Perce had pulled the sting out of that horror. Sabrina was sorry William was dead, because she felt he had been cheated of a life he enjoyed, but it was also true she felt a personal relief. That might not be good or moral, but she couldn't help it, and it would be stupid to lie to herself about it. Setting her private feelings aside, how was she to behave in public? She didn't think it would be possible to act the part of a grief-stricken wife. And Perce might misunderstand.

Perce would know best. Sabrina finished combing her hair in a hurry, coiled it unstylishly, which made her look as pure and perfect as a painted madonna, and went down. She had no time to ask Perce anything, however. The *regador,* with a gentleman who spoke fluent English, was already questioning Perce. Sabrina paused in the doorway, and all three men jumped to their feet.

For one moment Sabrina felt an unreasoning terror, but in the next she realized there was no threat to her in any of the men's expressions. Senhor de Sousa looked sympathetic. The translator, a young man, seemed rather embarrassed. Perce was even more expressionless than usual, but one lid closed slowly and deliberately over his round, glazed eyes as he came forward to lead her to a chair the *regador* had set for her.

All in all, giving her evidence was easier than Sabrina expected. She described hearing the shot that had killed Charlot and all the following events. However, it did take a long time—not because anyone asked difficult questions but because she was so frequently interrupted by expressions of sympathy and apologies for Dom José's behavior toward her. Clearly, Senhor de Sousa thought she had behaved just as she should by concealing her husband's affair to the best of her ability and not attempting to remonstrate with him.

In fact, the whole sticky question of why she and Perce had run away was treated by the *regador* as being entirely his fault. Sabrina spent more time assuring Senhor de Sousa that she did not blame him than explaining why she had not attempted to report and accuse the triple murderer.

When apologies on both sides had faltered into silence, Perce said flatly, "When will it be possible for Lady Elvan to claim her husband's body? It will be necessary to make arrangements to ship it back to England for interment. With Lady Elvan's permission, I will attend to any business on that score, unless my lack of Portuguese will create difficulties."

"Oh, thank you, Perce." Sabrina's voice trembled.

She had not thought of that necessity until Perce mentioned it. When he did, she had shuddered. It was very silly, but she could not help it. It was not so much that the body was dead, but because every time she had to deal with its physical presence she knew she would see William with his head all shattered. The worst of the horror of that vision was gone, but she was glad indeed that she would not need to think of it. Perce would take care of everything and would never mention it to her at all.

The *regador* had courteously assured Perce that Senhor

Mousinho would translate for him whenever necessary. The three men rose and consulted together quietly on what had been done and must still be done. Sabrina moved to a chair near Katy.

A few minutes later the *regador* and his translator made their farewells and left. As soon as the door closed behind them, Sabrina announced that since the question of William's death was settled, she had decided to remain in the dower house until Katy was ready to travel. Instantly the battle broke over her head. Every argument that could be used was used. All were equally in vain. Sabrina emerged quite unbowed. Finally, Perce pointed out that it was urgently necessary to inform Lord Strangford of what had happened.

"Good heavens, so it is," Sabrina cried, springing to her feet. "I will go and write to him at once."

Whereupon she fled from the room, leaving Perce and Katy to bewail her heedlessness and stubbornness. This relieved their feelings somewhat but was otherwise of little use, since neither could think of a practical way of forcing her to go.

"How dangerous is it for her to stay?" Katy asked.

Perce considered the question. When he had been in England, he had felt quite frantic over Sabrina's peril. When he rode up from Lisbon, he had barely been able to control his fear for her. Yet he had not heard anything in Prussia, England, or Lisbon that indicated the situation was acute. No doubt Bonaparte intended to take over Spain and Portugal, using the offer of partitioning the latter to engineer the peaceful invasion of the former. However, there was no indication that either faction of the Spanish court had yet agreed to the march-through of French troops. Furthermore, to be perfectly honest, the sensation of looming disaster was gone.

"I don't know," he answered. "Honestly, I don't believe

436

the invasion is a matter of days, possibly not even a matter of weeks."

"Are ye sayin' that to ease me, Lord Kevern? Please dinna. If I know for true, I'll manage better."

"No, I wouldn't lie to you, Katy."

That was the truth, but Perce realized he might have been lying to himself. Was all that anxiety simply a cover for his jealousy? Had he been too ashamed to admit that he did not believe Sabrina could resist her husband's efforts to woo her back into loving him? It was appallingly possible that was the truth, and the reason he no longer felt the French threat to be imminent was that Elvan was dead and he was with Sabrina. If so, obviously it was impossible to trust his feelings about the situation.

"In any case," Perce went on, "I can get the facts from Lord Strangford. I didn't bother asking questions when I was in Lisbon because it didn't seem to matter. I expected to have Brina out of the country within a week. Let's not argue with her any more until I have more information."

"It wouldna do any good anyway," Katy agreed. "She's set now, and more talk will only make her more stubborn."

"Will you tell Brina I'll be back for dinner?" Perce said next. "I must ride down to Lousa to see about a suitable coffin. Elvan'll have to be pickled in this heat. They used brandy for Lord Nelson. I have no idea what we'll use. I can't imagine there's enough brandy in a town like Lousa. And don't say anything to Brina about it, will you? She seems to blame herself for his death, so the less said about him, the better."

"You needna worrit. I'll not lie to ye, either, Lord Kevern. If I hadna broke my leg, I would've jumped for joy when I heard Himself was dead. Good riddance! And thank God it happened here. There'll be talk, but not half what there would've been if it happened in England. It was bound to happen, too. He was gettin' that careless. No, I'll say nothin' to her about him, and I'll keep her busy, never you fret."

So Perce rode off to see about a watertight coffin and a cart and team of horses strong enough to move it. After he left, Sabrina came down with her letter in hand. She was surprised to find him gone, but Katy engaged her attention with the problem of Perce's clothes. Sergei could give them a rough cleaning, but he was obviously no valet. Sabrina was dismayed. She had forgotten, not that Charlot was dead, but that his death meant all his duties would remain undone. In England his place would have been filled smoothly, if temporarily, from the large available staff until a satisfactory replacement was found.

"And if ye want to have dinner tonight, ye'd better go see what that fool is doin' in the kitchen," Katy added. "The only thing he seems to know how to do is empty a crock of that foul olive oil into everything. I swear he'd put it in the trifle if I didna stand over him."

"Heavens! I don't know how you managed. There seems to be so much to do," Sabrina said. "I'll go take a look in the kitchen first. Perce can wear William's shirt and neckcloths. You don't think he'll be sensitive about that, do you?"

"He'll not care if ye dinna," Katy said, watching her nursling.

But Sabrina was at the moment totally preoccupied with practical problems. She would have to oversee the cooking. There was no way a French or English trained cook could be found out here, and it was true that, left to themselves, the Portuguese cooks tended to swim everything in oil. However, she would need a maid to take Katy's place and a man to answer the door. There would be many notes and visits of sympathy or, perhaps, curiosity, but some reponse would have to be made. It was unfortunate that Sergei did not speak a word of Portuguese. Otherwise he could have served as butler. As the thought came into her head Sabrina burst out laughing.

Katy smiled in sympathy but was puzzled. "What is it, luv?"

"I was just thinking of Sergei acting as butler. Could you just see the looks on the faces of the ladies who visit when he opened the door and said, 'What do you want?' in his own inimitable fashion?"

"*Ach*, the big ox," Katy said, shaking her head but smiling, too. "I'll teach him better."

"Don't you dare!" Sabrina cried. "And don't you dress him up in any English monkey suit, either. Those Russian tunics are just right for him."

"I doubt I could get a proper suit to fit," Katy said, but her expression had softened, and there was more pink than usual in her cheeks.

"Really, it's best if he nurses you," Sabrina said thoughtfully. "You can teach him more English, and then I won't worry about you at all. Now, to whom can I write who could find a maid and butler for us for a few weeks?"

They had a brief discussion, after which Sabrina wrote a note explaining the situation and her needs and sent it off with a groom to the appropriate Lousa matron. She then went to the kitchen, where she had a protracted struggle with the cook, partly owing to the proclivity for olive oil but largely because of Sabrina's limited Portuguese. Although she was able to carry on a moderately fluent conversation about politics, dress, the weather, and other such social subjects, cooking was not a sufficiently ladylike topic. Thus, her vocabulary was totally unsuited for dealing with the cook.

By the time she emerged from the kitchen with some hope that the meal would be edible, Perce had returned. In fact, it was Sabrina who opened the door for him. He had accomplished his purposes without any difficulty, but while making sure the measurements for the coffin were correct, he had occasion to see Elvan's corpse. Perce had seen many soldiers with shattered heads, and he was particularly indifferent to Lord Elvan; however, during the short ride back to the dower house, he thought how that sight must have affected Sabrina, and he cursed himself for what must have seemed to her a cruel lack of sympathy.

This caused him to take Sabrina into his arms the moment he saw her. Sabrina's head, however, was full of the best way to explain the poaching of fish for the next day's luncheon to someone whose only method of preparation seemed to be boiling in oil. She returned what Perce had meant to be a tender and lingering embrace with a brisk hug, and said, "I know William's pantaloons are too short, but you can wear his smallclothes, can't you?"

Perce's tender, fragile image of suffering womanhood came hard against reality and shattered with a crash. It was a particularly difficult transition to make because no physical being could better fit the false image. Sabrina's angelic face was made more pure and delicate by the simple low knot into which she had twisted her hair. The few pale tendrils that had escaped curled gently over cheeks and forehead, increasing the impression of sweet innocence. Her lips were soft, unsmiling, and parted a trifle. It was her eyes that ruined everything. At the moment they were fixed with hard, calculating intensity on Perce's hips as she mentally measured him against her late husband.

"I am wearing his smallclothes," Perce said somewhat stiffly. The brusque way Sabrina had returned his gesture of tenderness and the flat practicality of her statement and thoughts at this time jarred him. "I am also wearing his shirt and neckcloth. I had no time to look for my belongings, provided Sergei packed any, and neither Katy nor Sergei is capable of restoring what I was wearing."

"Good," Sabrina responded, not really listening and detaching herself briskly from her lover's embrace. "That solves one problem. Now I've got to oversee that idiot girl while she sets the table for dinner. I swear, I don't know how Katy managed."

"Do we need a formal dinner?" Perce asked.

"No, of course not, but I want to talk to you about Sergei and Katy, and I can't very well do that in front of their faces. And also, I wanted . . . Oh, good gracious! Mourning! I wonder if that groom has come back from Lousa yet. If he has, he must go again and fetch me a dressmaker and some black material. Oh, and Perce, do you know—no, how could you! How ridiculous I am."

"What is it you want to know?"

Perce felt chilled. To him, the busyness seemed false, and combined with the brusque response his embrace had received, seemed designed to create a distance between himself and Sabrina. Was she implying, now that she was free and safe, that she wished to be free of him also? She was unaware, relaxed, and content in his presence and thus able to focus on the details of living.

"I need to know the customs used for mourning here. Do I have a hatchment put on the knocker the way I would in England? Should I receive visits of sympathy, or am I supposed to go into seclusion? I haven't the faintest idea of how to act."

"Must you act?" Perce asked, the chill increasing.

Sabrina blinked at the sound of his voice, startled out of her absorption, realizing that he was . . . angry? "I wouldn't at home," she said placatingly, "but here, I don't want to offend these people anymore. The incident cannot have made them think well of William. For all I know, I may be the only Englishwoman they've met, and I must try to ameliorate any bad impression."

"The perfect diplomatic wife."

Sabrina stepped back a pace. "If I am, it's nothing of which to be ashamed. It's what I was trained to be."

"Of course. I'm sorry, Brina. I don't know what's got into me."

He put out his hand, and she laid hers in it, but only for a moment. Almost immediately she repeated that she must oversee the maid and disappeared through the dining room door. Perce stood staring after her, appalled at what he had said. He started after her, but through the partially open door heard her speaking to the maid. It would be impossible to explain himself while the maid was there, and he didn't know what to say beyond what he had said already. He wasn't even sure Sabrina was hurt or angry. She had seemed more surprised and—could it be possible—relieved, almost eager to run away from him to her duties.

"Stunned" was a better word to apply to Sabrina's reaction than "surprised." She knew Perce had a temper, although it was usually masterfully controlled. And this was not the first time she had broken Perce's control. Various acts of mischief in which she had engaged had brought a hot blast of rage or a cold one of sarcasm, but this time she had done nothing. She told the maid where to set places and which wineglasses to put out, stepped into the drawing room to tell Sergei which wines to bring up, then returned to the kitchen to give a last check to dinner.

By then the shock had worn off, and Sabrina had very nearly convinced herself that Perce's nasty remarks had little to do with her. Everyone had irritable moments in which the nearest and dearest person was the one who caught a battering. What Perce had been doing had not been pleasant. He must have been more affected than he would admit, so, naturally, he had snapped at her. That was good, not bad. That bespoke a true intimacy, a reliance on her understanding.

Perce had said he was glad William was dead, Sabrina thought. Still, after arranging for encoffining him, Perce might have felt she was callous to urge her lover to take

442

the corpse's clothing, so to speak, before he was properly cold. Katy could have been wrong about that. Her people were poor and could not afford delicate feelings. Sabrina blamed herself for not taking Perce's finer sensibility into account. In order to speak to the *regador* and prepare the way for her, he had to use any clothing on which he could lay his hands, but he must have shrunk from the need. Now Sabrina remembered his reluctance to wear William's clothing in Prussia.

Sabrina realized she had overlooked a most important aspect of the male character about which Leonie had repeatedly warned her. Well-bred men, Leonie had explained, were basically much more romantic than their womenfolk. They tended to see women, and situations, too, in an idealistic light. It was necessary, Leonie had pointed out, not to shock the poor dears by allowing them to see the essential practicality of their "fragile" wives and daughters.

I did shock Perce, Sabrina thought. *He doesn't want me to grieve for William, but all the same he is shocked because I'm concerned with food and clothing and running the house. And then he thought I was being hypocritical when I spoke about mourning in accordance with Portuguese custom. On top of his feeling that he was, too literally, stepping into William's shoes, it was just too much. Well, I can explain that.*

Having worked out everything to her own satisfaction—barring a tiny, frightened uncertainty that she did not choose to deal with—Sabrina met Perce at the dinner table with a pleasant smile. Since his thoughts in the interval had been far from pleasant or satisfactory, this hurt him more than an icy hauteur or hot rage or even absence. *She doesn't care,* his shocked mind told him. *She's relieved to be rid of me.*

"I hope this can be eaten," Sabrina said, smiling encouragingly at the frightened maid who was awkwardly placing serving dishes on the table.

"It will be more edible than cheese and ants," Perce said, snatching at a chance to remind Sabrina of their nights in the forest.

Sabrina flashed a smile at him, but her eyes were on the maid. Perce's remark had set her more at ease. Everything was all right. He wasn't angry any longer. Her mind slid to the awkward girl and how to phrase corrections and advice in Portuguese, and that reminded her of her struggles in the kitchen.

"Taste before you commit yourself," Sabrina warned. "I was transmitting suggestions from Katy—who wasn't sure what the cook had already done—in language totally unsuited to its purpose to someone who didn't want to understand. A less propitious beginning would be far to seek."

That didn't work, Perce thought bitterly. Talk about someone who doesn't want to understand! Plainly Sabrina wasn't taking any hints that referred to the intimacy that had existed between them. Perce uncovered a dish and began to spoon contents from it onto his plate.

"Perce!" Sabrina exclaimed, "that's sauce. Take some meat and rice."

He said something under his breath that Sabrina politely did not hear, but she suddenly felt frightened and nervous. She had thought that comment about ants and cheese was a teasing reminder of their lovemaking, a signal that Perce was happy, but it seemed she was wrong. Had he resented the hardships of those two days? Was he reminding her that her silliness had enforced those hardships on them? It was very unlike Perce to do such a thing or to be so abstracted and bad-tempered. Again the unwelcome idea came into her mind that he felt trapped in a situation he had not expected. Well, who could have expected William to be murdered?

"I will leave for Lisbon sometime tomorrow," Perce said abruptly, "as soon as the arrangements I made today are completed."

"Lisbon!" Sabrina cried. "Why? I mean, why are you going?"

"Someone must go." Perce kept his eyes on his food, afraid to look up. Had there been a protest in Sabrina's voice, or was she merely surprised and hearing what she wanted to hear? "Since you refuse to leave Katy, I must speak to Strangford and find out exactly how bad the situation is. We must be prepared to move her in an emergency. And someone must explain William's death."

"Yes, yes, of course. I have finished the letter for that purpose," she agreed, and plunged into a discussion of practical matters concerning the journey.

Perce pulled himself together, ate as much as he could, and applied himself to attending civilly to talking about his own comfort while traveling, a subject in which he had less than no interest.

"I'll come back as soon as I can," he said at last, "but it may be a week or more. If you don't see me, don't worry. It may take longer than I expect to get to Lisbon or to make the necessary arrangements to have the coffin shipped home. And if Strangford has any expectation of new intelligence, I might wait a day or two to learn what it is."

"You must do what you think best," Sabrina said, her voice as colorless as her face.

But Perce did not see her face. He got to his feet suddenly, feeling that if he stayed, he would do something violent. Characteristically, his voice was pleasant and without expression when he spoke. "I'll ride into Lousa again and do what I can to discover the proper mode for mourning. The translator, Mousinho, should be able to tell me."

"Wait," Sabrina said, but he was gone.

He had heard her before he shut the door, she was certain. Sabrina rose slowly, steadying herself with a hand on the table. He had never given her a chance to explain that proper mourning for William was not a hypocrisy designed to win praise for herself. It was one thing she was sure William would have wanted. He had always taken his diplomatic duties seriously. Perhaps his overconfidence had blinded him to the danger of what he was doing, but he would have been glad and grateful, Sabrina was sure, if she could in some measure correct his mistake.

Only, Sabrina feared that Perce's controlled rage was not owing to disgust at her seeming hypocrisy. *I won't hold you, my love,* she thought. *If you don't want me either, I won't hold you.* Leaving everything, she went up to her own sitting room and just waited. At the time she did not realize for what she was waiting. Her mind was blank, except for an occasional mild wonder about what was wrong with her. She was beautiful; she was intelligent; she was not a shrew; she enjoyed and responded to lovemaking; she had tried hard to be a good and obedient wife. Still, William had tired of her, and Perce, dear Perce, who had tried to help, was so frantic at the thought of being tied to her for life that he could hardly be civil in his eagerness to run away.

The hours passed. Sabrina waited in vain. When she realized that her inability to see was not because her eyes were unfocused but because the room was dark, she tried to get up. It was not easy. She had sat still so long that it took her three attempts to succeed. Then she walked slowly to her bedroom and stiffly, like an old woman, took off her clothing, unpinned her hair, and went to bed.

She slept at once, or fell at once into the same unthinking, unfeeling state in which she had passed the preceding hours. It was not until she was wakened, or drawn back to reality, by Perce's and Sergei's voices beneath her open window that she began to cry. At that moment she realized for what she had been waiting. She had been waiting for Perce to come to her and to make love—but he did not want even that from her.

CHAPTER TWENTY-THREE

The voices that roused Sabrina were the tail end of a discussion that had begun the night before when Perce informed Sergei that he was taking William's body to Lisbon. Overnight Sergei had given the matter some thought, and as he accompanied Perce out of the house, he remarked that the corpse could wait; the dead were seldom impatient to be buried. Perce responded with a sharp order that Sergei mind his own business. But two years in Perce's service, wide new experience, and a large dose of Katy had changed Sergei. Despite the fact that he knew his master was seriously out of temper, he pointed out the fact that he *was* minding his own business.

"You are my business, and *she* is my business. Which shall I mind?"

Perce could not help laughing in spite of his misery. It struck him suddenly that he had never heard Sergei call Katy by name—a touching mark of respect, for in general Sergei named only equals or inferiors. But nothing could lighten Perce's mood for long. "Your business is to obey my orders," he snapped, "not to give me an argument every time I tell you something. There are other reasons for me to go to Lisbon."

"Does the great lady understand these things?"

"Yes, of course. Now you stay here and take care of the women. I doubt there will be any trouble, but if there is, just do what Lady Elvan tells you."

"Will it be safe for you alone on the road?" Sergei asked uneasily.

"I'm not exactly a small, defenseless child," Perce growled, "and I won't be alone. There will be the driver of the cart and his boy. Also, I doubt any bandit will want what we are carrying."

"Foreigners," Sergei remarked contemptuously. "And what of when you come back? Then you will be alone."

"I managed to survive for more than twenty-five years before I met you," Perce said in an exasperated voice. "I don't need a nursemaid. And even if I did, it would be impossible to leave Lady Elvan and Katy alone."

Sergei shrugged. "Well, be careful, and don't trust any of these foreigners."

Too unhappy to be amused, Perce mounted and rode away without replying. There was no need for him to leave so early. He had doubts that the coffinmaker would have the special casket ready before noon, but he could not bear to stay in the house with Sabrina any longer. When he had returned from Lousa with the information she wanted and he had not found her sitting with Katy, his worst fears had been realized. He was convinced she was staying in her own apartment to avoid him.

Perce had started up the stairs with every intention of walking in on Sabrina and telling her she had no right to behave as she was doing, but when he found his fists and teeth clenched, he detoured to his own room until he could control his temper. He was afraid he might have used force instead of arguments to convince her in his present state of mind. Once he calmed down, he thought, it would be best to confront Sabrina directly and ask what kind of game she was playing. It was, however, strangely difficult to calm himself. The rage would ebb, and he would begin to think what to say and find he was so angry again that he was having visions of beating Brina black and blue.

It was unfortunate that Katy and Sergei had been pre-occupied with their own affairs. They assumed, with knowing winks on Sergei's part and smiles on Katy's part, that the reason their master and mistress did not appear was because they were happier alone together. Sergei got a nice supper for himself and Katy. Since he had not a word in common with cook or maid, he did not ask and they did not try to tell him that neither Perce nor Sabrina had had any evening meal.

Neither of them was in the least aware of hunger. It was, in fact, about the time that Sergei and Katy were cozily consuming their tea that Perce had finally gave up the idea of trying to reason with Sabrina. If she was utterly determined not to see him, such behavior must be understood as a signal that his intentions were no longer desirable. It was clever, too. He had said he would be away for a week, so she signaled no trespass now, giving him a week to absorb the message, cool down, and come to terms with the facts before they met again.

On the long, slow trek to Lisbon, Perce tried—or thought he was trying—to do what Sabrina wanted. He told himself over and over that she had a right to some freedom, that it was reasonable after the end of an unhappy marriage that she should be afraid to commit herself again. However, instead of growing resigned, he grew angrier. He might not be new and exciting, but he was the best husband Brina could have. He could give her everything she needed and wanted. He knew her and understood her as no other man ever could, and he would not step aside and let her make another mistake.

The rage in him was stored away, totally undiminished, on his arrival in Lisbon. For two days he was too busy to reexamine his personal situation. There were reports to make orally and then to be written out, questions to be answered, forms to be filled in. At one point Perce asked

Lord Strangford what would have happened if not he but the grieving widow had brought back Lord Elvan's body.

"Why, then," the diplomat replied with twinkling eyes, "I would have had to write the reports myself. But, my dear Lord Kevern, you know the old saw 'Waste not, want not.' Having you here and doing all that work myself would surely be a waste. There is also the golden rule for all diplomats: 'Let George do it.' "

"My name," Perce said, blank and fish-eyed, "is Percivale."

"Percivale George," Strangford reminded him, with a comical, wide-eyed stare that mirrored his own. "And don't try to come the fool over me, Kevern. I've been warned about that face of yours." Then his expression sobered. "I am genuinely sorry that Lady Elvan is alone and needs your support. You left Lisbon so hurriedly the day you arrived that I had not had time, really, to study everything in the dispatch bag. Naturally, I was most concerned with the material that referred directly to the situation here in Portugal. But you come highly recommended, very highly. Moreover, Mr. Canning says you are attached, in a way, to the Foreign Office, and that if I had some use for you, he was sure you would be willing to serve."

So Canning had intended to keep him out of England if he could. Perce didn't mind that, and he was quite willing to be useful to Lord Strangford, but he had to make one responsibility clear. "My first duty must be to Lady Elvan. I am here, in a sense, in loco parentis. Her foster father, Mr. Roger St. Eyre, became very anxious about her when he discovered that . . . er . . . that Lord Elvan had insisted on her company when it was unlikely she could be useful and most diplomatic wives were being sent home."

"She is a very beautiful woman," Lord Strangford remarked, beginning to smile at the implication that a man needed more reason than that to want his wife with him.

Then he cleared his throat harshly when he remembered the circumstances of William's death.

"There may have been indications of . . . ah . . . dissatisfaction," Perce said stiffly. "I would not have been told that. However, since neither Mr. Roger St. Eyre nor Mr. Philip St. Eyre was at liberty to leave England, and as I was at liberty and have been a friend of long standing—I have known Lady Elvan since she was a child of eight—Mr. St. Eyre asked that I escort her home safely."

"Yes, indeed, naturally your first responsibility must be to Lady Elvan; however, there is no immediate danger. You did say she no longer intended to leave at once, did you not?"

"Yes. Lady Elvan's companion, her nurse actually, broke her leg when that madman Dom José pushed her down the stairs. Mrs. Petersen will not be fit to travel for some time, and Lady Elvan refuses to go without her."

"How long?" Strangford asked.

"A month at least, I imagine. In an emergency she could be moved, but the doctor believes that might cripple her."

Lord Strangford pursed his lips. "Let me describe the situation as we know it. After that, you can decide what you think is best to do. After all, Lady Elvan is your responsibility, but you have a duty to your country, also."

He then outlined the situation, which was still a stalemate as far as the Spanish court was concerned.

Perce frowned thoughtfully. "Yes, but one cannot rely on Bonaparte's patience or on either his word or normal military ideas of routes or times of march. Boney is quite unscrupulous, and absolutely indifferent to the loss of men and equipment so long as an objective is obtained. I would not be surprised if he marched an army from the border of France across Spain and Portugal in a week."

"I would," Strangford said dryly. "You haven't seen the terrain."

"You haven't seen Boney in action. I have," Perce replied even more dryly.

The two men stared at each other. Then Lord Strangford nodded.

"I have a use for you, Lord Kevern, and I believe it is important. In any case, no matter how fast Bonaparte moves, he cannot cross Portugal before we can get our people aboard ship. You may not have noticed, but we are amassing a fleet in the Tagus. Property is being loaded as is convenient, but we could get all British citizens in Lisbon aboard in a few hours, or a day at most."

"A day might be too long, depending on where the French army was when you were notified it was moving."

"Good God, you *are* a prophet of doom," Strangford remarked. "Do you recommend we run without even trying—"

"By no means!" Perce interrupted. "We must do everything humanly possible to assure us a chance to beat Bonaparte, no matter how far in the future. What I recommend is that you get your women and children out, then arm your men so that they can fight a rearguard action in the streets. I tell you, his troops move devilish fast."

"You are very convincing, Kevern."

Perce's face didn't change expression, but his eyes were bleak. "I fought at Austerlitz, at Pultusk, at Eylau, and at Friedland, my lord, and I cannot say how many minor actions. I have grown very aware of the abilities of Bonaparte's army."

"I would like you to speak to the prince regent, Kevern."

"But sir, I don't have a word of Portuguese."

"He knows enough French to understand what you will say. Our purpose, as you may know, is to persuade him to leave Portugal and take his fleet of ships with him. He isn't a brave or determined man. Anything you can tell him that will increase his fear of the French will be of use."

Perce smiled grimly. "Provided I can get an opening, I can tell him enough horror stories to make his hair stand on end. I saw the way Boney treated King Frederick William—like a piece of dirt on the road, something you notice just enough to lift your foot and step over. However, I must go back to Lousã. Lady Elvan will be—"

"She seemed to me to be a most capable woman," Strangford remarked.

Perce's heart sank. He knew that what Strangford wanted him to do was important, and he was the best person to do it. "Very well, my lord," he agreed.

When he had accepted the duty laid upon him, Perce hoped that, together with the other pressures on the prince regent, it would take no longer than a week or two to frighten him into leaving. However, João's indecisiveness was stronger. The deadline of September first passed, and the French fulminated but did not move. All through the month threat and counterthreat blew the prince regent first one way and then another, but he still clung to the ridiculous hope that he could find a solution that would satisfy irreconcilable enemies. Perce continued to tell him horror stories—quite true—about the contempt with which the defeated enemies of Bonaparte were treated, while Strangford cited cases of those who had yielded without a struggle and, for their reward, had been deprived of their thrones.

Meanwhile, Bonaparte was not wasting time. General Junot was ordered to form a new army corps for "the observation of the Gironde." Strangford pointed out that army corps do not, ordinarily, observe; João grew more nervous, but still he could not be convinced to leave Portugal, and Perce was still trapped in Lisbon.

After the first week, he had written to Sabrina to explain why he would be delayed. He had wanted to write a love letter, but there was a dreadful pressure in him, capping and storing rage. If he had allowed any emotion to color that letter, it would have blasted Sabrina to bits as effectively as gunpowder. Thus, he clung to formal phrases and to cold facts.

Before Sabrina received that letter, she had had moments of hope, moments when she convinced herself that she had misinterpreted what had happened. She was unintentionally assisted by her acquaintances in Lousa who came to pay calls of sympathy—and curiosity. There were times when, in spite of feeling totally lost and guilty, Sabrina could hardly keep from laughing. Some of the women were truly kind and concerned for her; others were merely seeking sensation. All were human, however, which made them more curious than monkeys, dying to know what Sabrina's reaction was to the manner of her husband's death and the public revelation of his unfaithfulness that came with it.

After Sabrina received Perce's letter, nothing could amuse her. She moved about in a frozen calm, attending to the household tasks she had taken over from Katy, packing and sending to the embassy for dispatch to William's brother in England those personal items she thought he would like to have, such as William's jewelry, razors, and hairbrushes. She had also to consider what to do with the part of William's property in which she, as widow, had a life interest. During September there were other letters from Perce, all equally formal. He had closed the house in Lisbon, he wrote, and sent Sabrina's personal possessions on board the fleet that was waiting in the harbor to remove all British subjects.

Meanwhile, Katy's leg healed. The doctor removed the heavy splints and replaced them with a lighter construction. With care, he said, she could travel now without real danger. Still Sabrina made no move to leave, although Katy and Sergei both remonstrated with her. She could not bring herself to go to Lisbon, where she would have to face Perce.

The days dragged by, Katy was moving around with a crutch, and at last Sabrina acknowledged she could delay no longer. It was growing cold in the mountains, and they had no proper clothing. She gave the orders to start packing and wrote to Lord Strangford to ask whether she would be able to stay at the embassy until it was time to debark or, if that were not possible, would he obtain lodgings for her.

Her letter arrived on the evening of the twenty-first of October and was a dreadful shock to Lord Strangford, who had forgotten all about her. He sent a message to Perce at once, giving him leave to escort her and urging him to bring her back to Lisbon as quickly as possible. There were rumors that the impasse in Spain was coming to an end.

Perce's fury had dulled into a leaden misery, but the knowledge that he would be with Sabrina again brought it to a new peak. Sabrina was a fool. Why should she have her own way? Was it best for her? He fell asleep with that question in his mind and woke with it before dawn. Since he knew he would sleep no more, he rose and dressed and was on his way at first light. As he urged his horse over a road that was becoming quite familiar, he wished he could talk the matter over with someone. Rage or no rage, Perce was aware that he was not unprejudiced on the subject. But who *was* unprejudiced? Roger and Leonie certainly were not. They were so besotted with love that they had already made one disastrous mistake. Perhaps they had learned a lesson, but what if Sabrina made another mistake? Would they be able to resist her pleas and tears any better this time? Probably not.

Besides, Perce thought with a sense of shock, Roger and Leonie no longer had a right to prevent Sabrina from marrying anyone she chose. As a widow, a rich widow, she was free to do as she liked. Doubtless she would be surrounded by fortune hunters the minute she showed her face. And, considering how she had fallen for Elvan's slimy charms, nine chances in ten she would fall victim to another practiced seducer. Then it would be too late. Sabrina was so stubborn, she made mules seem like the most reasonable animals on earth.

No! Perce gritted his teeth. Oh, no! Once was enough. Whether she loved him now or not, he was going to obtain a promise from her to marry him, if he had to beat it out of her. Sabrina might be a fool, but she was honest. If she promised, she would keep her word. She was softhearted, too. If she saw how much he loved her, she would love him in return once they were married. It was perfect all around. Roger and Leonie trusted him; Philip and Meg loved him. None of them had really been comfortable with Elvan. And it would solve any problems that might arise with Sergei and Katy, too. If he could only convince Sabrina that she had by implication promised herself to him. . . .

When the packing was complete, Sabrina had nothing more to do. She sat idly, emptily, in her own room, unable to bear the worried tenderness with which Katy regarded her. But avoidance of Katy brought another dreadful problem to her mind. If she did not marry Perce, what was to happen to Katy and Sergei? Would Sergei be willing to leave Perce? If not, would the marriage have to be put off? Given up? Or would she lose Katy? She could barely choke back the urge to run down, to cry, *Don't you leave me too*, but that would be a dreadful cruelty. The grief of Katy's going was one she must learn to accept, to welcome. In fighting her irrational terror of abandonment, Sabrina thought of a device that might help her. If she wrote to Leonie about Katy's forthcoming marriage, she herself might come to see it as the joyful event it was.

The letter was not as easy to write as Sabrina had

hoped. Her first lighthearted version, when reread, sounded like a vulgar joke. Sabrina tore it up and began again. The second attempt breathed bitterness and ill-usage, as if Katy were a traitor and had no right to an independent life and happiness. Sabrina destroyed that letter also and was sitting, pen in hand, trying to begin a third time, when she heard the knocker sound. She had lit the candles some time earlier. It was dark. Who would come after dark?

Sabrina uttered a gasp of fear and jumped to her feet. Her terror surprised her. It was unreasonable, yet her heart pounded, and her mouth went dry. Before her mind could fix on the cause—Dom José had been the only night visitor ever—she heard Perce's voice. Had Sabrina recognized the cause of her terror, it would have disappeared, but there was no time for that. Without thinking, she ran toward the help and safety that Perce had always meant to her.

It was not until she was at the head of the stairs and the sound of her hasty footsteps had drawn Perce's attention, that Sabrina realized equally that there was nothing of which to be afraid and that she had no right to fly into Perce's arms. She gasped again and, her wits completely addled by embarrassment and conflicting emotions, ran back toward her rooms.

"Sabrina!" Perce roared, starting for the stairs.

"Senhor!" the new butler protested, and valiantly, if unwisely, tried to interpose himself between a visitor he took to be unwelcome and his mistress.

Perce picked him up and threw him away. "Sabrina!" he bellowed, leaping up the stairs three at a time.

Sergei burst out of the sitting room just in time to see Perce's back disappearing up the stairs. He looked long enough to be sure that it was his master, and then calmly went to assist the half-stunned butler to his feet. The man broke into voluble Portuguese, of which Sergei understood not a single word, so he merely shook his head and shepherded the butler into the kitchen where Katy was getting painfully to her feet, calling out to know what was happening.

"Nothing," Sergei answered with a smile. "My master has returned to settle matters with your lady." He spoke mostly in English, only using the Russian words for master and lady because he could never feel that the English equivalents conveyed enough respect.

"But he was shouting at her!" Katy cried, her eyes wide with anxiety.

"So?" Sergei asked, eyes and voice still smiling, although his lips did not. "You know something has been heavy on the great lady's heart all these long weeks. He has come to tell her not to be a fool. When you are well and do what angers me, I will shout also. Women, even great ladies, are often fools."

"Not Brina," Katy averred without thinking.

Sergei laughed shortly. "Not even when she married that *chasseur des femmes*?"

"She was only sixteen," Katy protested, "and he swore up and down of his love. Even I didna doubt him."

Sergei laughed. "So? What says that for *your* wisdom? And why should your silliness make me think diffcrent of the great lady's wisdom?"

"Ye ignorant ox, what do ye think ye know of such things?" Katy sputtered.

"Another man can smell one of the dead lord's kind at a hundred yards," Sergei replied, his eyes twinkling, "but women are always fooled. Stop your talking, woman. Your lady desires my master—no? And he is sick for her—I know it. Whatever happens, even if he beats her—" Katy uttered a horrified exclamation, and Sergei laughed again. "He will find a way to soothe her bruises, never fear," he remarked.

Katy did not answer that but strained her ears. She heard nothing. Sabrina's rooms were above the dining

459

room across the corridor, and the walls, floors, and doors of the dower house were thick and sturdy. Still, both rooms were on the same side of the house, and Katy thought she would hear screams and furniture breaking. She made hushing signals at Sergei and the butler, who was still trying to find out who had come in and treated him with such violence. Even after the men were silent, however, Katy heard nothing.

At that moment there was nothing to hear. Nor had there ever been the kind of sounds Katy listened for so fearfully, although Perce was in a royal rage when he bounded up the stairs. Naturally the anger in his voice did nothing to calm Sabrina, who fled instinctively back into her own room. Indeed, her mental turmoil was so extreme at the moment that her thinking processes were totally suspended; her reactions were those of a helpless, startled animal. Had her bedchamber door been open, she would, like a ground squirrel or rabbit, have tried to hide in the dark. Perce arrived, however, at the open corridor door just as she reached for the door latch.

"What the devil do you think you're doing?" he roared.

Sabrina turned at bay, her back against the door, one arm raised as if to ward off a blow.

"Brina, what's the matter with you?" Perce asked more gently, seeing the blanched cheeks and lips, the fear-dilated eyes. "Darling, surely you aren't afraid of me?"

"I don't know," she gasped, and then, as if the sound of her own voice had wakened her from some nightmare, she blinked her eyes and shuddered. "I don't know," she repeated, but in a more natural voice, and her arm dropped. "When I heard the knocker, I was—I was terrified."

"My poor girl," Perce said softly. "I would never have gone away if I'd known you were afraid. Why didn't you tell me? But the man's dead, Brina. There's no one else in the world who could want to hurt you."

Her face cleared. "Oh," she exclaimed, "you always

make things right for me, Perce. How silly of me. Yes, that must be what frightened me. It was the knock at night. No one ever comes here at night." She found a small smile. "You mustn't think I've been flying into the vapors each time the knocker went."

"May I come in?" Perce was in, actually, but he was still standing by the door.

The smile disappeared. "Of course, but you must be tired and—and hungry, perhaps. Would you like—"

"I'd like to talk," he interrupted, walking farther into the room and shutting the door behind him.

Sabrina stood uncertainly for a moment, absorbing the fact that she must now act on the truth she had faced. Then she moved to the small sofa nearest her. She sat down and began a gesture of invitation that would have indicated an armchair. Perce ignored it, seating himself beside her. The gesture incomplete, her hand hung in the air for an instant, and Perce reached out and took it. He could feel it trembling, although the movement had not been apparent to the eye.

It was far easier, Perce discovered, to think about forcing Sabrina to do what was best for her when she was an image in his mind, ice-maiden perfect, cool and untroubled. Seated beside her, hearing her quickened breathing, seeing her pallor and the slight, pathetic droop of her lovely mouth, he only wanted to give her whatever she desired, no matter what the cost. He was now far less unsympathetic to the blunder Roger and Leonie had made.

At the same time the small remaining evidences of her fear roused a violent protective instinct in him. No one, he felt, had ever taken proper care of her. Only he could be sufficiently tender, sufficiently loving. His rational mind knew this was not true, that Roger and Leonie and Katy, if they could, would have prevented the wind from blowing on her too roughly or the rain from falling on her. But this had nothing to do with Perce's powerful conviction that Sabrina could be safe and happy only in his care.

"Brina," he began, "you just said I make everything right for you. I would like very much to be able to make everything right for you all of our lives. If you were my wife, that would be my right and my privilege."

Sabrina's breath caught, and she stared at the face she knew so well. Unfortunately, in his effort to control himself so that he would not frighten or distress Sabrina further, Perce had assumed the blank mask he so often wore. His eyes were down, fixed on the hand he held between his own. *He has disciplined himself,* Sabrina thought. *He believes himself committed and is making the offer he feels he owes me.*

"You don't have to," she whispered, fighting back tears. "It's all right. Just because we . . . It doesn't matter."

"Don't be a fool, Brina." Perce's tone firmed. He was annoyed by what he believed was an attempt to pretend their relationship had been no more than a casual love affair. "I know you've had a bad experience with marriage, but if you've begun to think I took you for a dissatisfied wife who was ripe for playing games, you're fooling yourself. I'm not a rake, and you know it. I've never looked at a married woman that way before in all my life—no matter how ready she was."

"No," Sabrina said, "it's not that. I didn't think you would. . . ."

Her voice drifted away uncertainly. The temptation to yield, to take what she wanted, was terribly strong, but her own words were echoing in her head. She didn't think Perce would have love affairs. . . . Or did she? He wouldn't intend to, but if he married her for pity and for duty, and his heart was empty, wouldn't his temptation be too strong?

"Then why?" he was asking. "Why won't you promise

to marry me? I know we'd have to wait until your strict mourning was over, but I—I want your promise."

His voice faltered over the last words. What the devil was he to say if Sabrina asked whether he didn't trust her? Sabrina heard the lack of sureness. *If Perce takes a mistress,* she thought, *I'll die.* It would be beyond bearing to be proved worthless and unwanted again. Terror gave her the strength to protest once more.

"I said it wasn't necessary."

Her voice was breathless and pitched higher than usual. The hand Perce held began to tremble more noticeably. He misunderstood what she said, thinking she meant the promise to marry him rather than his offer, was not necessary. The horrid suspicion that she had another man in mind occurred to him. She had been in England for months with the idea of annulment in her head. Perhaps she had gone to Portugal hoping to free herself of another love, let him make love to her in the hope she was cured, found she wasn't. . . .

"I don't understand you," he said harshly. "I thought it was understood that we would marry as soon as you were free. If you won't give your promise, at least I deserve the courtesy of being told why plainly and clearly."

Sabrina could bear no more. She tore her hand away from him and jumped to her feet. "Why? Because I don't want to be married for pity. I—"

"What?" Perce was on his feet too, blazingly angry. "Repeat what you said! I don't believe it!"

Sabrina began to shrink back, but Perce caught her wrist.

"Tell me again," he insisted, but his voice had softened, and he was drawing her closer. Rage was melting into amusement in his eyes.

"I thought," Sabrina quavered, "I thought you pitied me."

When Sabrina had first pulled away from him and given

her angry answer, Perce's own fears had made him mishear her to say she did not want to marry out of pity. Reasonably, Perce was violently offended. He knew he was no pattern-card of beauty, but also that he had nothing to be ashamed of as a man. Many women would have been tearfully grateful for an offer from him. But even in a rage it was impossible to misread Sabrina's expression. Before she had repeated her statement in an unmistakable form, Perce had understood what she meant.

Perce didn't know whether to kiss her, kill her, or, better, kill himself for being such a fool. To him Sabrina was so beautiful, so perfect in every way, that it had not entered his mind *she* might not appreciate how great a prize she must be to any man. Yet as far as she knew, sweet innocent that she was, every man might react like that hemchaser of a husband and grow tired of her as soon as he had her. He tipped her head up and kissed her.

"You birdbrained nitwit," he murmured when he broke the kiss. "You've given me six weeks of hell such as I never hope to live through again. Now, before you say anything else stupid, recite after me: I promise on my faith and honor that I will marry Percivale George Evelyn Moreton, Lord Kevern, at the very first opportunity decently available."

"But Perce—"

"I warn you, Sabrina, that if your next words are not the promise I have asked for, I will upend you and smack your behind." He tightened his grip and began to back toward the sofa.

"I promise," Sabrina said hastily, knowing that Perce was quite capable of carrying out his threat.

"Promise what?" he insisted, intent on leaving no loopholes.

"I promise to marry Percivale George—"

She got no further because he kissed her again, pulling her down on his lap on the sofa without breaking the embrace. When her arms came around him, Perce relaxed. Soon after, he lifted his head.

"Brina," he said seriously, "I had no right to call you a birdbrained nitwit, but I swear I don't know what I did wrong. Tell me, my love, what did I say or do that made you think asking you to marry me was a duty rather than a desire? I love you to distraction. I always have. I just didn't know that I wanted you for my wife. Be reasonable, Brina. I *couldn't* let myself think that way. Not while you were a little girl. And in the end, you grew up too fast. I didn't see soon enough that you were a woman."

She was holding his hands tightly, her eyes large. "It was William's fault, wasn't it?" she asked. "It isn't anything wrong with me, is it?"

Perce didn't answer for a moment, but his color rose, and Sabrina could see the muscles in his jaw jump as his teeth set hard. "I take it back," he said in a choked voice when he got his jaw loose. "I'm not glad that . . . I'm not glad Elvan's dead. I wish he were alive again so I could take him apart slowly. Brina, you're perfect! There's nothing wrong with you. You're beautiful, intelligent, and sweet-natured. If you weren't sometimes hen-witted and other times stubborn as an ass, you'd be an angel, and God would never have let you out of heaven."

She had been staring at him, wide-eyed, trying to believe, but on the last words she leaned forward and buried her face in his shoulder. Perce could feel her shaking, and he was about to beg her not to cry when he realized it was unnecessary. Something had struck her funny, and the release of her tension had sent her into a fit of giggles. He held her patiently, smiling himself because her laughter was contagious. At last she looked up, her eyes teardrenched.

"Well, what's so funny?" he asked. "It's very unromantic to laugh in a man's face when he's telling you that you're wonderful."

465

"I didn't laugh in your face," Sabrina pointed out. "It was that angel bit. I wouldn't be an angel even if I were wise as Solomon and as persuadable as Griselda. I'm dreadfully . . . dreadfully . . . Oh, dear, I can't think of a polite word. I'm dreadfully *lecherous*, Perce. And you know what God thinks of that!"

It was Perce's turn to laugh. "That's no fault to me," he exclaimed. "And I'll tell you something. I don't believe it's any fault to God, either—no matter what a bunch of bluenose zealots who don't know any better say."

"But it can be, Perce," Sabrina said, abruptly serious. "It can be a sin when—when it makes you hurt someone."

"My name is not William."

"I didn't mean—" She slipped off his lap to sit beside him.

"No, I know you didn't, but he hurt you, Brina, and you're sore. I've told you over and over. Chasing women is not my hobby, not even whores or opera dancers. I've used them—I'm human—but I've never kept one—"

"You're a *very* good lover, Perce, far better than William. Oh! I shouldn't have said that. It isn't . . . I wouldn't have said it to anyone else, but I never do think before I speak when I talk to you."

"That's as it should be. Nonetheless, you leave me speechless, or nearly." Then he smiled slowly. "I *think* that compliment was really an accusation. You're being henwitted again, Brina. Why should I bother to kiss a whore's toes or—or half kill myself to be sure she would always remember and crave my loving. I lay down my coin; she lays down her body. I don't need to please her. She'll lie down any time I put my hand in my purse. You're different, darling. The only way I can be sure you'll be willing to lie down with me, the only way I can reciprocate for the exquisite pleasure you give me is to give you—I would hope—just as much pleasure. I'm flattered that you find me so satisfactory, but I swear it's my imagination, not my experience, you should credit."

The conversation was having a predictable effect on Perce, and he shifted slightly to ease his position. He also restrained an impulse to look at the bedroom door. He felt it would be crude to suggest sexual congress at this moment, but it was all he could think of, so it took a few minutes before he became aware that Sabrina had not made any reply to what he said.

"Don't you believe me?" he asked.

"Yes. It's not that," she said finally in a small voice, but her eyes were lowered and her cheeks were unusually pink.

"Don't hide any doubts you have, Brina," Perce said, trying to keep the impatience from his voice. Sitting close as they were, thigh pressed to thigh and Sabrina's hand on his leg, Perce's condition was growing acute. If they were going to talk much longer, he thought, he would have to get up and move away, but that would probably hurt Sabrina. "Let's get down to the bare truth right now," he urged.

"Yes," Sabrina agreed emphatically, with a little smile, "the bare truth, that's what we need." Then, when Perce waited for her to go on, she glanced up, hesitated, and added petulantly, "For someone with such an active imagination, sometimes you're thick as a wall."

For one instant Perce was completely at a loss at this seeming non sequitur. Then he began to laugh, but that didn't prevent him from picking Sabrina up and carrying her toward her bedchamber.

"My lecherous little love," he murmured between chuckles, "I promise never to fail in imagination again."

CHAPTER TWENTY-FOUR

Both Perce and Sabrina slept after a very imaginative exercise with a very satisfactory culmination. However, Perce woke only an hour or so later, even though he had been tired by lovemaking and by the long ride. The more Sabrina was his, the more concerned he became that nothing he could prevent should hurt her. He was thus subliminally uncomfortable. Somewhere deep in his mind the fear of discovery troubled him. He had a vague memory, too, of the man he had pitched out of his way when he pursued Sabrina up the stairs. With an effort he pushed himself upright.

"What's the matter?" Sabrina asked, sitting up also.

"You lovely nitwit, I can't sleep here."

"Yes, you can. I'll tell the maid not to wake me tomorrow morning—"

"And not to do the bed in my room? Brina, be sensible."

He got out of bed and pulled on his shirt and breeches. Sighing, Sabrina gathered the remainder of his clothing and handed it to him. She slipped on a peignoir and opened the door to the corridor, which was empty but still lit up. Sabrina flitted across and opened the door to the principal guestchamber. It was prepared, the bed made, a small fire in the hearth, candles burning in the wall sconces and on the mantelpiece. Katy's instructions, no doubt. She went back and gestured. Perce stroked her cheek once as he passed her, and then the door closed behind him.

Sabrina was disappointed by Perce's refusal to spend the night with her. It was not important, but by morning the whole idea of avoiding scandal had started a new train of thought. No more unresolved questions, Sabrina vowed. So as soon as Perce entered the breakfast room, she said, "I know you intend to join the diplomatic service, Perce. Will it do you harm to marry William's widow?"

He paused inside the door, which he then shut carefully, and eyed her glassily. "No," he said. "No to everything in turn. One: If you are thinking of more silly reasons to allow me to go back on my proposal, my threat still stands. I will upend you and smack your bottom, since the lesson I gave you last night doesn't seem to have taken hold. Two: If you are trying to make me think you are afraid my affection is already wandering so that I will make love to you again here and now, I won't. I'm too hungry. I had no supper last night; the dinner at the inn I stopped at was inedible, and I had breakfast at four o'clock in the morning—such as it was."

Sabrina had begun to laugh at the end of item one. Now she sputtered, "Oh, Perce, don't be so silly. Come and sit down."

Without a flicker of expression, merely raising his voice to overpower hers, he continued, "Three: If that was a serious question, which I have begun to doubt you capable of, it is ridiculous. Of course it will do me no harm to marry William's widow. It will probably do me good, since your reputation as a diplomatic wife is excellent. Moreover, the marriage, in general, will be thought natural and suitable, even decorous, since I have been a family friend for a long time, and we are well matched in age, fortune, and breeding. Any more questions?"

"What do you want for breakfast?" Sabrina said meekly.

The mask shattered into delighted laughter, but in a moment he had sobered again. "How soon can you be ready to leave, Brina?" he asked. "That fool Strangford forgot all about you up here in Lousa, and he told me yesterday that the situation in Spain has changed. There are rumors that Godoy will sign the treaty with Boney any day now."

"Lord Strangford isn't a fool," Sabrina protested. "He has more on his mind than one woman. Fortunately, we're all packed. We can leave today. Sit down, and have breakfast, Perce. I'll tell Katy to order the carriage brought round and start the men loading."

But it was already too late. Even before Sabrina had accepted the necessity of leaving Lousa, on the nineteenth of October, Junot started his troops through the Pyrenees. On October twentieth, France declared war on Portugal. Word of these events reached Lisbon on October twenty-third. On the twenty-fifth, a convoy of fifty ships set sail, carrying all British subjects with their families and movable goods. But on the twenty-fifth, Sabrina's party was still twenty miles from Lisbon. By the time they arrived, the ships were well out to sea. Lord Strangford was distraught at the danger in which his forgetfulness had placed Sabrina; Perce was so angry that he left the embassy without a word, to walk off his rage. Sabrina, however, was delighted. She did not regard the danger as significant when British naval vessels were in the harbor, and anyway, Perce was there. Nothing could happen to her.

Nor was her calm shaken when word was brought to the embassy on the seventh of November that Portuguese batteries had fired on a British frigate. She felt sure Lord Strangford was correct when he said angrily that it was a childish attempt to pacify the French. And, indeed, when Strangford went to protest the insult—for the shooting was so bad that it was no more than an insult—Araujo, the foreign minister, assured the ambassador that it was only a mistake.

Nonetheless, further silly attempts at pacification were made. Despite what Araujo had said, the next day an order was published to confiscate all British property and arrest all British subjects. Again Lord Strangford went to court, this time to ask for his passport. The prince regent pleaded with him not to take offense and, indeed, seemed so frightened that everyone began to hope that João would, at last, agree to leave, but still he could not make up his mind. Strangford began to dismantle the embassy, but not in any violent hurry; he would not give up his attempts to remove the Portuguese fleet from Lisbon, without having it sunk, until the French were actually at the gates of the city.

Perce wanted Sabrina and Katy to go aboard one of the ships at once, but it was plain that no attempt was being made to enforce the order to arrest British citizens, and Sabrina protested that it was ridiculous for her to be uncomfortable and cause the myriad difficulties of having a woman aboard a naval vessel until it was absolutely necessary.

Two days later, on the tenth of November, both Strangford and Perce had cause to thank God that they had thought more of Sabrina's comfort and the sensibilities of the naval officers than of her safety. Nine Russian ships entered the Tagus strait. If there was to be a battle, a fighting ship was no place for a woman. In other ways Lord Strangford's troubles multiplied, too. Prince Regent João immediately forgot all about leaving Portugal, thinking that the Russians had come to protect his cities from the British ships.

Sabrina alone remained unshaken. She maintained that she was certainly in no danger as long as the Russians were in Lisbon harbor. Russian gentlemen were extremely chivalrous, and she had many friends among the Russian nobility. And she proved to be right. On the eleventh the Russian admiral came ashore. Since Sergei had already been out to the ships on a supply lighter, Perce was there to meet Admiral Siniavin, who was surprised and delighted to be greeted in his own language. He was also shocked when Perce asked whether the residents of the British embassy must consider him an enemy.

"You say our nations are at war?" He shrugged. "I must believe you, of course, and I deeply regret it, but *I* have had no official instructions, and Lisbon is a neutral port. We have come to take shelter from a storm, to make repairs and purchase supplies—and that is all."

Perce shook his hand cordially, and they smiled at each other. "There will be British ships coming in a day or two," Perce warned.

Far from looking worried, the admiral looked interested and eager. "Who commands?" he wanted to know. "Perhaps I will meet an old friend. I was trained in British ships, you know, and served in the Royal Navy."

"I don't know who the commanders will be, because I'm not sure which ships will be in this patrol," Perce said, grinning. "But if you would like to come to the embassy, perhaps Lord Strangford will be able to tell you."

This was easily agreed, although the visit had to be unofficial. Even so, it had most beneficial results. After the admiral's official call on the prince regent, João knew that his hopes had been in vain. The Russians had not come to support or protect him. They would put no obstacle in the way of anything the British wished to do. Nonetheless, João still dithered—until Bonaparte outsmarted himself. Because Junot's troops were already crossing Spain and it was obvious that Portugal was without leadership and defenseless, Bonaparte had published in *Le Moniteur* an imperial decree stating that "The House of Braganza has ceased to reign in Europe."

When he received a copy, Lord Strangford hastened to pass it along to the prince regent. It was then that the court and the royal family began to pack. Then Sir

William Sydney Smith arrived with six of the line and blockaded the mouth of the Tagus. The Portuguese fleet would leave under their escort or never leave at all. And still João doubted and lingered until, on November twenty-ninth, Colonel Le Cor rushed to the court for instructions and reported that the French had taken Abrantes.

Finally the prince regent and his family went aboard the flagship of the Portuguese fleet about noon and set sail as soon as they could. Sir Sydney and four of his fleet accompanied them, but the other two ships remained offshore, and the embassy party, including Perce, Sabrina, Katy, and Sergei, also went aboard. There were plenty of fishing boats going in and out of Lisbon and plenty of people who were ready to carry news to the British. They reported that General Junot entered Lisbon at about three o'clock on the thirtieth with fifteen hundred half-dead French troops.

"My lord," Perce said, "if we could land a force even a third of what they have, we could take them. They have not a single gun, or a cartridge that will fire. Boney has tripped himself at last, insisting that Junot take a road that did not exist. Let's—"

"No!" Strangford exclaimed. "I have no instructions that would permit me to order such an attack." Then he put a hand on Perce's shoulder. "Easy, now, easy. We aren't beat. You know it would do no good, even if we could drive Junot out of Lisbon. They have all the other cities. We couldn't hold on. We'll be back."

Perce turned away to stare over the rail, and after a moment Lord Strangford spoke again. "We'll be under way soon. Why don't you go below and see whether Lady Elvan is as comfortable as possible."

As soon as Perce entered the cramped cabin, Sabrina saw that something was very wrong. She asked anxiously, but when she heard the answer she was wise enough not to

473

voice her true feelings, which were intense relief and gratitude for Lord Strangford's good sense. All she said was
that she was sorry, and then, seeking to distract Perce,
added that she was glad he had come down.

"There's something I must talk to you about. You
know, we've been so careful not to be private that I
haven't had a chance."

Perce saw the worry in her eyes. "Good God, you aren't
breeding, are you?" he asked. He couldn't think of anything else that would require a private discussion. "It
would be a sin to pass the child as Elvan's, but—" Sabrina
was shaking her head, and he sighed with relief. "I was a
fool to spend into you," he went on, "but you drove me so
crazy, I didn't think. I won't do it again."

"Maybe it doesn't matter," Sabrina said. "That's what I
wanted to talk to you about. Perce, I know you will be
earl of Moreton and will need an heir, and—and I may
not be able to give you one."

"I don't care," he said immediately, pulling her into his
arms. It was the first time they had been alone since
Lousa. "I'm not marrying a brood mare. I have two brothers. But why do you say that, Brina?"

She rested her head on his shoulder. "I don't know. It's
just that de Conyers women don't seem to be fertile. Leonie is barren. It's the one grief in her life. And I only
conceived once. Then I lost the baby."

He held her tightly. "I'm sorry, darling. I didn't know."

"No, don't be sorry. I mean, don't think I was terribly
grieved. I—even then, I think I didn't want William's children, but I'll be dreadfully disappointed if I can't have
yours."

She never loved him, Perce thought triumphantly, never.
It was a final end to any fear that Sabrina's first marriage
would cast a shadow on their love. He kissed her nose and
then her lips, lightly. "Anyway, I suspect you're worrying

474

about a pack of nonsense. You did conceive. How often did you sleep with Elvan after that?"

"Not very often," Sabrina said thoughtfully, "that's true. But before that . . ."

"You were awfully young, Brina. Maybe it was something to do with that."

She sighed with relief, and her eyes were like stars. "Yes. You always make everything right for me, Perce."

He grinned down at her, his eyes lighting with mischief. "I'll tell you something. If you want to get with child, the best way is to make love right now."

Sabrina looked astonished. "Why right now? Do you think the sea air—"

His laugh cut her short, and he said, "Because now is the most inconvenient moment possible for you to conceive. It's far too late to have been Elvan's get, so it will make a horrid scandal. You know the rule: If there is anything you don't want to happen, it will not only happen, but it will happen at the most inconvenient time possible."

"Perce, you're crazy," she giggled, but she put her arms around his neck and pressed her hips against him. "Look at this cabin. Look at the bunk. We'll fall on the floor, and . . ."

Her voice drifted away as his lips moved down from her throat toward her breasts, and his hands slid down her back so he could press her harder into his body. Sabrina made a muffled exclamation and pulled back.

"There's something hard digging—"

"What do you expect?"

She laughed and pushed him away. "Idiot! Not there. It's your fob." Then she kissed his lips lightly. "There's no time as nice as an inconvenient one. Just open that cupboard. Our bearskin is in there, so we won't have to worry about falling on the floor."

AUTHOR'S NOTE

In general it is my practice to take no liberties with history
in any way. I must state here that I have done so in one
instance in this book. There is *no implication anywhere*
that General Bennigsen was in any way connected with
the leakage of the secret articles of the Treaty of Tilsit to
the British. If any evidence as to how that information
came to England existed, it does so no longer or is still
considered a state secret.

All that is known on this subject is that less than three
weeks after the treaty was signed, the content of the secret
clauses was known in London. There is no violation of history in making a fictional character carry this information.
Someone did so, but that person's name has not come
down to us. In these circumstances, it is a novelist's pre-
rogative to give the credit where it will best serve her
purposes. However, it is not really a novelist's right to
place the onus of this act on a man who most likely had
no connection at all with it. That I have implied General
Bennigsen was involved is solely for the purposes of the
plot of my novel.

My excuse for this liberty is my conviction that whoever
in the Russian or French hierarchy leaked this information
to the British performed a service to humanity—whatever
his or her reason for doing so might have been. Napoleon's concept of a unified Europe may have been a fine
one. If we do not destroy ourselves and our civilization,

we may some day see the fruition of this idea. However, unification cannot be engendered by force, nor can it be encouraged by the armed domination of one group over another.

Not only was Napoleon's concept ahead of its time—as was Alexander of Macedon's before him—but he was far less likely than Alexander to achieve his purpose. Napoleon ruthlessly drained the nations he conquered to support his imperial ambitions in France. Moreover, he did not respect the individuality of the people he conquered, but forced upon them foreign rulers (most often his own relatives) they hated and despised, as well as foreign laws and customs. It is not to the point whether or not these laws, customs, or rulers were better than their own; they were neither desirable nor acceptable to the people.

Had the secret clauses of Tilsit been put into effect, it is possible that Napoleon might have overcome the British navy and invaded England. Whether the invasion failed or was successful, it is not likely that Napoleon's empire could have endured. The constant waves of rebellion against him from 1804 through May 1814, when he finally was confined on Elba, indicate that the end result would have been the same whatever the route. Thus, implementation of the secret clauses of Tilsit could only have prolonged by a few or many years the bloody war that ended at Waterloo.

I wish to make clear that to the best of my ability the character and personality of General Bennigsen were portrayed as described in contemporary sources. He was said to be proud, touchy, and ambitious. Further, it is historical fact that he led the group that murdered Tsar Paul, and the events of Pultusk, Eylau, and Friedland are also fact. Under the circumstances, I do not feel that I have dishonored General Bennigsen by placing him in the role I did. If any differ from me in this opinion, I apologize to them and also to General Bennigsen's memory. It is in my fiction alone that he is connected with this intelligence coup of the British.

ROBERTA GELLIS
Roslyn Heights, New York
November 1982

From the author of *Evergreen*

RANDOM WINDS

by
BELVA PLAIN

From a quiet village in upstate New York to elegant house parties in the English countryside from the bedsides of the rural poor to the frenetic emergency room of a Manhattan hospital from war-torn London to luxurious lovers' hide-aways on the Riviera, here is the unforgettable story of three generations of doctors—and of a love no human force could surpress.

A Dell Book $3.50   (17158-X)

At your local bookstore or use this handy coupon for ordering:

| Dell | **DELL BOOKS** RANDOM WINDS $3.50   (17158-X)
P.O. BOX 1000, PINEBROOK, N.J. 07058 |

Please send me the above title. I am enclosing $ _____
(please add 75¢ per copy to cover postage and handling). Send check or money
order—no cash or C.O.D.'s. Please allow up to 8 weeks for shipment.

Mr/Mrs/Miss _____

Address _____

City _____ State/Zip _____

A love forged by destiny—
A passion born of flame

FLAMES OF DESIRE

by Vanessa Royall

Selena MacPherson, a proud princess of ancient
Scotland, had never met a man who did not desire
her. From the moment she met Royce Campbell at
an Edinburgh ball, Selena knew the burning
ecstasy that was to seal her fate through all eternity.
She sought him on the high seas, in India, and
finally in a young America raging in the
birth-throes of freedom, where destiny was bound
to fulfill its promise. . . .

A DELL BOOK $2.95

At your local bookstore or use this handy coupon for ordering:

Dell	**DELL BOOKS**	Flames of Desire $2.95 14637-2)
	P.O. BOX 1000, PINEBROOK, N.J. 07058	

Please send me the above title. I am enclosing $_____
(please add 75¢ per copy to cover postage and handling). Send check or money
order—no cash or C.O.D.'s. Please allow up to 8 weeks for shipment.

Mr/Mrs/Miss_____

Address_____

City_____ State/Zip_____